The Falcon Confession

THE FALCON CONFESSION

John V Norris

Dedication

To Raven, Maddy, and Isabel –

My light, my fire, and my inspiration

Map

England and the Frankish European Continent circa 1066

Prologue: Annora

May 15, 1051

The wolf's growl silenced the feasters in Dublin's royal hall. His brother's answering snarl caused even the drunkest revelers to stop and look. In the front of the torchlit chamber, the silver-coated animals started circling a chunk of discarded gristle. They captured every gaze and held every movement, save Annora's.

The sixteen-year-old thrall glanced over her shoulder to the entry doors. The hall guards watched along with the crowd, strain clear on their faces. Trying not to make a sound, she slid her tray of fowl carcasses on to the floor.

Queen Brigit, sitting on a raised dais far from the guests, launched up. "Danu! Dagda! Settle down now!"

Her pets – the guardian angels as she called them – bared their fangs and began circling the prize. The crowd whispered at this defiance; no one noticed Annora edge farther away.

With cheeks as red as her robe, the queen of Dublin slammed her fists on the dais. "Don't just stand there! Somebody stop them before they spill blood!"

The two hall guards rushed forward. "No spears," the queen shouted. "Just get them to the kennel master!"

The warriors laid their spears on the floor and continued the approach. Their fingers twitched more with each step.

The crowd began to rumble. These animals had

maimed two handlers since arriving from Norway last month; they wouldn't go easily now.

From the side wall, Annora spied the unguarded door. She needed just a few more moments.

Oblivious to the approaching men, the wolves crashed together in a tangle of clawing limbs and high-pitched whines. Their jaws snapped onto each other's necks and flanks. Tufts of silver fur floated in the hearth smoke.

In reaction, the guests sprang up as one, cheering, wagering, and wailing enough to shake the air. They grew even more feverish as six men joined the guards to encircle the thrashing wolves.

Annora receded to the entry doors amidst the uproar. When she pushed the iron door handle, night air seeped into her tunic sleeve and made her skin prickle.

Yet before she could move again, the doors were ripped open from the outside. Fergal, the court musician, stood before her with a grin curving the scar on his cheek. "Where you off to, pretty?"

Annora stifled a cry and forced her shoulders to relax. "Fergal...I'd heard of your return. I was on my way to greet you."

"But I greeted you first. Now, I'm mean to taste you." The bald singer pulled open her tunic neck-line, wrenched her head to the side, and slid his tongue across the tops of her breasts with a chuckle. He then yanked her away from the doors and headed to the nearest bench.

She succumbed to Fergal's grip with the saliva growing cold on her chest. Trailing behind, she saw the guards had removed the wolves and the hall had quieted.

Then, she felt the queen's stare. Fergal was Brigit's favorite entertainer. Annora's whippings always intensified after Fergal bedded her; tomorrow promised to be the worst yet. Fear and failure threatened to overwhelm her, but she drew strength by envisioning Aidan, her month-old son, resting in the servant's quarters. *I can't give up. We need to escape.*

Fergal's return complicated matters; his travels to the northern courts should have kept him away much longer. Now he trapped her, bedecked in the same gray tunic and mud-spattered vest in which he left. The object strapped behind him was the only addition. Wrapped in dark cloth, it traversed his back and jutted over his shoulder.

After finding a bench, he rested the object against a table and pulled Annora into his lap. He nipped at her ear lobe while emitting a hungry groan. She had to fight to stop her hands from pushing him off.

A herald's voice rang out: "All hail Diarmit, King of Dublin."

Fergal lifted his head at the announcement. On the side of the hall, the palace doors opened and Diarmit strolled in. He wore a green robe decorated with crimson flower embroidery and grease stains, a leather belt studded with rubies barely visible under his girth, and a thick golden crown atop his stringy black hair. "Loyal subjects, please forgive my absence. I trust you enjoyed the queen's entertainment?" The crowd roared as Brigit's eyes shot fire. The grinning king gestured for quiet. "Allow me to please you further: this feast of Saint Andrew has turned into a celebration of triumph. Our English mercenaries have trapped Callan ap McGowan and his outlaws in a cave near Ballymore. Dublin is now free of Callan's tyranny!"

Annora gasped along with the crowd. *Kill Bardan's murderer slowly, Englishmen. Make him suffer.*

She had not grieved alone; many in the hall had husbands, wives, or children who perished by Callan's hand. When the news settled in, the crowd leapt up and unleashed joyous cries. Fergal threw Annora off his lap to join them, but trapped her hand with a crushing grip.

The king's voice rose again. "So my subjects, raise a cup to Earl Harold Godwinson and his Englishmen. They may be fugitives, but their hunting prowess is beyond measure!"

Fergal reached for an ale cup with his free hand. "To Earl Harold," he shouted along with the guests and added under his breath, "the great hunter."

Everyone in Dublin knew the tale. Jealous rivals convinced the English king to banish Earl Harold and his family, and then hired Norman mercenaries to chase them away. The earl fled to Dublin and found the city in ruins after the raid. He and Diarmit struck a bargain: in exchange for Callan's death, the king would provide Harold with ships and men to force a return home.

He left before Annora ever saw him. The few servants who did said Harold resembled the pagan sun god, Lugh, in both stature and fierceness. Moreover, their tongues dripped of the earl's infatuation for his pagan wife.

Fergal's tongue, on the other hand, was infatuated with Annora. He leered at her again. "Now where was I?"

Glancing around the hall, she saw thralls refilling cups. "A moment, m'lord. The guests need more ale. If I don't help, the queen'll have me whipped."

"The whip shouldn't worry you, pretty. Deny me again and you'll have more pressing hurts."

The king cleared his throat to silence the hall and turned his beaming face to Fergal and Annora. While she lowered her head and cringed, Diarmit said, "It appears our honored scald has returned with fortuitous timing.

What say you, Fergal: Will you bless us with a victory gift?"

The singer released Annora's hand. "As you wish, lord king. In fact, I've returned to do exactly that."

He grabbed his cloaked object and sauntered to the head dais. When he removed the cloth, whispers swirled in the hall. "My god," a man said. "A golden lute..."

Annora sneered. *A gold painted lute perhaps.* Bardan had been the court's previous scald. She had cherished her husband's songs accompanied by his plain, time-worn lute above all things. "It's not how it looks," Bardan would say. "It's how it sounds."

Fergal strummed the strings, adjusted the tensions, strummed again, and nodded. "I learned this ode while on pilgrimage to Constantinople."

As he started singing, she had to concede his voice, not his lute, was a real treasure. The crowd welcomed his rich, clear verses like the earth welcomed rain after a drought. He sang of an ancient battle, where heroes used guile, not swords, to breach an impenetrable fortress. Brigit stared at her singer, dabbing eyes with her sleeve.

Annora stepped backward, yet no heads turned. The song flared in intensity, but never broke rhythm. With fear biting at her throat, she back-shuffled to the doors. Her hand reached the iron handle at last. And after a gentle nudge, she slipped into the night.

A chilling breeze carried the promise of rain. Clouds cloaked the stars, the half-moon, and the king's estate. No sentries paced the grounds and several torches had guttered. *Bardan is guiding my way.*

Enclosed by a giant wooden rampart, the palace precinct sat on a hill above Dublin Bay. It consisted of the palace, the servant's hut where Aidan now slept, a guest house, and a stone chapel.

Yearning to fly to Aidan, she headed to the guest house instead. One emotion dominated all others as she crossed the quiet yard: hope. Her husband's killer lay dying, she had delivered a beautiful boy into God's service, and she now approached the one person who could save them.

She reached the house with a pounding heart. After a glance to ensure no one watched, she cracked the door open.

Inside the circular room, a single candle flame danced on a table. The hot air held scents of sweat and beeswax. A form lay underneath thick pelts beyond the table.

"Lady Edith? I'm sorry for the intru—"

"Shut the door."

"Yes, m'lady. I'm sorry." She stepped in and closed the door behind her. Fergal's song fell to a muffled echo.

Annora smoothed her skirts and collected her wits. The first time she saw Earl Harold's wife, Lady Edith Swanneschals, she swore she gazed upon an angel. Tall and willowy, the noblewoman didn't walk so much as glide. Thick brown hair cascaded past her shoulders and bronze eyes shimmered like polished amber. Instead of Brigit's harsh company, Edith preferred to talk with farmers, brush horses, and play hide-and-seek with children. The insulted queen placed her in isolation, saying Edith needed protection from the rabble.

These memories emboldened Annora. "How are you feeling, m'lady?"

"I'm fine. You may go."

"Yes, m'lady. I...I do hope you feel better, but I wanted to ask a question. Well, it's not so much a question, but an offer—"

"I want for nothing. Please leave. Now."

Annora's gut tensed. *Has her suffering turned her?* While Edith and Harold escaped to Dublin, their three boys were rescued by other kinfolk and carried to a distant land. Then, after Harold left to chase Callan, the babe she carried in her belly didn't live to see his first sunrise.

Fighting back the doubt, Annora said, "Yes, Lady Edith. I just wanted to offer my services. I know what you're going through and I can help."

Applause from the palace broke Annora's attention. She panicked; the feast would be over soon. "We share a bond, m'lady. Our boys were born on the same day. That has to mean something to you; it does to me. I can help you. My boy will too, once he's old enough."

The noblewoman didn't respond. Embarrassment built on top of Annora's strain. "Please Lady Edith. I can't stay here. Queen Brigit hates me." Thoughts of Fergal's touch and Brigit's whip crept in. Tears made the room blurry. "Please..."

With her plan failing, Annora grew resolute. She'd steal away from the palace with Aidan and search for a nunnery. "I'm sorry to have bothered you..." She turned to leave.

"Wait."

Edith's torso rose. The pelts fell down, exposing her linen under tunic. "You're named Annora, are you not?"

The recognition jolted her. "Yes, m'lady. I...I wanted to come to you, but you've been guarded. Tonight, with everyone at the feast, I slipped out when Fergal started singing."

"The song's too much for me," Edith said, wincing. "How have you drawn Brigit's ire?"

"I've done nothing. She thinks I'm a temptress because I won't remarry."

"What happened to your husband?"

"The raid, m'lady...he died protecting me from Callan. Your lord husband has the bandit trapped now. I thought you'd like to hear that at least."

Edith rearranged her position to face Annora. "Yes...good. He should be returning soon then. How old are you, child?"

"I'll be seventeen this Christmastide."

"I see. Remove your headdress; let me look at you."

The order confused her, but she didn't want to renew Edith's displeasure. So, she unwound her head scarf and let her hair fall.

"You're young and pretty. But a temptress? Your eyes hold too much honesty for the title."

Annora began to catch her breath. "Thank you." Out of the corner of her eye, she spied a thick woolen robe draped over a nearby chest. "May I bring you clothes at least? The wind's picking up outside."

"You're so eager to serve me. Why?"

She crossed the room to hand Edith the clothing. "I felt my soul shatter after I heard about your little one. You deserve so much more."

Edith clutched the fabric. "How...how do you know my fate is undeserved?"

"Because..." Annora struggled for the right words, "no one deserves that, least of all someone as kind as you."

"Dear girl, you'll learn. Kind or not, our usefulness expires when God says so."

A gusting wind caused the candle to flicker. Edith's face broke into alarm.

"A spring gale," Annora said. "Nothing more. And

you're wrong, if you don't mind me saying, Lady Edith. God just loved your babe too much to wait for his company. That's what the priest told my sister when she lost her child."

The Englishwoman's head fell. "My Beothorn...he took three breaths. Three wonderful breaths..." She broke down, the sobs rising from deep within.

Without thinking, Annora lowered and embraced her.

"God is punishing me," Edith said. "I refused to marry Harold in a church and my family is shattered because of it."

"No, Lady Edith. Don't think like that." Their embrace grew tighter, more urgent. "Bardan and I were handfasted too. We—" A strange sound cut her off. "Did you hear that?"

"The wind? The music?"

"No...It sounded like...like bells ringing..."

A loud crack broke the door open. Fergal loomed in the threshold. He held his lute in one hand and a bloody dagger in the other. "There's my pretty. No one saw you leave, except me." His smile grew blade sharp as he stepped inside.

Annora couldn't find her voice; the open door framed too horrific a scene. The feasting hall's thatch roof had burst into flames and fighting raged everywhere.

Following her unbelieving gaze, Fergal said, "A beautiful sight. Callan does his work well." He turned back and advanced. "Don't look so confused, pretty. I slit the watchmen's throats and unlocked the gates before entering the hall. My song was all the distraction Callan needed."

"But...but he's trapped..."

"Ha! The Englishman should've hired more honest guides. He watched the cave entrance, never knowing it had a hidden exit." Fergal set his lute on the table and unclasped his belt. "Now, the great hunter twiddles his thumbs outside an empty hole."

Annora felt a stir behind her. Fergal's eyes widened. "What have we here?"

Lady Edith rose to her full height. "The great hunter, as you call him, is my husband. And if you harm me or my servant, he'll rip the heart out of your chest."

The scald's smile returned. He brandished his dagger and spoke to Edith with unblinking eyes. "By the time he finds your used corpse, I'll be counting my treasure far from here."

He pounced before either woman could react. Annora fell and her face went numb. When the searing pain spread moments later, she realized his punch had struck her cheek. She saw Edith on her knees, arresting Fergal's knife-wielding arm with both hands. "I'll sample you first," he said, straining, "then it's Callan's turn."

Annora rolled on the ground. Edith screamed, "Run!"

Struggling to rise, she bumped into the table and rattled Fergal's lute.

Edith wailed as the singer's strength wore her down.

A new instinct filled Annora: she had prayed too hard, endured too much, and cried too many tears to abide this. Grasping the lute by the neck, she stepped forward and swung. The instrument struck Fergal's skull with a sickening crunch. He fell against the wall and dropped the dagger. Without hesitation, she grabbed the blade and cut Fergal's throat with a harsh horizontal strike, just as Callan had killed her husband.

The traitor's eyes fluttered. He opened his mouth, but his song produced only red bubbles.

When he collapsed, her hands flew to her mouth and

the blade clattered to the floor. She looked to her new mistress, expecting to find an abhorred face staring back. Instead, the noblewoman lowered Annora's hands and said, "Don't fret; that beast deserved worse. Come. Let's escape before another brigand finds us."

Annora shook her head. "My boy. Aidan. I can't leave without him."

The room fell quiet as Edith absorbed her words. Then, without a hint of doubt, she said, "All right. You lead the way."

They raced into the courtyard. Cries from men, women, and children competed with the clash of steel, howling wolves, raging fires, and ringing church bells.

She led Edith behind the guest house where the rampart shadow hid them from firelight. At the main gate, however, the shadow gave way and they stepped over two watchmen who died with surprised looks on their faces. Annora's last remnants of shame for taking Fergal's life fled.

Crossing to the compound's other side, she noticed swords clashed less, the bell chimes lessened, and the wails quieted. Then, Annora stopped.

Edith looked at her, confused. "What is it?"

She pointed at the servant's hut. It wore a crown of flame.

"Come! We have to try!" Edith grabbed her arm and pulled.

Annora's heart hammered inside her chest. "No. Not my boy. Not my little boy!"

Wild shouts emitted from the shadows. In the next instant, brown demons jumped out. After a brief scuffle, Lady Edith disappeared and a grizzled, mud-covered man hefted Annora over his shoulder. She hung limp as the outlaw carried her to the yard.

When he tossed her down, her senses returned. Flames still engulfed the servant's hut roof. Lady Edith sat nearby. Captured feasting guests huddled together off to the side. The king and queen were separated from everyone and held at sword point.

A new voice rose over the din. "Is this the earl's wife, Diarmit?"

"Ye...Yes it is."

A lanky man with sweat-slicked blond hair, thin lips, and a hooked nose spoke. He wore leather armor like the others, but also a black cloak with gold embroidery. Annora's eyes deadened. *Callan.*

The outlaw crouched down to Edith. "Your husband's an admirable warrior; he chases us even now. We can't stay his sword, but I'll wager you can."

Edith glared back. "Take me if you must, but let these people save their loved ones."

Callan shrugged and pointed to Diarmit. "They followed that fat sow's orders. Now, their loyalty has turned to treason." From the folds of his cloak, Callan revealed Dublin's crown. He placed it on his head and rose.

His smile blocked Annora's view of the burning hut. In that instant, her new-found rage sparked. She rose and shrieked a death knell. Her nails bit into Callan's flesh. Her soul drank his surprised cry. She pressed deeper and harder and battle joy found her.

But then a burst of pain slowed the world. Her fingers ignored her will, relaxed, and slid away. She felt no panic even when bile coated her tongue, her back crashed to the ground, and numbness seized every limb. Looking down, she saw a slick, red stain spreading on her tunic under her breast.

Callan's face filled her vision again. "Well done, slut. You managed to break my skin. Diarmit's entire household couldn't even lay a ha—" He looked up. "No! How could that be? Where was my alarm?" The outlaw disappeared amid fresh screams, the renewed clash of swords, and the whinnying of horses.

Moments or lifetimes later – Annora could not tell which – a loud thump shook the earth. She turned and found Callan lying next to her. Scratch marks covered his face and a spear jutted from his chest. Strange shouts filled her ears, but she recognized one with ease: "Harold."

Faces and shapes flashed by. Lady Edith appeared, but soon hurried away. After a while, another face came into focus. This man had long straw-colored hair and a beard of russet. His eyes shone like blue flame. He cleaned her cheeks with warm hands.

"Brave soul," he said. "Without you, my Edith would've been taken captive."

"Lord Harold," she said, gripping his forearm, "My boy...the servant's quarters..."

"I know, child. We're trying. Rest now. Rest."

The earl ran off and someone lifted Annora's torso. Beyond leather-clad bodies lay the burning hut. She could only watch.

Her breath had grown labored when an infant's wail filled the night. The sound grew, yet she only allowed herself to believe when she beheld Lord Harold.

Soot covered his armor. His hair was matted and singed, yet his ash-covered face smiled. He held Aidan, who screamed from a blanket bundle. Lady Edith came up behind them, covered in soot as well.

When Annora pulled him in, Aidan's roaring softened slightly.

"He'll be okay, sweet one," Edith knelt and stroked Annora's forehead. "The fire didn't reach him, but a falling beam broke his foot."

She clutched her child tighter, not caring that tears and blood soiled his blanket.

"Annora," Edith said, "our time is short; you must listen. You not only saved me, but your attack on Callan distracted his men long enough for Harold to close in. Now, we can go home, clear our names, and reunite our family. How can we ever repay you?"

A torrent of pain forced her to squeeze Edith's hand. "Take him, m'lady. Please. After I'm gone, watch him for me."

The noblewoman brought their intertwined hands to her chest. "I swear, under the eyes of God, I will rear Aidan as one of my own."

A new height of joy seized Annora. "He'll watch after you too, Lady Edith. I know he will."

She tried to say more but her breath cut short. Darkness encroached and she grew too tired to resist. After a brief pause, an invisible hand lifted her from the ground. Looking up, she smiled. Bardan was striding down from the clearing night, lute in hand.

Chapter 1: Odo

June 30, 1065

Alone in the bed of his palace chamber, Bishop Odo of Bayeux flinched awake to the sound of squeaking door hinges. His weariness vanished in a jolt of fear.

The ensuing steps, however, held a familiar softness. His cry for help died in his lungs. *It is no murderer; it's my reward for last night's work.*

Torch light from the hallway illuminated Elise's young, lithe frame. "You've slept through Lauds, lord father," the kitchen maid said, her shawl muffling her voice. "I came to see if I could be of service."

Odo spoke in a whisper. "Did anyone see you?"

"The barons are gone. The palace is near empty."

"And the duke?" The barons didn't worry him. His half-brother, Duke William of Normandy, did.

"Left on a hunt at first light, lord father."

Elise hung by the door, her head tilted and her bewitching eyes daring an upward look. In daylight, they shimmered like green sunlit ponds; in candlelight, they hardened into polished oak orbs. Even in the darkness, her stare cast its spell. Odo had only seen one other woman with such eyes.

With the palace quiet, temptation coursed through his veins. *I deserve this.* The first stage of his plan succeeded last night. William had secured England's crown after King Edward's death...thanks to Odo's plot. He wanted this pleasure now, but his brother's presence loomed.

Discretion triumphed. "No. Now is not the time for this. Go before you are seen here."

To Odo's surprise, the girl hesitated. Then, he noticed the tears welling in her eyes. "What have I done, father? You turned from me last night and again now. I need your favor. Our son needs your favor."

Odo felt his heartbeat pause for the briefest moment. He sat up. "What do you mean?"

"I'm worried for his safety. I see people whispering. He has your blood, but not your protection—"

"Not about the boy. What do you mean about last night?"

Elise's lips quivered.

"Speak!"

"You turned from me, father. You saw me emerge from Lord Beaumont's chamber after the midnight bells chimed. I didn't want to go with him, but he forced me."

"*I* saw *you?*"

"Yes. You turned away and descended the stairs before I could call out. It...it looked as if you were angry."

"*Impossible!* I did not leave my chamber *all night!*"

She began shaking. "My lord, I...I..."

With a disgusted growl, he rose from the bed. "What did this *man* look like?"

"You! I...I swear to God." Her eyes strained. "It was just

a glimpse in the darkness, but he was tall like you and he wore your cloak...who else could it have been? Please don't hurt me, lord father!"

Odo tried to make sense of this madness. Half the men in Normandy wore similar garments. As he focused, Elise's mewling grew untenable. "Be gone! And keep your mouth shut, or a whipping will be the best outcome to befall you."

The maid shivered a nod and fled the room.

Alone, Odo stood in darkness. He had stayed up until dawn discussing his plans with his military captain, Egenulf D'Laigle. No one else had entered or left. Since Elise saw the man at midnight, she must have stumbled on a spy.

When he became bishop at the age of nineteen, rebels against William's authority infested Bayeux. The purge had taken the better part of his fourteen years in office and his tactics earned him the title of Beelzebub's bishop, but no soul in his domain – serf, merchant, or lord – would dare spy on him. *No one in my domain would...*

An answer forced his eyes to the door; he envisioned it breaking open then and there. If someone in the duke's employ overheard the conversation... *God could not be so cruel.*

The prospect spurred him into action. He threw his vestments on, raced out of the chamber, and descended to the palace's great hall. His feet had just reached the floor when an overwhelming presence accosted him.

"You seem in a hurry, Odo."

The Duke of Normandy sat at the head of the torch-lit feasting board, stiff and tall. He wore a dark tunic and blood-red cloak that contrasted his pale skin. His eyes – deep-set, dark brown, and covered by full, angled brows – showed complete steadiness.

"William. I...I was on my way to church. You've returned early."

"Very astute. Come. Sit next to me."

Flushing, Odo did as his half-brother bid. "Was the hunt unpleasing? I trust this has nothing to do with my guides or servants."

"Your servants mattered little...at first. All morning I chased through the woods, relishing in last night's triumph." He looked at Odo with a dark expression. "And then, just moments ago, I learned what you were up to."

"You learned—"

"Yes. And my disgust knows no bounds."

Odo clutched William's forearm. "I...I can explain."

"I need no explanation." William ripped his arm away. "The transgression couldn't be more naked. After all I've done for you, you repay me with subterfuge. I have half a mind to depose you right now."

The bishop thrust his hands out. "No. It's not what it seems."

"Oh? Tell me what it is then. The girl came crying down the stairs, rushed past my guards, and begged me to recognize *my* nephew. She had to be pried from my ankles."

"The girl? Your anger stems from Elise?"

"She knew your birthmark, Odo. If she hadn't seen it, another whore must've painted a pretty picture."

Collecting himself, Odo summoned his most penitent face. "I...I won't deny it. She bewitched me, William. I fathered a child by her, an abomination that spits in the face of my Savior and my family."

William sprang from his chair. "Devil's eyes, Odo! How could you be so stupid? I tasked you with solidifying

Bayeux, not scandalizing it. How many more bastards breathe?"

"None. I swear brother. I made one mistake. Just one. Please have mercy."

"If you were any other man, I'd gut you like a hooked trout. But my mother's blood runs through your veins and last night's feast was your idea. Because of those two reasons only, you will live to right your wrong."

"Yes brother. I'll do anything."

The duke folded his arms over his chest. "First, promise to do away with the wench and her spawn. I will *not* tolerate illegitimate branches growing from my noble stem."

"Yes brother. Right away." Odo maintained his beggar's face despite the smile threatening to form. William hated bastards, even though he was one himself. The result of a roadside dalliance between a tanner's daughter named Hereleva and Duke Robert of Normandy, William was nine years older than Odo. When Robert died on pilgrimage to the Levant, Hereleva passed into the arms of Odo's future father, a minor landholder named Hereluin.

"I'm not done," William said. "A detail from last night bothers me; it's why I returned early. I've tried to dismiss the agitation, but it persists."

"Well let me help. I may have been detained through the evening," Odo lied, "but I've been apprised of everything."

"It's Godwinson. He...he didn't seem himself when he pledged to support my claim. I wish to question him about it."

Odo feigned shock. "Alas, I fear you're too late. He's already sailing home, per your orders. But don't fret, brother. Nothing's amiss most like. From all accounts, the earl had his senses and spoke of his own will. Twenty barons witnessed his pledge."

William's face did not lighten. "Make inquiries anyway. We chased Godwinson to Ireland once, but he came back stronger and more determined than ever to keep Normans away from England's crown. This oath was supposed to tame him, but I fear he may have some recourse to stray."

Rising from his chair, Odo acted like the idea abhorred him. "Invalidate the oath...You think he'd do such a thing?"

"You never saw the fight in the man. The only time he looked docile was when he made that pledge."

Odo continued to calm. "Well, let's hope Harold's word proves true and we've spent our time on conjecture," he said. "Still, I should begin my inquiries immediately."

"Go with all haste." Odo tried to leave, but William held out a hand and blocked his way. The two brothers were of a similar height, but the duke's soldiery gave him the more powerful build. In Odo's thirty-three years on earth, no one made him feel smaller. "And remember one thing: *Never* keep secrets from me again."

"Of course, brother. And thank you. Your lenience is the greatest gift I could ask for."

After kissing William's hand, Odo crossed the hall and barged through the double-oak doors to the outside. Nervous sweat combined with thick, tepid air to coat his skin in perspiration.

He overlooked the courtyard separating his palace from Bayeux Cathedral. Construction tools, scaffolding, and chiseled stones were strewn about while dozens of workmen hefted beams, hammered nails, and yelled over the din. When finished, his cathedral would challenge any great house of God. The builders had already completed the sanctuary, transepts, and crypt, allowing for services ahead of schedule. *My church rises; my calling nears; and yet my doom is eminent unless I quiet this spy.*

Just then, Richard and Aubrey de Flers emerged from the cathedral's front entrance. The twin chevaliers walked side by side, each with a hand resting on a sheathed sword. Their chain mail coats and iron spurs gleamed in the sun. After guarding Godwinson for weeks, they had drawn the task of taking him to his ship this morning.

Odo stalked across the muddy yard and waved the warriors to a halt. "Well met, my sons. I trust the Englishman departed well enough?"

"Ye...yes, lord bishop," Richard said. Neither brother spoke much, an attribute laudable for gaolers but useless for informants.

"Did he seem distressed in any way?"

"Seemed exhausted last night, l...lord father, and..."

Both warriors hesitated and Odo's temper flared. "What?"

"And stricken by the de...Devil after he woke."

"Have no fear on his account," the bishop said. "Emotion from the feast drained him, that's all. Understood? If *anyone* asks, you say he left in fine spirits."

"Yes lord father," they said in unison.

After the brothers took their leave, Odo entered the church. Since the next divine office would not occur for some time, he knew it would offer a place of solitude. Crossing the nave, he assessed his danger. The twins had been set in line, so William wouldn't learn of the poisoning unless the spy told him.

Father Gilbert emerged from the northern transept as Odo neared the altar. He wore the gray robe of the Benedictine order and held a bible in his hands. The plump, tonsured priest should have returned to his monastic precinct by now. "What are you doing here?"

"The twins, Richard and Aubrey, needed a holy witness, lord father."

"A witness for what?"

"A sacred oath. They swore to resist all temptations of the grape for the rest of their lives after last night."

Odo stepped forward with his eyes leveled. "They *drank* last night?"

The priest's chin retracted into his neck. "Ye...yes. The kitchener offered a barrel of stale wine to the garrison. The de Flers had just a little, but woke greatly discontented."

Without having to ask, he knew the kitchener released the same barrel Godwinson drank from. If Richard and Aubrey had more than a few sips, they would have slept through Armageddon. A scenario formed in Odo's mind that unleashed a deluge of fear. "In this oath, did they say anything about their prisoner?"

"The prisoner? Nothing untoward, Bishop Odo. When they woke, the room key lay safe with Richard and the Englishman slept soundly on his pallet."

Odo's chest constricted. He had given the key specifically to Aubrey. They may have switched possession during the evening, but Odo knew in his gut they did not. Odo grabbed Father Gilbert by his robe collar. "Go fetch those sinners. *Now*. No oath will protect them from this breach of discipline."

After the priest scrambled out of the church, Odo turned to the sanctuary altar and fell to his knees. "Why God? Why did you let my secret slip into *Godwinson's* hands?"

Chapter 2: Aidan

July 1, 1065

In the forest surrounding the small fishing village of Bosham, Aidan struggled to keep pace with the long-striding Bishop Wulfstan. The fading dusk offered dwindling assistance. The trees seemed to enjoy throwing obstacles in his path. The fifteen-year-old boy felt besieged by snapping twigs, crunching leaves, and his own heaving breath.

"This way," Wulfstan called. The old man seemed to get more energetic by the moment. "Hurry Aidan. Don't fall too far behind. We're almost there."

"Yes father. Coming." He gnashed his teeth and pushed even harder. As he mounted a small incline, his deformed foot snagged on a root. He stumbled and averted a fall only by snatching a nearby tree limb. "God's bones!"

"I heard that. Three Hail Mary's. Now."

Shoulders slumping, Aidan pulled a rosary from his

robe and began the penance. He mouthed the rote prayer and chased the bishop once more. As he prayed, he wondered for the thousandth time why they rushed in the first place.

Wulfstan's nature had something to do with it, for certs. If Aidan had learned anything during his yearlong novitiate, it was Wulfstan of Worcester did not tolerate idleness. The two had met when Lady Edith sent Aidan to Worcester monastery for his education. Since that warm summer day, Wulfstan had instituted a rigorous schedule of study, chores, and prayer that mirrored the brotherhood's activities.

Five nights ago, however, the bishop flew into Aidan's sleeping cell. "Wake up boy. Grab your things, enough to fill two saddlebags but no more. We leave within the hour." They departed Worcester like thieves and spent every daylight hour in the saddle. During the entire trip, Wulfstan explained the journey by repeating one phrase: "God has called us to Bosham."

Now, as Aidan shuffled down this narrow path leading toward the fishing docks, he felt more baffled than ever. He assumed the calling involved Earl Harold, who was long overdue after a journey across the great channel. Similar villages lined Chichester Harbor, but Bosham claimed the earl's ancestral home and his most likely return port. But the village was empty and the earl was nowhere to be found.

So, after the prayers, Aidan asked God his own silent question. "Is this a punishment, Lord? I only smiled at the goldsmith's daughter once."

Up ahead, Wulfstan came to a stop where the forest thinned. He leaned on his staff, signed the cross over his chest, and fixed his stare on the distance. Aidan hobbled to the bishop's side and followed his gaze.

They stood at an opening to a crescent-shaped inlet fading into the blue blanket of night. The green water lay still and no sound disturbed the scene, save for the occasional jumping fish.

Then, beyond an old gray-wood dock, a snarling, black-eyed dragon head cut through the evening mist. The red-scaled monster bared its ivory fangs and lashed out with its stiff, forked tongue. Aidan recognized the prow carving with an audible gasp. *The Dragon of Wessex* was the same longship that carried Aidan from Ireland. Growing up in Lady Edith's household, he had spent several nights camped by its moorings. Earl Harold had indeed returned home.

"Father," Aidan said, his voice spilling wonder. "The longship...God was right all along."

Wulfstan stroked his beard from chin to navel. "The Almighty works in mysterious ways...mysterious, amazing ways. Come. Let's greet our old frie—"

A tortured yell broke the stillness. It came from the beach. After exchanging a quick glance, Aidan and Wulfstan raced toward the scream's source. The bishop rushed ahead as the boy raked his crippled foot over the uneven shore. With every step, shapes in the dark grew more definite. Then, Aidan heard frightened whispers.

He found two dozen men at the shore. Some sobbed. Others had fallen to their knees and were lifting handfuls of wet pebbles to the sky. "Thank you, God! Thank you," one man said as the pebbles sifted through his fingers and clicked to the ground. Most men huddled around an invalid who shook in uncontrollable violence with his back in the shallows. Aidan saw Wulfstan leaning over the afflicted person and hurried over.

What he saw shocked him to the core. Harold Godwinson, the Earl of Wessex, the *Subregulus* of England, the commander of the royal army, and the man who rescued Aidan from certain death, shook like a Devil-possessed child. His chest raised and lowered in disjointed breathes and his blue eyes searched everywhere and nowhere at once.

Earl Harold's head turned to the bishop. "F...Father Wulfstan?" His voice was as broken as the rest of him.

"Yes, dear son. I'm here. Aidan is as well. Your men say this sickness overtook you on the journey home. We must get you to a hearth. You need dryness and warmth." The bishop motioned for the men to lift him.

"N...No!" The earl convulsed and grasped for Wulfstan's Benedictine robe with ghost-white hands. "To church...to confession! God what have I done? This pain is too much...too much to bear!"

Aidan's whole body froze. He'd never heard this great man sound so desperate, so scared. Wulfstan, however, stared at the earl with narrowed, pensive eyes.

One of the crewmen looked up. "He's been rantin 'bout his sins the whole way home, lord bishop. It's a good thing you're here."

Wulfstan's eyes never left Harold, but he began speaking in calm, quiet certainty. "You men help the earl. Find him new clothes and cover him with fresh blankets if you can. If there's stew cooking in the manor's hearth, get him a bowl. My novice and I will prepare the parish church. Bring him when he's ready."

"Yes, father," the crewman said.

Wulfstan reached down and placed a reassuring hand

on his friend's shoulder. "Have faith, my son. Your burden will be before God soon."

He began striding toward the fisherman's path they followed earlier. Aidan swallowed a protest and shuffled behind. He wanted to stay and help his foster-father, but defying the bishop went against his training. He could not, however, abide any more mystery. "Father, what is going on?"

When Wulfstan turned, fear dominated his face. "Never, in my wildest imagination, did I expect this. The sins are driving him mad."

Aidan furrowed his brow. "Well, perhaps the confession will help ease his pain."

"I pray to God it will, but there's more. It appears God has called on us to do the impossible." The bishop led Aidan down the path. "What I told you about God's calling was true. He did lead us here...to perform a task. As I prayed alone in St. Mary's, a whisper flew into my ears: *'Go to Bosham and save the truth.'* I could just hear at first, but the voice grew until it drowned out all other sound. Since then, the voice relented, but did not disappear until Harold begged for his confession."

Aidan knew better than to doubt Wulfstan's story. The bishop could hear God whisper in a thunderstorm. "Save the truth? What truth?"

"Only the earl knows. Somehow, some way, we must save what he says tonight."

The path opened to show a view of Bosham's small huts and cots cloaked in a moon-lit evening. Before veering down the westward church path, Aidan prayed Harold's ancestral manor, which dominated a rise to the east, would help the stricken earl return to his old self. "Why don't we wait until he feels better?"

"Guilt is a terrible affliction and Harold's soul is rife with it," the bishop said. "I hope I'm wrong, but this confession may be Harold's last."

They rounded a bend and Bosham's parish church shined in the growing moon light. Not wasting any time, Wulfstan rushed to the entrance door and shouldered it open.

"But father," Aidan said, following Wulfstan into the stone-walled church. "How do you intend to save his words?"

"I don't know."

Inside, a lone torch sitting on a column sconce had yet to gutter. Wulfstan raced to the faint orange light, stood on the tips of his sandals, and nursed the flame with short, delicate breaths.

Aidan remained at the threshold. Ever since he could remember, fire stirred the depths of his soul. He understood flames had nurtured men for ages and many people considered it God's greatest gift. He also realized God himself had come to earth on more than one occasion in the form of fire. Yet no amount of warmth, protection, or light could alleviate the fear gripping him when a blaze came too close.

"Don't just stand there, boy. Help me light the..." The bishop paused. "Yes. Forgive me. I'll light the sconces; you set the altar candles."

Aidan nodded and traversed the nave. The only flame he could ever tolerate was the small, docile light of a candle. For without it, he could not write past sundown. Besides, a candle light could be snuffed with moistened fingers.

With the torches lit, Bosham's parish church took form. It ran no more than seventy paces long, but the stone walls stood taller than three grown men stacked high. Old wood support columns lined the empty nave. To Aidan's surprise, the altar displayed three panels of gilded oak. Each panel showed four apostles spreading their arms out to the congregation. Behind the altar loomed a life-sized wooden crucifix.

The sanctuary sparked an arresting guilt in Aidan's mind. Confessions were not meant to be saved. Once the ritual started, the sinner did not speak to a priest or clergyman; he spoke to God. Violating any part of the sacrament was unthinkable.

He did not hear Wulfstan approach the altar. "I think I've figured out how to save the confession," the bishop said.

"What do you intend to do, father?" He clasped his hands together to stop their shaking.

"God's orders were explicit: we must 'save the truth.' To disregard Him would endanger our souls. And He helped us; He guided you here through me... because of your gift."

"M...my gift?" He knew exactly what the bishop spoke of, but asked the question to buy time.

The proudest moment of his novitiate occurred on the day of his first examination. After Aidan presented his wax tablet etchings, Wulfstan's face had soured. "The other boys aren't half-finished. How did you do this?"

"I wrote as you spoke, father."

"Do not play games with me, boy. I read from a sermon of St. Gregory you could not have heard before. The task was to write down his main tenets. You've replicated the entire reading. Who let you read the sermon beforehand?"

"No one, lord father."

"We'll see."

Wulfstan read three more sermons. Each time, the words converted into their visible form just after hitting Aidan's ears. From then on, Wulfstan contemplated no other future for him except a monastic life where he could create books that glorify the Almighty's presence on earth.

Now, the bishop asked him to write words in defiance of the mother church's edicts. "If there's anyone who can save Harold's words, you can. You even brought parchment, quills, and ink to continue your translations."

"Please, Bishop Wulfstan, *don't* ask me to do this."

The bishop shook his head in slow, sweeping turns. "I know you're scared, Aidan. I am too. I've spent my whole life revering this sacrament above all others. I wish some other solution presented itself. But Harold may not survive the night and we're tasked with saving *his* truth."

Aidan tried to appeal with his eyes. "Father, I don't think I can do it."

"I absolve you from the sin, dear boy. Tonight's actions rest on my shoulders. Think of it as an examination, nothing more. Let the words flow like they always have."

"I...I still don't know."

Wulfstan sighed. "I won't order you to do this, Aidan. You must come to the task with a free heart. All I can say is you owe the earl your life. By following God's orders tonight, you may return the favor."

Aidan scowled as he thought. He would commit no sin; that burden would fall to the bishop. He would be following God's orders. And most importantly, he might help save Earl Harold's life. After a long, silent pause, he made up his mind. "I'll get my supplies."

Outside, the distant waves competed with the call of night insects. He paused to let his eyes readjust to the night and then headed to the riding ponies, which were tethered to a post outside the village. He concentrated on every step as a way to avoid thinking about the upcoming task. The journey took far shorter than he wished. Muttering and shaking his head, Aidan unstrapped the saddlebag containing a stack of lined parchment pages, two inkpots, and five sharpened quills. Hefting the bag over his shoulder, he began the return trip. Confusion and fear mounted with each moment.

At long last, he arrived back at the church and found Wulfstan kneeling before the altar. "Set your things down and come pray with me," his master said.

Aidan did as ordered. Kneeling next to the bishop gave him a comfort he sorely needed.

"Dear God, we know not what happened to our friend," Wulfstan said. "Yet he has returned as a shattered vestige of his former self. We will follow Your path though it threatens the holy sacrament of confession. We will turn this sinner back toward Your good grace although he swears he is cast out forever. Most of all, we will endeavor to save his words even though we fear them as we fear the end of days. God have mercy on our souls. Amen."

The creaking door announced Harold's arrival. Both he and the crewman who supported him still wore the drenched clothes from the seashore. The earl's gray tunic and brown breeches clung to his skin, revealing a man with half his former strength. His red-gold beard hung wild from his chin and his eyes still searched for solace.

"Lord bishop, the earl refused new garb and would take no food. He keeps warning of great sins, of England and even the Holy Land on the brink of destruction—"

"*God, what have I done?*" The scream echoed in the empty church.

Wulfstan approached and hooked one of the earl's arms around his neck. "I can take him from here, my son."

"Yes, lord bishop. The voyage," he said with a shaking head. "I just don't know what happened."

The bishop regarded the crewman for a long moment. "You speak with a strange accent, friend. Are you new to the earl's service?"

"Yes and no," the man said. He stood near as tall as the earl and almost as broad. "He came to my rescue when—"

"Father?" The earl convulsed and almost fell. "Confess me now!"

"All right, my son. All right."

The crewman excused himself as Aidan rushed forward. "Earl Harold, it's me. It's Aidan."

The earl craned his neck to regard him. "Is it really you, boy? Is Edith here?"

"No, lord." He hooked the earl's other arm around his shoulders. "She's back in Nazeing with your sons and daughters." Lady Edith told the story many times. After Beothorn's death, she thought she was barren, yet the bravery of Aidan's mother instilled in her new confidence, resulting in two beautiful daughters named Gytha and Gunhild.

"My family..." Harold began to shake. "I cannot wait, Wulfstan. My mind is berserk."

They reached the space before the altar and lowered the earl to his knees.

"Just a moment more," Wulfstan said. "I know you're stricken, my son, but you must listen to me." Wulfstan breathed deep. "I knew to arrive tonight because God sent me."

Harold's head snapped back and he regarded the

bishop with bewildered eyes. He then cast his gaze to the crucifix in the sanctuary. "He told you to come? Why?"

"I was ordered to save the truth."

"The truth. But the truth is my confession."

"I believe so, yes. Therefore, with your permission, I will hear you out as Aidan records every word."

Harold closed his eyes and hung his head. "I prayed the whole way home for an answer..." He clasped his hands tight in front of his face. "Thank you, Lord. Thank you!" When he regarded Wulfstan again, his eyes had calmed. "This is my chance, father. We must follow God's order."

"We'll begin as soon as Aidan is prepared."

Trembling, Aidan left the earl and took his saddlebag to a half-table on the side of the altar. Unlike his writing desk in Worcester, the flat table had several knobs jutting from the surface. In the following heartbeat, he panicked. *If I miss a word, there's no going back. If I interrupt, I am breaking the sacrament. If I fail, I have disobeyed God.*

His training rushed to his defense. He imagined his writing desk on a sunny day. Instead of a confession, he imagined Wulfstan reading a Psalm. Opening his mind, he prepared to ignore the breaks, pauses, and stumbles that plagued man's speech and to focus on the words. He could go back and add the formalities of a dialogue later; the words were paramount now. His fingers stretched wide and every muscle in his arm tensed.

"Then we are prepared," Wulfstan ascended the two small steps to stand in front of the altar. After one last breath, the bishop began the ritual he loved, respected, and would now violate. "In the name of the Father, the Son, and the Holy Spirit. Amen. What ails you my son?"

From his kneeling prostration, Harold flung his arms

open and lifted his head so he stared through the church's roof to Heaven.

"Forgive me father. I have sinned..."

*

When Aidan put the quill down at last, songbirds were welcoming the dawn outside. Both hands curled in pain after hours of frantic work. He lifted the edge of the parchment page and blanched; he found no more beneath it. If the confession had continued for just a few more sentences, those words would have disappeared.

Wulfstan approached. His steps held no relief or gratification. Aidan knew what was coming next; the bishop was going to burn the pages and their damning contents.

"Are you finished?"

"Yes, father."

"Give them over."

Aidan closed his weary eyes and offered up the stack. He envisioned the bishop holding them to the nearest torch, uncaring about God's orders, the hard work, or the resulting flames.

While Wulfstan rolled the pages into a bundle, the stiff, disheveled earl rose. "What will happen now, old friend?"

The rolled pages shook in Wulfstan's hand, but he made no move toward a torch. "Now, we pray you can defeat the Normans and avert this destructive course. You are the only man who can save us."

"So I am forgiven for breaking my Norman oath?"

"You are, my son. And you can make it known to the world. But I task you both," Wulfstan pointed from the earl to Aidan, "to keep the rest of the confession in total secrecy. The world is not yet ready for the horrors it contains."

But father," Aidan said, pointing at the pages in confusion. "How are we going to keep that secret? Shouldn't we…"

"Destroy it? No. I've risked God's wrath enough this day. Until a clear path opens to us, we'll have to guard these words with all the steadfastness in our hearts."

Aidan sat back in his chair, hardly believing the bishop's words. He had only wanted to help Earl Harold and obey his bishop's request. Now, after a terrifying night, he had peered into a future of blood, iron, and godlessness.

It should have overwhelmed him. He should have stood up and said he wished no part of it. Instead, one thought overcame all others to keep him quiet: *goldsmith's daughters don't smile at cowards.*

Chapter 3: Edith

July 10, 1065

Entering London through the Bishop's gate, Edith felt the familiar, portentous stir of intuition writhe inside her.

"A glorious morning, m'lady," her servant Renweard said. The old man rode next to her on a sturdy plow horse.

A smile crept on her face. She took a breath of damp summer air. "It is, my old friend. And a long-awaited one." The tickle in her stomach worked its magic. She'd first felt it two decades ago when her father welcomed a young earl to the Maypole festivities at Nazeing Manor. The resulting union with Harold had laid her life's cornerstone. She felt it again when the thrall, Annora, entered her chamber during the Irish exile. Their brief friendship healed her womb and brought Aidan into her life.

An agitated sigh emitted from Eanfled, Renweard's wife and Edith's handmaid for the short trip from Nazeing. "Long-awaited or no, this is not proper." The rotund woman, who wore a beet root-colored dress and matching wimple, sat pillion to her husband. "Your arrival should fit your station."

Dressed in a natural-colored dress, wimple, and veil, Edith looked more like a merchant's wife than an earl's. Her horse, a gray gelding named Offa, gave no hint to her status. Only the saddle that allowed her to stay horsed with both legs hanging over one side betrayed her wealth.

But unlike Eanfled, Edith cared little for propriety. She had not seen Harold since his return from the continent. Duty had kept him in London for several days and his messages gave no hint when he might leave. So, Edith summoned her two servants and set off for this surprise visit. Now, her smile turned devilish. "Chide me again, Eanfled, and my arrival will emulate Lady Godiva's ride through Coventry."

The serving woman's face creased with disgust. According to legend, Godiva rode naked through the streets to protest her lord husband's unfair taxation. "My lady, such jests are beneath you."

"Jest? I do no such thing. Godiva's tactics won her husband's attention. I can only hope to repeat her success."

Eanfled's mouth hung open. "And if King Edward catches you?"

"Peace, woman!" Renweard snapped around to glare at his wife. "Her ladyship knows what she looks like. She'll change before any royal audience."

Edith chuckled at Renweard's veiled barb. "As long as we stay away from Westminster, the king is none of our concern." Lying far outside London's walls, the great cathedral and palace had become the Edward's eternal gift to England. In fact, the sixty-one-year-old king spent his days lording over the builders instead of the realm.

But the servants did have a point, so Edith sped the

pace. Getting caught in such a state would supply more fodder for her detractors. No matter how secure Edith felt in her marriage, many powerful men dismissed her. Folk who clung to the heritage instilled by their Viking fore-fathers – like her parents – understood the union with Harold as a handfast marriage. Yet because they married in a forest grove instead of a church and because Edith's father led the ceremony instead of a priest, folk blinded by hate-spewing clergymen, including many nobles, called it concubinage.

They crossed over Cornhill and headed for Watling Street. In times past, she arrived at Harold's side to an end-less crowd of supporters, messengers, and merchants. She earned a just a few second glances today.

Compared to Nazeing's tranquility, London both ter-rified and excited her. The thoroughfares teemed with unfortunates begging for alms, burghers hocking their wares from corner stalls, and servants scurrying to com-plete chores. Most of the traffic flowed west, toward the hammering and chiseling of Westminster. An increasing number of stone houses had sprung up amidst the wattle and daub huts. Clanging metal mixed with incessant live-stock brays and human shouts.

Making their way south toward the Thames, the houses grew in density, as did the overpowering stench of dung. Harold's manse took up four plots of riverfront just west of London Bridge. As she approached, Edith's pulse quickened.

After dismounting at the stables, Renweard and Ean-fled left to buy supplies at the market. Edith turned to the weathered-timber manor roofed with golden thatch. Sol-diers, servants, and scribes milled around the entrance, but she felt no fear. These were Harold's men. *With any luck, this will be their last glimpse of me today.* She felt her skin prickle.

Finding the thick entry doors unlocked, she stepped inside. The hall was dark except for a hearth fire at the far end. Edith had expected more men to fill the feasting board and line the walls, but only one figure sat with his back to the doors. In an instant, the writhing grew so strong Edith put a hand on her stomach to calm it.

"Harold?"

He turned and Edith's smile vanished. She faced a ghost of her husband. He sat on a bench in a plain, rough spun tunic, his head leaning to the side. "Edith. What are you doing here?" His voice held cold surprise.

"I...I wanted to see you." A weight in the back of her mind made her walk slow. "None of your messages said when you planned to come home."

He offered a weary nod. "I haven't fully recovered from my journey."

"What afflicts you?" She reached him, yet he made no attempt to rise; he hardly even met her gaze. "Come home," she said, sitting on the bench and feeling his damp forehead. "Let me take care of you."

"No." He turned his head away. "The malady's fading and I'm needed here."

"Edward can live without you."

"I'm fine. Truly. How are the children?" He stretched his legs to rest by the circular hearth.

Edith moved closer, trying to spark energy back into him. "Godwine spars with the smith's son, Rand, every day. Magnus and Edmund watch them like hunting cats. Gunhild has..." She trailed off as Harold gazed into the flames. "Forgive me. Am I boring you?"

His eyes fluttered. "No, no. My mind's scattered. That's all."

Edith placed her hands in her lap. Throughout their marriage, she had made a point to stay out of his affairs. Today, however, she couldn't bear this enormous distance between them. "Does my arrival upset you?"

"Of course not. I just spent too long away. Matters of the realm preoccupy me."

"What delayed you anyway? You said your hunting trip in Ponthieu would last a few weeks. You were gone almost three months."

His sigh almost ached. "The trip unfolded under a curse. My friend, Count Guy...well, he changed since I saw him last."

"That was eight years ago. Of course he changed. Did he harm you?"

"No. *He* did not."

She touched his tense shoulder. "Did someone else? You look as if you lost your soul."

"Edith, I told you. It's just a passing illness." He clasped her hand. His palm felt cold and dry. "At one point, I feared for my life, but Wulfstan chased away the malignant spirits—"

"Wulfstan? When did you see him?"

"He met me in Bosham."

"Was Aidan with him?"

"As a matter of fact, yes."

Edith removed her hand from his grasp. "Jesu Harold! You know I've been guilt-ridden since I sent him to Worcester. How's the boy faring?"

From the time he could speak, Aidan's mind had proven insatiable. He had learned to write and speak Latin before any of her boys could sign their names. So, praying for Annora's approval, she had sent him to learn from England's fairest and most demanding clergyman: Wulfstan of Worcester.

"The little firebrand's well." Harold smiled for the first time. "He's grown some, although I fear he'll always be slight. Wulfstan says he'll join the brotherhood in the spring."

"The brotherhood?" She shook her head. "We call him firebrand for a reason, and it's not just because he emerged from a burning hut. He was supposed to learn from Wulfstan, not follow the bishop's footsteps. Why didn't you tell me about this?"

"Other matters have taken precedence. Besides, we agreed to let Wulfstan run his education and this is what the bishop decided."

The answer fired her anger. "These pressing matters have blinded you. The boy won't last the year in a cloister."

"Look Edith, I'd hoped to avoid this bickering—"

"I don't mean to bicker; I'm just worried about Aidan...and you."

His neck stiffened. "Well, there's no need. This last journey has opened my eyes in many ways. Wulfstan is to be trusted without question and I...I won't have much time to return home from now on."

"What? Why?"

Harold met her irate eyes and showed the first glimmer of fight. "I'm sworn to secrecy, Edith. Stare at me all you want, but I won't relent and neither will Wulfstan."

"There must be something you can say. How will I explain this to our children?"

He turned to the fire and measured his words. "England is under assault. The armies are as yet unseen, but they're assembling. Given Edward's age and ineptitude, I will mount the realm's defense. Until the battles are fought and won, I must guard our shores."

The sound of crackling flames filled the hall as the intuition in her stomach twitched. "I'm not asking you to disregard your duties. If anything, coming home will help. How can you be steadfast with a weak constitution?"

"You misunderstand me. My path leads into the unknown, but I have promised God I will make every sacrifice to guard the land."

Every sacrifice...Dear God! "You plan to sacrifice us. Is that what you mean?"

His pained face told her all she needed to know. Making things worse, he lied. "I have no such plans. You know I love you and you alone. I just meant that matters of state will occupy me for the foreseeable future."

Unbidden tears streamed down her cheeks. "After all these years...What happened? Why forsake us now?"

"I'm not *forsaking* anyone. But winning a war takes precedence over everything; you must understand that."

"Can't you see?" The strength in her voice fled. "You're threatening to abandon your family."

He reached out and cupped her chin. "You're more wrong than you know, Edith. I'm protecting my family and countless others." Without warning, he rose. "Now, I must ride to Westminster. Important messages need my approval. Will you stay in London tonight? We can talk more after I return."

"I...I cannot stay here one moment more."

Bowing his head, he reached out to brush her cheek. "My love, I...I'm sorry for my harsh words. I didn't expect you and spoke without thinking. I won't forbid you to leave, but please know this: I love you and the children as much as I ever have."

It was too late and not enough. "When will you come see us?"

He rubbed his temples. "Perhaps after the emissaries from Flanders leave..."

She smoothed her tunic and stepped away. "Our sons and daughters would appreciate your visit, my lord. I'm sorry to have delayed your important business."

Without looking back, Edith turned and stalked out. She slammed the doors behind her, shocked her intuition had led her astray. *Some stranger has returned from Ponthieu in place of my husband...*

The Confession

July 1, 1065

The earl: Forgive me, father, I have sinned. The worst of my crimes will result in the destruction of all I hold dear, unless I make amends.

The bishop: Calm down, my son. Tell me how this hunting trip sent you into such a fury.

The earl: There was no hunting trip. I journeyed to Ponthieu, hoping to right a terrible wrong done to my family. I kept the true intent secret, for my success depended on stealth and speed...or so I thought.

The bishop: What did the men of Ponthieu ever do to the Godwin clan?

The earl: Nothing until my arrival. The wrong I sought to address lay at the feet of the Normans. Count Guy of Ponthieu offered a path to recompense.

The bishop: Heavenly father preserve us all. You still haven't given up on your kinsmen? They're are as good as dead, Harold. They have been ever since your return from exile in Ireland.

The earl: Their screams plagued me day and night. How could I give up on them?

The bishop: Screams? You never told me you heard them scream.

The earl: Before, I could not face the shame of my failure. Now, deeper sins afflict my soul. I heard them scream shortly after returning from Dublin. The Norman mercenaries had captured the toddlers, and held knives against their necks as they escaped. I hunted the hostage-takers all the way to Dover, but stormed the quay a moment too late. The cries of my kinsmen carried across the sea as they disappeared into the channel. Every year after, I sent a delegation to Normandy to win their return. Some offered gold; others threatened war; one messenger even got on his knees and begged. None had any success. This past year, I turned to action.

The bishop: Count Guy...

The earl: I met him eight years ago while attending court in Flanders. Our friendship ran deep. He loved hunting, hated the Normans, and treated women with reverence. He sent me a message last May. The boys were held in the fortress of Eu, which sat on Ponthieu's border. My friend said the fortress lay vulnerable if I acted with haste and secrecy. The opportunity answered my prayers. The next day, I begged leave from the king under the guise of a hunting expedition.

The bishop: Of course! The crewman who helped you to the church. The resemblance almost shouted at me.

The earl: Hakon made it back. My other little kinsman did not.

The bishop: So the raid turned violent?

The earl: It never took place. Unbeknownst to me, I sailed headlong into a trap. When we made landfall, Guy met me alone. The tall man's posture stooped and he possessed more gray hair than I expected, but he seemed well enough judging from his golden cloak broach. We embraced like brothers, but he didn't release me when I tried to pull away. Before I could cry for help, a host of soldiers sprouted from hiding places under beached ships to surround me.

The bishop: But why would Guy do such a thing?

The earl: Standing dumbfounded on the harbor sands, I asked the same question. Guy said the safety of his borders outweighed any friendship. In that instant, I realized my true captor's identity. You should not look so vexed, Wulfstan. It's the same enemy I've fought for more than a decade.

The bishop: William of Normandy.

The earl: Yes. In all the previous years, I sent emissaries instead of going in person because I feared I would fall into his hands. Yet impatience led to carelessness. I never suspected Guy would betray me, but I should have. Why would he have risked inciting a Norman war for the safety of two foreign boys? Even a blind fool would have known better, father...

The bishop: Acting to save family is no sin, Harold. The sin lies in pride. A more humble man would have been more cautious.

The earl: A more humble man would have been most welcome. Yet I committed more egregious errors on this trip than putting my faith in Count Guy...

Chapter 4:
Aidan

July 14, 1065

Having finally escaped the bishop, Aidan limped along Worcester's High Street. The novice disregarded the ominous clouds overhead and the gusting wind at his back. He knew God would not rob him of his reward after the ordeal in Bosham.

He arrived at the market well before closing time at Vespers. Held in the city square north of the old Roman wall, rows of tented stalls sold everything from livestock to precious stones. Aidan's excitement surged after he entered the narrow alleys between stalls. Arms, shoulders and heads popped in and out of view. The smell of mystic spices, exotic powders, and foreign men overpowered the air. The constant droning of crowds and animals sounded deafening compared to the silence of St. Mary's cathedral.

The goldsmith named Thunor had set up shop near the northeastern corner. "Well, look who's come back," he said when Aidan hobbled up. The goldsmith was a stump of a man with fading shoulder-length brown hair and a well-trimmed beard. "Been traveling with the bishop?"

"Just returned recently." Aidan picked up a bracelet off the counter, not wanting to tell the full truth. The earl's confession had come with them to Worcester. Neither he nor the bishop knew what to do with it. *The words haunt me, but the cure is right here.*

Aidan twirled the bracelet through his fingers. The gold band showed almost no hint of hammering. The amethyst on its crown winked with daylight. The item no doubt cost a heavy purse. Luckily, the boy didn't need jewelry; he just needed an excuse to linger.

"Isn't she beautiful?" Thunor's smile stretched like a red crescent moon.

"She most certainly is," Aidan allowed himself a moment of joy. Thunor's daughter, Eadburga, stood a few yards away.

"Not sure what the brotherhood would do if you walked into the cloister with that around your arm, Aidan. Wouldn't be good, for certs."

"You're right, Thunor. She's beautiful... and forbidden." He returned the bracelet to the counter and dared a glance. The short, skinny girl polished a hammer. Her head hung to the side. A strand of curly blonde hair escaped her beige wimple. The tip of her tongue edged just past the corner of her strained lips. Her green eyes winced with focus. Then, they flicked up and locked onto Aidan's gawking face.

An earth-shaking shiver took hold. "I...I had best be going."

Thunor's stepped forward, blocking the view of his daughter. "You sure, lad? Stay and browse some more. The church's Eucharist chalice looks a bit worn if you ask me. I have several to choose from."

Aidan began to reply, but God cut him off with a crack of lightning.

The goldsmith's eyes shot to the sky. "Saints preserve us all! I'm sorry young novice. I'd best cover up my wares." He wheeled around. "Ebba, help me with the chests!"

The market transformed into a flurry of folding tents. A drenching rain descended moments later. Aidan was watching Ebba when a thought broke through: *the pages!*

He hurried back to the monastery precinct. When they returned from Bosham, Wulfstan ordered him to store the confession in the undercroft of the bishop's palace. The musty smell was overwhelming down there; moisture had clearly seeped in. But with no better idea, he put the rolled-up sheets in a box, and then hid the box under a pile of old monk's robes.

Aidan accessed the undercroft via the door on the side of the palace. The earthen floor felt slick with mud and the air reeked of decay. *This can't continue.*

After stumbling in the dark and undoing all his work, he tucked the pages into his robe sleeve. In the pelting rain outside, he crouched to protect his sleeve and hurried into the palace.

The bishop's voice rang out when he entered. "Don't track mud into my hall. The rushes were just swept."

"Yes, father." He took off his filth-covered sandals and approached the bishop's solar. Wulfstan sat at a round table, staring at a golden chalice.

"Father, we need a new hiding place for the confession. Your undercroft is too damp."

The bishop nodded, but never took his eyes off the cup.

"Is that a new Eucharist chalice, father?"

"A gift from Harold. He wanted to thank me for saving his life."

"Very generous…"

The bishop shifted in his seat. "Generous? Hardly. I need no reward for doing God's work."

"I'm sure the earl didn't mean to offend—"

"His intentions don't matter. I cannot accept payment for taking a confession, be it life-saving or otherwise. I'll send this *gift* back tomorrow."

Aidan regarded the goblet. "It's a terrible pity. Our chalice is chipped in a dozen different places."

"It still holds wine well enough. A member of our congregation will donate a proper vessel to further God's glory, not commend me for mine. Now, what did you say about the text?"

"Your undercroft is too damp…" Aidan trailed off. Something about a gift sparked an idea.

"Where else can we put it? The cloister? A brother would find it within the hour."

"True. But I may have a solution. What if we give them back to Earl Harold? He has treasuries and hidden chests all over England."

Wulfstan stroked his beard. "The idea has merit. Harold was in no state to guard them after that terrible night, but his health returns with every day."

"Yes, but the confession in its current state is at risk no matter who guards it. Let me bind the pages into a book. It could be a gift of sorts."

"A gift…" The bishop nodded slowly. "God ordered the words written. It makes sense to create a book worthy of His honor…" He trailed off, lost in thought.

Sensing his chance, Aidan stayed quiet. Then, as if

kissed by an angel, he had an idea. "We could use the chalice as material for the cover, father. Thunor the goldsmith could melt it down for us. We could turn it into gold leaf. Christendom will never know a more beautiful cover."

After one last pause, Wulfstan smiled. "Your mind is as fast as your feet are slow, my son. Go about your plan."

The novice unfurled a smile of his own. He could now create a most glorious gift...and visit Thunor's house.

Chapter 5: Odo

August 1, 1065

Bishop Odo walked through the drizzle to intercept the messenger. He kept his countenance relaxed even though every nerve in his body twitched. Wearing his plainest garb of natural colored wool, the bishop approached without his staff of office or his mitre. His lone chance hinged on humility.

The stables lay clear across the cobblestoned bailey of Rouen Palace. Odo saw the messenger hand his reins over to a groom and then stare in admiration of the three-story central keep. The reaction was a good sign. *The more awed he is, the more malleable he becomes.*

After arriving at the port town of Dieppe earlier this morning, the messenger claimed he carried a message from Harold Godwinson and requested an audience with Duke William straight away. The riders sent to prepare the audience had reached the palace an hour ago.

When he heard, Odo panicked. William would receive the messenger, learn of Godwinson's knowledge, and hunt down the men responsible. Sheer pride made the bishop resist flight. He had stayed in William's company every day with the secret intent to intercept this message. He had to try.

His harbinger of doom offered a glimmer of hope. He was not some stern, righteous, old stickler, but a young, doe-eyed monk. His habit looked several sizes too large and his cowl engulfed his head. Most importantly, the rider Odo spoke with had not lied. The monk's cheeks held the tell-tale green pallor.

Halting a few paces away, Odo spoke in Latin. "Welcome friend. How was the crossing from our island neighbor?"

"Not well in truth. I fear the voyage quite upset my constitution."

Odo glanced over his shoulder. No one emerged from the palace. "It happens I have a quick remedy for just such an affliction. Follow me, brother."

The monk winced and shook his head. "I'm sorry, friend, but I'm on urgent business. Duke William awaits."

The bishop nodded and remained patient. "Forgive me, my son. I don't know your name."

"I am Adelhelm, a brother of the Benedictine house at Christ Church in Canterbury. Now please, either lead me to the duke or stand aside."

A nearby groom overheard Adelhelm's tone and a look of dread filled the boy's face. Confused, the monk asked, "And who are you?"

Odo maintained his grin. "I'm Bishop Odo of Bayeux, the duke's half brother."

The monk went still for a few heartbeats before falling to his knees. "Forgive me, lord father. I had no idea."

The bishop lowered his hand. His fingers felt bare without their rings, but the disguise had performed its task. The monk would do anything to repair his insult. "You are forgiven, my son. Clearly, the journey has affected you. Of course I'll show you to the duke. However, my brother can be...harsh when holding an audience, especially with weak messengers. My remedy will no doubt restore your vigor."

The monk glanced up, clasped Odo's hand, and kissed the back of his palm. "I am yours to command, lord father."

"A smart choice, Adelhelm. Now, let's be rid of this drizzle."

Hunched over with his elbows locked to his sides, the monk followed. Odo led him to the kitchens, which lay half-way between the stables and the palace. Tucked behind a wattle and daub wall, the rooms held salted meats, harvested vegetables, and grain stores. No one, other than servants, would interrupt them. The two sat on a bench inside the entryway. An overhang of woven sticks kept the rain away.

"You're in luck, Brother Adelhelm. I remember my first sea voyage. Came back scalier than a fish. Stomach in utter rebellion. The sole cure was a home-made stew from this same kitchen. Cooks have come and gone, but the recipe has endured to this day. Sit here and I'll have a bowl brought out."

Adelhelm held the sides of his head. "I'm sorry, lord father. Your riders led me here at a feverish pace. My insides still shake."

"No need for apologies, brother. Your elixir will be out shortly. My men let me know of your arrival. They also told me you bear a message from Earl Harold."

"Yes," the monk stifled a gag. "They are correct. It...it is solely for the duke."

"Of course," Odo said. "Do you have this message on your person, or is it spoken?"

"It's right here." The monk produced a folded parchment from his habit. A red wax seal in the shape of a snarling dragon's head bound the paper shut.

Part of Odo rejoiced when he saw the note. Godwinson's accusations would be kept to William's eyes alone. The other part of Odo wished to snatch the message from the weakling and rip it to oblivion. Of course, that action would just hasten the bishop's journey to the gallows. Adelhelm's arrival and mission were no secret. Neither the message, nor the messenger could disappear. So, Odo nodded at Adelhelm and returned to silence.

A servant appeared with a bowl on a tray. Scents of pine, sage, and oxtail filled the air. The mistletoe was undetectable.

"Ah. The cure for your ailment."

Adelhelm's greenish hue intensified. "Forgive me, lord bishop, is this meat broth?"

"We raise some of the finest oxen in the world here, brother. You should be honored to receive such sustenance."

"Yes. Thank you father. Only we don't often eat meat, Bishop Odo. Saint Benedict's rule is very strict on that point."

Odo sighed deep and leveled a scowl at Adelhelm. "The brothers should have taught you some manners by now. I ordered this stew for you. I have sworn it will cure your condition. Disregard me if you wish, but God will no doubt observe your ingratitude."

Adelhelm's head bent lower. "I meant no disrespect, lord father." He picked up the spoon with a trembling hand and took a small sip.

"There now," Odo said. "It takes a few moments, but you'll know when it starts to work."

"I...I think it's working already." The monk began slurping the broth. "Yes. I think I..."

The bishop cocked his head sideways. "Brother? Has it taken effect?"

Heaves shook Adelhelm's entire body. The first wave of nausea splashed out in a yellowish mucus. The message fell onto the bench.

"Well don't just sit here fouling my kitchen entryway, brother. Run around back and expel the demons. It's the only way. You'll feel better in a little while. I'll guard your message until you return."

The monk scurried behind the kitchen rooms. When Odo heard the first uncontrollable retch, he snatched the note and fled to his private quarters on the palace's first floor.

He locked the door behind him and placed the note atop a small table. Tearing the seal would, in effect, damn him. So, Odo removed a knife from his belt sheathe, carved the paper around the seal, unfolded the message, and read.

William,

This will be my last correspondence on the matter. God has forgiven my sins and assigned me the penance of stopping you at all costs. For like me, He is reviled by your true plans for England and Bishop Odo's intentions for the Holy Land. My soul is prepared. Is yours?

Odo's heart fluttered as his mind poured over the words. He had precious moments before Adelhelm recovered. He began to sweat despite the cool dampness inside the keep. Then, his breath caught in his chest. He realized an opportunity.

The Englishman confirmed no more messages would be forthcoming. So, without this parchment, Godwinson's defiance would remain veiled. Odo stroked his clean-shaven lip, exploring every possible solution. The monk would need his message back...or at least *a* message back. *That's it!*

Odo raced to a chest by his bed. Inside, he found a sheaf of parchment reserved for his correspondence. Since Benedictine houses made both pieces, they were similar color and thickness. Using his knife, Odo carved the blank piece to a similar size. He then sorted through the chest for his quill and ink pot. Returning to the table, he mimicked Godwinson's handwriting from eyesight and copied the message with one important omission.

William,

This will be my last correspondence on the matter. God has forgiven my sins and assigned me the penance of stopping you at all costs. My soul is prepared. Is yours?

The bishop appraised his work. The handwriting didn't match well, but no one could identify the earl's original writing. The message, however, served his purposes; it implied Godwinson's faith, not his discovery, led to his opposition. If no more messages passed between them, the secret would stay locked in England. Odo would gain vital time to plan his next action.

Satisfied, Odo folded the new message. Taking the intact seal from the table, he affixed it to the fold and waved a candle above the wax while catching the drippings with his hand.

"Please God, let this work."

The dripping wax scalded his hand, but the bishop

winced and endured. The flame heated the wax just enough to cling to the new parchment without destroying its dragon shape.

"Thank you, Lord. Thank you."

He then held the original to the candle. The evidence of his error turned to embers.

Rushing out of the palace and back to the kitchens, he reached the entryway as Adelhelm stumbled around the corner. "Feel better, brother?" Odo hid his short breath and held out the fabrication.

The monk snatched it and the signed the cross over his chest. "The broth was quite effective, lord father. Thank you."

"Servants of God must help each other," Odo said, putting a gentle hand on the monk's back and pushing him along. "Now, let's go find Duke William, shall we?"

The palace great hall also served as William's throne room. Tapestries adorned every wall. Some dazzled with colors of cerulean, maize, ochre, sapphire, and scarlet. Others depicted mythical hunting scenes where the heroes appeared to reach out from the fabric. With tables cleared and torches lit, the long stone room with its high-beamed ceiling looked cavernous.

Norman lords stood on either side of the central aisle. They watched Adelhelm in silence.

The monk had taken the room, the lavish adornment, and even the crowd without a shiver. When William of Normandy appeared before him, however, his feet froze. The duke sat with a forward lean. He used a propped elbow on his knee to support his chiseled chin.

Odo employed his church service voice. "Brother Adelhelm of Christ Church in Canterbury, my lord duke." Quaking, Adelhelm stepped forward.

Watching from the back of the hall, Odo's blood raced faster with every step the monk took. If William assessed the melted seal with a discerning eye, would he call it into question?

The monk fell to his knees at the foot of the throne. "Most honorable Duke William, I have sailed at the bequest of Earl Harold of Wessex to deliver this message." He held up Odo's note.

A servant transferred the parchment from the kneeling monk to the duke. William received it without ever taking his eyes from Adelhelm. Odo stood straight as his brother inspected the seal. A twinge of relief slithered down the bishop's spine when he heard the familiar tear and pop.

William read the note, glanced up, read the note again, and then crumpled the paper. "It seems the good earl has forgotten our hospitality. My lords, return to your estates and warn your men. Unless this traitor changes course, we are headed for war against England."

The crowd rumbled as William leaned back on his ducal throne. Odo, however, stayed silent. He knew the look on his brother's face. Harold Godwinson and his ill-gotten secrets were as good as dead.

The Confession

July 1, 1065

    The bishop: We will get to each of your sins in good time. But continue: how did Count Guy act after taking you hostage?

    The earl: Standing on that hell-ensnared strip of beach, he acted amiable enough. He took our weapons, but led us to his castle without harassment. There, he quartered us in a clean barn and bade me to dine with him. Over supper, I begged for my release, offering all I could give: falcons, horses, fully outfitted longships, chests of silver coin. Temptation spilled from his face, but when he opened his mouth, Guy spoke of Maine.

    The bishop: The county lying between the duchy of Normandy and the kingdom of France? Why would Count Guy speak of such a place?

    The earl: Because some villages still smolder after William's invasion. Guy did not want the same attacks on Ponthieu and releasing me would have incited them. So despite all my pleadings, he removed me from my men and passed me, like chattel, to Hell's hound.

    The bishop: Do not demonize Duke William, Harold.

The earl: I swear, Wulfstan, God could not create such a being. When I first saw him, he looked more like a ghost than a man. He wore the trappings of an unadorned warrior, not a grand statesman. His men followed his orders not in mirth, nor derision, but in fearful silence. After taking possession of me, he made a great show of cutting my bonds.

The bishop: He freed you?

The earl: Not in the least. Norman warriors surrounded me. I was free to breathe, no more. He just wanted the world to know I was in his debt.

The bishop: Where did he take you?

The earl: Rouen palace, where I spent several weeks in an incarceration infuriating for its cordiality. They bid me to attend the duke's courts and councils, but ignored my requests to speak. They quartered me in a lavish apartment on the palace's first floor, but two armed stewards attended me while I slept, ate, prayed, even when I pissed. I was a training hawk allowed tethered flight so the hunter could assess my instincts.

The bishop: How did you endure such a trial?

The earl: With mettle. If William and his retainers wanted to judge me, I determined to pass their tests. I turned patient at their councils. I shared wine and wench stories with my stewards. I even won respite for my men by promising William they could build him a hunting lodge worthy of his person. All the while, I prayed for the moment when I could win our freedom, either through deeds, coin, or death.

That moment arrived three weeks later. Hoping to shock me with a display of might, William took me on campaign. Wearing an ill-fitting tunic and riding a borrowed horse, I followed hundreds of Norman chevaliers across the dukedom to break a Breton siege of Dol. On the march's fifth day, we reached the tidal flats near Mount St. Michael, which were only passable by a narrow land bridge. My stewards and I were the last to cross.

No sooner had we ridden twenty paces when the tides began to rise. By the halfway point, the surging current covered our horses' shins. I reached safety just in time. My stewards, however, were swept away. "Let them go," I heard a Norman say, but I could not sit and watch them die. Flying off my horse, I dove into the icy water. With no armor to drag me down, I swam to their limb-flailing forms and held them aloft. Warriors on the bank cast us lines and pulled us to safety. I remember lying on the cold, wet ground and gazing up at William. For the first time, his face registered wonder. It was the one moment when I believed freedom could be won.

After arriving at the besieged Norman town, I built on my success. Heedless of my unarmored, weaponless state, I charged into the fray. By God's provenance, I wrestled a sword away from a Breton and unleashed all my frustration on the unsuspecting enemy. They fled like hunted herons.

The bishop: How did Duke William react?

The earl: He awarded me a new sword and a chain mail hauberk in front of the entire army. And despite all the eyes on me, I refused the gift. Accepting would have been tantamount to enslavement. Instead, I asked to return home with my captive kinsmen. In front of his entire army, the lying bastard agreed. I should have known better. I could not have won my freedom had I conquered the horsemen of the apocalypse. From the moment he took me, William knew the price of my liberation...

Chapter 6: Orrin

August 15, 1065

From his vantage point above the Peterborough downs, Orrin Geirson spotted the falcon before anyone else. The forty-year-old thane of Fritton Village regarded his traveling companions with a teeth-bearing smile and pointed toward the cloudless sky. "You see friends? The earl has raised his most glorious banner for us."

Orrin shook his horse's reins and led seven other East Anglian thanes into the tree-spotted farmland below. They had left their homes to answer Harold's summons for a folkmoote. No one knew the reason for the assembly, and some grumbled at the abrasiveness of the order. For his part, Orrin needed little excuse to visit his old friend.

The smile never left his face as he watched the raptor circle above lush green foliage. Even from this distance, he could see the blade-shaped wings; cream-colored under-feathers; dark, fanned tail; and yellow, hooked beak of a mature Peregrine.

He shook his head in wonder. Many knew Earl Harold, the righteous lord and fierce warrior. Orrin knew something more; if God turned the Earl of Wessex into a pauper, Harold could make his way as a falconer in any kingdom.

The raptor ascended heaven-ward while unleashing an ear-splitting screech. In a blink, she crested her ascent, folded her wings, and plummeted toward land like an angel cast her down. Half-way to the tree line, the raptor crashed into her prey, an unsuspecting songbird by the look of it. Orrin's heart bounced in his chest. The Peregrine tumbled in a momentary free-fall with the prey trapped in her talons. When her wings shot out from her body and she glided below the trees, he began to breathe again. The distant sound of barking dogs and shouting men grew. With exhilaration pumping in his veins, the thane galloped to find the hunters.

Orrin had met the earl in this same forest on a hunting trip with King Edward twenty years ago. He and Harold hawked while the king and his entourage coursed stags. Befitting his station, Harold held a Peregrine Falcon named Lady Anwyn on his arm. Orrin hunted with his ruffled old raptor, a Goshawk named Oliver. Upon seeing the majestic Lady, Orrin almost withdrew from the hunt out of embarrassment. "Nonsense," Harold said when Orrin admitted his shame. "I think old Oliver could teach my Anwyn a thing or two about getting her talons dirty." The earl proved correct that day; Oliver matched Lady Anwyn kill for kill. At the end of the hunt, both men were breathless from running down their birds' prey, but the exhaustion paled in comparison to Orrin's pride. Now, as he rode through these memory-filled woods, his pride surged anew.

He found the hunting party in a forest clearing. Harold looked as if he'd hunted through the night. His tan tunic and dark leggings showed tears and dirt marks. He sat on his horse with the falcon perched on a leather-mitted arm and the hint of a smile on his face.

Harold's brother rode with him. Tostig Godwinson, the Earl of Northumbria, sat atop a black destrier with golden harness clasps. He wore a red tunic with gold edging, lightly damp with sweat. His smirk wrinkled the side of his face.

"Brother," Tostig said as Harold tended to his raptor. "Did you call for a cup of wine?"

When Orrin became thane of Fritton, the title included a longship moored at the nearby port of Lowestoft. His first voyage took him to Rouen, where a merchant offered to pay him a chest of silver to transport five wine casks back to Norwich. This first agreement grew into a thriving trade, the envy of burghers in London and nobles throughout the realm—Tostig being the worst of the lot. "You may not have ordered wine, lord earl, but your Northumbrians keep my vaults overflowing with coin."

"My Northumbrians?" His smirk flattened. "Perhaps a new tax is necessary then. One that would dissuade such behavior."

"From what your men tell me, your taxes dissuade everything already."

Harold stepped forward. "You two bicker worse than my daughters." He passed his raptor to a falconer. "And you will stop. *Now.*"

"Forgive me if I offended, Earl Tostig," Orrin said. The

two had traded insults many times. The conversations always ended in Orrin's insincere apology.

"You're too baseborn to offend me, Orrin. Now, this talk of wine has made me thirsty for some ale. Come Harold, will you share a cup?"

"I will after I'm done speaking with Orrin, brother."

Tostig shot Orrin a rueful stare before trotting off.

Harold welcomed the Norfolk thanes and directed them to his hunting lodge, where food and drink waited for them. When the others left, the two friends dropped pretense. Orrin dismounted and embraced Harold like the brother he never had.

"You look tired. How long have you been hunting?"

"Not long. My strength still wanes after a sickness this summer."

"I heard of no illness, although affairs in Fritton have kept me cloistered off for months. I trust Edith has nursed you back to health." Orrin had heard of Edith's beauty five years before ever laying eyes on her. Even then, she surpassed his expectations.

Harold did not lighten as he typically did at Edith's mention. "I've scarcely seen her. Thanks to Edward's church building, I need to be in London for every decision. But I didn't call you here to complain about the king or my marriage. I want to ask you a question, but I'd rather keep it amongst us alone. May I have a word?"

"Of course."

They walked under a canopy of wide-leafed oaks that provided a gentle comfort against the sun. After several steps, Harold said, "How goes your trade?"

"It's well. The summer rains'll make for a plump harvest. Ought to be a banner vintage."

"And your search for a wife?"

Orrin's wife, Saegyth, died five years ago. The marriage brought him good land south of Fritton and a woman who worshipped him, but no children. Now, no one – not even Harold – knew Orrin's plans in this regard. "Same as always, Hal. The fruitless quest continues."

The earl walked along wearing a pensive look. "And what news of Normandy? Any incidents these past weeks?"

Orrin felt like he had dodged an axe strike. *If Hal had offered me a bride, what would I have done?* "None that I'm aware of. What's all this about? You're making me nervous."

They reached a felled oak tree. The wide, jagged stump sat a hand-length over the grass. The fallen trunk lay rotting next to it. "It's about loyalty." Harold propped his foot atop the stump and looked at Orrin. "I must find out who'll help me and who won't."

"You know I'll help." He tried to lighten his friend's melancholy. "Are we rebelling?"

Harold smiled. "Rebel against whom? King Edward can't stand against a strong wind."

"Well you're planning something," Orrin said, chuckling. "What's this moote about?"

"I'm holding these assemblies throughout the realm. Men need to hear my voice, see my face, and take my news of Normandy to heart."

Pausing, Orrin sat on the tree trunk and fought his unease. "Normandy?"

"Yes. I visited earlier this summer."

"I would have met you if I had known."

The earl waved away the apology. "No one knew. God sent me to look the Devil in the eye so I would know my enemy."

With fear kindling inside his chest, Orrin said, "What enemy did you find?"

His friend stood tall. "Duke William eyes England's crown like my falcon eyes songbirds."

"Now wait one moment, Hal." He gripped the rotted bark so hard it frayed in his hands. "What makes William so devilish that you're willing to cross him?"

"I've learned many things about him and his followers. They see England as a stepping-stone to a higher cause. To reach their aims, our land will suffer."

"You must be mistaken." He stood up fast. "William's claimed to be Edward's heir for more than twelve years. Can't you settle this quarrel amicably?"

"The course is already set. Someday soon, William and I will meet in battle. Will you fight beside me when that day comes, Orrin?"

He stayed quiet for several moments, choosing instead to listen to the forest leaves rustle in the warm breeze. Hal watched him the entire time and finally wore him down.

"Of course I'll fight for you, Hal. But does this mean the end of my wine trade?"

"No." The earl's eyes turned grave. "Quite the opposite, in fact. Until war is declared, I'm asking you to heighten your attention while on Norman shores."

"You...You want me to *spy* for you?"

"I'm not asking you to break into Rouen Castle in the dead of night. Just keep your eyes more open than normal."

"It sounds an awful lot like spying to me."

"If the request is too much..."

"I...I'll do my best. It's just I'm a neophyte in this work."

"They won't suspect anything as long as you keep your

wits. Don't hide under bushes, count troops, or steal maps. Your observations of Fecamp harbor ought to earn a hefty purse."

Orrin calmed. The task sounded docile enough and the purse would always be welcome. "When do you need me to sail? I'd hoped to stay through the harvest and depart after All Saints."

Breathing deep, the earl nodded. "That should serve. William won't attack until the throne becomes vacant and Edward's hale enough for now. Will you join us at Nazeing for the All Saints feast? We can talk more of your journey then."

"It would be my honor, lord."

"Good. I feel somewhat ashamed. For days now, I wondered if you'd agree to my request."

"I'll be by your side come the reaper of souls, Hal. You know that." Orrin managed a smile, but his mind envisioned his ships moored in the bays of Normandy.

The earl's shoulders fell as he gazed deep into Orrin's eyes. "Good. For I fear that's exactly who is coming to England."

Chapter 7: Edith

October 20, 1065

Edith pressed on her temples with a thumb and forefinger, but the searing pain didn't relent. "How many people are expected?"

Renweard stood at the end of the table with his hands behind his back. "A multitude, m'lady. The earl didn't provide an exact number."

Sitting at the table's head, Edith looked around Nazeing Manor's narrow feasting hall. It had thick timber walls and a fresh thatch roof held up by sturdy rafter beams. Aside from the table dominating much of the room's length, it had a smattering of chairs and benches, a layer of lavender-scented rush straw, and a stone fireplace that filled the back wall. Harold hired a Flemish mason to construct the hearth years ago. In the past, the mere sight of the beige, gray, and reddish stones, with their plethora of deer antler trophies would warm Edith's soul. Today, she wished it gone.

This home had passed through Edith's family for generations. It held plenty of feasts in its day, but she could remember none equal to the one her husband asked for. "The *earl* should pay better attention. We'll have to prepare for the entire court." She sighed long and deep. "But he *did* confirm King Edward will not be in attendance?"

"The earl was clear on that point, Lady Edith. The king wishes to pray through the evening, but his court will be free to join our celebration."

Her headache eased somewhat. Still, this massive undertaking would stretch the limit of her manor's stores. "Very well then. Kill the third ox and bring up the tables from the London residence. We'll make do somehow."

"As you say, my lady. Should be a grand display." He bowed and left the hall. The entire household looked forward to the event, Edith knew. Families from all over England would arrive to celebrate not just All Saints Day, but an end to a successful harvest. For any other wife, this feast would offer a chance to show what a happy, bounteous home she kept. Edith, however, just feigned excitement. There would be no quiet evenings with her husband and children until Advent, at the earliest.

True to his word, Harold had stayed preoccupied since his mysterious summer voyage. The days he did not spend with the king were spent ensuring men's loyalty across the realm. Edith had tried to discover what happened to Harold during the summer, but learned just unconfirmed rumors. Some said he'd been taken captive by a pagan baron and forced to renounce God in exchange for freedom. Others whispered he had sailed all the way to Constantinople to forsake Pope Alexander for the favor of the Byzantine Emperor. The most absurd speculators said Harold pledged away his lands and titles in exchange for

Norman honors. Edith stopped asking after she heard that filth.

Lately, her husband showed recovery signs. He spent the Feast of the Cross with the family. His messages became more frequent and informative. Most importantly, she heard no news of a second marriage and those fears receded into nothing more than frightful night visions.

Sitting in her ancestral hall, the All Saints feast became her most frightening vision. Many of these guests had slandered Edith in times past because of her unsanctified marriage. For a moment, she thought of begging Harold to call the gathering off. Their grain, meat, ale, and wine supplies would be ruined. Their guesthouses were inadequate to host noble lords.

Yet even with all these reasons, she couldn't refuse her husband out of hand. Such an act would no doubt stretch the distance between them. Perhaps they could hold one feast in Nazeing for the family and another at Harold's London manor for the nobles?

The sounds of excited laughter filled the quiet hall. Her two daughters and youngest son barged in moments later. Loads of greenery dangled from their arms. The children had spent the morning bunching mistletoe leaves, holly bushes, and pine garlands to create feasting hall decorations.

Unlike most noblewomen, Edith required her children to help around the manor as much as any servant. This way, they would know the toil of running their own houses. Her two eldest boys, Godwine and Magnus were the exceptions; at their age, servitude would demean their station.

A wintry gust swept through the chamber. White light glowed from the door opening. Springing from her seat,

Edith helped lessen the load from her youngest child, Gunhild. "Come in quick. We'll all catch cold from this unseasonable chill."

Her children were half-frozen already. Wrapped in thick woolen cloaks, their teeth chattered and their cheeks reddened. When the three unloaded the decorations onto the table, the scent of pine mixed with lavender from the straw.

"Is this enough, mother?" Edmund asked. The burly fifteen-year-old blew on his fists. "Can I go to the training yard now?" Like every manor in England, Nazeing had a yard where men trained for their fyrdsmen duties. That way, all the local forces would have a basic training for battle. If Edmund wished to go to the yard, no doubt Magnus and Godwine were there too.

"You may go," Edith said, cupping her blue-eyed boy's chin, "but just to tell your brothers I expect them for the midday meal."

The zeal fled from Edmund's face; his brothers would not appreciate the message. Still, venturing out seemed preferable to decorating the hall. He nodded his assent and bounded away.

Gytha and Gunhild had moved to the fireplace to warm their hands. The two girls giggled as they stood with their back to their mother.

"What are you laughing about?"

Their grinning faces snapped around. "Nothing, mother," Gytha said. The older sister was tall and slender. Her hair fell straight down, and her brows framed perfect blue pools. Edith liked to think she looked similar when she was thirteen, but doubted she was ever so striking.

"We were just talking about the guests," Gunhild added as she warmed her hands. Edith's youngest child at eleven was plumper than her older sister and bore none of Gytha's reserve. Her hair fell in curls and her eyes were a darker, more solid blue. Watching the giddy girl, Edith could think of no being with more energy, save a hummingbird.

"What about our guests?" Edith tried to summon the strength to disappoint them.

"We're excited to serve them. That's all," Gytha said. Warm now, the girls crossed the hall and began to untangle the garlands on the table.

"Especially Rand." Gunhild said. A sharp elbow from her sister caught her arm.

Edith could not suppress a smile. Her daughters had good taste. Last month, Rand joined the ranks of Nazeing's huscarls, the manor's warrior band dedicated year-round to the land's defense. The twenty-year-old smith's son was tall, muscle-wrought, and could handle an axe with brutal precision. Both Edith and Harold agreed he would excel much more as a constant warrior compared with intermittent fyrdsmen service. But the match would never happen. Noblemen's sons lay in the offing for both her daughters, not tradesmen's ilk.

"I'm excited to serve all our guests, mother," Gytha said, fighting back her blushing cheeks. "And to see Aidan as well."

Wulfstan's note, which said he and Aidan would attend the feast, provided Edith's one source of brightness.

"Will Queen Eadgifu come, mother?" Gunhild asked. "I'd like to meet our aunt."

"Your father said 'no,' little one. She wishes to stay with the king." *And I pray she doesn't change her mind.*

Harold's sister, a gaunt, joyless woman named Eadgifu,

had married King Edward two decades ago. Although she had failed to provide an heir, the queen had no trouble wielding her moral authority. In fact, she only addressed Edith as "Harold's current companion." Standing at her dining table with handfuls of pine needles, Edith realized her true fears stemmed from facing guests who shared the queen's spite.

"So without the king or queen, you and father will run the court during the festivities," Gunhild said as she strung out a long garland line. "Should we begin hanging, mother?"

Edith stared at Gunhild. *From the mouth of a child.* Deep in her chest, a new courage welled. If Harold's summer voyage was a test of their union, they passed it unsettled but intact. This feast offered another challenge, but also an opportunity to rule over court for a short while. *This could be his way of making amends.*

A smile widened on Edith's face. "I'll get the ladder. We'll need to cover every beam."

*

November 1, 1065
The contented rumble of guests filled her ears and the scents of mint and chive intermixed with roasted swine, but Edith couldn't stand the way this All Saints feast had unfolded so far. After greeting the guests, Harold had disappeared into the bower to hold private audiences with individual thanes and freemen. Every time one person emerged, another would enter.

Godwine and Magnus flanked Edith's head table seat. Her two eldest sons looked like regal Athelings in clean blue tunics and red cloaks. They had bound their hair behind their heads and trim their rust-colored beards. If they noticed her agitation, they had the grace to ignore it. Instead, they conversed with those who sat next to them.

An overpowering laugh snapped Edith's attention away from the bower door. Harold's brother Tostig approached. "Lady Edith," he said between snickers, "I think it's high time we visited the other side of the board to ensure our guests' enjoyment."

Tostig's green and brown tunic reeked of mead. She wanted to send him back to his seat, but he was not just Harold's younger brother. As the Earl of Northumbria, Tostig could command her to grovel if the thought occurred to him.

"Yes brother. How thoughtful of you." She rose and took Tostig's arm.

From the look of it, the revelers had enjoyed her hospitality. The trenchers were bare and the hounds under the table sniffed the floor in disappointment.

Tostig walked next to the benches, laughing and slapping men on their backs. All the while, his wife, Judith, trailed behind in submissive silence.

"Where is my brother?"

"I wish I knew," Edith said. "He's been locked away since the feast began."

"Well then, I'll have to assume the host's role until he surfaces from his king play."

"It's no trouble. Perhaps you should sit down, Tostig?"

"Nonsense. We'll just pretend we're the married ones."

Judith mumbled behind them. She was the Count of Flanders' daughter, and Edith did not need to decipher her native tongue. "Tostig, we won't pretend anything."

A biting voice rose from across the table. "The problem, m'lady, is our revered earl can pretend better than he can do anything else."

Tostig's arm muscles constricted. When Edith found the speaker, she covered her smile with her hands.

Orrin Geirson, the short boar of a thane from Fritton, stood from his seat. He wore a tunic of interwoven blue and gold thread. Dozens of silver bands wrapped around his arms. His richness made Edith feel unrefined. She didn't dare imagine how it made Tostig feel.

With a level stare, her brother-in-law said, "You should be more careful, Geirson. Your angel isn't here to guard you."

The thane kept his oval, blunt-nosed face emotionless. "Forgive me, m'lady. The earl and I have an understanding. I chide him and he robs me blind."

"Rob," Tostig said with a laugh. "It's my right to tax Northumbria. The king said as much in his charter."

"We both know Edward signed that charter with you guiding the quill."

"Are you accusing me of a crime, Orrin? Or are you just insulting our king? Either way, I take offense to your words." Tostig's hand fell to his sheathed dagger.

Fuming, Orrin turned to Edith. "Thank you for a delightful feast, my lady. I'm afraid I will have to take my leave. My stomach can't handle such succulent pig."

Edith stifled another laugh. Orrin had made no comment on the feasting fare. "I bid you good night, Orrin Geirson, and thank you for your kind words."

The thane bowed deep and stalked out of the hall.

"Harold be damned. I should kill that man," Tostig said loud enough for Edith to hear.

"There will be no such talk in my hall."

The earl furrowed his brow and met Edith's gaze. A devious grin spread on his face. "Women don't speak to me this way. Even my brother's woman."

"The hostess can speak however she wishes, Tostig."

Two men stepped to the fore. Gyrth, the third eldest Godwinson brother, placed an arresting hand on Tostig's shoulder.

"And I suppose you would fight for her honor, Gyrth?"

"Both of us would." Leofwine Godwinson stepped forward. At thirty years old, he was the youngest of Harold's siblings and most similar to him in appearance.

Edith loved these two brothers almost as much as she loved her husband at the moment. But still, she had to stem the brewing storm. "No one is fighting. Come brothers, let's share a cup of wine and forget this unhappiness."

Renweard stepped forward with a flagon and a stack of cups. The brothers stood in a triangle, none daring to look another in the eye.

"To family," Edith said. The brothers murmured a concurrence and drank.

After a quick sip, Edith glanced toward the entrance. Her heart lightened. "If you'll excuse me, I have to greet an important late arrival."

Wulfstan and Aidan appeared in the doorway. The bishop looked just as he did when Edith first met him, except his hair and beard had turned white. Shaped like a barrel on stout legs, he wore a plain brown Benedictine habit with the cowl down and held a non-descript bishop's staff.

Aidan, on the other hand, had changed. He still had narrow shoulders and his gait still hitched with his deformed right ankle, but the faint shadow across his upper lip, the thick tuft of blond curls, the increased sharpness of his green eyes, and the linen sack in his hands all surprised her.

She bowed to Wulfstan and wrapped Aidan in a fierce

embrace. Feeling his arms around her again, her mind flashed to the infant she rescued from the burning hut in Ireland. *Could that really be fourteen years ago?*

The bishop surveyed the feast with unveiled shock. "It looks as though Harold invited all of Sodom and Gomorra. I hope we're not too late to sup."

No, lord father. There's plenty for all. Aidan, you look famished."

"Part of training, m'lady. I'm to end my novitiate in April. Father Wulfstan thought it worthwhile to fast along with the brotherhood. I haven't had meat, milk, or cheese in weeks."

"How disciplined of you. His training goes well, Wulfstan?'

"The boy shows promise, no doubt. His focus wavers on occasion, but God seldom grants success without hardship."

The boy hardly listened, choosing instead to track the servers carrying around heaping trays of roasted swine.

Edith smiled. "Right now, I'd say he's *very* focused. He has my permission to break his fast. Does he have yours, lord bishop?"

"He does, but after our audience with the earl."

"He's in the bower. I'll see if I can catch his atten—"

A strange man wearing chain mail and a sword at his side entered the hall behind Aidan. He had long bangs covering his forehead and a close-cropped haircut otherwise. The newcomer's face showed no joy. Several guests sneered at his arrival.

Not recognizing this new entrant, Edith stepped forward. "Forgive me, friend, servants are asked to stand outside."

"I'm no servant, woman. My name is Egenulf D'Laigle

and I carry a message from Duke William of Normandy." He patted a sack bundle carried under his arm. It made a metallic *chink* when he hit it.

Wulfstan's voice broke the hall's silence. "Normandy must be a bleak land if her men act like spoiled children before their hostess."

"Old man, I've braved the great channel at its foulest to bring the liar his message. Formalities are lost on me."

"God cannot respect those who show no respect, Egenulf. You had best change your tone."

Edith's mind raced. It seemed like no two men could speak to each other without instigating a fight. "Lord bishop, our Norman lord is most welcome. His curtness is my fault. I mistook him for a servant. Come, Lord Egenulf, enjoy the evening. Earl Harold will be out soon. My one caution is to refrain from slighting him again. We cannot tolerate hostility."

The Norman shook his head. "Hostility *is* my message, woman."

Tostig's voice boomed through the air. "And you have delivered it. Now leave!"

In a heartbeat, a dozen men splayed Egenulf to the wall. The Earl of Northumbria led the way. "My dear sister-in-law, your feast is beyond reproach. There's only one delicacy missing: tongue." He slammed the Norman's head against the wall, cracking the timber beam. Edith screamed and the hall erupted into chaos.

"THIS ENDS NOW!"

Harold stood just outside the bower doorway, casting a menacing glance at the entire hall. The head of the God-winson clan stalked to the Norman messenger. "In honor of the saints we celebrate and the protection under which you travel, Norman, no more harm will be done to you. Now, follow me and deliver your message in private."

Egenulf spat blood. "No need, liar." His red lips creased up. "I'm here to deliver the armor Duke William gifted you this past summer." The sack dropped to the floor. A gleaming coat of mail fell out. "The duke wishes to remind you of your pledge."

Harold composed himself even though he had turned redder than holly berries. "I declined this gift once already. *Remind* your duke of that." He took the bundle and slammed it into the messenger's torso. "Your kind should learn to stay across the channel. Now be gone before my brother's dagger slips."

As Tostig and the other men carried Egenulf away, Edith stood a few steps from the cracked timber, trembling. She remembered the wild speculation about the past summer. *Was there truth to it after all?*

Harold surveyed the guests and paused on Edith's shocked face. "I'm sorry for that. None of it is true." He then noticed Wulfstan and Aidan for the first time. "God is good after all. You're most welcome, friends, as are all good-hearted men and women this night. Let the feast recommence. Don't let that dog ruin our celebration."

Most guests found their seats and spoke in anxious whispers. Edith's nerves made the ground feel unstable. Grabbing the table ledge for support, she turned back to Harold to ask one of her thousand questions, but he had returned to the bower with Wulfstan and Aidan in tow.

Chapter 8: Aidan

As Earl Harold shut the bower door, Aidan's heart throbbed. Murder had been avoided by the slimmest of margins. He licked his dry lips, thanked God for making his soul a peaceful one, and hugged the sack to his chest.

The three had the room to themselves. Candles on a central table illuminated tapestry covered walls and tidy sleeping pallets.

"Rotten cur!" The earl glared at the shut door. His fingers twitched and his neck muscles strained to the utmost.

"He lacked manners," Bishop Wulfstan said. "No doubt Tostig will teach him."

"Even so, I'm not sure my trip to Normandy can be kept secret any more, old friend."

Aidan stayed off to the side of the room. He had seen the curious looks on the guests' faces. They would most certainly seek their own answers regarding Normandy and the armor.

Wulfstan sat in a chair and stroked his beard. "Perhaps the time has come to reveal the ordeal you experienced over the summer."

The earl's eyes widened. Aidan's head snapped to the bishop as well.

"Your confession has three parts," Wulfstan said, gesturing for patience. "The first is the ordeal; the second is the revelation; and the third is the threat. You can divulge the first. The others...we'll pray they stay secret for eternity."

"Am I to compound my sin with half-truths, Wulfstan?" Harold said.

"I swore you to secrecy for a reason. The world is not ready for your whole confession. Unfortunately, Duke William's version of events will skew the truth toward his aims. So, we must combat him with our truth where we can. Speak of the capture and incarceration. Speak of the feast and the ill-gotten oath. But I implore you: go no further. If men learn of those tidings, the gates of Hell will open."

Aidan clutched the sack even harder. Wulfstan made sense; the earl's entrapment could not be kept secret. Yet he could also see the source of Harold's frustration. The story held much more than his incarceration.

"Very well," the earl said, hanging his head in resignation. "I hate to admit it old friend, but remembering what happened is a chore in itself."

"Ah, your gift may help your efforts. Aidan, show the earl what you've been up to."

Limping forward, his heart beat louder than a whinnying horse. Offering up the sack, he said, "I've worked every day on this since returning to Worcester." Memories of the past months flashed by: straining his eyes in candlelight; the noxious scent of ink dye and cured leather; the snap of brittle quills; Thunor's incessant begging for more time, money, and direction; and the one day when Aidan summoned the courage to speak with Ebba. The conversation lasted just a few sentences, but the thrill stayed with him still. "I hope it pleases you."

After letting his eyes linger on Aidan's face, Harold pulled the book from the sack. His mesmerized inhale was Aidan's first reward. The earl traced his finger over the golden falcon medallion dominating the cover's center.

"It's remarkable. The raptor looks like he's ascending to some great height, while forming the shape of a cross at the same time. And the leather! Aidan, how did you create such a rich crimson color?"

"Cured with beet root, m'lord. It smudges on the fingertips somewhat, but the inside cover is unstained so it won't bleed."

"But the size...it's not like a bible or a Psalter. It's actually manageable." He bounced it on one hand to prove his point.

"Yes, lord. The parchment was originally destined for a simple book of hours."

"And the eyes! The amethysts actually glimmer." He shook his head in wonder. "It is almost the perfect gift."

Aidan's brows creased. "Al...almost, Lord Harold?"

"Yes. It's missing something important, but the fault's not yours." Tucking the book under his arm, the earl crossed to a chest. He lifted the top and rummaged around. When he stood up, he held a red wax candle and a latched box. "It lacks my seal."

Moving to the candles on the bower table, the earl lit the red candle and set it aside. He then unlatched the box, unfurled a cord of ribbon, and withdrew a golden ring.

"We'll affix the ribbon tomorrow," he said. "For now, I want you both to witness this."

Wax dripped over the ribbon. When a pool formed, he took his ring and pressed it in. When Aidan recognized the red dragon of Wessex, a new height of pride soared through him. He opened his mouth to voice his thanks.

No words escaped. Instead, the bower door crashed against the wall and Earl Tostig traipsed in. "What was that all about Harold? Why did that bastard try to give—" His eyes caught the book. "Good Lord, Wulfstan! What is that?"

"Earl Harold's gift. One that was meant to be delivered in private."

The Northumbrian earl could not stop staring. Harold hid the gift behind his back. "We'll speak of the Norman later, brother. Why don't you return to the feast?"

"May I see it?"

Harold and Wulfstan passed a glance between them. "Not now," Harold said.

Aidan could see Tostig flush with new anger. "What is it? A book of psalms? A collection of sermons? Why would you hide it from me?"

"It's nothing..." Harold kept his gaze steady.

"Go ahead and tell him, Harold," Wulfstan said. Aidan knew the bishop prodded him to speak of the Norman ordeal.

Harold did not lose the meaning. "It's an account of my journey to Normandy this summer. Come, I'll tell you and the guests all about it."

Tostig stepped forward. Only a few hand-widths separated the brothers. "I'll read it for myself, thank you."

"Tostig, do not press me. You have no need to read it."

"Really? Ever since your *hunting trip*, you've built up

an astounding war chest without declaring the slightest intention. Perhaps this book reveals your true aims."

"True aims?" Wulfstan stepped closer. "What are you accusing us of, Tostig?"

"Be quiet old man." He stood so close to Harold their noses almost touched. "Produce the book or I'll take it from you."

Aidan retreated against the bower wall, assaulted by a pang of guilt. *My pride has led to this.*

Harold, however, kept his voice level. "Think before you act, Tostig."

"Are you rejecting my offer, brother? I won't issue another."

"Perhaps you should go home. You'll see how petty you've been once the ale fog lifts."

"Petty is it? I know treachery when I see it."

Without another word, the Earl of Northumbria shoved his brother with one hand while grabbing for the book with the other. Harold stumbled back and looked certain to fall. But with a dexterity Aidan had just seen in cats, the Earl of Wessex re-planted his feet, ducked Tostig's swinging arm, and devastated his brother's jaw with an elbow. Tostig collapsed to the ground in a heap.

Heart convulsing, Aidan stood rooted in place. Wulfstan raced between the two brothers. "Stop this! You are leaders of men. Act like it *now!*"

Murmurs and shouts filled the room. Tostig had left the door open and guests crowded into the frame, Lady Edith among them. Earl Harold noticed them too. He stalked to a chest on the far side of the bower and placed the book inside.

The Earl of Northumbria rose to his knees with a growl. Blood dripped down his chin from a bloody lower lip. "I've had enough of your secrets, Harold. You're no brother to me."

"Tostig, please." Wulfstan tried to help him rise.

"Do not touch me, priest!" The earl launched his arm up to fend off the help. His elbow caught the bishop's midsection. Wulfstan bent and grunted. The crowd gasped in horror.

Tostig swiveled to them, humiliation clouding his face. After one last sneer in Harold's direction, he shot to his feet and shoved his way out.

The room fell silent. Aidan rushed to help Wulfstan, who stood doubled-over in the room's center. Harold came to his friend as well.

"I'm fine." Wulfstan said, lifting his head with a wince. "He didn't mean to strike me."

Aidan looked up to the earl. "Forgive me, Lord Harold. My gift caused all this."

Harold stared at the open door. "No, boy. You could have given me a tree branch and he would have demanded it. Your gift is beautiful, and I will cherish it always. Tostig's head will cool tomorrow, I'm sure. Now, I owe my guests a story."

The Confession

July 1, 1065

    The earl: After lifting the Dol siege, two significant changes infuriated me. First, William kept me at arm's length. Every attempt I made to discuss my release met with dismissals or avoidance. Secondly, the stewards I saved were replaced by two mute behemoths who knew nothing except how to bar my way. So, I became no more than an observer as the Breton campaign continued.

    The bishop: What led to these changes? Why promise to discuss your release and then evade you?

    The earl: He is nothing if not shrewd, Wulfstan. He saw his men regarding me with respect. More eyes looked at me that way every passing day. By gifting me promises, he showed benevolence, but more importantly, superiority. He then shut me away to avoid those promises.

    The bishop: Why didn't he just send you back to Rouen?

    The earl: How could he demonstrate his vaunted army's might if I were not there to witness it? At Dol, I thwarted him by leading the charge. He would not make the same mistake twice.

As the feast of St. John the Baptist passed, I helplessly followed as William fortified border towns and leveled enemy villages. Then, after the Breton town of Dinan crackled in a blaze behind him, we marched to Bayeux.

The bishop: The capital of his brother's bishopric. Did you ever meet Odo? By all accounts he is the living embodiment of our mother church's wretched state.

The earl: I expected to meet Odo at the victory feast set for the evening, but he was delayed. Neither he, nor God, nor any of his angels attended this foul gathering.

The bishop: What happened at this feast?

The earl: A servant led me to the palace's great hall. Twenty of Normandy's barons lined the table, ten to a side. William sat at the table's other head, flanked to the right by his seneschal, William Fitz Osbern. The whole assembly reveled in the feast's merriment, save the duke and I. Neither of us so much as smiled.

After the trenchers were cleared, Fitz Osbern offered a toast to, "the most honorable English earl, without whom victory would have proven much more elusive." Every cup in the hall rose up. What choice did I have but to raise mine? I tasted the bitter potion right away. No amount of water could wash it off. The hall grew dim, words stretched into incessant rumbles, and my chest jumped in fits and starts. My world in a fog, hands lifted me up. Two reliquary chests appeared on the feasting board. My hands fell on their cold, metallic lids as William's voice rang out. "Do you, Harold Godwinson, pledge to be my vassal, to protect my claim to the English throne, and to commit your soul to all my future campaigns?"

The poison twisted my senses. Spices from the stewed lamb burned my throat. The leathery, musky smell of the Normans roiled my stomach. Every bench creak, fire crackle, cough, and snigger burst in my ears. A thousand eyes peeled away my skin, pulled my ribs apart, and stared at my beating heart.

Of countless thoughts rampaging through my head, one reached the forefront: Edith. I thought of her power, her courage. I had to make the pledge in order to see her again, so the words fell from my mouth like falling stones. "I do so swear."

Like a bear baiting, the hunter had slain the beast and the blood-sated crowd left to discuss the kill elsewhere. William led them out and left me in the hall alone. Yet Edith still dominated my thoughts. Even in my poisoned, dejected state, I prayed for God to somehow let me return to her.

The bishop: So this is the reason for your madness. Listen to me, Harold, an oath made under duress holds no validity in the eyes of God. This mummer's trick is invalid.

The earl: I wish it were so, Wulfstan, but as events later in the night would prove, God had stopped watching over me...

Chapter 9: Edith

November 20, 1065

From the darkness of the bower, Edith heard clopping hooves intrude on the driving wind and constant rain. She sat up, straining her ears to follow the sound. It was well past midnight, she judged, and the rider must have an urgent task to brave the foul weather. So she rose, donned a thick woolen cloak, and slipped out the door without waking the children.

Outside, lightning set the sky afire and wind battered the surrounding trees. Rain pelted Edith's skin and cloak, soaking her through in moments. The sheep-eaten grass surrounding the manor house had turned to a mud slick; her frozen toes seeped into the ground with every step. Huddling against the manor wall, she upbraided herself for venturing out. Whatever the news, it could wait until morning.

Yet the single light flickering inside the stable entranced her. *Perhaps Harold has sent a message?* Ever since All Saints, her husband had acted as a man possessed.

And after learning of his Norman incarceration – along with everyone else in England – she had to excuse him. Still, her heart did not forgive. She had no idea why he kept the Norman disaster secret from her or why he refused to come home. Making matters worse, the children had begun to show their dejection. She caught Godwine beating a serf for failing to meet his grain tribute. Gunhild had broken down in tears a few nights past after a nightmare in which her father had disappeared.

So, instead of returning to the dry manor house, Edith ran to the stable.

After reaching cover, she lowered her cowl and wiped her dripping face. Wind still howled and streams of water fell from the thatch above, yet warm torch light glowed from the far stall.

She froze in place when she beheld the messenger. Harold spoke to the head groom, Tobias, about instructions for his mount. His drenched hair, purple cloak, and brown leggings clung to his body. He spoke in hushed tones and his eyes held the look of utter helplessness.

She waited for Tobias' departure before daring to speak. "Jesu, Harold. You look like—"

He stalked forward and embraced her, nuzzling his cold, wet nose into her neck. His desperation shocked her, but she returned the affection with tenderness. "What's wrong, love. I've never seen you like this."

When he pulled his head back, Edith saw redness surround his fire-lit blue eyes. "I had to do it, Edith. I had no choice."

"Do what, Harold?" She gripped him hard.

"Tostig's been exiled by my command."

A burst of fear enveloped her. She hadn't heard anything of Tostig since he embarrassed himself at the feast. "What did he do now?"

"He failed to *think*. Instead of speaking with me, he tried to raise his own war chest through more taxes. His people rebelled and threatened civil war if he remained in power. In reaction, the blundering fool tried to summon the royal army. He sought to rain fire and sword down on his own people, but I stepped in and convinced Edward I could negotiate a solution."

"And the end result was exile?"

"Thousands of saved lives in return for one bloodless banishment. I had to do it, Edith. I had to." His head shook in the crook between her neck and shoulder. "Good God, what would my father think of me now?"

The great Godwin of Wessex weathered the lives of four kings to create one of the strongest dynasties in Christendom. Harold lived every day to preserve his father's work, Edith knew. "You avoided war. Your father would be proud of that."

"I...I came here straight from the council. I needed to see you. I feel so lost."

They embraced again, this time with more force. His kisses soothed the hurt in her soul. She let him unclasp her robe and cover her neck with hungry lips. "So lost without you," he said.

Edith shuddered. Pulling Harold's head away, she kissed him so hard they fell to the ground.

When they finished, they lay intertwined atop the stable straw. He stroked her hair as she listened to the rhythms of his heartbeat. Contentment filled her for the first time in months.

"I'm sorry for this past year, Edith," he said in a tired voice. "My mind won't let me rest. Every time I try, visions of those vile Normans attack my conscience."

"It was hard for me, Harold, but harder for the children. They miss you more than I can describe. Still, we understand. You're married to the realm as much as to us."

"It's good of you to say, but I can hear your tension. I wish it were different. I really do."

"It'll get better. You're here now; that's what matters."

"I will try—"

Tobias' entry cut Harold short. "My lord, I'm sorry to disturb, but Hakon's arrived. He said King Edward's fallen ill, gravely so in fact."

She felt her husband flinch and her previous contentment vanished.

"I'll be right out, Tobias," Harold said. "Tell Hakon to wait just a moment longer."

Alone again, he turned to her. "Is there anything I can say?"

"No. Do what you must."

"There's something I should tell you first." He engulfed her in an embrace. "If the king passes, it'll just be a matter of time before the Normans make their claim. I'm sworn to defeat them, and I may have to go to extreme lengths to do so."

Lying naked in the stable, Edith should have felt freezing cold, but Harold's warmth protected her. "Extreme lengths? What do you mean?"

"I'll take the crown myself before I let William have it."

Her mouth fell open. Never, in her wildest dreams, did she imagine being married to a king. She knew this was no time for fear or questions. "I'll love you still, Harold, whether you're a king or a carter."

"Thank you," he said, tightening his embrace. "With all these threats about me, you're my only solace."

"Nothing could threaten us, love," she said, pulling his head in for a final kiss. "Nothing."

Chapter 10: Odo

December 14, 1065

Odo stirred his bowl of pottage as the Duke of Normandy gnawed the carcass of a once-steaming capon. The blues and oranges of dusk poured through Rouen palace's solar window, and frigid winter air penetrated from the open shutters. The two half-brothers sat at a small table in the center of the room with no sound save for the crunch of bird cartilage.

When William began to lick his grease-glistened fingers, Odo could take no more. "Must we sit in this infernal cold much longer?"

"I'm not finished my supper."

"If there's any meat left on those bones, it's invisible. Let's start a fire and close the shutters. Tostig's been waiting too long."

The duke glanced up from his bones. "You seem excited to meet him, Odo. Believe me, it's no pleasure."

"I don't need a companion for my cups, brother. I want his information."

"And he wants us to have it." William pushed the carcass aside. "It's his sole currency."

"But keeping him outside this long will incense him."

"You forget, brother. I've known him several years. His wife is my wife's sister. We've been equals in all our previous meetings. Now, he is a man without a title or a home. His comfort is the least of my concerns."

The mention of Matilda warmed Odo's blood more than any fire could. Still, he grasped the advantage in keeping Tostig off balance. An irritated guest would be easier to manipulate than a collected one. "And after this lesson, will we imprison him like we did his kin?"

William sipped a cup of water and shook his head. "Our aim is served best by Tostig's freedom. The more battles Harold fights, the weaker he'll be when he faces us."

"Then why agree to see him at all? If we anger him too much, we may have two Godwinsons to fight."

"Perhaps, but Tostig poses no threat to us. Harold is my true enemy. I'm holding this audience to please my wife, no more." William bent his head for the after-supper prayer. Odo issued a quick blessing, seething all the while.

The duke turned to the servant by the door. "It's time. Send him in."

When he entered the solar, Tostig's thin cheeks held a reddish hue. He wore fine, cross-gartered brown hose and a thick woolen tunic dyed in lush green. "You're stubborn as an ox, William," he said without bowing.

"At least an ox can lay claim to a plot of land, lord earl. That's more than I can say for you. Have you met my half-brother, Bishop Odo of Bayeux?"

The two exchanged cold nods. The bishop held the exile in little regard. He seemed a wispier, more effeminate version of the man who stole his secrets.

William did not ask Tostig to join the table. So, the disinherited earl stood with his hands clasped behind his back. "It's high time we discussed my plan."

"Plan to return to England, I gather," William said.

"Yes. I'm afraid it won't be a happy reunion."

"What makes you think you can return so quickly?" Odo asked.

"With Norman swords and ships, not even an army of arch-angels could prevent me."

William sat back in his chair. "Do you hear this Englishman, brother? He seems quite assured of his Norman might."

Odo nodded, wondering where William headed in this game. Tostig's reputation as an army general was undeniable; several kings from Ireland to Rome would rejoice if he offered to lead their armies. At the same time, Odo knew William, and William alone, would lead a Norman invasion of England. So, he ventured deeper into the fray. "If I didn't know better, lord duke, I'd say the esteemed earl is asking to make his Norman might a reality."

Tostig shifted his weight. "Give me five thousand men and Harold won't live to see Lent. It's no secret he disavowed your oath and stands poised to dispute your kingship. The only way you'll become King of England is through battle. Let me conquer the country for you."

Odo leaned forward. It was the expected offer and the tempting argument.

"An ambitious plan," William said in an unmoved tone. "What's your price?"

"The opportunity to gut my brother for one. But after my victory, I'll need a longer-lasting reward I'm afraid."

"Like what?"

"I want my earldom back. It's only fair, William. Harold robbed me of it without cause."

Your first mistake will be your undoing, Tostig.

William pointed a black-gloved finger at the earl's face. "Better men have offered to conquer Jerusalem for no price but the honor to serve me, you sniveling serpent. How dare you talk of conquest and service when all you chase is your own gain?"

Odo sat back and enjoyed the exile's twisted face.

Tostig began to stutter. "Y...you ask me to win England without recompense?"

"Recompense?" William's lip curled as he spoke. "I will honor service when and how I see fit. Right now, I'd rather honor the cook who prepared my capon. Now get out of my sight before I throw you from my window."

After a tense pause, Tostig sidled toward the door. "You are madder than my brother. To hell with you both!" Turning hard on his boot heels, the former earl exited.

The duke turned to Odo. "The poor dolt should know better than to insult his host. Go and look after him. Make sure he leaves without major injury. My wife would never forgive me if I killed her sister's unarmed husband."

Maybe Tostig should meet an unfortunate accident, then. "As you wish, lord duke." Odo flew from the solar and down the stone steps. As much as he'd like to drive a wedge between William and Matilda, he needed to question Tostig without prying ears nearby.

The Englishman's voice rang out from the palace bailey. "Let me go you fucking whoresons! You can't treat me like this!"

Four guards carried Tostig's flailing body between them. "Hold for a moment," Odo said. "Master Tostig, you have more to say?"

"Get these rat-infested shit mongers off me!"

Speaking French, Odo asked the warriors to let go. They dropped him like a sack of grain. He then told them to guard the hall entrance.

The Englishman sat on the ground, adjusting his fine livery and scowling at the Normans. "Thank you lord bishop. It seems there's one Norman with a sane mind."

"My half-brother can be vexing when the mood strikes. I'll see if I can quell his anger. In the meantime, I was hoping you could tell me why the Earl of Wessex broke his oath. We gave him no cause to think ill of us."

A thin smile creased Tostig's lips. "No cause to think ill? He swears the oath was made under duress and his lack-wit confessor absolved him of the sin."

Odo's throat caught on a swallow. "Confessor?"

"The higher-than-all Bishop Wulfstan of Worcester."

"How do you know of the absolution?"

"Because Harold could turn into Judas and Wulfstan would still absolve him. The story must have caused a stir in Wulfstan's holy mind, for he documented it in writing."

"*What?*"

"It's true. At the All Saints feast, Wulfstan gifted Harold a text. A pretty work, I admit. It had the most splendid falcon medallion affixed to the cover. Wulfstan wanted to transfer the gift in private, but I interrupted. And it's good I did, for their treachery became clear that day."

"What does the book contain?"

Tostig rose and dusted off. "I don't know for certain. Harold said it detailed his Norman incarceration, but refused to let me read it."

Odo began pacing in the bailey yard. "The bastards have some sort of false account..."

"The disgrace is beyond measure, but it's just the beginning. Edward is dying and won't last much longer. When he passes, Harold will not sit idle, I assure you. He already has spies in your ranks."

"Who? I need names."

Tostig stood tall. "I see. Now you need my information. You'd do well to tell your duke how helpful I'm being."

"Who?" He stepped forward. The time for games was over.

Tostig retreated a step. "Orrin Geirson, a wine trader based out of Fecamp. Do with him as you please, just make sure he suffers."

Odo repeated the name in his mind; the man was as good as dead. He then returned to the real threat. "Perhaps this book contains more names. Are you certain you could identify it?"

"Without question. Wulfstan's pet scribe created it. The boy's an abomination, but has a most vivid imagination."

"How many people know of the text?"

"I don't know. They were terribly secretive. My guess is they're waiting for Edward's death and then they'll unveil it."

Odo wanted to cringe, but forced himself to remain unbent. "They keep it secret while they formulate more lies! Rest assured Tostig. William won't stand for this once he's king. Thank you for your assistance." He turned to go.

"What about helping me, Odo? Will you talk to William on my behalf?"

The bishop honored Tostig with a gentle smile. "Guards," Odo called. "We must help Master Tostig. Take him to the stable and set him on our fastest horse. If he refuses to leave, chase him out."

Chapter 11:
Aidan

December 17, 1065

Thunor threw the stylus down and his wax tablet clattered to the floor. "These conjurations'll be the death of me if this cursed leg doesn't kill me first!"

"They're called verb *conjugations*," Aidan said, leaning under the goldsmith's splinted leg to pick up the etching tools. "And you'll never learn to write Latin without them. Do you need a drink before we continue?"

They sat in Thunor's pine-adorned hall. Because of the powerful chill outside, his servants had stoked the hearth to a stifling heat. Aidan made sure to stay well away, whereas the goldsmith planted himself in front of the flames.

Mopping sweat from his brow with a cloth, Thunor said, "No no. Let's continue. It's just this blessed splint is sending me mad." He shoved thick fingers between the splint frames running from his upper thigh to his ankle.

"The itching is a result of the poultice." Aidan put his

hand on the exposed flesh above Thunor's knee. He felt no excess heat. "You're healing well, although you'd heal better if you'd sit still more."

"Any more still and moss would grow on me. How do you do it, boy?"

Aidan sat back in his chair. He enjoyed speaking with Thunor. Moreover, he wanted to stay in the house as long as possible. "I figured out long ago I have a better chance of writing a beautiful letter than winning a foot race."

"Ha!" The short, fair-haired man slapped the table. "I'm in your same boat now. Even if this splint comes off, my racing days are done...the Devil take that rotted ladder peg."

Just after the start of Advent, Thunor was climbing into his barn loft when the top ladder peg gave way. Luckily, he knocked his head so he didn't hear his leg bones snap. Wulfstan and Aidan rushed over when they heard. They found Thunor abed, seized by an unrelenting fever. Even more heart wrenching, Ebba cradled her father in her arms and sobbed without restraint. Then, just as Wulfstan began the last rites, the goldsmith blinked awake and his fever broke.

"God works in mysterious ways, Thunor. Had your daughter fallen from the ladder, the world would be missing a brilliant light right now."

"True words, novice of Worcester." He unfurled a wide grin. "You'll make a good monk soon enough, I'd wager, and an even better teacher. Wulfstan was loath to send you from the precinct, but I think you've found your true calling."

Aidan laughed to cover his unease. The bishop had seethed after learning of Thunor's request last week: "Just because you worked on that falcon medallion together, he thinks you're *his* apprentice. If he hadn't come so close to death, I'd box him about the ears." In the end, Wulfstan acquiesced to one of the city's wealthiest merchants, although he filled Aidan's head with rules: no wandering through the city, no handling money, no discussions besides education and the injury, and no – under any circumstances – interaction with women. After one-and-a-half lessons, Aidan had managed to heed all of them...although his eyes darted to the hall entrance at every noise.

"It seems your tirade has passed," he said, sliding the tablet and stylus back to Thunor. "Let's get back to the lesson. Habeo, habes, habet. Habemus, habetis, habent."

He continued the conjugations, making sure to keep a level voice and allow plenty of time for Thunor to etch the words. Besides the occasional servant refilling the water skin, no one bothered them.

They were finishing the verb "laborare" when the cathedral bells tolled. A shiver ran down Aidan's spine. "Vespers! Forgive me Master Thunor, I was supposed to be back by now. I'll return tomorrow if I can." Before the goldsmith could reply, Aidan fled the hall.

He scuffled down the dusk-lit alley, each bell chime weighing heavier on his shoulders. Wulfstan's punishment would be drastic at best and damning at worst. Rounding the corner to High Street, he doubted he'd be allowed to keep teaching.

A high-pitched voice broke his concentration. "Novice Aidan! A moment please!"

Without thinking, he spun around. Eadburga ran after him, wrapped in a thick cloak with the cowl pulled overhead. The sight stunned him silent.

"Father sent me after you," she said as she came close.

Aidan smelled the pine scent of her cloak. "You forgot your writing kit." She held out the tablet and stylus.

The bells had stopped ringing, but Aidan no longer cared. "Thank...thank you, Sister Eadburga." He received the material. The cowl could not hide her dimples and bright red lips. *She's smiling.*

"My mother called me Ebba...when she was alive. So does my father and all my friends. Sister Eadburga doesn't sound like me."

"Forgive me...Ebba." His heart sang. "It was good of you to chase me down." He tried to calm himself. While he did interact with a woman, it still pertained to education.

She giggled. "You're not the fastest novice, so the chase wasn't too difficult. Still, you were racing rather hard."

"Racing? Yes. I...I should've been back for the Vespers office."

"Well then, I won't keep you." Her smile lessened and her words lost their playfulness. "I'm glad we spoke though. I wanted to at the last lesson, but father kept me away."

"You...you wanted to speak to me?"

"Yes. After father fell, you came rushing to our house. I was crying so hard my chest almost burst, but your presence," her head turned to the side, "helped me. I wanted to say thank you for that as well."

"There...there's no need to thank me sis...Ebba." Aidan wanted to jump out of his skin. "I did little, in truth."

"No," she said, stepping forward. "You've done more than you know."

The sixteen-year-old girl leaned in and brushed her lips across Aidan's cheek. Slack-jawed, all he could do is look up. As she withdrew, he could see underneath her cowl. Her grin slanted to one side and her eyes pulsed in the fading daylight. "I hope to see you again soon," she said. With that, she turned and ran back to her house amidst the dwellings of Sidbury Lane.

The next hours passed in a fog. With the kiss planted on his cheek, he spent the rest of Vespers alone in his cell, half begging for forgiveness and half rejoicing in unrepentant rapture. When the office finished, however, he forced himself to the bishop's palace. His one chance to keep teaching was to confess the truth straight away...or most of the truth. He could not bring himself to say the word "kiss" out loud, much less to a raging bishop. Besides, Ebba may get in trouble if he did.

A tumult of activity greeted him in the palace. Servants bustled about, packing chests and bags. He found Wulfstan administering orders to the gangly, somber Brother Coleman.

"Yes. That's right," the bishop said, oblivious to Aidan's arrival. "I want no drop-off with the scribing work while I'm gone. I'm just taking five monks and Aid—" He turned and discovered his audience. "Ah, there you are."

"Father, I'm so sorry." He got down on his knees. "I ran long with the writing lesson. I have no excuse save my own stupidity." He lowered his head and braced for the worst.

"I don't have time to deal with your groveling right now, boy, and you don't either."

Aidan looked up, baffled. "You're not going to punish me, lord father?"

The bishop crossed the hall to load papers into a chest. "Oh, you'll be punished, just not here and now. We're heading back to London."

Not now. Not after today! "I thought you wanted to

spend the nativity in Worcester after traveling to London for All Saints."

"With all my heart, I wish I never had to leave at all, but Harold sent word. The king is ill and may not recover. Apparently, he hangs on for the sole purpose of consecrating his abbey. This is a Christmas Court I cannot miss. So, you and five monks will form my retinue. You'll earn your penance on the way."

"Now lord bishop, is this wise?" Coleman's contempt sat plain on his face. "This novice committed a serious offense. Should we reward him for missing a holy office by including him on this journey? Leaving him behind may be the fitting punishment."

Aidan lowered his head once more. Coleman had embraced monastic life after Welsh bandits destroyed his family farm. At twenty-four years old, he exuded enough rigidity for a village of crones and it now cost him dearly.

The bishop's face darkened. "Perhaps I should stand aside and let you run my monastery, brother. You seem to know what's fitting and what isn't."

The monk trembled. "I'm so sorry, lord bishop. That's not what I meant!"

"Go back to your cell and pray for better sense. Brother Alfstan will retrieve you at the appropriate time. Maybe then, you'll grasp how effective my punishments can be."

"Yes, lord father. Thank you, lord father."

Aidan listened to Coleman's sulking steps. He then felt the bishop's eyes on him. "You heard me," Wulfstan's voice had yet to calm. "Go prepare!"

Vaulting to his feet, Aidan bowed and fled the palace. A torrent of emotions coursed through him. First and foremost, he needed to send a message to Thunor. The lessons were delayed, but not cancelled by any means.

*

True to his word, Wulfstan made Aidan pay. Riding atop a gray donkey named Walter, the novice spent every moment of the first day reciting psalms, chanting hymns, or quoting prayer. If he stopped for any reason save to drink water, catch his breath, or concentrate while navigating a treacherous stretch of icy road, the bishop would count to three. If Aidan didn't commence his protestations before the end of the count, he would miss the next meal.

By the second day, his throat had grown hoarse and his tongue wagged in exhaustion. By the third day, the other monks joined his penance from time to time out of pity. Yet when Wulfstan finally relented on the journey's fourth night – just two days from London – Aidan fell asleep with a hidden smile on his face and a hand covering the cheek still tingling from Ebba's lips.

*

December 24, 1065

Just west of the city, Aidan's courage surfaced. He let Walter fall behind until he rode side-by-side with the bishop. "Lord father, there's something you should know."

"What is it boy? If you're cold, wrap the cloak around tighter."

"No. The chill is fine. I...I've been having doubts about joining the brotherhood."

The bishop's face grew sour. "Oh? What stirs this doubt?"

The boy paused. He needed to phrase his argument perfectly. "A fear...A hesitance."

"Hesitance often demonstrates intelligence, boy. A certain amount of trepidation is natural, especially for someone like you. You've tasted the secular world. You know what the sacrifice entails. This is good. When you say your vows, they will have more meaning and God will reward you all the more."

"Letting go is terrifying, father. I'm not sure I can do it."

They had come up on the humble monastic enclosure called St. Clement's Well. A slight flurry began to fall.

Wulfstan's frown lessened. "Overcoming fear is a learned skill, just like writing. The trick is to identify the source and confront it. When you think of your vows, what scares you the most?"

Aidan thought about divulging everything: his feelings for Ebba, her feelings for him, their intimate conversation, and her mesmerizing eyes. The notion of resisting her for the rest of his life seemed untenable. Still, he could not reveal the entire truth. "The vow of chastity. I...I am unsure about foregoing a family in my future."

A knowing, sharp smirk formed on Wulfstan's white-bearded face. "Ah. The union with God can often seem a lonely pairing." They wended their way past St. Clements and onto the muddy path known as the Strand. "I've seen more novices than I can count struggle with chastity. I remember one specifically. Like you, he was destined for God's service. Every cornerstone of his life, from his family, to his village, to his education pointed him in God's direction, yet he ran away the night before his vow-taking, intent on finding a woman. The brotherhood searched for him for hours, before they found him nearly frozen to death by an icy stream. After the brothers nurtured him back to health, the novice realized what a fool he'd been. The monastery may have scared him, but the outside world proved much harsher."

Aidan regarded the bishop with wonder. "It was you, wasn't it, father?"

"No. It was my brother, Alfstan. I still cannot fathom why he did it."

"Oh. I see." *He doesn't understand at all.*

"And besides, boy, monks are lucky men. They get to spend their days in houses of worship. Some of these houses," he gestured over his pony's ears, "are closer to heaven than anything else on earth."

Following the bishop's gesture, Aidan beheld Westminster Abbey for the first time. Built on Thorney Island – a stretch of dry land that bisected the Thames River– the white stone cathedral gleamed from the reflected torchlight in the flurry-filled night. The spire soared to the sky and huge window panes glimmered. Aidan tried to speak, but words escaped him.

The bishop, however, remained undaunted. "Now, let's pray for mercy. I fear the king's state will make this a most arduous midnight Mass."

"Aren't you going to help perform the ceremony, father?"

Wulfstan shook his head. "Not tonight. I am just one of the sheep bleating at the shepherd in a most exquisite fold."

The Worcester retinue made their way inside to join the perfumed crowd in the nave. Aidan expected to be awed by London's citizens, but the new abbey superseded their brilliance. Tapestries of every color covered the white-washed stone walls. The chapels in the transepts shimmered in gilded oak. Behind a screen of wrought iron flowers, the altar, choir stalls, crucifix, and lecterns glistened in mosaic gold leaf. A cloth of virgin white draped over the altar, which displayed jewel-encrusted Eucharist vessels, an illuminated bible, and reliquary boxes painted garnet and emerald.

The nobility took their places of honor just below the sanctuary. Aidan caught glimpses of Earl Harold and his brothers, distinctive by their broad backs. He found no sign of King Edward or Lady Edith anywhere.

"Come," Wulfstan said. "God can hear us from the back just as well." They found their places moments before the procession began. The Westminster monks streamed into the sanctuary, lined the choir walls, and began the opening hymns.

As they sang, England's two archbishops proceeded down the nave's center. Dressed in fine robes of purple and gold, Stigand of Canterbury scowled down the makeshift isle. Ealdred of York, on the other hand, seemed like he wanted this moment to last forever. Wearing a white robe embroidered with crimson satin, he meandered down the nave, blessing all those who came within reaching distance. When he spied Wulfstan his smile grew. Ealdred had been bishop of Worcester before his elevation to the archbishopric and Wulfstan often said he would know less about God than driftwood had it not been for this mentor. After the archbishops found their places next to the altar, William, the Bishop of London, appeared under the great entryway and marched to the chancel swinging an orb of burning incense. The sweet fragrance mixed with the crowd's sour perfume.

When Bishop William ascended the sanctuary steps, everyone in attendance knelt. Aidan snuck a glance forward, and saw the bag of bones that must have been King Edward. Hunched, gray, and pale, the shadow of a man sat front and center, wrapped in a gigantic bear fur.

Called the Angel's Mass, this first holy service of

Christmastide emphasized how the light of salvation appears to the faithful even on the darkest moment in the depth of winter. Aidan prayed for the king's salvation, for he certainly faced his darkest hour.

After the service, Wulfstan led Aidan and his monks toward the front of the nave. The king had left just after the service, but Ealdred and Earl Harold remained to greet those around them.

"I wondered where you were hiding, old fox," Harold said after meeting them by the sanctuary screen. The earl looked resplendent in a floor-length blue tunic fastened with a belt of silver filigree.

"The fox never strays too far from the chicken coop, Harold. Especially a coop as remarkable as this one. Edward's church impresses even my pastoral bones."

Ealdred's grumbling voice emitted from over Harold's shoulder. "Your pastoral bones had better be more than impressed, Wulfstan. Judging from my last visit to Worcester, you'd be well-served to hire some of these masons to help fix St. Mary's."

"A greater churchman than me built St. Mary's, your grace. It is a sin of vanity to assume I can improve upon it."

"St. Mary's will have to wait one way or another," the earl said. He then clasped Wulfstan's forearm. "Thank you for heeding my message."

"Your words didn't lie. The king's fallen mightily these past weeks." Wulfstan said.

Harold sighed and looked to the stone floor. "Ever since Tostig's exile, he's hardly spoken or eaten. He loved my brother dearly, I'm afraid."

"He loves you more, Harold," Ealdred said. "You've proven your loyalty to him ten times over these last years."

"I wish he'd love me enough to speak to a scribe. The

old man needs a will. If his last wishes go unrecorded, how will we prove his choice for the crown?"

"A troubling situation," Wulfstan said. "Has he made his choice clear in any other way?"

"He muttered just last week that he wants me to protect the realm after he's gone, but every time a scribe gets near, he falls asleep. No written proof exists."

The bishop shook his head. "Your enemies in the Witan are aware of this, no doubt."

The Witan was a council that advised the king on matters of the realm. They also affirmed successors to the throne. Aidan knew the main members well enough: Earl Harold, his brothers Gyrth and Leofwine, and the earls of the north, the brothers Edwin and Morcar Aelfgarson. He didn't know who Earl Harold's enemies were or why they wished him harm.

"Some already accuse me of being the hungriest of the carrion crows," Harold said, passing a look to Wulfstan that Aidan caught but Ealdred did not. "They say I chase after the Atheling like a hawk chases a heron."

Edgar the Atheling was Edward's fourteen-year-old grand nephew and the last scion of the house of Cerdic. By blood lines alone, Edgar stood to inherit the crown.

"Those accusers do not know you, Harold," the archbishop said, "and seem to forget you have sheltered Edgar for many years now. When the time comes, they'll see you mean Edgar no harm. Now, if you'll excuse me, I must go ensure Stigand does not rob the alms box."

After the archbishop left, Harold spoke in a low whisper. "Edwin and Morcar have come down from their northern perches, the greedy bastards. They love my family little, Wulfstan."

"Have you met with them?"

The earl's face curdled. "Yes, and they've been thinking about the succession as well. They'll back me, but the price..." Harold glanced at Aidan, frowning. Then, he took Wulfstan aside and spoke out of earshot.

Aidan knew his place, so the screaming question in his head remained silent. *What could they possibly have demanded that needs to be kept secret from me?*

December 27, 1065

The news was not surprising, but still shocking to hear: King Edward was too ill to rise from bed. The city, which normally overflowed with Christmastide revelry, remained subdued and quiet. Wulfstan rode to the newly-built palace at Westminster as Aidan stayed in the cloisters of St. Clement's Well. In between Masses, he made his way to Earl Harold's manse to pay a visit to Lady Edith, but servants told him the lady had stayed in Nazeing.

Speaking with her about Ebba seemed so right, so natural. She, more than anybody, would help him find the true path. So, he decided to make the afternoon-long journey to Nazeing Manor.

Yet when he arrived at the city gate, the sentry turned him back.

"Sorry, young novice," the guard said through shivering blue lips. "Earl Harold's orders. No one's to leave or enter the city without permission."

"Do you know the reason?"

"No, and I if I did, I wouldn't waste time 'splainin it to people. Now get back to church little monk."

Having nowhere else to go, he returned to St. Clements. As he approached the little church enclave, he heard the monks singing. Any other time, the sight of the snow-dusted, candle-lit church emanating with celebration would have brought a smile to his face. Now, he felt like too much of caged animal to smile at anything. Making matters worse, he had no idea why the gates were closed.

Wulfstan did not emerge the next day or the day after that. The St. Clements brothers treated him well and welcomed him into their rituals, but none cared a seed about the outside world. Aidan began to wonder if Wulfstan had left him there as a lesson. Even the sensation of Ebba's kiss began to fade.

On the night before the Epiphany, the bishop returned to the cloister. Aidan opened his mouth to speak, but Wulfstan's grim look silenced him. "The king has left us. God have mercy on his soul."

"I'm so sorry, lord bishop. I know how much you respected him. Were you there...in the room when he passed?"

"Yes, boy, right next to the weeping queen. It was a portentous moment, to be sure. Edward commended his wife and England into Harold's protection."

Aidan squinted to decipher the words. "Isn't that the same as choosing a successor?"

"As near as any of us can figure, yes. We've held the city gates closed since Christmas Eve, preventing the nobles from escaping before they perform their duty to acknowledge the new king. The moote was held this morning. With the support Harold gathered combined with Edward's designation, few questioned the choice."

Aidan retraced the years. The man who saved him, provided him with a nurturing family, and set him on the path to learn next to Wulfstan would now become King of England. The shock spread to his fingertips. "When will the coronation take place?"

The bishop scoffed and shook his head. "Harold wishes it done tomorrow, just after Edward's funeral. He argues the longer England goes without a king, the more vulnerable it becomes to William of Normandy."

Aidan brightened. "So Lady Edith and her children will be arriving from Nazeing, then. May I go stay with them, father? I'd like to spend some time with her before I take my vows."

To Aidan's surprise, the bishop shook his head. "She won't be coming down, boy. It's best if we leave her be."

Chapter 12:
Edith

January 6, 1066

Edith used her finest cloak of woad-stained wool and her temper to fight off the bitter wind. She traversed the frozen grass in Nazeing's courtyard alone, her prim stride telling everyone to stay well away. Yet Renweard approached nonetheless.

The servant met her at the stables and addressed her with a lowered head. "Will you be taking the gelding to London, m'lady?"

"No. Fetch me Scramasax." Her black stallion stood forty-five hands high and conquered rides in half the time of any gelding. Her servant slinked off to do her bidding.

A pang of guilt softened her posture. She hated acting this way, but events had reached their breaking point. Harold had not returned since the day after Tostig's exile, nor had he asked Edith or the children to join him in London. She had accepted the situation well enough, but now

London's church bells rang in honor of King Edward's passing. She knew what Harold aspired to and meant to be there when he acted.

Renweard had just brought up the stallion when she heard the gallop of a far-off horse. Looking down the manor road, she saw a single rider approach at full-tilt. Her heart fluttered. He had long, golden hair, a russet beard, and anvils for shoulders. *Harold?*

When the rider entered the compound, she veiled her disappointment with a courteous smile. Harold's younger brother Leofwine dismounted and crossed to Edith in long, supple steps. He wore a tunic of embroidered gold under a thick red cloak. Edith could smell the fresh leather from his boots even though he stood several hand-lengths away. His hair and beard were brushed, washed, and trimmed. The rings on his fingers and bracelets around his arms shone in the fading daylight. *Proper attire for a king's funeral.* "Hello, brother. You'll forgive my surprised state. I've learned not to expect visitors."

She had known him since his toddling days. He had the kindest blue eyes of any Godwinson, so she grew wary when a flicker of pain dimmed them.

"Aye," he smiled, covering his unease. "Hal thought you might be angered. Come, let's get inside. This cold'll eat right through me if we stay out."

Edith held one hand on Scramasax. She could feel the stallion urge her to mount and burst away. It tempted her, but she could not disregard Leofwine. She loved him too much to humiliate him like that. "Yes, of course. Come inside. The children will be—"

"Best to keep the young ones away for now. Hal's message is for you, not them."

Edith's intuition screamed in warning. Maintaining

the last shred of poise, she said, "Very well then. Will you at least greet them before we talk? They haven't seen any of you since All Saints."

Leofwine suppressed an impatient look and acquiesced to her request. When they entered the manor, the stoic earl of Hertford and Kent switched to a doting uncle. The girls blushed as he cupped their cheeks and the boys laughed as he joked about their scrawny muscles. He evaded all specific talk of Harold. "He's fine," their uncle said. "He misses you all terribly."

Hoping to delay as long as possible, Edith let the children surround him. After a short while, however, he threw an even-eyed glance at her. The time had come. Edith asked the children to adjourn to the bower with a quiver in her voice.

Instead of sitting, Leofwine stood next to the table, close to the doors. He wasted no time after the children left. "First, let me say Hal desperately wanted to come himself. Events, however, demanded his presence elsewhere."

"Events have demanded him for several weeks now. You can see why I'm upset, can't you? My children miss their father and I miss my husband."

"It hasn't been an easy Christmastide on anyone. Edward invited every noble worth a penny to attend Westminster's consecration. The feasting alone is bound to kill us all if the blood feuds don't do the job first. Every meal, we break bread with someone who, at one point or another, has wanted to slit all our necks."

Edith nodded. "I understand the importance of this Christmas court...especially now. I know of Edward's death, Leofwine. Harold means to take the crown doesn't he? Does he send for his whole family, or just me? When is the coronation?"

Leofwine reset his feet and shoulders. "The coronation occurred just after Edward's funeral. Hal's been king since Terce."

Edith wrapped her hands around her stomach. "He's king already? Why didn't he summon me?"

"He didn't summon anyone. All the nobles were already there and he couldn't open the city until he had their allegiance. If he hesitated, even for a blink, it all might have unraveled."

Edith began to recover. Affairs of state took precedence. "This is remarkable! King Harold...I can hardly believe it. This is incredible!" She sprang forward. "I can't wait to see him—"

Leofwine kept his voice low. "You'll have to stay here with the children for a little longer."

Confusion flooded in. "He's my husband. I'm not some country whore he threw a silver and then forgot about."

"Be reasonable, Edith."

"I am being nothing but reasonable." She pointed a shaking finger toward the bower. "What *reason* do I give my children when I tell them we are barred from seeing their father and their king? There is no reason to exclude us unless he intentionally does so. Why can't we see him?"

Leofwine's massive shoulders slumped. "He's gone. After the ceremony, he left in a royal march bound for York."

"York? What could possibly be waiting for him there?"

When he looked up, the whites of his eyes had turned red. "A betrothal."

At first, she thought he misspoke, but the word rolled through her mind like a stampeding herd. The insinuation it carried made the torch-lit hall grow dim. She wanted to act dignified. She wanted to demonstrate grace and power.

She wanted to do anything, except ask the question that escaped her lips. "Betrothed to whom?"

"Alditha, the younger sister of the northern earls, Edwin and Morcar Aelfgarson. A maid of sixteen years."

Edith sat down and tried to find steadiness by holding her head. The name sounded familiar. Fighting the blanket of pain and anger wrapping around her, Edith searched her mind. When she found the memory, she shuddered in her seat. "The young widow? That makes no sense. Harold killed her husband last year. Why would he marry *her*?"

"Hal doesn't want to and I'm sure the girl is incensed, but the earls wouldn't support our claim without the betrothal. Edwin and Morcar are slow and fat, yet they're ambitious. This marriage joins their blood to the royal family."

"This can't be. Harold already has a *family*."

"Not a Christian one..."

She jolted from the table. "Harold *loves* me. He *loves* our children."

Leofwine's face drained of all color. "Forgive me, I spoke without thought. I know he does. That's not what I meant. It's just this new marriage has the church's blessing."

The walls started to close in. She turned to Leofwine, imploring him with her eyes to make some sense of this. "I ask you now to swear to me, as the brother I always wanted, that I am still Harold's true wife."

He lowered his head and spoke in a close, tender voice. "I've loved you since I was a boy, Edith. You know that. So has Gyrth. Tostig," he paused, "well, Tostig never had much love for anyone, but he envied Harold for having such a beautiful, dutiful wife. Hal still loves you too, Edith. He told me to tell you so."

"His words mean nothing. I want to see him. Take me to York, *now*."

"I can't. The northern earls wouldn't stand for it. They may even break the agreement."

"These men play games with my life!" She slammed a fist down on the table. "What have I ever done to them?"

"Nothing, but they want no question that Alditha's son will be Harold's sole heir." Leofwine reached out to comfort her shaking shoulder. She wrenched away from his hand. "Crowns are seldom won for free. He had to sacrifice you. I'm so sorry."

Her throat constricted. In their stead emitted loud, anguished sobs. She never heard her children re-enter the hall, but they attempted to diffuse the wailing with an embrace. Their efforts proved futile.

She let her head fall. Her intuition, which stirred like serpents in her belly so many times before, lay utterly dormant. The future, which she always looked to with such hope, vanished into a gray, murky haze. The house where she had birthed, raised, and cherished her five children now felt cold and stark. Most of all, the life she had built with her husband – the laughter, love-making, crying, celebrations, and late-night whispers – felt like a lost dream...and she could do nothing about it.

Chapter 13:
Orrin

February 20, 1066

Orrin helped load the final barrel aboard *The Maid of Valmont*. After securing it to the hold, he patted the deck rail of the seventy-foot knar. "Soon, old friend. We'll go home soon." God offered a perfect day to sail: calm seas in Fecamp Harbor, crisp air, and a cloudless sky. Temptation coursed through him for a brief moment, but it didn't last. Life had changed for Orrin in the past months; he could no longer act on impulse.

A young crewman named Ralf approached. "You staying with the crew tonight, m'lord?"

"No," Orrin said, smiling. "I'll ride to Hesilia before sun down."

The courtship concluded after the Epiphany feast. Hesilia, the daughter of the Vicomte de Valmont, brought him dowry lands and revenues equal to his English estate. His gifts to her were less tangible, but heartfelt nonetheless. He renamed his flagship from *Blackspear* to *The Maid of Valmont*. He also allowed her to rename his other vessels: *Bloodfire* became *Windsong*; *Golden Wrath* became *Redemption*; and *Silver Storm* became *Evening Star*. The twenty-year-old girl giggled as she decided each name. When she finished, Orrin wished he owned more ships to offer her.

"Suit yourself," Ralf said with a sheepish grin. "Might find meself some warm arms for the evening."

"You don't have the coin for warm arms. You could barely afford a goat's stall."

Ralf finished the last mooring line knot. "Well, if my esteemed captain would ever give the order to sail home, my purse would grow heavier."

Orrin yanked on the nearest line. Ralf's knots didn't budge. "Patience, friend. If we stay just a while longer, you'll need a bigger purse all-together." Duke William had summoned all Norman magnates to a great council in Rouen at the beginning of March. If he could discover their decisions, Harold's rewards would know no end.

"Tough to stay patient what with all the war-mongering going on hereabouts, m'lord."

"There's nothing to fear on that front. We're just innocent wine traders." He gave Ralf's shoulder a reassuring pat. Neither Hesilia nor the crew knew of his spying; they all deserved ignorance's protection. Yet even without their help, he had learned enough. The Norman invasion force promised to be Christendom's most powerful. Men from as far away as Sicily flocked to William's banner for the chance to win English spoils.

Despite all he learned, Orrin knew in his heart England would win. Harold controlled the entire country now; an invasion fleet would find no safe beachhead as long as he patrolled the shores. Watching Ralf heave his sack over his shoulder, Orrin felt an intense thrill. *The next time we sail into this harbor, we'll arrive as conquerors.*

Something among the dock posts and gray buildings lining the harbor caught Ralf's eye. All color drained from his face.

Perplexed, Orrin followed the crewman's terrified eyes. A swarm of armored warriors stormed toward *The Maid's* quay. A clergyman in shining red robes led the contingent.

The priest stopped at the end of the knar's gang plank. He looked familiar with his thick black hair and chiseled chin. "Orrin of Fritton," he said with a voice as rich as Burgundian wine. "Come with me and answer for your crime."

Orrin swore under his breath. Local officials always tried to squeeze money from foreign traders. Yet thanks to Hesilia, he had more power than this over-dressed parish priest knew. "I'll do no such thing. I've done nothing wrong. Now leave us alone."

"We do not leave spies alone, Englishman."

The response slammed Orrin in the gut. Still, he tried to bluster his way out. "Spy? You must be a fool, not a priest. There's no spy here."

A soldier pointed his spear point at Orrin. "Insulting the Bishop of Bayeux will make your execution all the more painful."

The bishop was not a greedy local prelate; throughout Normandy, people feared Odo like they feared the sweating sickness.

Despite the up-swell of panic, he maintained calm. Pretending to scratch his stubble, Orrin turned to Ralf and whispered. "If I don't find you in the morning, tell Hesilia about my demise. Go now before they take you, too." He turned back to his accuser. "You have the wrong man,

Lord Odo. Just let my crewman pass and I'll prove my innocence."

The bishop said nothing, but stood aside. Orrin said a small prayer of thanks as reticent footsteps clunked on the plank. *At least Odo has a sense of decency.*

The sailor had just reached the dock when Orrin caught the glimmer of sunlight-reflected steel.

"No!" He raced forward, but far too late. One quick puncture in the back made Ralf slump to the dock-boards. As two warriors heaved the body into the harbor's shallows, two more boarded Orrin's knar and seized his still-unbelieving arms.

The bishop's soft feet scraped aboard. His feverish blue eyes never left Orrin's face. "Humble him."

Fists descended like a purge of Devil-thrown stones, catching Orrin's forehead, cheeks, nose, chin, chest, ribs, gut, and groin. When they relented, his eyes had almost swollen shut. Sticky, hot blood coated his tongue, chin, and lips. A desperate urge to retch seized him, but his stomach hurt too much to accommodate.

"I will ask these questions once," Odo said. "Displease me and you will join the sailor."

Even though movement unleashed bursts of pain, Orrin lolled his head up and down.

"How many times have you reported to the usurper?"

"N...none." His tongue felt larger than a bread loaf.

"Too busy conquering Valmont, it seems. I wonder what your new father-in-law would say if he learned about your spying...or perhaps, he knew all along."

"*No!* They're...innocent...I swear."

Rough hands lifted Orrin's head. The bishop's rumbling whisper entered his ear. "You can save them, Englishman, and yourself as well. Just tell me the names of the other spies. Are any of them currently in Normandy?"

"I...I don't know."

A fist slammed into Orrin's stomach with a breath-robbing force. After a raging coughing fit, he said, "Beat...beat me all you want, Odo. I'm tell... I'm telling the truth."

"Perhaps. Then again, you may be protecting your friends at the cost of your new family."

Orrin's knees went limp. "Leave them alone, I beg you. They're *not* involved and...I...I know no other spies." He realized the slip too late.

"No *other* spies? You admit your crime."

He crumbled to the deck and hocked a glob of blood-filled spit into the sea. "There's no use denying it. Yet be...because of Hesilia, I haven't yet committed the act." The truth, Orrin prayed, would be his best defense.

Odo sighed long and deep. "Were it left to me, your head would hang from the harbor gate already. Yet my brother believes you may be of service still. You will be offered one chance to clear your name and save your family."

For a singular moment, all his bodily pain disappeared. "What must I do?"

"Switch allegiances of course."

"That...that is ridiculous. Why do you care about me?"

"To win a war, Englishman, one must weaken the enemy's greatest strength. In our case, we must weaken Godwinson's ability to win men's loyalty. So, killing you holds less value than using you to embarrass him."

"Embarrass him? I'd rather die."

"And what of sweet, virtuous Hesilia? The life of a spy's widow holds little promise."

His mind flashed to the day when Harold asked him to swear his loyalty. It seemed so clear, so perfect. Now, he lowered his head and spoke. "I'll do anything to protect her, lord bishop."

"Will you now? Let's put that to the test. Go back to England. Proclaim your Norman loyalty to anyone who'll listen and return with as many men as your fleet can carry. Then, and only then, will the dagger fall from Hesilia's neck."

"But Harold will kill me."

"All the better if he does," Odo stepped onto the plank without looking back. "Who would fight for a man who kills his own friends?"

The Confession

July 1, 1065

The earl: I awoke in the dead of night. Every word of the pledge hit me with more force than a smith's hammer. The last promise baffled me the most. What future campaigns had I sworn to?

I needed answers, so I dared an escape. Up to this point, I knew any such attempt put my life and my men at risk. But that night, I did not intend to flee from William; on the contrary, I sought him out.

My Norman gaolers reeked of sour wine and snored louder than barking hounds. A full moon shone through the barred window, illuminating the door key hanging from a small pouch on one of their belts. I crept to the guard and lifted the key just before the sod turned to snore in my face. The latch proved the most harrowing obstacle; the rusty iron lock could have woken the earth's other side. By chance or fate, the Normans slept on and I flew into the inner sanctum of Bayeux Palace wearing nothing more than an under tunic and a worn cloak.

Assuming William slept upstairs, I skulked to the second

floor. At the top of the stairs, my name floated from behind the nearest chamber door. Thinking I could learn my answers, I pressed my ear to the crack between the door and frame.

Two men spoke: William's half-brother, Bishop Odo, and a minor Norman lord named Egenulf D'Laigle.

The bishop: But you said Odo did not attend the feast.

The earl: He did not. Instead, he stayed in the kitchens to administer the liquid that muddled my mind. When I arrived at the door, Egenulf was regaling him with a description of my affliction.

The bishop: What did they say that haunts you so?

The earl: After they had their laugh, they toasted to the true victory of the evening: Odo believes William will reward him with the title of Subregulus once he's king.

The bishop: But how could that be? You are England's Subregul...Oh, I see.

The earl: As you've discovered, my pledge of Norman loyalty is a glorified death sentence. And I won't be alone; after William takes the crown, they plan to methodically remove every Englishman from power. William seeks nothing less than a Norman empire with enough might to challenge the kingdom of France.

The bishop: We cannot abide by such evil. Do not fret about the oath, Harold. While I understand your pain, the words weigh less than grains of sand. We must defy these wicked men at all costs.

The earl: I have come to the same conclusions, lord father, for more reasons than I have admitted so far. Prepare yourself: on this night I discovered a plot so horrific I shake just thinking of it...

Chapter 14: Aidan

April 24, 1066

From his position on the side of the choir, Aidan stole a glance toward the nave of St. Mary's when he rose to sing the recessional hymn for Vespers. He found Ebba among the dozens of Worcester's lay folk. She wore a light gray tunic, a white veil, and a look of true devotion...or was it true sadness?

He forced the welling passion from his heart into the hymn. His voice soared as he begged for forgiveness yet again. He had run out of time. Before the service of the Great Litany tomorrow morning, the novices would take their vows. The culmination of his education, the vows would seal Aidan's fate as a Benedictine monk. Once he said the words, he would enter a new world of learning. He would gain access to countless libraries across England and Europe. The life Wulfstan laid out for him would take a giant leap toward fruition. Yet despite all of this, he could not stop stealing glances at Ebba.

Wulfstan stepped forward from the lectern to give the benediction. "Lord, guide us and protect us and lead us in thy grace. Wherever life may take us as we go our separate ways, help us share with others the love we've shared in Your service. In Your name we pray, amen."

The words made Aidan's throat clench. All this time, he looked for a sign to guide him. He needed just one signal from the Lord to let him pursue Ebba. But it never came.

As the faithful recessed out the west end of the church, Aidan's love turned her back. He cast his eyes up to the rafter beams and asked God to take mercy on his deplorable soul.

Then, frantic yells from the courtyard burst into the church. One woman's voice rose above the other shouts. "My God, the fiery star's returned! The end of days has arrived!"

The lay folk clogging the entry doors quaked in fear. They began pushing one another to get out. Enveloped by the laity's desperation, the monks broke their silence and started panicking as well. In his mind, Aidan pictured a giant fireball engulfing all of Worcester.

The bishop unfurled a furious scowl. "No one move." He then strode out the nave and ordered the doorways clear. Everyone left in the church whispered, prayed, and tried to follow the bishop's orders. Aidan fought the growing wave of fear and curiosity in his body.

Wulfstan returned. The scowl had shifted to a look of awe. "You may go see, as long as you stay calm." Gray-robed monks streamed down the choir and out the now-empty nave. "God loves and treasures us all," Wulfstan said as they passed. "There's no reason to fret."

Aidan pulled up next to Wulfstan and they exited the

church together. The bishop's mere presence cast a reassuring air.

Stepping onto the entryway landing, he heard intensified wails and shouts. Torches in the courtyard illuminated a sea of shadows. Some had fallen on their knees. Others shook their heads in wonder. Everyone craned their necks upward.

The waning moon had taken its normal seat in the evening sky, yet it wasn't alone. A star the size of an eclipsed sun lorded over the darkening western horizon. It blazed blood red. Three long, straight tails of smoke stretched from the fireball half-way up the sky. The night, which should have been dark and clear, could not conquer the new star's mystic, red-tinted light.

The sight scared Aidan to the core. Holding his breath, he waited for God's cleansing of the sinful to begin. He imagined an army of demons ripping down Heaven's gates.

The bishop stepped to the fore, raised his arms, and demanded the crowd's attention. "Have faith, friends. We know not what this omen portends."

"I know what it means." It was the voice Aidan first heard inside. He shifted to see the speaker. Two men helped Beda, the oldest person in Worcester at eighty-seven years, move to the forefront. The bent-backed hag walked with a knobby cane. "I remember when last it came. It was the year of the scourge, the year when the Danes laid waste to the entire kingdom as punishment for our sins."

Townspeople shrieked. Wulfstan stood on the church steps, gesturing for quiet. For her part, Beda seemed to enjoy knowing something Wulfstan did not.

"Good people," the bishop said, "Our venerable elder

has endured much over her life. Let us learn from her. What year did the star last appear, Sister Beda?"

The woman scrunched her face and her lips moved in silent counting. "Eleven springs before the turn of the century."

Wulfstan leaned his head and nodded. "Unquestionably an awful time for our realm. Do you remember, venerable sister, who sat on England's throne during those turbulent days?"

Aidan had heard this tone hundreds of times. Wulfstan knew the answers, yet he wanted to push his unknowing student toward enlightenment.

"Ethelred, lord father. Such a hapless king is hard to forget."

"Very good, sister. Do you see, good citizens, the difference between then and now? When the star last visited, it prophesied years of torment and fear because an unfit king sat on England's throne. Ethelred, may God bless his incompetent soul, could not have fought his way out of a barn. Now, the star comes again, but I argue it could portend an era of joy. We have a most glorious monarch at long last. What has King Harold done since ascending to the throne? Our land prospers. Bandits quake in fear of his justice. Churches sprout like weeds in burgs from here to Norwich. Even the northlands bask in grace thanks to King Harold's marriage with Queen Alditha."

The news of the king's marriage still confounded Aidan. Part of him wondered if this omen was not a sign of God's wrath, but Lady Edith's. Still, Wulfstan's confidence made him look back at the sky. He saw the celestial orb hanging mischievously, like it enjoyed the people's confusion. Perhaps the star contained an army of archangels descending to slay the Devil in his lair? Perhaps it was a gift from God to enable crops to grow at night?

Perhaps, Aidan thought with a jolt of realization, the sign he prayed for had arrived.

Sensing the crowd's apprehension waver, the bishop infused more hope into his words. "Mark me, faithful followers. This star may be God's sign to strengthen, not shy away from, the pursuit of our heart's true path." The bishop descended the stairs, lifted his arms, and turned his palms upwards in a gesture of peace. "Return to your homes and pray, loyal citizens of Worcester. God alone determines the future and our prayers may yet sway his decision."

Aidan nodded. *A sign to follow my heart's true path.*

The bishop wheeled around to the brotherhood. "*Praise ye the Lord.* Sing it now."

Responding at once, the monks formed a cluster on the landing steps. Aidan ensured he stood off to the side, close to the ledge. A plan to follow the star's calling had formed in his mind. The singing commenced:

Praise ye the Lord:
God heals the broken in heart,
and binds up their wounds.
He counts the number of stars.
He calls them all by name.
Great is our Lord, and mighty in power.
His understanding is infinite.

Aidan maintained the song as he glanced about. The brothers around him closed their eyes and threw their souls into the words. A multitude of people swarmed the bishop, begging for alms or blessings.

His heart beat slowed; his one chance had come. With

every muscle calling for speed, he leapt off the landing. He landed in a clump. Pain flooded his twisted ankle, but he pulled his cowl tight overhead and shuffled toward the dispersing crowd.

Staying on the periphery, he spotted Ebba walking with her father. Just before they exited the precinct, he walked up behind and nudged her with an elbow. Ebba glanced behind and they locked eyes. He subtly tilted his head as he limped by. Her eyes popped open and she shook her head. Then, Thunor stopped at the gate to speak with two townspeople. Aidan almost crashed into Ebba's back as she stopped a few paces away from her distracted parent. It was all the opening he needed.

"The grove," he said, pretending to glance up at the sky. "As the Vigilis office bells toll."

He dared to meet her eyes. When she gave her quick, slight nod, Aidan's heart trembled. He shuffled out of the crowd as she returned to her father.

Scanning the courtyard, Aidan saw the monks returning to the cloister. He hurried to join in before anyone noticed his divergence through the crowd.

Limping behind the brotherhood, he controlled his breathing. A vision descended that felt so real he could almost touch it. Back in Nazeing, he escorted Ebba down the well-trodden path after a church service at Waltham Abbey. The grip of her arm felt warm and solid. A brood of children ran ahead. Their laughter lifted his smile. One called him "papa."

In that moment, he realized his last hours at Worcester monastery were at hand.

The rule of Saint Benedict forbade any talking in the cloister, so the monks and novices used a series of hand signs to communicate. Tonight, their hands fluttered like birds' wings. Clusters gathered all through the torch-lit archway and on the cloister green. No one knew what to make of the red star's appearance.

Aidan made his way to the cupboard containing writing supplies. Taking fresh parchment, quills, ink, and writing board, he found a space on the covered floor.

He began by depicting the star. Underneath the drawing, he wrote...

My most esteemed lord and father,

As you said today, the star is a sign to follow my true path. While I have tried hard to serve God, I have also found a call emitting from my heart's innermost chamber. Choosing a life of worship is a beautiful and pure pursuit, but it requires too much of a commitment for my curious soul. Therefore, I cannot in good conscience take my vows on the morrow.

Throughout my tutelage, you have sought to show me the power of God's love. At times, I have felt His profound influence. In the pursuits of writing and bookbinding, you have shown me how to access our Lord's divine provenance. Yet I've never felt anything more striking than my love for Eadburga. It consumes and defines me. She consumes and defines me. Life without her is no life at all, and there is no future for me without her. I would not be able to live if I ignored my true feelings and a monastic life would require me to do just that.

Thinking of your reaction sends stabs of anguish through me, but I must write these words. I wish I could repay all the kindness you bestowed upon me, and maybe someday I can return to your good graces. For the time being, staying in Worcester and saying false vows is no way to honor you or God. So, all I can do is depart and beg, with every moment of my existence, for your forgiveness.

Your servant forever,
Aidan

After setting his quill down, he found an empty cloister through wet eyes. Time had gotten away from him. He wiped tears from the note and his cheeks, returned his unused supplies to the cupboard, and fled the cloister.

As he exited, he passed a torch sconce. The flame seemed to jump out at him, as if it had arms that wanted to pull him into its searing hell. He pulled his cowl lower over his head and hurried away.

He crossed the now empty courtyard in the red hue of the night. After rounding St. Mary's, Aidan headed to the bishop's palace. No guard or monk gave him a second glance. As far as they knew, the bishop's most favored student could go where he wished.

Inside, candles lit the great hall and a roaring hearth fought the growing chill. Aidan listened for any sign of Wulfstan, but heard nothing.

Entering the bishop's bower, he crossed to the chest at the end of the straw mattress. It contained Wulfstan's personal prayer objects: a silver crucifix, a kneeling pelt, a small bronze chalice, and a reliquary box containing relics of Saint Oswald's knuckles. Aidan laid his note on top, knowing the bishop would find it after his rest.

No sooner had he closed the chest when voices filled the hall.

"Can the messenger be trusted?" the bishop asked.

"With certainty, lord father. The man carried the king's seal." Brother Coleman's high-pitched voice made Aidan's skin crawl. Still, they spoke of King Harold, so Aidan paused.

"God be good. Maybe this is an ill-omen after all," Wulfstan said. "Tostig has lost his mind if he thinks these raids will work. When are they expected to begin?"

"Soon. The fyrd is positioned to defend the Sussex coast."

"Harold should be preparing to defeat the Normans, not his *brother*. This could lead to disaster! Fetch me quill and parchment from my bower, Coleman, at once."

In an instant, Aidan grew frantic. He had nowhere to hide. At the last moment, he spied the hide-covered window on the far wall. Without thinking, Aidan rushed across the room and lunged out. He hit the ground with a bone-rattling thud. Fighting over the blooming pain, he scrambled to his feet. Instead of running, he pressed his back against the palace wall. Coleman's footsteps approached the window and for a few terrifying moments, Aidan saw a skinny nose protrude from the opening. Then, the folds of hide were pulled tight and the footsteps disappeared. He let out his breath and wasted no time in fleeing.

He wished he never overheard the conversation. *Could the star signify something terrible?* His excitement, however, quelled the doubt. *For me, it still points to a life with Ebba...it has to.*

Thanks to Wulfstan's insistence on herb lore study, no one at the stables questioned him when he took Walter from the paddock; he had done the same on too many previous evenings for this night to seem irregular. As the pony clopped through the dirt-covered streets, guilt ripped at him. *I'm not stealing. I'm borrowing Walter and he'll be returned after we reach Nazeing.*

Just past the North gate, the bells for the Vigilis office tolled. The sound shattered Aidan's attempt for stealth. He pushed Walter into a stilted canter. If he didn't reach the grove before Ebba left, his whole plan would fail.

The forest grove lay near a stream northeast of the city.

Hidden by dense oak trees, the damp, leafy floor was perfect for hidden lovers. They had first stumbled upon it on a spring evening when he should have been picking thornapple and cotton grass. They had stopped here and kissed for the first time. Ever since, the grove had become their designated meeting place.

Driven near to madness, Aidan pushed Walter through tall grass and brambles until he reached the grove. When he found Ebba waiting for him in the red night, he could have screamed in relief. Instead, he dismounted, approached with a heavy breath, and stopped an arm's-length away. "Thank God," he whispered. "I thought I was too late."

Her smile slanted. Ebba liked these clandestine meetings. "Almost, Brother Aidan, but such a daring summons deserved every chance. What's so urgent?"

He looked deep into her eyes. "It's our sign, Ebba. I know it is."

"Really, good novice of Worcester Abbey? I thought our sign would involve angels singing, you changing into freeman's garb, and us finding a fortune buried in the ground. Summoning spectacles in the sky is a poor substitute, I think. Have you spoken with the bishop yet?"

This had always been the turning point. They had discussed running several times before, but dealing with Wulfstan always stopped such talk. This time, however, he had an answer. "He knows. I've delivered a letter."

Her small mouth gaped open. "I can't believe it," she said.

"It's true. Are you ready? I want to take you away before Thunor marries you off to the first merchant's son he deems worthy."

"But I just can't run away. My father's here. My life's here."

"But I won't be. I've left the monastery." He stepped closer. "Everything I've ever promised is here for the taking. Now. I even know where we can go. Lady Edith'll take us in. She'll love you like another daughter. I know she will. So I ask you again: are you ready?"

Ebba's eyes narrowed. "I don't know. Are you sure we could make it?"

"Walter's stubborn as a stone, but he'll get us there. We've no bandits to worry about, thanks to the king's justice. The weather's held up for weeks, so the roads should be in good condition. Moreover, God has given us a sign, so we can go with guiltless—"

She stepped to him. "I'm ready, or as ready as I'll ever be."

They embraced and kissed. Aidan slid his hands down the sides of Ebba's warm, curvy body. She offered a slight whimper. He watched her closed-eyed face yearn for closer contact, more gratification and he wanted nothing more than to grant her wishes. He reached up to caress her face with his hands and to pull her down to the lush green grass. His soul, his body, and his mind had never felt more whole.

And then he heard the voice. "WHAT IN GOD"S NAME IS GOING ON HERE?"

The novice whipped around. Wulfstan stood before him. Coleman lurked behind, holding a torch that lit his abhorred face.

Aidan thrust Ebba behind him. He realized his hands shook and could hear Ebba's sobs. "We just...I...father, I know what you think..."

"There is no thinking here. You have defiled this

young girl, yourself, and me!" He held up a piece of parchment. Even in the red night, Aidan could see his star drawing at the top.

"I found the note when I looked for the bishop's quills," Coleman said. "Racing back to the window, I saw you crossing the courtyard, Aidan. We had to follow and stop this crime."

"You have brought shame on the entire monastery, boy," Wulfstan said. "You have forsaken your chosen life!"

With all his heart, Aidan wished to argue. He had never chosen this life. He never had any idea what he wanted, until he met Ebba. Wulfstan would not understand that clarity, nor would he accept it. Yet despite all the anger and frustration built inside, Aidan bowed his head. "It was my cross to bear, father. I thought God wanted us to be together."

"If you are so easily swayed, you are no pupil of mine."

"Please, I meant no disrespect. I just couldn't..."

"There is no defense. Fornication for novices is forbidden. It is rampant enough in the church already. I will not have it!"

Ebba continued to sob behind Aidan. "What will happen to her, father?"

"The girl will be returned to her house. Thunor will deal with her punishment."

The sobbing behind him paused. "I beg you lord bishop," she said. "Not my father. Please."

Aidan's heart broke in that moment. He fell to his knees. "Do what you must to me, lord father. Spare her from Thunor. She's innocent."

The bishop stormed forward. "You both are guilty as sin. I can see it in your faces. She *will* be sent home. As for you, Aidan, I cannot stand your treacherous air. Since you're so filled with lust for flesh, perhaps Harold can make use of you..." He turned to Coleman. "I'll take the goldsmith's daughter. You take the sinner to his cell."

Too stupefied to argue, Aidan watched Wulfstan lead Ebba away. Then, when he felt Coleman's grip around his arm, he followed without a sound.

Outside the grove, the red star glowed like a garnet. Aidan took another look at this beguiling sign. Somehow, it had formed a devilish smile with fiery lips.

*

Eight days later, Aidan and his escort arrived at Tunbridge Wells. The star was still visible in both the day and night sky, but it had lessened from a red orb into a white pearl.

They approached the English camp from the north. Aidan had never seen so many tents. They dotted the wind-swept rolling hills as far as the horizon allowed. He didn't know which was more daunting: the endless sea of canvas or Brother Sigmund, the escort Wulfstan had chosen who hadn't said five words for the entire trip.

The fyrd's outriders led them to a large pavilion tent. Sigmund's perpetual frown did not change as he gestured for Aidan to dismount and follow him inside.

"Brother Sigmund of Worcester Monastery," announced the guard, "and his novice, Aidan Bard—"

The monk's head snapped to the guard. "He is *not* a novice anymore."

Both Aidan and the guard cringed.

"Thank you, good brother," A voice inside the tent said. "He may not be a novice, but I know who he is anyway. Hello, my young Bardanson."

King Harold stood next to a table covered with maps.

Aidan bowed on one knee and bent his head. Sigmund's stiff body followed moments later.

"I assume Wulfstan sent an explanation."

"He did, lord king," Sigmund said.

Aidan heard the rustle of parchment and the break of a wax seal. He trembled. Would it be banishment, castration, or the gallows? The punishments for disobedience were endless.

"Brother, the king said, "adjourn to the chapel tent, please. I wish to compose a reply. In the meantime, I will deal with your companion."

"Yes, my king." Sigmund's joints cracked and then his steps faded away.

"Rise, you troublesome boy."

Keeping his head down, Aidan followed orders.

"Look at me."

Wincing, Aidan looked up. King Harold addressed him with a brimming grin. "You're not the first adventurer caught in Wulfstan's wrath. Nor will you be the last. This episode has shaken you?"

"More than I thought possible, King Harold. I didn't want to harm anyone. I just acted on God's sign. I thought He was telling me to be with Ebba."

"I'll tell you a secret, boy. I don't think God can give signs pertaining to women. He's as baffled as the rest of us." The slap that hit Aidan in the back made him jostle forward. "Come." The king started walking down the tent rows. "We'll treat this reunion as our own sign. So monastic life didn't suit you? Well, my writing office could use another good quill. Besides, Wulfstan's storms never last long. You'll summer with me and we'll revisit Worcester after the harvest. I'm sure his feathers can be smoothed over. And boy," he faced Aidan again. Before he could bow, the king had grabbed him and looked deep into his eyes, "your heart will mend if your intentions were true. They were true, weren't they?"

Aidan lost his composure. "Yes! I love Ebba..."

"Good. Then you have nothing to worry about. Now come with me. There's no shortage of messages to write."

Aidan hurried to catch up in both mind and body. He faced no punishment; the king seemed happy to see him; and he would work in the royal writing office. By all rights, this should have been a happy day, but his heart did not respond. In fact, it hadn't responded at all since Aidan left it in the forest grove.

Chapter 15: Edith

May 3, 1066

Osgod Knoppe waddled to the center of Waltham Abbey's sanctuary to give the homily. On great feast days such as this, the celebration of the finding of the true cross, the dean of Waltham's secular canons should have performed the ceremony, yet Osgod showed no signs of turning around. To her left, Edith's children stood tall and attentive amidst the throng filling the nave. Silently, she begged God to soften the upcoming harshness.

The clergyman wrapped his hands behind his back and surveyed the congregation. His silken red vestment gave him the appearance of an arrogant apple. Sure enough, he began to speak after fixing his two beady eyes on her.

"Loyal followers, we have gazed in wonder at the red star for more than a week now. Last night, its true meaning dawned on me in a fit of revelation and I'd like to profess it now."

Edith shifted her weight under the scrutiny of Osgod's stare. Since coming to Waltham from Canterbury five years ago, he would be kind to Edith with Harold present and assail the sanctity of handfast unions at the services Harold did not attend. Her husband had laughed it off, saying Osgod aimed his sermons at lay folk, but she always sensed hate in the man.

"As you can see, the Holy Rood sits next to the altar. No church in England holds a more precious relic, especially on this day. After all, within its marble casing resides the true cross."

Edith relaxed somewhat. *Perhaps Osgod will focus on the rood instead of me.* According to legend, monks found a life-size flint cross buried in the earth hundreds of years ago. Declaring it the Holy Rood – the true cross – they ordered a team of oxen to take it to Glastonbury. The beasts refused and instead bore it to the then-ramshackle church at Waltham. Interpreting the journey as a holy sign, the town encased the flint in marble, added an invaluable silver statue of a crucified Jesus, and built a shrine for the relic. Now, thanks to Harold's benevolence, this shrine and church had become one of England's most sacred pilgrimage destinations.

"What does the Holy Rood have to do with the red star? In a word: everything. Our cross demonstrated God's favor of Waltham and the red star confirms it. I know this because the sign appeared the same day as our beloved, *Christian* queen, Alditha, learned she was pregnant."

A boiling heat filled Edith's blood and prevented her from reacting.

Osgod's sickening smile widened. "That's right, friends. Waltham's most generous benefactor, King

Harold, has ensured England's future by creating a family worthy of our Lord's praise."

She looked to her children again. Their faces emanated confusion and embarrassment. Godwine, especially, stood taut as a lute string.

Anger won out. "We're leaving," she whispered as the lay folk celebrated the news. "Now." She pushed through the delighted masses to the narthex, suffering Osgod's triumphant gaze the entire time.

Outside, the fresh, cool spring day couldn't disperse the heat in Edith's skin. She dared not react honestly, not in front of her children. "I'm sorry," she said. "The news overjoyed me."

"Is it true, mother?" Gytha asked. She wore a green tunic and a red veil, looking every bit the grown woman. "Is Queen Alditha pregnant?"

"I don't know, sweet one. I'm sure your father will tell us in person."

Godwine did not hide his frown. "What does it mean for us if she is? Will we be forgotten?"

"No," Edith said with all the authority she could summon. "Never. Your father loves us. This is not some disaster to lament. The babe would be a joyous addition to our family."

"I wish father'd come home," Gunhild said. "We haven't seen him in months."

Edith brushed her youngest child's cheek. "I know my sweetness. It's easy to feel dejected, yet we cannot fall into that trap. We have to believe he loves us. It's all we can do." Gunhild nodded, but Edith realized her advice rang hollow. "Now come. Let's go home and rest."

Waltham lay just a short distance from Nazeing. The family mounted their horses and rode home in somber silence. After they crested a small hill, their manor appeared in the valley below.

Godwine stuck his arm out. "We have unexpected visitors." He pointed to a strange pack of horses tethered to a post in the courtyard.

"I'm sure it's fine. No one wishes to harm us." Edith hoped her voice sounded definite. Without Harold's protection, she felt more vulnerable than ever.

They trotted down to the manor house. Unease swirled in Edith's mind. These visitors could be the queen's men, here to vanquish her rival once and for all.

Upon reaching the yard, Edith grew even more anxious. Leofwine waited for her. He wore chain mail and had a bloodstained battle-axe slung behind his back. Fifteen huscarls had come with him.

The memory of Harold's coronation day flooded back. She would not show her misery like that again. So, she raised her posture and greeted the man who was once her brother-in-law with a thin smile and stiff bow.

After the children had their greetings, she sent her daughters to prepare supper. Her sons, she decided, would hear Leofwine's tidings first-hand.

"Is father coming too, uncle?" Edmund asked. Her youngest son's eyes still showed hurt from Osgod's homily.

"I wish so. He's with the fyrd, shadowing a fleet of raiders along the Suffolk coast."

"Who dares attack?" Magnus asked. He looked ready to defend the shores himself.

Leofwine assumed a rare seriousness. "Your Uncle Tostig leads them."

The blunt answer wiped the bluster from Magnus' eyes. Edith rushed into the deafening silence. "Don't worry, my sons. I'm sure your father and your uncle will settle their quarrel amicably. Come inside and we can talk more."

"I wish I could stay," Leofwine said, "but I'm needed in London. I've come with a message for you and a gift for Godwine."

He handed Edith a wax-sealed parchment. Wanting nothing more than to shred it into pieces, she snapped it open instead. Harold had written another note begging for forgiveness and promising no love existed between him and Alditha. It made no mention of the queen's pregnancy. "We heard exciting news in church today, Leofwine." She tapped the parchment against her palm. Is Harold expecting a child from Alditha's womb?"

Harold's tender younger brother grimaced. "So she says. Nothing's confirmed yet."

"Well please tell Harold we eagerly wait to hear from *him* on the matter."

Godwine stepped forward, clearly disgusted by the topic. "What's my gift, uncle?"

"Your father's spread thin, boy. Traitors infest East Anglia, the fyrdsmen near rebellion because they've exceeded their service time, and meanwhile, no one's home to farm."

Edith cut in. "Who dares rebel?"

"Orrin Geirson returned from Normandy weeks ago. He's been recruiting men to Normandy's banner. We just learned of it. *Orrin!* The man would've been worth less than dirt without Hal. Well," he spat, "he'll get plenty of dirt after we're finished with him."

The news confounded her. "Even our friends turn against us..."

Leofwine seethed through his blond whiskers. "Aye.

England needs good men now more than ever. That's why the king's decided Godwine should take up a lordship."

Edith body jolted. *No.*

Her son's eyes flashed. "Where?"

"You're to receive three estates in Somerset, near Glastonbury. They're small, but fertile beyond doubt."

"This is unbelievable." Godwine looked ready to whoop for joy. "When can I join father's army?"

Edith stepped forward. She would *not* let that happen.

"Don't be over-eager, young cub," Leofwine said. "Somerset has answered our call and sent a great number of fighting men. As a result, no one is left to manage the planting and harvest. The king commands you to rule your estates with a just hand. If your sword is needed, he'll call for it."

Godwine's puffing chest caved, but he summoned a lordly grace nonetheless. "I am the king's to command." Then, he turned to Edith. "Mother, can you believe it?"

"I certainly cannot. This...elevation...is quite the surprise." She pretended to straighten a fold in her tunic. Most mothers would feel surges of pride if their sons received such a gift; Edith felt wholly unprepared.

Her other sons shared none of her reticence. Magnus embraced his elder brother. "If England needs good men in Somerset, I'll go too," he said.

"As will I," Edmund bounced.

Edith stood speechless, unbelieving every word.

"Are you feeling well, mother?" Edmund asked. "You...you look ill."

"No. I'm fine...Just shocked by your father's generosity." She crossed to her oldest son. "You've been given a wondrous gift. But it's a responsibility in equal parts."

Never one to voice his emotions, Godwine embraced

his mother formally. "I know it's sudden, but having Magnus and Edmund would help. I...I'm not sure I can run an estate alone."

She clutched his face. His eyes beamed with a mix of eagerness and apprehension.

Leofwine cleared his throat. Do you give your blessing to the boys, Edith?"

Her other sons showed bright, expectant faces as well. Calling them to her, she said, "Your father has relied on his brothers during every campaign. You should do the same." She turned to the awestruck Magnus and Edmund. "You will take care of one another, you hear me? No matter the enemy, nothing is to come between you."

She gathered them into an embrace, partly because she needed to feel their touch and partly because she could better hide her tears. *It seems Harold needs everyone, except me.*

While her sons made final preparations later that night, Edith supped with her daughters.

"When the boys head off, I will go on a journey as well. It's past time I visited the monastery at St. Benet's. The monks always supported my parents, yet I've ignored them for too long. During my absence, you two will run Nazeing."

"Yes, mum," Gytha said, keeping her eyes on her untouched trencher.

"You have a question?"

"I'm just worried about you. Godwine is off to become a great lord. Shouldn't that make you happy?"

"It does," Edith lied. "Your brother has received his rights. Why wouldn't I be joyful?"

"So this trip has nothing to do with Godwine leaving, the queen, or our father?"

"Absolutely not. I'm upholding my family traditions. The monastery looks to me for benefaction, as it did with my father. God will frown upon me if I ignore my duty."

The half-truth roiled in Edith's stomach. She needed to escape, and the remoteness of St. Benet's offered the perfect place to do that until she could face her abandonment with some semblance of dignity.

"But the abbey is so far away." Gunhild said. "Are you sure it's safe to go with all this talk of raids?"

Edith paused. In her haste, she had not considered that. "I suppose I'll need an escort."

"But we'll be lost without Renweard and Eanfled." Her young daughter's voice grew even more desperate.

"Eanfled will be my hand maid. She loves the abbey near as much as I do. Renweard, however, will stay here with you."

Gytha followed the conversation with a look of growing dread. "Then who'll protect you?"

Edith knew the answer would hurt Gytha, but the time had arrived to break her young infatuation before it careened out of control. "Rand will come with me as well. He can protect us better than ten fyrdsmen."

"But..." Gytha's hands spread flat on the table. She appealed to Edith with her eyes.

"But what?" Edith met her daughter's gaze. She had been denied at every turn this day. Others would have to learn disappointment too.

"Nothing mother," her eldest daughter said. "I just hope your trip is brief."

"Me too, sweet one, but I'll be gone for as long as it

takes the brotherhood to prepare for winter." *And to prepare for my winter as well.*

Chapter 16: Orrin

May 16, 1066

Orrin rode out of his manor house stable in full battle armor. He headed into Fritton's deserted cluster of huts, barns, and sheds. No clouds shrouded the warm morning sun and the wind carried a cool breeze. The fiery star had failed to show for the first time in weeks. He understood the meaning of this change with certainty. *At least I picked a good day to die.*

The sound of a galloping horse lowered his eyes. One of his scouts approached fast. "They're coming from the south, Lord Valmont. It looks like all of them."

"Thank you, Jean." Lord Valmont still sounded strange. The names of his Norman sailors sounded even stranger, but he could do nothing about that. For better or worse, his life and family depended on them. "You had best run ahead. If Harold catches one glimpse of your Norman hide, it'll be the death of us all."

The sailor nodded and disappeared down the foliage-covered path that led from Fritton to Lowestoft, the village where *The Maiden of Valmont* lay anchored. They had practiced the escape for days. It offered little chance for survival, but at least some type of chance existed.

Since returning to England, Orrin had honored his agreement with Bishop Odo. In every corner of East Anglia, he spoke loud and often of Duke William's prowess and his will to obtain the English throne. Most men ignored him, some chased him away, and a few even believed him.

None of it mattered to Orrin, for his antics achieved their true goal. He had drawn Harold's army down upon him; confrontation would occur today.

The thunder of hooves grew louder and Orrin turned to face the oncoming horde. His heart begged to flee, but his mind forbade any movement.

Harold charged down the road, a cloud of dust in his wake. He wore freshly-sanded chainmail, but his helmet-less head let his sweat-stained hair flow. The sight of his friend sent a pause into Orrin's chest.

When their eyes met, the king signaled for a halt. Hundreds of warriors behind him obeyed. Save for the sporadic horse whinny, a tense silence fell over the village.

Orrin bowed his head. "Lord king, Fritton welcomes you."

"You may welcome me, but the rest of Fritton seems oddly absent." Harold issued an aggravated sigh. "I prayed, with all my heart, that the rumors were false. I envisioned arriving here and finding an assembled fyrd ready to join my service. Instead, I find you alone. What am I to make of that, Orrin?"

His horse sensed unease and began side-stepping. He

calmed the mare with soft mane strokes. "It couldn't be helped, Hal. I was given no choice."

A rumble flowed through the warriors at Orrin's tone. Harold, however, maintained his composure. "In honor of the friendship we shared, I will give you the chance to surrender. Take it and you'll die quickly. Refuse, and my men will have their way."

Orrin prayed Jean had prepared everything. Feigning a struggle for control, he trotted his horse a few paces toward the eastern road of the intersection. "Your army looks fierce enough, although I'm surprised to see a novice monk amongst your host." The boy had caught his eye the moment the English army arrived.

"He's my scribe and he holds more loyalty in one finger than you hold in your entire body. *Now give yourself up!*"

Looking at his old friend, he thought for a moment of remaining loyal. Then, a vision of Odo slicing Hesilia's white neck chased all thoughts away. "I'm sorry," he said. "I fight for William of Normandy now, England's true king!" Without waiting to see the declaration's effect, he wheeled his horse and raced down the eastern road.

Shouts erupted behind him. Javelins and sling stones whistled past his head. Orrin dug his spurs into the mare's flanks and urged her forward.

Overgrown maple and oak trees lined the narrow path to Lowestoft. One rider held an advantage over an army in racing through it. Still, Orrin figured he had just a few moments before the chasers caught him. A voice rang out, closer than Orrin expected. "You're as good as dead, you Norman cunt!"

He felt a hand clutch his billowing gray cloak. An instant before the warrior yanked him from his saddle, Orrin unclasped the cloak broach and let the cloth fly. He heard a muffled scream and an ear-splitting crash. Daring a look back, he saw a horse and rider upturned on the side of the path, struggling to kick off the cloak. Then, a rush of warriors filled the void.

After rounding a sharp bend, he came up to a bridge spanning two steep banks of a creek. His heart stopped shaking in his chest as the horse raced across. "Now!"

Jean and another of his sailors emerged from their hiding spots with axes in hand. As Orrin reached the other side, the sailors slid down the bank and hacked the bridge supports underneath. They were mostly sawed beforehand, so the collapse occurred after just a few swings.

Against his instincts, Orrin stopped and watched. *If my sailors fail, I'll be caught anyway.* The hoof falls and shouts grew louder. A *Crack* burst into the air, followed by several louder *Snaps*. The wood cascaded into the creek just as the first rider reached the opposing bank. A stream of screeching horses and screaming men tumbled into the creek.

The Normans scrambled up. Jean reached his horse, but Luke fell with an axe blade jutting from his back.

Before he fled, Orrin cast one last look back at England. Harold sat mounted where the bridge used to be. He neither shook his head nor yelled. He just stared with piercing eyes. No action could have hurt Orrin more, save an assault on Hesilia...who was now safe if Bishop Odo held his end of the bargain.

Chapter 17: Aidan

The warriors returned from the chase, red-faced and empty-handed. For his part, Aidan fought to hide his excitement. The king had paid him a high compliment, even if it was spoken in the heat of argument.

"We'll rest here for the night," the king said after he emerged from the forest path. "At dawn, we ride back to London."

"But what of Tostig and his fleet," one soldiers asked.

The king shook his head as if it weighed more than a mountain. "The coast is guarded all the way up to The Wash. From there, Edwin and Morcar will have to earn their earldoms. It's clear the Normans are preparing to sail, and if I'm not there to meet them, we won't ever get them out. Now leave me. All of you." The king retreated into Fritton's great hall, his grief plain to every eye watching.

That afternoon, King Harold found Aidan in the camp. "Get your pages and come with me."

He knew the pages King Harold spoke of. After grabbing the parchment stack from the tent that housed the royal documents, Aidan hurried to follow.

Fritton lay near the marshlands of Suffolk. Thick tangles of greenery and swamp dominated the landscape. "If you know where the clearings are," the king said, "this is some of the best raptor hunting in all of England."

After finding a wide stretch of land, King Harold removed the hood from a majestic hawk perched on his wrist and let him fly. The raptor screeched, unfurled his wings, ascended with four flaps, and stopped just above the tree line as the tether reached its slack. Unleashing another caw, the hawk rode the wind.

"Do you see the shape of the wings as he glides, Aidan? Make note of that. You can tell he's ready for full flight. Maybe next week. Maybe sooner. He's full grown, but is he fully trained?"

Without looking down, Aidan converted the scene into a sketch. He wrote on a flat writing board and dipped his quill into an ink pot holding a mixture of ground coals, water, and lye.

"Are you getting this boy? See how he circles? One wing flap can last several seconds without him ever losing height. He's doing well, this one."

The raptor bestiary was Aidan's top priority. It aimed to encompass every aspect of falconry. As far as Aidan knew, nothing like it existed in the world.

"Now for the real test," King Harold said, reaching into his saddle bag. A small bell glinted in the late afternoon sun. The king rang it three times and held out his leather-gloved arm.

Above, the hawk gained speed coming out of his final turn before diving down. This part always made Aidan's heart jump: the hawk flew with such force, such focus, that Aidan felt sure he would attack. Descending from the tree line, the hawk landed on King Harold's gloved wrist with an audible *thud* of talons gripping leather.

"He's ready I'll wager. Next week, we'll set him free..."

Aidan finished his sketches and looked up. He expected to see jubilation, but instead found a somber, pensive man.

"It's it the traitor, isn't it King Harold?"

He nodded. "I had wanted to show Orrin the manuscript. He was...he *is* a fine hunter."

"It doesn't make sense to me, lord king. Why'd he side with the Normans?"

"Money, land, fear...I'm not certain, in truth. One of my spies told me Orrin wedded a daughter of a Norman baron. If that's true, then he acted to protect her. Part of me cannot fault him for that." The king offered a morsel of heron flesh to the hawk sitting on his wrist.

Aidan stacked the papers into an orderly pile. "What do you think will happen next?"

"I wish I knew. He had hoped to embarrass me with the display today, and in that regard his plan failed. My men are spitting fire. Many have sworn to stay past the harvest with the hope of skewering him on the battlefield."

"Is that why we're heading back south? You'd rather fight the Normans than fight your brother, and so would the men."

"You're learning how to think like a warrior, young novice. Tostig doesn't have the strength to invade England. I'm certain of it. He may raid a few coastlines, but his hoped-for uprising will not form. So, I'll let Edwin and

Morcar get their hands dirty. Tostig's a better fighter than both of them combined, but their Northmen can handle my brother's meager invasion fleet. I cannot get caught away from the south when William's ships land."

They returned to camp with the sun half-set. Aidan found his fellow scribes sharing a horn of mead around a fire. He loved the sweet taste of the drink, but could not stand the proximity to the blaze. So, he begged leave from them, curled up on his pelt, and tried to fall asleep. They had a long march in the morning and his rump still ached from the race up the coast. Still, rest evaded him. Ebba would not leave his mind.

At dawn, the host began the two-day march back to London. After re-supplying, they traveled to the Isle of Wight, where the king intended to wait until Judgment Day for William of Normandy to invade. Upon reaching the windswept, chalky cliffs, the king learned Edwin and Morcar's forces had repulsed Tostig's landing attempt on the banks of the Humber. Several invading ships lay strewn on the muddy shore and Tostig had fled toward sanctuary in Scotland.

Aidan marveled when he heard the news. Events unfolded just as the king predicted. Yet while the rest of the army celebrated with food and drink, Harold's tent lay quiet all night.

With the army encamped, his tutelage in secular affairs commenced. Clerks taught him how to keep treasury rolls. He learned how to write charters, writs, and wills. The king himself showed him maps and drawings of the wider world.

At night, he often wandered through the camp with his fellow scribes, talking with huscarls and fyrdsmen alike. Without the Benedictine order's strict regulations on food and drink, he experienced a new level of taste. He imbibed mead, ale, and strong wine, discovering his fearful memories dulled after the third cup.

A camp of whores had set up next to the army. Most nights it danced with the sounds and sights of sin, yet Aidan never once entered, even when other scribes tried to drag him. He just wanted Ebba, and spent his resting hours devising what he would say at their next meeting.

At the beginning of June, a small host of soldiers arrived from London. Aidan realized they escorted a young woman to the king's tent. She wore a striking emerald cloak with a matching veil and a circle of gold around her head.

"The queen," said a passing fyrdsman. "Come to show her pregnant belly to the king."

The army had whispered about Alditha's unborn child for weeks. Only the king stayed quiet on the subject. Some guessed he wanted to keep the secret until he could be sure the child would survive. Others said he did not father the child; her brother Edwin had performed the task so his unsullied blood could sit the throne some day. The mere thought of another woman besides Lady Edith giving birth to one of the king's sons filled Aidan with contempt, but since no one confirmed the pregnancy, he had hoped the rumors would be dispelled. Now, with the queen in camp, he had a chance to find out.

He hurried to the king's tent, but the guards blocked his entry. When he turned to go, the king's voice rose from the closed tent flaps. "Aidan: saddle two horses and gather the manuscript. We set off within the hour."

After he brought the horses around, they rode from camp yet again. The king broke his silence only to issue terse, one-word commands.

The king let Wulfcyning – his vicious male gyrfalcon – fly at the edge of a cliff overlooking the great channel. The tethered raptor soared above the cliff in the late-morning sunshine.

Aidan ventured the safest questions first. "Should I pay attention to any particular trait, lord king?"

"Just draw, boy."

"Yes, King Harold. Wulfcyning looks stronger than a dragon today."

A grunt was all he received.

"The day could not be more perfect for a hunt. Perhaps we should summon the falconer and let some caged herons fly?"

King Harold turned his back, forcing Aidan to quell his curiosity.

After an hour of silent flying, the bell chimed and Wulfcyning returned to his master's wrist. The king turned his horse to go home. As custom dictated, Aidan bowed his head, but he caught a glimpse of the tear-stained face before he lowered his eyes.

He expected to hear horse trots, but only the distant sound of the sea hit his ears. Looking up, Aidan found his king looking straight at him.

"Edith's found out by now. She must have."

Aidan infused his words with innocence. "Found out what, King Harold?"

"You're a terrible liar, Aidan, but thank you for the courtesy. I'm sure every tongue wags about the queen's pregnancy."

"I...I'd heard rumors. I guess they can be correct sometimes."

"Correct but slow. The queen's womb failed her."

Aidan lowered his head even closer to the ground. "I don't know what to say..."

"That's good. The less you say the better." Stirrups jingled as the king dismounted. "I cannot keep this to myself, Aidan, but it cannot reach anyone else's ears. Look at me and swear you will take this knowledge to the grave."

Aidan raised his head. King Harold stood before him with Wulfcyning on his wrist and the sun lowering behind him. "I swear, King Harold."

"You have an amazing gift, boy. You're right easy to confess to."

Pride mixed with guilt as Aidan blushed. "Father Wulfstan's training, lord king. He said listening is the most important aspect of learning. Listening and watching."

"What I wouldn't give to have him here now. In a sense, part of him *is* here. Edith too, for that matter. Are you ready? This won't be for the faint-hearted."

"Ye...yes, lord king."

"All right then." The king breathed deep. "The child who died in Alditha's womb was born from my seed, but not my heart. Her brothers, the northern earls, are as ambitious as they are greedy. Marrying Alditha didn't win their loyalty. They wanted her wedded *and* bedded. The night of our wedding, Edwin and Morcar entered our chamber and watched the consummation. Alditha couldn't help but cry, yet her brothers watched without remorse."

Aidan's eyes stretched wide. He had no reply.

The king stared to the sea. "Crowns are seldom won without cruelty. The sad fact is I need those bastard brothers right now. Had I not done their bidding, they would've killed me in my marriage bed. You know what I learned in

Normandy. You know why I fight. I could not risk my life just to protect my honor. Does that make sense, boy?"

Too scared to speak, Aidan nodded.

"It won't make sense to Edith." The king snapped a twig in two and hurled the pieces over the cliff. "She'll see it as a betrayal, and she'll be right. I'm scared I've lost her, Aidan. Ever since I became king, I've been unable to go to her. The earls wouldn't allow it."

The two watched the horizon for long moments. Finding his voice, Aidan said, "Still, lord king, I'm sorry for your loss. The queen must be devastated..."

"It's worse than devastation. She's scared out of her young mind. Once Edwin and Morcar find out she lost the baby, there's no telling what they'll do."

"They wouldn't hurt their own sister, would they?"

"Not if I have any say in the matter. I may not love her, but she's my wife all the same. My assurances did nothing to ease her fear. She begged me to bed her again. Another pregnancy, she said, would protect her, nothing else."

Aidan smoothed the parchment atop his writing board. He never knew such evil could exist. "So what are you going to do, King Harold?"

"I bedded her once against my will. I cannot do it again. Edwin and Morcar may rage and spit, but their thanes won't rise over one failed pregnancy. With any luck, I can keep this alliance through William's invasion. Once he's vanquished, I'll rid Alditha of her fears once and for all."

The next morning, Aidan was working on the falconry manuscript by a snuffed-out campfire when he heard the ordered rumbling of hooves. A caravan headed toward him. In between two lines of mounted huscarls, the queen rode a gray stallion and wore her emerald cloak with the hood pulled down.

They locked eyes for a heartbeat. She had creamy skin, rust-colored hair, plump red lips, and eyes to rival the sparkling green of her cloak. Judging from her furrowed brow, the presence of a crippled scribe had caught her off-guard. Yet neither her quizzical look nor her features startled him as much as the wet streaks running down her cheeks.

The caravan thundered by, leaving him alone once again by the smouldering fire. He tried to return to the manuscript, but the vision of the weeping queen transformed into Ebba, sobbing in the red night. Putting his quill down, he closed his eyes and winced. *I'm no better than any of these men. In fact, I may be the worst of the lot.*

Chapter 18: Odo

June 25, 1066

Archdeacon Gilbert of Lisieux hunched onto his knees in the bailey of Rouen Castle. "A moment's rest is all I ask, lord bishop."

Odo regarded this younger churchman with open impatience. As Gilbert panted, sweat poured down his neck and dampened his fine red tunic. He smelled of sour garlic and horse dung. The satchel hanging over his shoulder, however, looked dry and undisturbed and that was all Odo cared about right now.

"Lives are lost in a moment, Gilbert. And so are opportunities. Follow me."

Without looking back, he crossed the cobbled bailey and traversed the lowered causeway. The sun beat down on his shoulders, neck, and bare head. Outside the palace ramparts, the archdeacon scurried to a water barrel set amongst a pile of wooden bins and dunked himself.

Nonplussed, Odo used his sternest voice. "Father Gilbert, attend me *now!*"

Gilbert was tall, athletic, and limber. His vitality was the reason Odo had sent him on the important mission he just this past hour returned from. It also was the reason for Odo's current ire.

When the dripping archdeacon bounded back, he bowed his head low. "I'm sorry, lord bishop. It couldn't be helped. I've ridden in this heat since sunri—"

Odo struck Gilbert across the mouth. "Show me the satchel. If any of it is wet, I'll throw you head first back into the barrel and not let you up."

Gilbert presented the satchel. Odo inspected the contents. "You're lucky nothing's damaged. Now, wipe the blood from your lip and *follow* me."

Odo and Gilbert continued their walk along the main castle road. Few others dared the heat today, but the sounds of horses, carts, and shovels grew louder as they wended their way through Rouen. After passing through the city gates, they emerged at the base of a large plain. Normally, these fields would contain fertile green pastures and tree clusters. For the past month, however, white and beige canvas tents stretched to the horizon.

After the spring planting, William had assembled his invasion army on this plain. Thousands of men spent day and night cutting trees, hammering metal, and drilling for combat. The sight exhilarated Odo to no end. *These warriors are the instruments of my salvation.*

The bishop's luck had held; Godwinson had sent no messages, save official rebukes to William's accusations. Even after he usurped England's crown, he kept his eavesdropping to himself. The silence baffled Odo, but it also bought valuable time. With his work in discovering English spies – he had disposed of twelve to date – Odo rose above the duke's seneschal, William Fitz Osbern, to the forefront of William's curia table. And with Gilbert's arrival today, he looked to enhance his gains.

They heard the duke before they saw him. "Tell those men to stay in order or they'll stay in Normandy! Do the drill again. We won't stop until these pigs charge the right way!"

They neared his command tent, or what was left of it. An overturned table, shards of clay goblets, and the shattered remnants of a camp chair covered the grass under the canopy. Odo could see William standing at the far side, where the open flaps framed a view of the practice yard below. He wore chain mail despite the heat and his gloved hands gripped his hips as he watched the drill. Off to the side, his usually stoic servants visibly shook.

The duke's seneschal emerged from the shadows. Fitz Osbern was nine years Odo's senior. Tall, gaunt, and reserved, this man had served the duke since they were boys. People often called him the brother Duke William deserved all along. Odo hated him with every fiber of his being.

"Well met, lord bishop, honored archdeacon," The seneschal squinted in confusion at the drenched Gilbert. "Now may not be the best time. Perhaps after the midday meal..."

"We do not wish to disturb, lord seneschal. But may I enquire what has troubled my brother?"

"News from the King Louis. France has refused to support our invasion. He said because of the questions surrounding our claim and the Bayeux oath, the venture falls too close to unfounded aggression against another Christian kingdom."

Odo spread a white-gloved hand over his chest. "But the king is our liege lord. He's honor-bound to help us, or at least you led us to believe so in the last council meeting." He bit his tongue to keep from smiling. *This may be easier than I thought.*

"The decision cuts deep, I know. Combined with the refusal of the Holy Roman Emperor and the Count of Flanders, we have precious few allies in this endeavor."

"Lord seneschal, these tidings distress me to no end. Please: allow me to bless the duke. This is a trial set forth by God. He needs to remain steadfast. If he does, these lords will soon learn the error of their ways."

Fitz Osbern raised his eyebrows and stared deep into Odo's honest face. After moments of indecision, he stepped aside with a slight headshake. "Your blessing had best work, Odo, or else you'll end in worse shape than his camp chair."

Striding past the curious seneschal, Odo approached the duke. Without turning, William knew who was coming. "I have no patience for your scheming today, brother. If you've found another spy, torture him as you see fit."

"No schemes today, William. Just honesty. I've come to beg your forgiveness." Odo knelt in the grass and assumed a penitent's pose.

The duke regarded him with irate, weary eyes. "What have you done now?"

"Knowing of the troubles to rally allies around our cause, I took matters into my own hands. I sent an emissary to my old mentor. Hildebrand is Pope Alexander's chancellor. If anyone could help rally men to us, I thought he could."

William stepped in front of his kneeling body. "Tell me we can recall this emissary. There is nothing stopping the papacy from ruling against us. If word leaks out, my own Normans may not fight for *me!*"

Despite his brother's tone, calm filled Odo's body. "The emissary cannot be called back. In fact, he's already returned." He glanced over his shoulder toward Gilbert, who had waited outside the tent with Fitz Osbern.

William followed Odo's gaze. "You sent the archdeacon of Lisieux? When?"

"The day after the red star appeared in the sky. I believed the star was God's way of telling me to follow my heart."

"What response did he get?"

"He can tell you himself."

After the duke beckoned him inside the tent, Gilbert knelt down next to Odo. "Lord William," he said, "His Grace, Chancellor Hildebrand, sends his warmest regards. He also gave me this satchel. It contained tokens of the papacy's favor."

"*Favor!*" William snagged the satchel and ripped it open. Odo began to smile.

Half-stumbling, the duke reached for an overturned stool, stood it upright, and sat. "Servants, bring me a table."

When the table was provided, he spread out the satchel's contents with more care than a mother tends to a mewling child. He found a papal bull declaring William England's rightful king, a banner displaying the white cross of St. Peter on a field of purple silk, and a necklace of bone relics.

Odo rose. "Despite my insubordination, brother, I think this may be our turning point. With the papacy's support, our numbers should swell."

William looked up from the items. Sweat beaded on his forehead and his eyes had lost their sharp edges. "You did well, Odo. I should never have doubted you. When

I claim my kingdom, your rewards will be astounding to all."

"My dear brother, service to you is reward enough."

"This is remarkable!" William's voice grew as close to excitement as Odo had ever heard. "Did you have any idea Hildebrand would be so definite in his support?"

Raising his eyes to the tent ceiling and opening his hands, Odo pretended to speak to Heaven. "I trusted in God's judgment and the chancellor's ability to interpret it." He looked back to his brother. "We can discuss the papal plea later. I believe we should resend the messengers, don't you?"

"Yes. There's no doubt this changes everything."

It certainly does. And when I'm King of Jerusalem, you will bow to me.

The Confession

July 1, 1065

The bishop: What plot did you discover?

The earl: After they spoke of William's plans for England, Egenulf and Odo turned to their own sickening calling. Each word is branded in my memory. It went thusly:

"I am writing a letter to Hildebrand concerning tonight's accomplishment," Odo said. "You are to take it to Rome on the next ship."

"As you say," Egenulf said, sounding doubtful. "But what if the Englishman breaks his oath?"

"Then he will face the combined wrath of Normandy and Saint Peter's throne. Hildebrand will no doubt convince Pope Alexander to side with us. In fact, the chancellor has assured me His Holiness shares our vision. No matter what he tries, Godwinson won't long outlive his king. Then, it will be a matter of time before our war against the infidel."

"Glory," Egenulf said, his voice spilling hope.

"Our heart's desire," Odo agreed.

In these small moments, the fog of confusion lifted and the depth of my sin pushed even deeper...

Chapter 19:
Edith

July 15, 1066

Sitting by a small hearth in the corner of her one-room hut, Edith wondered how much longer she could endure.

A pile of church vestments from St. Benet's Abbey lay on the floor. Her hand cramped from hours of sewing. Night seemed darker in the Broads of Norfolk and despite the height of summer, chilling moisture infested everything. Even the hearth smoke smelled like damp rot since it spewed from logs of peat instead of wood. Yet without even so much as a pause, she folded a patched monk's habit and picked up a red chasuble with fraying white borders. Daylight would come soon enough, and the abbey's monks would need their mended clothing.

She had worked to the point of exhaustion since her arrival. Part of her felt the charity was her God-given responsibility. After King Canute established the Benedictine Abbey here decades ago, the estates in the surrounding areas experienced a litany of peaceful, productive summers. Some called it a coincidence. Edith's father, who owned two of these estates, called it divine provenance and swore to help the abbey always. When he died, Edith inherited both his estates and his oath.

Yet the main reason she worked herself to the bone stared back at her every time she dared a moment of inaction to gaze into the orange turf logs, white ash, and leaping yellow flames. There lurked visions of Harold holding his young bride in his arms or her sons lording over the maiming of a thief. The sleeping hours were the worst. Instead of restorative bliss, the visions would roll by in unrelenting cycles.

So, as Eanfled filled the room with her snores, Edith pressed on. After she finished the pile of clothes, she intended to help the village women bake the day's bread. Then, she would walk to the Bure River and help wash beggars' feet before they crowded the monastery gates for alms.

Just when she folded the last tunic, birds chirped their daybreak welcome. The women would gather around the communal ovens shortly. So, she stretched out her curling fingers; wrapped herself in a thick, gray cloak; crept around her snoring handmaid; and exited the hut.

With the sky lightening from black to dark blue, she walked across the sopping, sheep-eaten grass toward the cluster of huts that made up Horning Village. The brotherhood forbade any women from staying within the precinct, so Edith stayed at her father's house with Eanfled. She enjoyed the dwelling where she spent several childhood summers, but it stood far apart from the rest of the village. *Just like me.*

Compared to the damp smokiness in the hut, the outside air held scents of moss and pine gum. Just a few birds broke the morning's silence, yet Edith appreciated each high-pitched warble. In Nazeing, a heartbeat never passed without one of her children raising a sound storm. Here, a whisper was considered shouting.

The chirping birds helped her reach a conclusion: she needed to leave. The healing she expected here had proven elusive. Instead, she felt more secluded, more forgotten, with every passing day.

Standing in the burgeoning dawn, she imagined her return to Nazeing. The manor would be half-empty of loved ones and filled with memories that twisted the invisible knife in her back. *I can't stay here, nor can I go home. So where will I go?*

A raptor's call, emanating from high above the tree line, scattered the morning birds. It also provided Edith's answer. She had to find Harold. If she could speak with him, perhaps the misery would ease. Perhaps she could even convince him to come back. The new direction flooded her with warmth and spurred her to continue her walk.

The villagers had set their houses against a wide swath of marsh forest. Stilts elevated many dwellings so the fickle bog or flooding river would not trouble them. As she walked, however, a new sound echoed in the morning. A man grunted, an axe chopped, and a tree fell. After a short pause, the sounds replicated. *Who is felling trees now?* She strained to locate the source, and then followed the sound into a cluster of moss-covered trees.

The sky now held shades of pink, gray, and azure, enabling her to pick her way through the heavy, musky foliage. The noise grew louder as she waded farther in.

After a few dozen steps, the trees gave way to a small

clearing. At the clearing's far end, a tall, sinewy man dressed in no more than a loin cloth whirled and attacked a tree with a single-bladed axe. The sapling snapped in one strike.

Rand began his ritual from the middle of the clearing with the axe held out front. He progressed through a series of poses by shifting his arms, legs, torso, head, and axe in smooth succession. Every move led him closer to the ringing tree-line. Had he been holding a girl instead of a weapon, she would have thought he danced. *In a way, I guess he is.* The ritual finished when he assumed a half-crouch, the axe braced over his head. With a deep grunt, he sprang at a thick pine tree. The blade cut the air with an audible *swooooosh.* When the blade met bark, it sunk almost to the handle. Growling like a bear, the huscarl wrenched it out of the tree and began the series over again.

Without a word, Rand had added his support to Edith's decision. He looked more like a caged wolf than a patient guardian.

She thought for a moment about talking to Rand about the return journey, but then realized how improper it would be. In addition to his half-nakedness, she wore a threadbare tunic under her cloak and no headdress. She also realized any conversation with him could lead to a departure that day. The idea was still too fresh for such quick action.

So, she left Rand to his blade work and retraced her steps back to Horning. By now, the village women will have already kneaded the dough and set the first loaves to bake.

She found more than just the local wives when she arrived at the village square. A man, tall as a gnarled oak in a gray monk's robe, watched the baking from a respectful distance. His cowl was lowered, so Edith saw his skinny neck, bushy fair eyebrows, and thinning, tonsured hair.

"Greetings Abbot Athelwold," she said, offering a slight curtsey. In her mind, she upbraided herself for not wearing better clothing. "Forgive my appearance. I did not expect you."

"Do not trouble yourself, Lady Edith. My return from the coast took everyone by surprise." He smiled and bowed his head. On Harold's recommendation, Athelwold ascended to the abbacy little more than a year ago. A native of Bosham, he had grown up as kin to the Godwin-sons, making him nearly kin to Edith. His kindness added to her desire to come to St. Benet's. But Harold had taken the Abbot away from her too; he assigned Athelwold the task of leading the Norfolk coast's defenses.

"A happy surprise, I hope," Edith said. "The abbey has grown so secluded, the sky could have fallen in London and we'd never hear of it."

"The sky over London is sound, by all reports." He flashed a warm grin. "But if God wanted to send it crash-ing down upon that walled shit pot, he'd get no argument from me."

Edith could not help but laugh. She'd forgotten about the good Abbot's hatred of court.

"But now that you mention it, my return holds a hap-piness of sorts," he said. "The coast has seen no attacks in weeks, so I took the opportunity to call on my abbey's most generous benefactor."

"You came to see me?" She pulled her cloak tight around.

"Of course. You didn't think a year's worth of praying would make me forget our friendship, did you?"

"No. Not at all. I just don't think I'm worthy of such a compliment." Inside, Edith felt a new burst of warmth.

"After all you've done for my remote, little church, the least I could do is take the time to offer you thanks. Will you walk with me?"

"It would be my pleasure."

Athelwold escorted her down a well-trodden path leading to the river. They walked side-by-side as the sun lifted to wholeness. "How goes your charity work," he asked, regarding her with sincere interest.

"In truth, it's almost breaking me. How do the brothers rip so much clothing?"

"It's the damp. It turns metal to rust in a blink and treats fabric with even less regard. But you know, my lady, no one is forcing you to break yourself over our chores. The abbey is not without helping hands and I'd much rather not report to Harold that you have a bent back due to my abbey."

At the mention of Harold, Edith's smile dimmed. "He's *not* worried about me, Athelwold."

The path ended at a river dock. The monastic precinct rose on a flat plain across the flowing green waters. During heavy rains, the river would rage and flood the land bridge to the precinct gates. Since the sun had held firm for days, though, the river now rolled harmless and tranquil.

The Abbot gestured for Edith to walk onto the dock. "Now we reach the heart of the matter. Your face doesn't lie, not to me. Hal's marriage is the event that's breaking you, not this charity work."

"It...it's been difficult, but I have always served my husband loyally—"

"Edith, don't raise the veil."

She leaned against a dock post and stared at the river.

As if carried by a sudden gust, all the pain and heartbreak broke free. "Why shouldn't I be angry? I've done nothing to deserve this. He becomes king and I get vilified as a whore! He then has the audacity to order my sons away from me, in the name of the realm. It's too much." She hung her head.

Athelwold stepped to her and signed the cross over her chest. "God loves you, Edith. He's blessed you with beauty, a healthy family, and a strong husband...handfasting or no. He knows you are struggling with your sacrifice, but you should know it is bearing fruit."

"How do you mean?"

"His marriage to Alditha united the realm stronger than ever before. He can race from the tip of Sussex to the top of Northumbria without one thane barring his way. Your sacrifice, Edith, is saving England."

"So that's it then? I am to sacrifice my soul for the realm? I never asked for this." She began shaking in her cloak.

"No you didn't, but I couldn't think of a stronger woman to take on this great task. Earlier, you asked me why I returned from the coast. While I wanted to see and comfort you, I also came to tell you this: resign yourself to your new life. You are free to stay at the abbey for as long as it takes. Under no circumstances should you seek Harold out. If the besotted northern earls even catch wind you've returned to Harold, they may withdraw their support."

"I will not let these men dictate my life. I am Harold's wife, not theirs."

"Edith, please. Think of your sons. If the northern earls rebel, Godwine, Edmund, and Magnus will hold swords for the rest of their days."

Edith felt as if a vice clamped her stomach. "I cannot believe this is happening. I am to stay here as prisoner?"

"No. You may go whenever you wish. All I ask is that you leave prepared to live the rest of your days without Harold. You hold the course of war in your actions."

She looked up at him. His gentle blue eyes held complete honesty. She felt her throat tighten as she tried to speak. All she could manage is a weak shake of the head.

"I'm so sorry," Athelwold said. Breaking every law of propriety, he embraced her. "It is necessary...for all our sakes. Will you try?"

Separating herself from the abbot, she looked across the river to the monastery. It looked as peaceful as Heaven. "You ask me to do the impossible...but the only other choice is war."

Chapter 20: Orrin

August 1, 1066

Sitting on the earthen floor of Valmont Castle's undercroft, Orrin watched the encroaching torchlight. He knew he should try to clean the empty bottles around him, or at least rise to his feet, but he chose to have another drink instead. He tilted his head and opened his throat. The strong wine dripped down his gullet, lips, and chin. Its sweet, fruity aroma combined with the smells of the undercroft's mold and urine-filled rushes. Most importantly, the accusation in Harold's blistering eyes dimmed and the roars of his ex-countrymen muffled.

The torchbearer rounded a wooden box stack to discover him propped against the stone wall. Before shielding his eyes from the searing light, he caught a glimpse of Hesilia's incredulous face. One of her hands held the torch, but the other rested atop her bulging belly. Their child would be born in two months if the midwives could be trusted.

"You promised you'd try, Orrin."

"I did try, sweet one, and failed miserably." His effort to stay sober had lasted from when he rose at dawn to when he finished his breakfast an hour later. Under the weight of Hesilia's stare, he realized he had no idea how long he'd been drinking.

"Are you well enough to stand?"

"My legs should work, although I'm not inclined to use them. Can't your father drill his men without me today?"

When Orrin returned to Normandy, Bishop Odo kept his word and removed the conroi from Valmont Castle. Yet the episode's effects lingered. Hesilia's father, Ranulf, called every able-bodied man in his dominion to join his invasion force. "The duke doesn't trust us because of you, Englishman," Ranulf had said. "But I'll earn his favor back if it's the last thing I do...and you will help me." So, Orrin spent his sober hours teaching Norman farmers how to kill his English countrymen. Lately, his sober hours had grown few and far between.

"My father is the reason I'm here," Hesilia said. For the first time, Orrin noticed the uneasy flutter in her voice. "He's hurt."

"What? How?" The pain in his head came screaming back.

"He had left to hunt earlier this morning on a new horse. The stallion wasn't running right, so father dismounted to check the shoeing. Just as he lifted the back hoof, a stag bolted from hiding. A groom..." She paused and Orrin heard her sniffle. "A groom hollered and spooked the stallion. The hoof caught father on the side of the head. He was wearing a helm, but we needed a smith to pry it off his head. The blood...God God husband, the blood was everywhere..."

Lurching to his feet, Orrin used the wall to get balance before stepping to her. The violet smell of her dress fought the undercroft's staleness. His eyes had acclimated by now and her pale cheeks glowed orange from the torchlight. She wore a light-colored tunic that tented over her round-ness and a loose-fitting head scarf. When he reached her, he brushed her cheek with the back of his hand. Warm wetness covered his knuckles. "How much time does he have left?"

"They...they've called for a priest. They don't expect him to last the day."

He lowered her torch and embraced her. "I'm so sorry."

Cradling Hesilia, memories of his father-in-law chased away the plaguing English voices. His spying had almost cost Ranulf the lordship of Valmont. By rights, the vicomte could have cast him out or even killed him. But instead, Orrin was allowed to stay by Hesilia's side and drown his sorrows. "If I hurt you, I hurt her," Ranulf had said, pointing to his daughter. "And her mother, God rest her soul, would never forgive me."

Orrin lifted his head off of Hesilia's shoulder, and this time, she brushed tears off his cheek. "I know you've been sorrowed, love," she said. "I've tried to give you time and leeway to heal, but now...I need you. He needs you. He's called for you."

"Me?"

She nodded. "Please, drink this." A water skin hung over her other shoulder. "Clear your mind."

The cold, clean water sent a shiver of gratification through his body. He drained the skin without pausing.

After wiping his mouth with his sleeve, he asked, "What does he want with me?"

"I don't know, but we'd best hurry."

He led the way up the stairs to the castle's first floor. Ranulf's father built the square, stone keep during the tumult that marked the beginning of Duke William's reign. Luckily, Hesilia's grandfather had never wavered in support of the young duke. If he had, the two-story structure would have been reduced to a pile of stones long ago.

The water combined with the fresh air above ground to fight Orrin's drunkenness. Objects stopped blurring and his hands moved in better control. His blue tunic and gray hose were filthy, but there was nothing he could do about that.

When they ascended to the lord's chamber, the familiar stench of death hit his nose. Hesilia noticed it too and squeezed Orrin's hand even tighter.

Ranulf lay face-up on his straw mattress. A single sheet covered him up to his neck. He had heard their footsteps. "Hesilia? Is that you?"

"Yes father," she said, rushing to his side. Orrin's wife bent down and listened to her father's whispers. Her sobs started soft, but grew fiercer as the whispering continued until she draped over him, unable to control her wails.

Orrin watched in grief-stricken silence. Ranulf managed to lift an arm and stroke his daughter's heaving back. "It will be all right," he said with a husky voice. "God loves you almost as much as I do."

Hesilia's wails began to lessen. Keeping her hand intertwined with her father's, she stepped aside.

"Come here, Englishman," the vicomte said.

The window on the adjacent wall allowed a hot summer breeze to cover the bed. It also cloaked the vicomte's head in sunlight. White linen wrapping covered most of his face and head. On the right side above the ear, a bloom of blood spread to the crown of his skull. The wrapping covered his right eye, so one blue orb stared at Orrin. "Father," he said, kneeling. "My sorrow is...inexpressible."

"Save the sorrow. Use your mind if there's anything left. Do you rem...remember what I said the day you came back from England?"

"You said you would win the duke's favor back."

"And what else?"

"That I would help you."

"Well, it seems—" He stopped and cringed as a wave of pain washed over him. When he spoke again, his voice strained. "It seems my time has run out."

Orrin lowered his head. *On his deathbed, he will lay his shame at my feet.*

"But your time has not." Ranulf continued. "You can still help win the duke's favor."

"How, my lord?"

"By serving him *loyally* as the Vicomte of Valmont."

Orrin's head snapped up. The dying man's lips were smiling. "You want me to inherit your title?"

"God..." Another cringe made Ranulf shudder. "God decided to gift me with Hesilia and her alone. Unlike you English, the Normans prohibit women from inheriting land. If you don't take my title, one of my neighbors will."

"I...I am unworthy of the honor, Lord Ranulf."

"I know you are. You are a drunken sot who used to spy on Normandy before turning traitor. You also happen to be the light in Hesilia's life."

"She is the light in mine, too." He stroked the stomach that held his unborn child.

"I know, which is why you are still alive to receive my

lands. But now, before I die, I must tell you how to honor me for this gift."

"I will do anything, father."

"Good, be...because it won't be easy. Pre...prepare yourself, for you will join Duke William's army in my stead. And when the time comes, Englishman, you *must* win the duke's favor. Do you understand me?"

Orrin looked into Ranulf's one eye. He had planned to stay behind when the invasion sailed. The thought of raising a sword against an Englishman had driven him to the wine bottle as much as the voices in his head. "You want me to fight my own people."

"No." He pointed a shivering finger in Orrin's face. "I want you to conquer them. You must get it through your wine-filled skull; the English are no longer your people."

"But I—"

"But nothing. For some reason, God has smiled on you as much as he has frowned on me. England is doomed, Orrin. No army in the world can withstand a charge from a Norman conroi. You must make sure you are never on the wrong side of one." Ranulf breathed heavy and his eye spread wide and wild.

Looking from his wife's weeping face to his father-in-law, Orrin felt his heart shift. "I will do my best, for your sake and for my family's future."

"Good...good. If Hesilia births a son, the duke's favor is the best gift you could bestow upon him."

Behind Orrin, a man cleared his throat. At some point, a priest had entered the room. The gray-haired, white-robed man stepped to the bed and said, "It's time for the rites."

Rising off his knees, he stepped to his wife's side. As the vicomte surrendered his soul, the priest prayed and

Hesilia wept with all her might. Orrin, however, stood tall. A new voice had entered his mind, and this one did not plague him. On the contrary, it whispered salvation.

Chapter 21:
Aidan

September 17, 1066

A steady, warm wind blew in Aidan's face as he arrived at the king's tent atop the cliffs of Sandown Bay. He embraced the unbound, yet finally complete bestiary manuscript to his chest.

Open flaps allowed morning sun inside the king's tent. After the guards let Aidan through, he found King Harold and his brothers breaking their fast on bowls of stewed deer meat. Shuffling to the side, Aidan waited to be called on.

"It's the same cursed wind again," Earl Gyrth said, shaking his head at the bowl.

"May keep up until the winter storms." Earl Leofwine ripped a chunk of bread from the loaf sitting between them and mopped his bowl edge. "If so, no fleet'll pass the channel 'til spring."

Aidan knew what they discussed; the fyrdsmen spoke

of little else. The same southern wind had blown for weeks. At first, the men rejoiced because it provided a needed respite by pinning the Normans across the sea. Their joy turned to grumbles as the wind continued into the harvest season. In response, King Harold allowed thousands to return to their crops. Now, the remaining men wanted to fight, and as the earl said, the wind might thwart any crossing.

"I sent an advanced guard to London earlier this morning," the king said, pushing his empty bowl aside. "If no changes occur before Michaelmas, we'll move there. I fear our stay has ravaged this poor island." When he looked up, anger poured from his face. "The bastard's luck defies *reason...*" He glanced in Aidan's direction for the first time. "Oh...Aidan. I didn't hear you come in. Some stew to warm your belly?"

Aidan had passed the iron cauldron on the way inside. Remembering the aromas of simmering meat, rosemary, and basil made his eyes lids flutter all over again. "Thank you, lord king, but I should give you the pages first. I finished the last sketch yesterday."

"Finished!" The king's previous strain vanished. "Bring them over. Gyrth, Leofwine: look at this. I'll wager a fortune you've never seen such beautiful work..."

Warmth expanded in Aidan's chest, more filling than any stew. He crossed over to the trestle table and pushed the manuscript away from his torso.

Just as the pages hit the king's hand, a messenger appeared at the tent entrance. His clothes were stained with sweat and mud. "My lord, the realm is under attack!"

King Harold shoved the pages aside and launched from his chair. "How could that be? Where'd the bastard land?"

"Not the Normans, lord king. It's your brother.

Tostig's returned at the head of a vast host, along with the King of Norway. Even as we speak, three hundred ships sail up the Humber toward York."

"Tostig's allied himself with Hardrada and the Norwegians...Do the northern earls act?"

"They've assembled a host of their own and mean to chase the invaders to the gates of Hell if they must."

The king tensed his hands into fists. "*Damn them all!*"

Gyrth's face turned puzzled. "Isn't that what they should be doing?"

"Three hundred ships! Tostig and Hardrada have brought *several thousand men!* There's no way Edwin and Morcar can win an open battle, damn their over-eager hides! Assemble the men. We sail for London tonight and will march for York within the week. We'll gather men as we go."

Earl Leofwine gestured for his elder brother to calm. "We can't just leave the south coast undefended. What if the wind changes?"

King Harold looked through the open tent flaps to the sea. "God may yet protect us. And I don't mean to tarry in the north for long. So if the winds do change, William'll have little time to secure his landing. Now, prepare to sail. There's not a moment to lose!"

The king and his brothers ran from the tent, leaving Aidan behind to collect the scattered pages and his scattered mind.

The sail to London introduced Aidan to a foe more challenging than hand cramps or drink headaches. The open sea stirred his gut and infested his skin with a clammy sweat. For two nights and a day, he retched every hour. When the sailors offered him ale, he retched even more.

Disembarking at Thorney Island's dock, he fell to his knees and offered thanks to God. The prayer felt strange and removed, but the ordeal's survival demanded it.

He helped unload cargo after the prayer finished. As he hefted a small document chest from the deck's hold, he noticed a cluster of monks outside Westminster Abbey. A wave of guilt washed over him, but their panicked cries and flailing arms pushed it down. "Disaster," they yelled. "The scourge has begun again!"

Hurrying as fast as he could push his weary body, Aidan joined the crowd listening to the squat, pig-nosed monk.

"The Viking scourge has returned to England! Harald Hardrada and the traitor Tostig have routed Earl Edwin's army! York is theirs for the taking! The earl and his brother managed to escape into the sanctuary of the city minster, but their forces lay annihilated..."

Aidan glanced at the crowd. Heads shook and mouths hung open as the monk grew more lathered with each word. His mind flashed to the courtyard outside St. Mary's on the night of the red star. *Old Beda was right after all...*

Later in the evening, Aidan was settling his stomach with some wine-soaked bread in the abbey refectory when the king appeared. Respecting the rule that prohibited speaking in this room, King Harold motioned for Aidan to meet him outside.

The night felt calm and still as he approached King Harold by the empty abbey steps. He began to kneel when the king stopped him. "We're both too tired for formality, boy. Judging from your supper, the sea turned your stomach inside out."

"Yes, lord king. I was happy to reach shore until I heard the news. I...I'm terribly sorry."

Dressed in chain mail and brown, loose-fitting hose, Aidan's foster father shook his weary head. "It's the trial God presents. Only a coward would hide from it, yet some of my counselors recommend I do just that." He shrugged away the irritation. "I didn't come to lay my troubles at your feet...not this time anyway. I came to apologize."

"You owe me no apol—"

"Well I haven't finished speaking yet. First, you were just about to show me the manuscript when the messenger came. I'm sorry our audience finished the way it did."

Aidan's face flushed. "Thank you, lord king. Do you wish to see the manuscript now? I could go get it..."

"No. I need to return to the army and you need to prepare for the journey."

"Journey, lord king?"

"You're coming north...Don't look at me like that Aidan Bardanson. All summer, I toyed with the idea of cataloging the upcoming battles. Now, with the fight so close, I think a chronicle *must* be written so my children and grandchildren will know how I fought for them. I trust no one for this task more than you."

"But King Harold, The sea voyage *broke* me. How will I make it through a race to Yorkshire?"

"With strength, boy. And strength can be gleaned from more than a sword arm. Do you know what pushes me forward when all else fails? I picture Edith as I saw her when we first met. The vision still thrills me. I'd wager you have a similar memory to draw from."

Aidan's head lowered to cover his smile. He still

thought of Ebba every night. "I...I will try my best, lord king."

The next day, thousands of men charged up Ermine Street. Riding in the back of a covered cart, Aidan hugged his aching frame as it bounced and jostled, thanked God for every brief pause, and lost himself in thoughts of Ebba when the travel threatened to overwhelm him.

September 24, 1066

King Harold called for a halt outside Tadcaster, just south of York. There, a scout told him of York's surrender. Edwin and Morcar, the scout said, planned to deliver the city's keys to the invaders the next morning at a ford of the River Derwent called Stamford Bridge. The king stood still as he received the news; his lips, nose, and eyes pressed as if he was imagining every scene unfold. "Stamford Bridge..." After dwelling in his thoughts for several more heartbeats, he whirled toward the town gates. "Summon my thegns to the great hall," he said.

Left alone with the other scribes in the baggage train, Aidan tried to make the world stop spinning after the constant march. He ravished a bowl of gray, lumpy pottage, and washed it down with a cup of strong ale. He then began preparing the king's war text. Parchment sheets were lined and folded. Ink viles were filled, organized, and secured. Lastly, he took his knife and filed down a batch of quill points.

The king walked up as he bundled his supplies into a riding satchel. "Are you prepared to write your first entry, Aidan?"

"I think so, lord king."

"Good." The king's eyes held no levity. "My brother

expects keys tomorrow. He'll find something sharper, I'm afraid."

*

No war horns blared. No one sang songs of courage. Warriors whispered as their horses trampled the soft turf and now and again, the metallic slither of chain mail escaped into the gray morning. Aidan watched from the back as this silent wall of death approached its prey.

Inside, his organs rattled with a mixture of fear and thrill; he'd never been this close to battle. At the same time, King Harold's orders dominated his mind: "Stay by the baggage, write what you see, and run like there's no tomorrow if you see the enemy advance."

A call for a halt crashed through the morning. Aidan could see nothing, but he could hear. A bevy of panicked foreign shouts rang through the morning, followed by the rustles of thousands of feet.

Moments later, the fighters surged forward and the battlefield opened before his eyes. Remembering his purpose, Aidan pulled out his writing board and began drawing.

Made of mortared stone and weathered wood, Stamford Bridge arched above the banks of the fast-flowing Derwent. On the far bank, tall conifers in the distance framed a hill of dew-glistened grass. Most of the invading army stood here; Harald Hardrada had staked his banner – a black raven flying on a triangle of whitened canvas – at the hill center.

The English warriors halted at the bridge entrance. A throng of foreign soldiers blocked the crossing. Aidan's quill trembled when he noticed the enemy wore no armor.

A few chain mail coats and leather chest-plates were visible, but most wore cloth tunics. He then realized King Harold's plan. The Vikings expected a city council to arrive, not a spear-wielding army.

At King Harold's call, the English swarmed onto the bridge. Aidan's view grew hopeless, so he used his ears once more. Axes crashed onto wooden shields, making a *knock* sound followed by a shower of wood chips *plinking* into the river. Metal scraped on metal in between the underlying beat of drums. Bodies splashed in the river shallows. Shouts, curses, prayers, and pleas fell like rain drops. Once, he swore King Harold's voice conquered the entire field. "Kill the Vikings! Spare the English!"

Then, silence shrouded the fight. Aidan took his eyes off his drawing to look—and the sight took his breath away.

One God-like warrior stood alone in front of the entire English army. His long limbs and wide shoulders gave him the appearance of an oak tree. His black beard fell in a tumble past his blood and leather-covered chest. He barred the way with a gore-encrusted double-bladed axe and an even more vicious-looking scowl.

A single shout restarted the tremors of war. Through the thinned-out line, Aidan saw an English hero rush the bridge. Hakon, the nephew whom Harold journeyed to Normandy to save, vaulted over bodies, his sword high in the air. His ululating cry sounded half-bloodthirsty and half death-resigned.

Despite Hakon's courage, his assault looked like a child charging his father. The scowling enemy hefted his axe to the side and waited without a sound. When Hakon got within three arm-lengths, the Viking swung the axe in a devastating side arch.

King Harold's voice burst out. "Beware!"

Hakon crouched low, ducked the blade, and pounced with his slashing sword. His enemy blocked the blow with the axe shaft and stumbled backward.

The royal army erupted into a cheer. Aidan dropped his quill to join in.

With a grin on his face, Hakon stepped forward and raised his sword high. In the brief moment before he struck, the Norwegian thrust the butt of his axe into Hakon's chest.

As Aidan's cheer died in his throat, the king's nephew stumbled over a body and fell in the middle of the bridge. Before he could rise, the Norwegian coiled his axe behind his back and hurled it down with demonic force.

Time slowed. The king's cry, "NOOOOOOOOOOO," sounded like a war horn. As the axe cut its vertical arch, a small fishing punt came into view from up-river. A sickening *crunch* echoed in the air and a shower of blood spewed from Hakon's body. The far embankment roared in triumph, and the Norwegian champion lifted his axe over his head. The scowl transformed into a chiseled grin.

"Now!" King Harold's voice rang out again.

The champion on the bridge staggered forward, hushing the cheering invaders. His smile scrunched into a confused look and his axe fell to the bridge floor with a *clang*. When he crashed to the ground, a woody *snap* echoed.

Through the celebrating English line, Aidan saw a single spear shaft sticking through the bridge boards. Moments later, Leofwine and Gyrth emerged on the other side of the river in the fishing punt. The incensed English surged over the bridge toward the Raven banner on the hill.

With the fighting on the far bank, Aidan could use

his eyes to continue drawing. The enemy fought hard, but could not overcome their lack of armor. After every swing, an invader fell. Within an hour of Hakon's death, the raven banner wavered and toppled.

"Yield!" The king yelled, but no answer emerged. Swords still clashed at the far corner of the hill.

"YIELD!" The king screamed, but the fighting continued.

"For the love of God, Tostig! Put up your sword!"

The exiled earl found his voice. It was filled with the same spite Aidan remembered from Nazeing's bower. "You took everything," Tostig said. "You ALWAYS took everything!" Steel slithered on steel once more.

"What do you want? You can have your earldom back. You can have more. Just put down your sword."

"I want..." Tostig said between pants, "I want what you have." Men grappled, a scared scream lifted to Heaven, and the English army engulfed the last corner of the hillside.

*

The victors arrived outside of York's walls just before sunset. The city welcomed King Harold as a savior. Edwin and Morcar met him as the gates flung open; the two smiling brothers opened their arms and waited for the king's embrace. Along with the rest of the warriors, Aidan watched in astonishment as the king walked right by them and knelt before Ealdred, the Archbishop of York and Wulfstan's oldest friend.

For two days, the army recuperated in a camp outside the gates.

On the second night, Aidan waited to fill his cup at an

ale cask set amongst the army tents when he felt a tap on his shoulder. Earl Gyrth stood behind him. Remembering how this man helped avenge Hakon's death and win the battle, Aidan bowed low in honest reverence.

"The king summons you, young scribe. He wishes to finish his falcon text."

"Is he inside the city, Lord Gyrth?"

"No. He came back to the army this afternoon. He can't stand to be anywhere near his brothers-in-law and I can't blame him."

Nor can I. "Thank you for the message, lord earl. I'll attend the king right away."

After one last look at the ale cask, Aidan dropped his cup, retrieved the manuscript, and made his way to the king's tent.

When he pushed through the canvas flaps, the outside merriment dulled. Just a few candles lit the near-empty pavilion. Still in his armor, Harold sat on a tall-backed wooden throne, massaging his temples with his left hand. An open book lay in his lap.

"You wish to finish the text, lord king?" He held the manuscript pages out.

Rising from his seat, the king slammed his book shut. Aidan caught the glimmer of the falcon on the cover. *Why was he reading his confession?*

Without a word, the king stowed his book in a nearby chest. Then, he approached without a hint of joy in his steps. "Is this my bestiary?"

Lungs constricting, Aidan managed a meager head nod.

"Give it to me."

Taking the bestiary, the king gazed at it with a strange sadness. "I'm sorry, boy."

Before Aidan could react, diagonal, vertical, and horizontal dagger slashes sent parchment shards and months of toil flying through the air. When the king finished, he slumped back into his chair. "Instead of hunting all summer, I should have been with her. I should have cherished her."

Aidan sat quiet and tried to control his shaking. *Has he gone mad?*

"Do you hear them, Aidan?"

"The men? They're jubilant, lord king."

"They don't know what you and I know. This is their victory. I wish it had never happened."

"You...you just vanquished the Norwegian horde. For decades, English kings have tried and failed to achieve what you did in a morning's work."

"A morning's work? I didn't till a field, boy. I just took hundreds of lives. I took *my brother's* life!"

Sitting on the soft grass, Aidan kept his eyes down. "He was a traitor..."

"My heart cannot assign him that title. He was a jealous soul. A strong-willed, able-bodied jealous soul. And no matter what else he may have been, he was my own brother. When Aelfwyn's sword cut his throat, it cut my father's flesh and my mother's blood."

"King Harold, you are being unfair to yourself. Had the situation been reversed, he would have killed you."

"There's no way to be sure. He looked at me just as the death blow struck. In that quickest of moments, I didn't see a hell-consumed traitor. I saw my scared, disoriented brother realizing what a mistake he'd made."

After several quiet moments, Aidan found the words he thought would sooth the king's soul. "With time, perhaps, the pain will fade under the glory of the accomplishment."

"Time is a fickle friend, Aidan. Tell me, has time eased the pain of your own tragedy?"

"A brother's death isn't comparable to my...mistake." He cringed the moment the final word escaped.

"Love is not a mistake, boy. In troubled times such as this, love is the solace, the joy. It matters not whether a love lasts for two moments," he nodded to Aidan, "or two decades. Once you wrap your hands around it, you hold it for a lifetime."

The king stared into the shadows, lost in thought. Aidan wondered whether he should leave him in peace. He was desperate for a pot of ale. He took two small steps toward the entryway. As he walked, he stepped over the remains of the bestiary.

The tent flaps parted and a mud-covered messenger stormed in. "My king! News from the south. Norman ships have landed in Pevensey Bay."

At first, Aidan thought he had misheard, but the desperation on the messenger's face confirmed everything. He began to shake; God had forsaken them. The English army sat bloodied and exhausted at York, and now a fresh enemy arrived at the complete opposite end of the kingdom. All of Sussex and Wessex lay open to the Norman advance.

King Harold showed no such weakness. If anything, the news seemed to fortify him. "Very well, lad," he said to the panicked messenger. "Do you know when the bastards arrived?"

"Two days ago, lord king. A relay of four us riding night and day brought the news."

"Go rest, boy. You've done your job well."

After the messenger left, the king said, "I told you time is fickle, Aidan. As much as my heart aches for Hakon and Tostig, the time for wallowing is over. We march at dawn."

Confusion sprouted in Aidan's mind. "March? You mean to confront the Normans? The army—"

"You said it yourself; the army just vanquished the Vikings from England. Now, we have the chance to devastate the Normans too, and right several wrongs along the way." He strode to Aidan and placed a hand on his shoulder. "Make sure you find a good horse."

"Where are we going, King Harold?"

"Nazeing. To make amends. From this moment on, I swear to lose my own life before hurting another loved one."

Chapter 22: Odo

September 30, 1066

Odo swiped his finger across the altar inside the parish church of Hastings. It came away coated with cold, sticky blood. Turning, he held his soiled finger up to the enormous chevalier standing behind him.

"Forgive me, lord bishop. Some of the English fighters ran for sanctuary, but we had our orders."

Using the warrior's mantle to clean his finger, Odo frowned. "What did you say your name was again?"

"Urse D'Abitot, lord bishop." The man stood still, but fear filled his voice.

"Urse D'Abitot," Odo repeated, etching the name in his memory as he surveyed the church. Overturned tables, ripped tapestries, and broken glass were strewn all over. Blood coated the altar, the stone walls, and earthen floor. At the western entrance, the doors were propped against the frame, right next to their ruined hinges. *This man does his work well.* Still, Odo could not let this transgression pass unpunished. "Who ordered you to despoil this church?"

The warrior cleared his throat. "No one, my lord. The orders were to grant no mercy."

Odo slapped him. "Grant no mercy to the English, you blood-crazed cretin. To the church, you are expected to show the utmost respect. These puny townspeople were just the first to taste our justice. More battles face us, and you've risked God's favor for the whole invasion with this defilement."

"Yes, my lord. But...but the sanctuary. They could have held out for days."

"You broke the doors, D'Abitot." Odo thrust his still blood-stained finger toward the entrance. "But you didn't have to butcher them in the church. Next time, *drag them outside*. Am I understood?"

Urse fell to his knees, quaking. "I beg forgiveness from God and from you, Bishop Odo."

"God will accept or deny your forgiveness in due time. As for me, I require your complete loyalty for the duration of this expedition. Serve me well, and you'll earn my forgiveness. Fail me, and I'll send you to Lucifer myself."

"What do you command, lord bishop?"

"First, clean this place. All of it. The duke means to hold a war council here within the hour. We'll speak more later."

The warrior scrambled to his feet to summon his men. Odo stalked outside; he needed to calm himself before the council.

When he stepped into the fresh air, Odo breathed deep. A strong sea wind had dissipated most of the smoke, even though some houses still burned. The confiscation of Hastings had been quick and absolute. After arriving in

Pevensey Bay, William chose to attack this small port town first. With its pier-filled harbor, city walls, and church, it offered an ideal base. It also lay at the end of a well-traveled road leading to London. Yet instead of setting out to begin the invasion in earnest, William ordered the army to construct a castle within the city walls. The delay infuriated Odo more than words could describe.

He walked through the city square outside the church. The sounds of digging, hammering, and sawing joined the ocean waves. Men bowed as he walked past, but Odo paid them no mind. Harold Godwinson dominated his thoughts. After the spying earl took the throne, Odo worked to cast him as a usurper in the eyes of Christendom. When he learned Tostig had attacked Yorkshire, a surge of righteousness flowed through his body. When the winds shifted and the Normans set sail, he could almost taste his revenge.

Yet God continued His vexing ways. After reaching these shores, William stumbled and fell as he disembarked. In that moment, thousands of excited men hushed. Knowing the superstitious nature of warriors, Odo rushed to save face. "You see, good lords," he shouted so all men could hear. "The king embraces his new land with open arms!"

A quick snigger gave way to light chuckles throughout the crowd. When William raised his head, he continued to disarm them with a smile. "My half-brother has the right of it. I've been here but a few moments and am already one with my land." The chuckles turned into full, if still nervous laughter. They avoided a crisis, but the omen was unmistakable.

Then, just before their assault on Hastings, they learned of Tostig's crushing loss at Stamford Bridge. As a result, the men had grown an uneasy edge. Had William not unleashed them on Hastings, they may have begun fighting one another.

While the army's morale hung by a thread, Odo's secret battle threatened to undo him. He lived in constant fear of the usurper's damning accusations and the existence of the falcon book tormented him. He prayed every night for Godwinson's death and the book's destruction. For the death, Odo knew he had to rely on the swords of men like Egenulf and Urse. For the book's destruction, he had no idea who could help.

Just as his frustration began to exhaust him, the church bells rang. The council was set to begin.

When Odo re-entered the church, he saw Urse had done his penance well. The blood stains had dimmed, the altar appeared clean, and the smell of entrails had lightened. The Norman barons who made up William's war curia packed the nave.

A haggard-looking William made his entrance and stalked to the front of the altar. Long ago, he told Odo how to deal with the proud, fickle baronage. "Let them speak, but make up your own mind silently. That way, they feel involved and you learn their true intentions."

The portly, fork-bearded Count Brian of Brittany stepped forward to speak first. "Honored duke, I sense a trap. The usurper has allowed us to land, which means he plans to harry us instead of engage in open battle. We cannot survive the winter under such duress. Perhaps we should consider returning home?"

A few murmurs of agreement filled the church. Odo spewed silent hatred at the cowards; Count Brian garnered the most damning curse.

"My lords," said William Fitz Osbern, "we have it on

good authority the English army is far to the north. They have not *allowed* us to land. On the contrary, they were not here to prevent it." The tall, thin man wore chain mail, held a helm under his arm, and regarded the other barons with his sharp nose turned up. The seneschal spoke with his own voice, but the words reeked of Duke William.

A young, strapping warrior named Roger de Beaumont rose. The son of William's greatest baron, Roger had been the first to charge into the enemy ranks outside Hastings. "I say we strike London. Let's have a look at that lying, thieving English pig as he stands helpless outside his own city." Odo nodded, hoping William agreed as well. An assault on London would allow access to the royal palace, one of the places that may house the falcon book.

Yet Fitz Osbern raised an arresting hand. "I'm as eager to win this war as the next man, but a march on London is fraught with risk. If the city refuses to open its gates, we're committed to a siege. With Godwinson still lurking about, we could be crushed against London's walls."

"Perhaps we should send an envoy to the usurper," counseled wise old Bishop Geoffrey of Coutances. "He could return to us with knowledge of the English army's state."

"The army's state doesn't concern me." The sound of the duke's voice quieted the church. Odo braced for the decision. "The usurper's strategy does. No doubt he's being counseled to refrain from conflict. He's also basking in the glow of a great victory. But you forget, honored lords, I spent a summer with the man. He is not one to accept inactivity, no matter how advantageous that course may be. Isn't that right Orrin Geirson?"

Along with everyone else, Odo turned to the back of the church. The Englishman whom he found in Fecamp stood near the broken entryway. He looked to the floor as he spoke. "Yes, King William. I...I doubt Har...the usurper relishes the idea of hosting a Norman army over the winter any more than you wish to be his guest. He'll strike at some point, though I know not when."

Lord Roger fumed. "Why should we trust this man? He spied for the English once. Who can say if he isn't still serving them?"

An air of indignation swept over Orrin's face. "I may not have earned your trust, Lord Beaumont, but I have served Normandy with outright loyalty since my marriage. And you talk of service. I do not deny my past service to Harold Godwinson. Have you ever served him, lord? Can you speak of his mind, his mettle? If so, please enlighten us."

My my. A plan took root in Odo's mind.

Beaumont's mind, however, lost control. "You disrespectful cur!" He unsheathed his sword and stormed forward.

Almost as if an angel struck him, Orrin remembered his place. Fear overcame indignation and he reached for his sword as well.

Fitz Osbern and a host of other barons stepped between them. The heir of Beaumont hurled curses and taunts that echoed off the stone church walls. For his part, Orrin held his ground with a red face and silent mouth.

The guards who lined the walls wrapped their spear butts on the floor. The nave returned to order as William spoke again. "I will speak of this disturbance to you later, Beaumont. As for you, Geirson, you'd do well to respect my nobles."

Both men mumbled, "Yes, lord king."

"Now, back to the matter at hand. I agree with Geirson:

the usurper will strike soon. He knows I'm not some passing Viking here for loot and glory. If he doesn't act, every village in his beloved Sussex will sport a castle he'll need to uproot before he can consider himself safe. Every day he lets us stay, we can imbed ourselves deeper into his heartland."

Odo saw heads that once shook in doubt now nodding in agreement.

"Yet I agree with you in one respect, Count Brian," Duke William continued. "We need to meet him soon. With that in mind, we'll turn our ravagers loose in the coming days. No village, no shed, not even an over-turned skiff will be left alone. Only a gutless swine would hold back from trying to stop the carnage, and the usurper is anything but gutless."

After the council concluded, Odo approached his half-brother. "And so the final days of the Godwinson scourge have arrived. Are you satisfied with the lords' morale?"

"They're starting to believe. I would never have convinced them had it not been for the English traitor. Did you see how he bit at Beaumont? I could not have paid for a more convincing show."

"Yes, a curious man to say the least. Did you select him for any of the raids?"

"No. If he were to betray us in a bout of guilty conscience, I'd look like a fool."

Odo checked to make sure no one listened. "When we first arrived, I helped you out of a tough fall. Now, I'd like to redeem the favor, if I may?"

"What would you ask of me?"

"I think Orrin Geirson may be quite useful. He's among his own people again; if you send him on a raid, he may convince them to lay down their weapons."

The duke stroked his stubbled chin. "It'll never work. He's a proclaimed traitor; no Englishman would listen to him."

"There's no harm in trying. If he succeeds, our cause looks peaceable and righteous. If he fails, he'll have to kill the villagers; I can think of no greater test of loyalty than that. As insurance, send him with men of unquestioning allegiance and light regard for hesitance. Urse D'Abitot, for example. Even if Geirson falters, Urse will not."

"Fine. As a favor to you and a test for him, he'll be allowed one raid."

"Fair enough." Odo nodded his thanks and turned to go.

William's scraping voice called after him. "This fascination with the Englishman is unlike you, brother. What are you up to?"

Spreading his arms out in a gesture of innocence, he met the duke's accusatory stare. "Tests of faith intrigue me to no end, William. I will pray for Orrin's success." *And his knowledge of the usurper's secrets.*

Chapter 23:
Edith

October 10, 1066

Edith raised high in her saddle as she crossed the stone cairns marking the boundary of her Nazeing estate. Spying a farmer scything in one of her golden wheat fields, she covered her encroaching misery with pride. "That's the first harvester we've seen in days. At least we have the good sense to prepare for winter."

Rand rode atop an old bay gelding. Wearing a leather vest, green tunic, and brown woolen breeches, he basked in the morning sun. His sheathed sword dangled from his hip and his chainmail hauberk chinked in the packed bundle behind his saddle. "Aye," he said with an eager grin. "Safe to say the cold is far from many minds."

She could not deny it. The countryside resisted its annual fate and clung to its lush green prime; the sun defied the season-changing chill; and the sky offered nothing but clear blue instead of autumnal gray.

Eanfled nodded from atop her straining brown pony. "God is rewarding all our good work at St. Benet's, m'lady."

Edith turned to hide her sneer. *Is this a reward for relinquishing my husband and sons?* In the weeks since Athelwold's visit to St. Benet's, she prepared for the journey home. The time arrived with the onset of harvest season. Gunhild and Gytha would need help during the upcoming toils. Even so, she shied away from cities on the trip back to savor her last quiet moments before re-entering the storm.

With each trot, the storm grew closer. As the crossroad between Waltham and Nazeing approached, harvesters, carts, and grain sacks filled the rolling fields like ants in a rotted log.

"Look there," Rand said, gesturing to the scene. "Even the field hands enjoy the fine day."

Everywhere Edith looked, tattered, sweat-soaked harvesters waved and cheered with brimming grins. A peasant boy – named Jarl if she could remember right – burst from the fields and offered a brilliant purple poppy. Edith received the flower and returned all the greetings with warmth, but these reactions put her on edge. The nibbling feeling broke through as the estate came into view. The harvesters were all women, young boys, or old men.

After hastily giving Rand and Eanfled leave to return to their families, Edith galloped the rest of the way home. As she dismounted by the barn, Gytha and Gunhild emerged from the manor. Gunhild raced up and engulfed her in a smothering embrace. Edith had just caught her breath before the questions descended. "How was your trip, mum? Are you tired? How was St. Benet's?"

She wrapped her arms around her youngest child.

You're all I have left. "The abbey's well, little one. A place of peace and restoration, as it always has been." Her feet now firm on the ground, Edith felt each of her forty-four years as her pilgrimage concluded. She must have looked as disheveled as she felt, standing in dust-covered riding skirts and an unwashed red tunic. She peeled away from Gunhild and unwound her wimple to cool her sweat-soaked neck.

By this time, Gytha had reached the barn. "I'm glad you're home," Gytha said, embracing her mother formally. "You'll never believe it."

"Don't keep me waiting. The men have disappeared, and the remaining lay folk act as if angels had fought off judgment day."

"Not angels, mother," Gunhild said, bouncing up and down. "It was father! While you were gone, he defeated an army of Norwegians!"

Edith's heart unfolded in exhilaration, confusion, and panic. She grasped Gytha's arm. "Your brothers. Did they take part in the battle?"

"No mother," Gytha said with a calming grin. "We've had word. They're still with the western levies."

"God be praised." Edith let her shoulders go slack. "So tell me what happened."

"The armies clashed at a place near York called Stamford Bridge," Gunhild said.

"Three hundred ships brought the Vikings to England. Just *twenty-four* took them home," Gytha added.

Edith covered her mouth. It all made sense now. Her men, and those of the estates on the way home, had joined Harold's army. They all now reveled in victory. Edith tried to rejoice with them, but every thought fell to a common, terrible vision. She saw a euphoric Harold riding to the embrace of his new brood mare of a wife.

Feeling her daughters' expectant stares, she removed the hand from her mouth and managed a smile. "St. Benet's grows more reclusive by the day. When did this remarkable battle occur?"

"Just a day before Michaelmas," Gytha said.

"More than ten days ago? Shouldn't our men be home by now?"

Gytha glanced at her feet. "Come in and refresh your-self..."

"You are hiding something from me. Out with it."

Strain crossed Gytha's eyes. "They're not home because another battle looms. A Norman army landed in Pevensey Bay."

Edith stood dumbfounded. Two of the world's most powerful armies had invaded in two week's time. Harold had broken one, but the second attacked England's opposite end before he could possibly have recovered. "Your father's an amazing man," she said, masking her shock. "The Norwegians learned a hard lesson at his hands, and no doubt the Normans will too. Come. You can tell me more inside. I think I need that refreshment now." And somewhere to sit before I faint.

Gytha led the way as Edith fought to control her thoughts. She focused on walking tall, maintaining calm, and hiding the one emotion overriding everything else: inconsequence.

With its entry doors open, the great hall breathed the fresh morning. New tallow candles burned from their wall sconces. Fresh straw covered the floorboards. The wall tapestries had been aired, beaten, and brushed. Pine garlands adorned the wooden columns and rafter beams. At the far wall, the hearth Harold built welcomed her home. With leaden eyes, she turned away and sat at her feasting board.

Gunhild had run off, but Gytha sat with her. The oak table emitted familiar hints of grease, rosemary, and chive. Her daughter filled a washbowl from a clay pitcher and the sound of trickling water broke the silence. My house was never so quiet.

As she brooded, Gunhild entered with a tray and placed it before her. It held a bowl of stewed boar's meat, a plate of soft goat cheese, and fresh bread. Edith scowled the moment she saw the fare. "What's this?"

"Your meal, mum. You've been traveling so much I thought you'd be hungry."

Edith flushed with a sudden, uncontrollable anger. "Stewed boar? My good cheese? I suppose you opened the Burgundian wine as well. Have you lost your wits? I don't care how warm it is or how well the harvest is going. You would've exhausted our stores before Advent. Do you know how to survive on beechnuts and bush berries? Run a house like you have, and you'll find out!"

As Gunhild repressed tears and took her seat, Gytha's eyes widened. "This is unfair."

Edith met her daughter's incredulous stare. How dare she oppose me? But some underlying strength in the girl's tone held Edith from raising her voice. Still, she pressed forward.

"Tell me daughter: what is unfair about prudence?"

"It's *unfair*," Gytha's tone bit hard, "because we had an unexpected visitor...Our father."

Edith tilted her head and regarded Gytha with disbelief. "How? He's in York with his army."

"No, mother. Father's already come back." Gunhild

said, pleading. "He came to Waltham to pray for victory against the Normans. Then, he came here for supper. It was just last week. He asked about you, too. We saw it, didn't we Gytha? He grew wroth the moment he learned you were away."

"Harold came here..." Confusion collided with astonishment in Edith's heart, yet just one question formed on her tongue. "Who...who was he with?"

"He was all by himself, save his hearth guard. Some thirty men in all." Gytha said. "Uncle Gyrth and Uncle Leofwine had gone with him to Waltham, but they lodged in London. Other than the feast, we've tried to save all we could."

Relief filled her body; at least Harold kept Alditha away from Nazeing. Rising from her seat, she walked to her daughters and kissed both their cheeks. "I'm so sorry, young ones. The journey exhausted me. I spoke too soon. Did your father have any message for me?"

"Yes mother." Gytha nodded, reached into her tunic, and produced crinkled, folded parchment with a red wax seal binding the fold shut.

Edith bit her lip and removed the parchment from Gytha's outstretched hand. The message felt strange...heavy. She placed it on the board, not ready to open it yet. "You both have done well. Now, return to your chores. We'll speak more of these battles during supper."

The girls rose from the table and left the hall. Alone, Edith nibbled on a bread heel and searched the hall for some distraction. Every thought, however, returned to the note. She took a deep breath and ripped it open.

Come to me before the battle. I have a precious gift you must receive from my hands. Please do this. If not for your husband or your king, do it for the love we once shared.

Edith leaned forward. *A gift for me?* Her pulse quickened at the prospect of following his orders. She would have to leave for London at first light. If he had already left the city, she would need to race to catch him. A second thought crept in, forcing her back in her chair. *Is this some trinket his whore rejected as inferior?* All of the sudden, her exhaustion and anger welled up, strong as a summer storm. More riding was unthinkable. Her daughters needed her here. If Harold wanted to give her a gift, he would have to come back.

"Forgive me, m' lady. A private word, if you please?"

Edith found Renweard standing in the doorway. "Yes. Of course. Please sit with me," she said, folding Harold's message shut.

In mud-spattered tunic and hose after hours in the fields, Renweard's nimble feet padded to the feasting board. As he sat, a pained expression crossed his face. "Guess the lasses told you 'bout the king's battles." He sounded soft, almost scared.

"I couldn't believe it," Edith said, putting the message down and picking up her water cup. "For months, I sat at home, still as a scared deer. Then, a great storm erupts after I leave. I'm afraid to ask if anything else happened!"

The servant nodded and his face tightened into a joyless smile.

"Renweard, did something else happen?"

"Well, m'lady, it's more rumor 'n anything else. Just didn't want you t'be caught off-guard an' I didn't have the heart to tell the lasses. Heard it from a ceorl comin in from the north." His face twisted, but Edith urged him on with a nod. "He...he said the king's gone mad."

Edith's clay cup banged down on the oak table. "Why would anybody say that?"

The servant opened his hands as if the gesture would help him explain. "He said the king's besot with grief after slayin Master Tostig at Stamford Bridge."

Edith's body went limp and breathless. She remembered the night when Harold last visited Nazeing; the feelings of his desperate hands, her needful embrace, and their last lovemaking came rushing back. The memories filled her with sheer pain. *Is Alditha comforting you now, Harold?*

Renweard's soft, nasal voice continued. "The ceorl ate an' drank more 'n his fill, but he shared plenty of the fight. Said he saw Tostig fall with his own eyes."

"Tostig fought with the Norwegians...Have you verified the truth?"

"No, m'lady. The king'd already come an' gone. Now, from what I saw, no madness gripped him. He walked with a heavy heart, for certs, but he's still got his wits. No more's come down 'bout Master Tostig."

"Well, we'll have to find out soon. The girls love their uncle. They'll need to be protected from this rumor, if it *is* a rumor."

With the world outside Nazeing in a tempest, Renweard turned the discussion to the manor itself. Most of Nazeing's fighting men had joined Harold's army, but some had missed the call. The king had taken a healthy swath of their food stores, but left enough until the men could return. Of most import, Harold hadn't taken any of Edith's fifteen horses from the stables.

"Horses are worth their weight in gold to armies," she said. "Why didn't he take any?"

Renweard looked nonplussed. "I offered 'em, m'lady,

but the king said you may need 'em. I didn't fight too hard. We do need 'em, what with the fewer harvest hands."

He then began to catalog the efforts to till the fields, but Edith paid cursory attention. Harold left the horses not for harvest use, but for her. He wanted her to catch up and bring the men he missed.

The servant excused himself and returned to the fields, leaving Edith alone with her thoughts. She felt an irrepressible need for fresh air. Walking into the bright afternoon sun, Edith closed her eyes, breathed deep, and sought to find reason. *Gift be damned, I'll not run to him like a hound runs for scraps.*

Just then, Rand galloped back into the compound. He vaulted from his saddle, walked straight to Edith, and knelt. "It's true, isn't it Lady Edith? King Harold plans to fight. May I have your leave to join him?"

Edith stood straight and gestured for him to stand. The child she remembered in swaddling clothes now dwarfed her. Remembering his practice session outside St. Benet's, she said, "Yes, my boy...my warrior. Your king needs you and Nazeing. I ask you now, as your lord and lady, to assemble every willing man to join the king's army. You'll need to hurry, so I offer up the horses from my stables."

Rand returned her stare with an unflinching one of his own. His raven-black hair blew in the slight breeze. "We won't fail you, m' lady. We'll cut those bastards to the quick and be back for All Saints."

Edith summoned a grin, although grief renewed its attack on her soul. *Now, even Rand leaves me.* "I hope you're right, dear boy, for all our sakes." She released his hand. "I've another task for you. When you reach the army, tell King Harold I...tell him my place is in Nazeing with the girls. He can deliver his gift after the victory."

His brown eyes registered confusion and obedience. "As you say, m'lady. Now, by your leave, I'll gather the men. We'll head for London at daybreak. If the king's not there, at least we'll learn the muster point."

"I'll be here to see you off. Go now with God's speed."

Rand knelt again and kissed Edith's hand. As soon as he did, she could see over the top of his head to the fields. Gytha stared at them, holding a basket of wheat stalks at her side. When Rand rose and turned to go, Edith could sense they had locked eyes. If...when he comes back, perhaps there will be a wedding after all.

*

That night, Gunhild rattled questions. "Why does father need to fight again so soon? Will our brothers take part in the battle? What about our uncles? Why are the Normans attacking us?" All Edith could say was that Duke William was a power hungry madman who has coveted England for years. This answer did nothing to stem the tide of questions throughout the rest of dinner. Gytha, on the other hand, sat in a smoldering silence.

Exhausted, Edith retired while her daughters mended clothing next to the fireplace. After entering the bower, she undressed into her light tunic and then said a quiet prayer.

"Dear God, my husband, my sons, and my people need Your guiding hand. For years, I thought myself a guide as well. But my efforts have done nothing but drive those I love away. I have learned my lesson and will guide no more. All I ask is that you keep my loved ones safe. In Your name I pray, Amen."

Crawling under her furs, she doused the candle and

closed her eyes. She expected another restless night, but soon found herself drifting away.

In her mind's eye, she hovered over a field outside a snow-dusted city. On top of the field, a silver blanket rippled in the wind. Looking closer, she realized it was no cloth blanket, but a host of silver armored warriors prostrating toward a crimson-clad prelate. With a ground-shaking roar, the army dissolved into thousands of silver serpents. They slithered to the walls of a tan-stone city with a domed church at its highest point.

After a crack of lightning, Bishop Wulfstan appeared outside the city gate, or at least an apparition of him did. He wore his austere robe and his skin glowed like night stars. The serpents coiled, but the bishop halted them with an outstretched hand. They hissed and lashed out, but the old man grew young and nimble and evaded their every attack.

Edith screamed and they all turned to stare at her; the bishop's eyes flashed ice blue and the snakes' eyes burned with blood. Looking down, she found a crimson book with a gold falcon on its cover resting in her hands.

The snakes attacked, venom spewing from their fangs.

The bishop fell to his knees, his hands clasped in prayer. "Save the truth." Harold now stood beside him, bleeding from a dozen ghastly wounds but begging her to obey nonetheless.

She ran. Her pursuers sounded like an army of scythes threshing wheat. She pushed with all her strength, but they entangled her legs. Just before she fell, the corner of her eye caught a familiar-looking boy limping alongside her. In the last gleams of light, Edith felt a weight lifted from her hands and heard a voice reading bold and strong, like Harold's voice.

At dawn, the men arrived to take their leave. The cadenced jingling of weapons and armor filled the yard. They halted in a line. Breath of both horses and men misted in the pre-morning coolness. Then, Edith made her entrance.

"M' lady," Rand said, "you don't look prepared to give our parting blessing."

She rode atop Scramasax and wore the leather and wool of a traveler, not the silk and linen of a lady in state.

"I prayed last night, Rand, and told the Almighty I would no longer meddle in His affairs. He answered me with a dream. Now," she shook her head, "I think I'm needed more than ever."

The Confession

July 1, 1065

The bishop: You said the fog of confusion lifted when you overheard the Normans, but I remain shrouded. What glory does Odo seek against the infidel?

The earl: To put it plain, Odo, Egenulf, and the papacy seek to destroy the Islamic realms.

The bishop: How can you be so sure?

The earl: The papal chancellor once called on me to lead a similar campaign. I rebuffed him and now Odo and his Normans seek to make me pay.

The bishop: Wait one moment, Harold. The papacy once offered you the chance to lead an army of Christ?

The earl: Yes. I met with Hildebrand during my pilgrimage to Rome eight years ago.

The bishop: Why didn't you ever tell anybody?

The earl: Because I knew others would yearn for this disgusting calling. If I had tried to preach against it, I could have sparked the movement by accident. Besides, I didn't want to incur the wrath of St. Peter's throne. The closest I ever came to *telling anyone occurred upon my return. I whispered the entire tale to Edith as she slept.*

The bishop: What did Hildebrand offer?

The earl: He said I could earn undying glory. He even said the Pope would name me Edward's successor as long as I chased the infidel from the world. The idea abhorred me. If Hildebrand had asked me to protect Christian pilgrims and churches, I would have accepted without doubt. But he asked for annihilation; he sought the slaughter of an uncountable number of innocents in the name of Christ's glory. When I refused, the chancellor's eyes darkened. They escorted me and my small band out of the city the next day.

The bishop: It seems Hildebrand found a replacement for you.

The earl: Yes. Odo intends to lead the campaign and destroy me along the way. If the Normans gain control of England, the majority of Hildebrand's great calling will be paid by subjugated English toil. With the gold, silver, ships, and power Odo will gain if he becomes Subregulus, he could hire an army for his purpose. My heart aches at the thought...

Chapter 24:
Orrin

October 12, 1066

He peered from behind the verge to assess his target. At the end of a muddy track, a smattering of wattle and daub huts surrounded Bexhill's circular great hall. No walls, fences, or palisades protected the quiet village. A small wharf with moored fishing punts jutted out into green-gray waves, but no sign of a longship existed. It looked like a typical, serene fishing village with one vital exception: this one determined his destiny.

A steady breeze infiltrated his new riding cloak; the crimson cloth, Hesilia's hand-sewn parting gift, held her faint violet scent. Orrin breathed deep, channeled her memory into his fingers, and gripped his sword's polished wolf-bone hilt. The gesture eased his trepidation, but couldn't snuff it completely.

Gulls cawed from above; Orrin followed their flight through the cloud-spotted sky. His English mother's voice filled his mind, sounding as it did on her deathbed. *"Stop. Find your friend. Fight for your country."*

Tearing his eyes from the sky, he looked to his conroi. Fifteen veteran chevaliers rested spears on shoulders. No one spoke. No horse acted unruly. Unbidden, the voice of his dead father-in-law came to him. *"No army in the world can withstand a chevalier charge. Make sure you're never on the wrong end of one."*

All summer long, Orrin felt certain the invasion would falter. Harold patrolled the coasts; William would never find a landing point. Their arrival at an unguarded Pevensey Bay made him all the warier; Hal knew how to launch surprise attacks better than anyone. Yet when he learned of Stamford Bridge, his certainty of an English victory dwindled. The real fight would come soon, and it would pit a rested Norman army against an exhausted English force. Orrin's father-in-law may have been right after all.

Returning his gaze to Bexhill, Orrin spied a child darting from a hut to the great hall and cursed under his breath. He had hoped the tall nestle of trees extending from the forest would mask their approach.

Urse D'Abitot, his second-in-command with chain-mailed limbs thick as tree trunks, saw the boy as well. The warrior dismounted and ran to Orrin in a half-crouch. "Is our surprise lost?" Behind his helmet nose-guard, the edges of strain crept into his square jaw.

"Did you see the panic in the boy's step? They know we're here. But it doesn't matter. There's no longship, no fortifications. This shouldn't be difficult."

"And what if axmen lurk in the huts?" The huscarls fought with long-shafted, single blade axes. They were responsible for the edge on Urse's face. If Bexhill had a band of those renowned warriors, the raid – and their lives – would end today.

Yet Orrin didn't waver. "Huscarls don't hide, Urse. If they were here, we'd know."

"But we could continue up the coast and find another village, one that hasn't prepared—"

"No. Bexhill may look shabby, but Harold often spoke of its overflowing granary. With any luck, we'll return with a huge bounty."

A clatter jolted Orrin's attention back to the great hall. The hide-covered entrance parted, and English warriors marched out. They looked fierce at first, dressed in rusty mail, iron half helms, and bits of leather. The edges of their round wooden shields were hacked and frayed, suggesting an experienced warrior band. Their weapons – some swords, a few pitchforks, a wood axe or two – looked deadly sharp. The defenders formed a shield wall across the muddy track and waited in silence.

The shield wall gave them away as an untrained gaggle of fishermen and farmers. Men failed to stand still and gripped their weapons to the point of strangulation; some of the largest, strongest looking fighters lined up away from the center, which meant they were fat and worthless; most tellingly, they deployed in two thin lines to cover the entire track. A trained, experienced, band would have tripled or even quadrupled the ranks.

Urse's voice rose from its doldrums. "I almost shit my breeches over these mud-growers? Let's have at them."

"Stay here," Orrin said with a sigh. "I need to talk to them first; perhaps they'll show some sense and release their stores peaceably."

"You'd have more luck trying to bed the holy virgin."

Orrin raised a single finger in front of Urse's face. "Just

stay here and prepare the attack. Lead the way on my signal. The ground's soft, so watch your spacing. Aim for the right side; it's the weakest from the look of it."

After rounding the hedge, he made a slow approach. The rabble immediately braced for battle, so he raised his empty hands and stopped twenty paces away. "Who's in command?"

"Who wants to know?" The nasal voice came from the left side of the line.

"My name is Orrin Geirson. And while I'm a Norman soldier, my mother birthed and raised me here in England. So I ask you now – as your countryman – to surrender and save your loved ones from grief. You and your families can continue with your lives by swearing allegiance to your rightful king, William of Normandy."

A barrel of a man lowered his shield; he had long silver hair and black holes where teeth used to be. "Call me a countryman? I call you a traitor, and so does your whore of a mother. As for William of Normandy, the only right he's got is to the pointy end of my pitchfork. Now crawl to whatever hole spit you out and leave us alone!"

Orrin stood unflinching. He looked deep into his insulter's eyes and waited, but no one superseded the fool. After long, tense moments, his patience flagged. "You've had your chance. As a favor to you all, your loved ones will never learn you had the opportunity to avoid death."

With memories of his mother's dying face and Harold's disappointed glare, he dropped his arms. "Chargez! Leur Attaque!"

Behind the verge, Urse's bellow erupted. The fishermen began to charge, but froze when the furious rampage of horses met their ears. Orrin stood deathly still as the earth began to shake and the pang of realization sprouted in his opponents' eyes.

The conroi flew past. Just as they reached the enemy, Urse forced his horse to leap. Englishmen howled in fear as bone crunched under hoof. Not one Norman fell, yet several bodies collapsed to the ground.

The shield wall broke apart as Orrin reached the fight. The mounted Normans encircled fragmented batches of Englishmen, hacking down with ruthless abandon. The calming, warm surge of victory flowed in his veins...and then he heard the English leader shout, "NOW!"

From the corner of his eye, Orrin saw a hut door fly open. Before he could react, the two chevaliers nearest to him crashed to the ground with arrows sticking from their necks. Ice replaced the victory in his blood. He never expected to lose a man, nor did he think the villagers would resort to the poacher's weapon: the bow and arrow. It had been outlawed in England for decades.

With dread cutting his breath short, he dove for a dead Englishman's shield and huddled behind it. "The hut behind us! Archers!"

Three arrows thumped into his shield. With his head down, he could see nothing, but more Normans cried out in agony. Finally, after moments that felt like lifetimes, English shouts reached his ears, followed by the tell-tale grunts of death. "Got 'em," Urse said with a panting breath.

Looking up, Orrin saw the giant chevalier standing at the hut entrance, wrenching a bevy of arrows from his shield. Three more Normans littered the ground, along with every Bexhill defender. *I've lost five men. This bounty had better be worth it.*

"Check the other huts." Orrin said over the agonized moans of the dying. "I'll check the central hall."

He stalked to the draped cowhides. Steps away from the entrance, a bursting sense of fear shot through him. He swiveled around just in time to see a pitchfork-wielding Englishman slide out from his hiding place behind a wood pile.

Years of training took over. He jumped back and leaned away, narrowly dodging a brutal strike. As his opponent recoiled, Orrin spun to the side and threw his entire weight into his slicing sword arm. The blade bit deep into a leather-covered shoulder and rib cage. He yanked it free and the Englishman fell in a clump.

Breathing hard, Orrin kicked the man's helm off. He found a bloody-mouthed, labored-breathing boy with matted blond hair and peach fuzz under his lip praying to God for salvation. Guilt almost crushed Orrin's chest. *There's no going back now.* He stabbed down, and the praying ceased.

Inside the hut, streams of light poured through the shoddy thatch roof, illuminating mud walls and filthy straw on the earthen floor. Stepping across the threshold, he sensed movement behind a long feasting board. He braced for battle once more, but the action drew only shrieks of fear. He had found the village's women and children.

Sensing no danger, Orrin turned to his task. The roof held no supply loft and no undercroft hatch was visible. *Strange...*

Urse stormed in, his bloody sword still drawn. He shouted over the renewed screams of the village women, "There's nothing. Not one kernel anywhere!"

"Where's the grain?" Orrin said, pointing to the nearest woman.

"The...the men took it," she said, quivering. "When they left to join the king's army."

Orrin slammed his fists onto the dining board. *I was so sure.* He looked back to her; for a single moment, she wore his mother's face.

"Well let's return their generosity," Urse said, his eyes brimming with hunger. He turned and addressed the men gathered at the entrance. "Have at 'em boys. Whatever you find, you keep, even if it's the syrup at the mouth of an Englishwoman's legs—"

The instinctive, angry slap sounded crisp in the silent hall. Urse stumbled back in shock while Orrin pointed a bare, tingling finger at each wide-eyed man. "There will be no rape, no murder. You can protect yourselves if they attack, but you will face my wrath for any woman or child harmed without cause."

His finger stopped in front of Urse's face. The huge, stunned Norman held his cheek with one hand and his blade with the other. For a brief moment, Orrin feared attack. He had no hope against such a ferocious opponent.

But D'Abitot was still too new, too unsure to contemplate mutiny. "Yes sir," he lowered his sword and head. "What do you command?"

Orrin let his stare linger. "Search the homes, take what you want, and then burn every building."

Turning to the captives, he spoke through tensed lips. "Go to your loved ones. Bury them. When you finish, leave this place. The next raiding party will not be so merciful."

His men ran off for their plunder and the women left to dig graves. Urse hung back, looking at Orrin with a pained face. "Forgive me; I overstepped my bounds. But the men need something. We'll have little to show for this raid."

Staring at his ungloved hands, Orrin felt fear stir in his soul. "You're right. I've failed."

The conroi returned to the Norman camp with dusk fast approaching. After washing the blood and mud away, Orrin stood over a water barrel and stared at his grim reflection. *What have I become?*

A rich, almost joyous voice hit his ears. "Don't like what you see?"

Bishop Odo stood behind him. He wore a long-sleeved crimson robe, a golden circlet atop his cropped dark hair, and a devious grin.

Orrin wiped his dripping cheeks and prepared to face his failure. "Forgive me, Lord Odo. The raid proved messier than I had hoped. We lost five men and returned empty-handed."

"Oh dear. Distressing results to say the least. My brother won't be pleased." Odo's grin disappeared. "Did you knowingly lead your men into an ambush?"

"No! I swear. We made them pay, lord father; none of their men remain alive and we burned every building. Would a traitor do that?"

The bishop's eyebrows creased up. "You showed no lenience?"

Orrin winced and hung his head. "I...I let the women and children go free."

"A benevolent decision, albeit a weak one. Still, any softness on your part could be construed the wrong way and William loves to make examples out of failures."

Clasping his hands, Orrin abandoned dignity. "My

family's future hinges on this invasion, lord father. I'll do anything to make amends. Please, help me save my standing."

"I may be able to help you, Geirson, but my aid comes at a cost." Odo leaned on his golden staff. "We'll start with a payment now, and if I deem it satisfactory, I'll do what I can to forestall William's wrath."

A sudden breeze made Orrin's skin prickle. "Payment, my lord? I...I don't understand."

"A payment of information. You may have divulged all you know of troop counts and supply lines, but I require something more. I'm specifically interested in the usurper. The man's lies are a plague on Christendom and I intend to administer the cure."

With the chill turning into a shiver, Orrin wrapped Hesilia's cloak around his shoulders. "What would you like to know about him?"

Odo lowered his voice. "Is he a man of letters? Spoken lies fly with the wind. Written lies can last for eternity."

Orrin squeezed the bridge of his nose to alleviate the crushing pressure in his head. He had already betrayed his homeland; now he was asked to betray his friend. He thought about lying, but then he caught the faint scent of violet. "He cherishes learning and writing over every other pursuit, my lord, even more than falconry. In fact, a scribe rode at his side when I last saw him in Fritton."

Odo placed a rough hand on Orrin's shoulder. "Would you, by chance, be able to recognize this scribe when the time comes? The usurper's writs and charters interest me greatly."

"I believe so, father. He was a frail, odd-looking boy."

"You did well to remember this secret, honored

vicomte." His hand shook Orrin's shoulders. "Have no fear about today's test; no punishment shall befall you.

"Thank God," Orrin said, unleashing all his tension.

The bishop wasn't finished. "And provided you survive the upcoming battle, a man with your unique knowledge will earn several more chances for glory."

For the first time in what seemed like ages, hope welled in Orrin's mind. "Your trust is the greatest reward I could earn."

Chapter 25: Edith

October 13, 1066

The Nazeing contingent entered the Andredsweald forest at a gallop. No one complained or begged for a slower pace, for every moment had become precious. Harold had called a muster for tomorrow morning at the hoary apple tree along the road linking London to Hastings; the fighting would begin shortly thereafter. They needed to race without rest to make it in time.

Edith rode Scramasax at the head, her thoughts pulsing with every stride. The dream that thrust her on this journey had receded to her memory's shadow. She still felt haunted by its affects, but the visions lay a hair's width farther than her reach. Curiosity over Harold's mysterious gift, however, filled the void. *What could it be? Why do I need to receive it from his hand and his hand only?*

After a bend in the forest path, they spied a carter up ahead blocking the way with his wide, slow pull-cart.

Edith's shoulders tensed as she signaled for a trot. "What imbecile would take such a large cart on a forest road?"

Rand pulled alongside her. "He'll move...or we'll move him."

They began hailing the carter. The man rose from his bench, turned, and pulled down his hood. Edith gasped; as much as she wanted to, she could not just pass by this man whose position demanded courtesy, even if his person begged for spite.

Osgod, the sacristan of Harold's beloved Waltham Holy Cross, curled two wormy lips into a smile and hailed them back. "A most fortuitous and unexpected encounter, Lady Edith. God is good to re-unite friends on the road."

"Hello, Osgod. Are you riding to the king's army as well?"

"Indeed, my lady. What glory could our good king aspire to without the presence of his most beloved church?" He smiled sweeter than honey. "He has even decreed the army will pay deference to our house by using 'Holy Cross' as a battle cry."

"God's favor continues to shine upon you, I see," Edith glanced down the road impatiently. The self-important fop had yet to move his cart.

"Truer words have never been uttered, my dear. Have you heard the miracle the Holy Rood bestowed upon the king during his last prayer?"

"No. I have not."

"I would not believe it, except I saw the proof with my own eyes," Osgod thrust his ample gut forward and stood tall. "Before leaving our humble church, the king turned at the end of the nave, bowed one last time to the Holy Rood, and asked for a sign. With morning light pouring onto our precious relic, the silver Christ bowed his head to the king."

Edith's warriors whispered and rumbled behind her. "A sign," Rand muttered. "A sign of victory?"

"Yes my boy. I inspected the cross myself. Our Savior's head, which once lay against his shoulder, is now bent down. Our prince in Heaven paid deference to our king on earth." Osgod made the sign of the cross and all the warriors followed suit. Edith did not. She had prayed to this crucifix several times; the only way the statue bowed its head is if someone took a hammer to it. She did not put it past Osgod to do so.

"A remarkable development," she said, unable to cast doubt on Osgod in front of her awed warriors. "And with such an unmistakable sign, you saw no danger in journeying to the battlefield."

"Perceptive, Lady Edith. With God's blessing, victory is assured. My fellow canons have sent me to oversee the joyous day and collect any gifts He wishes to bestow." He patted the wooden cart.

Edith had heard enough; she tried to move on, but the sacristan wished to bless her warriors before they went to battle. Then, he insisted they break bread together. By the time he said farewell, they had lost half the morning.

Her party resumed the journey, heartened by the story. Edith, though, pushed even harder than before, driven by the delay and her desperation to gain distance from Osgod.

October 14, 1066
As the first fiery hints of dawn crept into the sky, Edith and her small band emerged from the Andredsweald.

Ahead, the road plummeted into the endless gold and green hills of eastern Sussex. Amongst the patches of trees and verge, she spied plowed fields, fallow ground, occasional fence lines, and even a barn. With the sun breaking over the horizon, her eye caught a hill, far in the distance, jutting higher than any other peak. This hill looked pock-marked with small tents; she had found the English army at last.

"Do you see them, Rand? Are we in time?"

With a *click-click* of his tongue, her young warrior walked his horse forward. Where the others wore tunics of boiled leather or thick wool, Rand wore a chain mail shirt that draped down over his knees. His gleaming iron helmet added a hand-length to his height. Edith regarded him with awe. *He looks every bit like Nazeing's champion.*

"It's the camp, m'lady. Still too far away to see if we're in time."

Taking one last respite, she smoothed her own armor. This morning, she had donned her richest, rose-madder dress and a fresh linen head scarf. A dozen golden arm clasps covered her sleeves and a necklace of interwoven gold chains hung down to her chest. Edith secured her clasps, set her necklace, and led the way into the valley.

With the end in sight, they charged along the road as it led them over hill after hill. Edith's cloak flowed in the draft, but her nerves made her impervious to any chill. *In a few moments, I will stand before him.*

The track became wide and muddy as the group reached a steep uphill climb. Halfway up, the camp came full into view. Edith pulled hard on the reins, and Scramasax reared onto his back legs to halt.

Canvas tents billowed in the breeze, as did ramshackle shelters made of torn cloaks erected on tree limbs. Camp fires smoldered and the occasional chicken clucked. Then, her heart sank. She didn't see anyone. *Are we too late?*

The answer reached her ears before her eyes. Above the tents, on yet another rise in this endless hill, a shout rose up; the shout turned into a clamor; and the clamor cascaded into a tumult. A pinnacle of waving axes, spears, and swords basked in the morning sunshine. In the middle of the warrior wall stood a thick apple tree with long wiry limbs forming a bushy finger-tipped hand.

"Come good sirs," she said, willing herself to sound bold. "The king awaits."

They dismounted and hurried to join the muster. Atop the hill, the thick, musky smells of leather, lard, and sweat permeated the air. Despite her full-length tunic and cloak, she felt bare compared to all these chain-mailed bodies.

Harold stood on the lowest bough of the tree, one hand braced on the trunk and the other on the hilt of his sheathed sword. His silver armor radiated sunlight while his bear-skin cloak seemed a chasm of blackness. He bowed his head while a priest concluded a prayer for victory below him.

When the priest finished, Harold's roar echoed loud and pure. "FOR GOD AND ENGLAND!"

Whipped into a delirium, thousands of men hit metal on metal and screamed at the top of their lungs. The sound assumed a force; she huddled down, covered her ears, and prayed it scared the Normans as much as it scared her. She waited for the racket to dissipate, but when she looked up, a flow of humanity enveloped her as the army broke from the muster.

Rand grabbed her hand and pushed through the rising warrior tide. The faces flashed by like ghosts; some looked at her with curiosity, but most wore the distant expressions of preoccupied men. Laughs, prayers, and shouts filled her ears.

The pre-battle energy cast simultaneous pangs of fear and exhilaration through her. She felt the edges of fright emerge; these men would die today for her, her family, and countless others.

A different emotion sprang forward when she heard the familiar voice say, "Well, what have we here?"

Rand knelt on one knee and Edith stood face to face with her estranged husband. She realized she should curtsey, or at least bow, but anger relegated her to staring at the man she thought would love her forever.

He was still handsome, which made her all the angrier. His bronze hair fell unbound past his shoulders and his well-cropped beard showed few specks of gray. His eyes – the same effervescent blue Gytha inherited – did register surprise, which comforted her somewhat, but she felt their familiar warmth nonetheless. She wanted to rush to him, to hit him until he reclaimed her, but she couldn't. *His men deserve better than that, and so do I.* So, she straightened her posture, unclasped her cloak broach to reveal her dress, and prayed for strength. "My king, I've brought Rand and more Nazeing fyrdsmen to fight with their English brothers."

After a lingering look that dove into her eyes, the king stepped to the prostrated huscarl and raised him by the shoulders. "Rand my boy! How's Godric?"

"Father's well, lord king, but he's right devilish 'cause his achin' leg won't let him fight."

Harold unfurled a wide, beguiling smile. "Ha! I'll bet that ol' hammer's livid! Well, I'll be sure to tell him all about his son's bravery when I see him next. Gather your warriors, Rand. You'll fight with me in the center line. I also relieve you of your charge. I'll look after Lady Edith for the moment."

Rand began to take his leave, but Edith stepped to him. "May victory smile upon you."

"It will, m'lady. After we've won, I'll be sure to tell you the news myself." He withdrew, bowed deep, and hurried down the hill. She watched Rand leave, all the while sensing Harold's eyes on her back. She forced herself to turn.

He began by reaching for her hand. Too confused to resist, she let him intertwine his fingers with hers. "I'm happy you came; you look beautiful. Is that the Flemish riding tunic I bought you?"

The flattery incensed her. "Even scorned women must do their duty, Harold," she removed her hand from his grasp. "Besides, you sparked my curiosity. Why do you need me now? Is your new wife too precious to parade before the men?"

Harold rewarded her with a hurt look. It lasted just a moment, but she could still read his face. "If God is good today, we'll have time afterward to discuss Alditha." He looked into her eyes. She looked away.

"Listen," he said with a hint of frustration. "Battle preparations are pressing; my time is short. Will you walk with me?" He gestured to a path.

"I serve at the will of my king...and his queen."

Harold's face darkened. He gestured to the path again.

"Where are we going?"

"You'll see."

They walked in silence a safe distance apart. After several paces, Edith could take no more. "Tell me you did not summon our sons to this conflict."

"I did not. I've had two miserable weeks to assemble an

army. Half the country hasn't heard of Stamford Bridge, much less this fight."

She said a silent prayer of thanks and kept walking.

"You've heard about Stamford Bridge, haven't you?"

Keeping her eyes straight, she nodded. "A great victory—"

"Oh yes; the scalds will sing of it for centuries. Is it a great victory when one brother kills another?"

"So it's true?" Her heart fluttered in her chest. "Tostig fought against you?"

"The battle had ended, Edith, but he kept fighting. I begged him to throw down his sword, yet vengeance obsessed him. He cut down three of my best huscarls, but Aelfwyn slit his throat right in front of me."

Despite her shock, Edith set her jaw. "We live in terrible days. Brother or no, the traitor deserved Aelfwyn's judgment."

Harold waved his hand, as if his troubles encircled him. "The first traitor of many. Orrin fights with the Normans. Edwin and Morcar, my supposed brothers bound by marriage, trail behind me like scared sheep. Even if they arrive, their armies are decimated." He seethed an exhale. "May I confide in you, like I used to?"

She stalked several paces away, flush with new heat. "Like you used to? I counseled and comforted you after every one of your battles, but no longer. You have a new, blessed wife. Cry to her."

His eyes flashed. "Edith, I've barely seen her since that connivance of a wedding. The only woman I've ever loved is you. I married *her* to ensure the allegiance of her miscreant brothers and even that's falling apart on me. Now may I speak to you in confidence, *please*."

She felt an unbidden lump form in her throat. "Say what you must."

He walked to her side. "What I tell you now has been heard by no one and cannot be repeated." He leaned in close; Edith could feel his breath. "This battle needs to be fought, but I have never faced sterner odds. At times, even my courage has wavered."

A vision dawned in Edith's mind of Harold standing in front of a walled city, bleeding from wicked gashes on his face, neck, torso, and legs. She blinked it away and, half realizing it, gazed into his eyes. "If such peril exists, if you are so unsure, then don't fight. If your army's not fit, wait until it's stronger."

"The situation is more complex." He escorted her down the path with his hand at her back. "My men have stood at arms all summer and are desperate to return home. I cannot afford to keep them much longer."

"So, appeal to their hearts, Harold. You never had trouble rallying men before."

"There is even more. The Normans fight under the papal banner. William has convinced Pope Alexander that he should be the rightful King of England. Given time, my men may question my authority."

She felt a sudden chill. A new vision descended of a crimson-robed man preaching before an army of silver serpents. "How...how did William win the papal banner?"

"I've known for some time they were in league with each other, and the Bayeux oath provided the excuse they needed to align against me."

"The oath? But that's a lie built on air."

A thin smile crossed his lips. "Apparently, my story hasn't reached the pope's ears. It's just one situation I hope to remedy after today." They arrived at a small tent on the outer rim of the camp site. An overpowering burst of stale mead hit her nose.

"Aidan," the king said. "Come out here."

A young man in a soiled, frayed Benedictine robe emerged. *That can't be my Aidan.*

The novice took one look at Harold, fell to his knees, and bowed to the ground. "My king," he said with his nasal voice muffled. "I didn't expect you."

"Have you forgotten your manners, boy? Did you not see Lady Edith?"

He glanced up for a brief moment. "M' lady, I...I expected you even less than the king."

Edith walked over, and like Harold had done to Rand earlier, raised the boy by the shoulders and embraced him. "My dear firebrand, I didn't expect to find you either. Is Wulfstan here too?"

Fear clouded Aidan's face as Harold let out a deep breath. "There was an incident," the king said. "I don't have time to go into it, but Aidan now works in my writing office." He shook the boy's head with his massive hand. "It's time to display your work."

As Aidan disappeared into the tent, Edith looked at Harold with unveiled disproval. "The boy is lost. Why did you take him from Worcester?" She kept her voice down, but judging by the paper rustling inside the tent, Aidan would not have heard Heaven fall.

"Wulfstan sent him to me five months ago after discovering some dalliance between the boy and a goldsmith's daughter. I welcomed him with open arms; he's not just a gifted scribe, but his talents extend to book binding and illumination too. Sure he's a little unkempt, but boys need to be boys, Edith. I haven't had the time to cluck over him like a mother hen—"

Harold cut short as Aidan emerged with a flushed face and heavy breath. "My apologies, lord king. With all this marching, it's been difficult to keep your documents in order. I found it well enough, though." He handed a text to the king, who hid it behind his back.

"Thank you Aidan. Now please go see if any of the men need help arming. I must speak to Lady Edith alone now."

After Aidan limped off, Harold turned and presented the gift with a neutral face.

Her whole body began to tingle. The thin book ran half the length of Harold's forearm, and the cover shocked Edith's soul. The dyed leather created a pure crimson backdrop. Centered on this blood red field flew a dazzling falcon. Etched in gold leaf and detailed with silver, black, and copper filigree, the medallion glistened like the sun. The wings, talons, and tail all stretched out, as if the falcon ascended to some mythical sky. Two small amethysts gleamed on each side of the beak, giving the impression the raptor could see. From the bottom of the book, the king's red wax seal dangled from a chord of leather.

Harold stepped closer. "It's for you. A token of my faith."

Edith flushed with a joyful thrill. After her fingers gripped the cover, however, a different sensation arose; she began to shake.

"Edith?"

The entire dream rushed back like an unstoppable flood. "I had a vision. I wasn't going to come, but I couldn't stay away after these terrible scenes infested my mind. This book," she shook it before Harold's face, "played a vital role. It saves you...somehow. I don't know how but it does."

"War plays tricks on the mind. I know that better than anyone." He grabbed the book to stop her hand from shaking. "We can talk of your visions later. Now, you must see what I offer."

Foreboding clenched her body. She forced herself to bring the text in and spread the cover open. She read just a few lines, her eyes growing wider with each word. "You recorded a confession? For what purpose?"

"It's much more than a simple confession," he said, standing close. "It is now the lone proof to combat the powers arrayed against me. Today's battle has grown from seeds sown in this text. If I defeat the Normans – and I have no intention of leaving the field until I do – I will win the chance to right several wrongs." He brushed her cheek. "If I die, it becomes me; it becomes my legacy and I want you to guard it."

Still holding the book, Edith looked up. She did not see a regal king, just the blushing boy who courted her in Nazeing's feasting hall. "Why me? There must be someone stronger, more powerful—"

"In the wrong hands, this book is worth less than firewood. The only hands I trust are yours and Wulfstan's. But his faith is in God; yours has always been in yourself. With all that has befallen me, I trust you more than God." He cupped her chin. "Do you accept this gift?"

A torrent of emotions coursed through her: confusion from the dream; anger from Harold's betrayal; joy in the trust he showed in her now; pride in her country; uncertainty over the day's outcome; and underlying it all, fear for her husband's life. "You still insist on fighting, even with all these evils working against you?"

"It will all vanish when the Normans break. I cannot let them escape me today."

Removing a hand from the book, she clasped his forearm and said the words true to her soul. "Then you must go with an unburdened heart: I accept your gift."

Harold's whole body relaxed and his eyes glazed over. "My God, I have dreamed of this moment for so long." He then embraced her. "Thank you," he whispered into the crook of her neck. She felt warm tears dampen her skin.

"Thank me by returning from the field alive."

"I...I will do my best." He nuzzled her one more time, then held Edith out by the waist. "Once the battle starts, this camp won't be safe. I'll send some men to escort you to my garrison in Romney."

Harold's forearm provided the only solidity; the thought of letting it go, even for a heartbeat, filled her with dread. But then, as if another woman filled her own skin and used her mouth, she agreed to leave. "You can't spare a single sword and you know it. I'll ride with Aidan."

He honored her with another smile. "The countryside's near empty and Romney's not far; it should be safe enough...Now, I must go." He stood tall, turned, and walked down the path. Edith felt her heart deaden with every step. She embraced the supple leather-covered book, as if it could protect her against the future. After just a few paces, he spun around. "Will you wait for me in Romney? I'll ride to you the moment the battle is over."

Her heart pounded the book still clutched to her chest. "I will...and I pray my wait is short."

Chapter 26: Orrin

"Saint Gabriel's mercy," Urse said with a sneer, "when do we charge?"

Orrin could only shake his head at the spectacle in front of his eyes. "This is no time for impatience. Harold's set them atop a natural fortress."

After marching at dawn, the Normans followed the London road until they reached a steep hill. At the crest of this incline, they found a silver, axe-wielding, spear-bristling crown that glinted in the morning sun and howled wilder than any pack of wolves. On the far side of the slope, thick swaths of sloppy bog left two options for the invaders: attack straight up the slope or retreat. The duke had ended any debate by calling the army into battle formation an hour ago.

While the English resembled a steel wall, the Normans resembled a sinister sea at rising tide. Rows upon rows of infantrymen formed the first wave. They took confession from passing priests, sharpened weapons on whet stones, adjusted helmet and shield straps, or stood in stoic patience. The chevaliers formed the second wave. In all his dreams, Orrin never imagined such power. Three thousand mounted warriors stared up the hill in calm preparedness. The smell of manure and hay added a heat to the cool morning air and spirited stallions whinnied their own taunts to the English. Behind them, a third wave of archers stood ten lines thick; England may have outlawed this weapon, but Normandy had not.

"We've been mounted too long," Urse said, shifting in his saddle. "The call *must* come soon."

"Soon enough," Orrin said distractedly. Near the front, a striking chevalier addressed Talifer, a magician turned soldier renown in the Norman camp for making even the most secured belt purse disappear. The mounted man wore tunic and breeches of quilted wool checkered crimson and black. His stallion looked sculpted from black stone. The magician lifted his helmeted head while the chevalier reached down and sketched a cross over his forehead.

The sight threw his mind into a new tumult. He watched Bishop Odo, not some resplendent chevalier, and after Bexhill, the bishop had become Orrin's salvation. *He should be blessing me, not some fool-hardy jester.*

Just then, William of Normandy emerged from his command tent, armored in shining mail from head to leather boot and riding a pristine white stallion. Even the English howlers quieted.

He rode to the fore and faced his army; the conviction in his eyes could have frozen fire. "Today, I rip my destiny back from the usurper's cold, dead embrace. These bones," he shook his loose hanging necklace, "are relics of a host of saints. Pope Alexander sent them to me as a symbol of my claim's righteousness. That pretender has no such relics; he has no such right!

"You are my avenging angels. We will attack until my banner – the gonfanon of St. Peter – flies atop the usurper's ridge. Fear not death, for His Holiness has promised that any man who dies this day in my service will ascend to Heaven clean of sin."

The Norman army unleashed a landslide of cheers; Orrin could not resist joining in. *To return to Hesilia as a conquering hero clean of sin...*

William raised both hands in the air as if he beckoned the clouds to fall. The Normans quieted. "So strike with the power of the Almighty, my army of conquest, for the usurper's day of reckoning is nigh at hand."

He thrust both of his arms down, and a volley of Norman arrows darkened the morning sky. The English raised their shields and the arrows achieved little, but the signal was unmistakable: the battle for England had begun.

No sooner had the arrows flown when a Norman atop a black stallion charged the hill. He sang at the top of his lungs.

"My God," Urse said, spellbound. "The lunatic seeks immortality."

At first, Orrin thought a Devil's knife had pricked the man. But as the words floated to him, he recognized Talifer performing *The Song of Roland*. It was a song of sacrifice, duty, and death, memorializing Charlemagne's nephew who sacrificed himself so his uncle could escape the ambushing infidels. Orrin realized this was no random act of bravery. *Is this the price of Odo's blessing?*

The English responded, drowning out Talifer's song with their shouts. "Ut! Ut! Ut!" Half way up, the mad magician tossed his sword to the sky. Orrin's eyes bulged, yet Talifer answered his unspoken question when he reached up and caught his blade by the hilt without breaking stride.

A lone huscarl stepped out to meet Talifer's challenge. He swung his giant battle axe just as the horse reached the crest. The blade caught the beast's chest, stopping him in mid-gallop and sending foul screeches into the blue morning. The magician spilled from his dying animal. Orrin thought him done for, but Talifer surprised him again. He controlled his vault and landed in a crouch several paces behind the Englishman but several paces in front of the rest of the army. As the unsuspecting huscarl dislodged his axe from the carcass, Talifer ran him through from behind. The magician wailed in triumph just as the English line engulfed him.

While every other Norman cheered for their champion, Orrin visualized himself in Talifer's place and remained silent.

A deep, booming horn sounded, and the first sea wave on the valley floor advanced.

"Infantry first?" Urse sounded as if he had already taken a wound.

"Patience friend. Our turn will come soon enough."

Knowing his charge grew closer with every infantry step, Orrin stroked his horse's mane. Sylvan was an agile, responsive bay stallion, the best destrier from Orrin's stables at Valmont. "If you get me through this young friend," he whispered into Sylvan's ear, "you'll never want for carrots or brood mares again."

The English front set their shield wall atop the crest. When the foot soldiers neared the hilltop, they smashed into the shields with a ferocious crash. Axes sprouted up between English shields, chopping and swiping at the invaders. On lower ground and without cover, the infantrymen faltered; those lucky enough to escape scrambled down the hill.

A tense pause blanketed the field as both sides recovered from the first assault. During the gap, a rich, seductive voice emanated from behind the Norman cavalry. Bishop Odo shouted so the whole army could hear, but Orrin felt the words were aimed for him.

"Armor your heart against doubt. When you fly to the fray, you are God's chosen. Strike with the power of Archangel Michael, for you attack the most egregious sinner in Christendom!"

A double horn blast sounded as commanders shouted, "*Laissez Coré!*" Orrin gave Urse a curt nod and received a grin of pure joy in return.

The charge was absolute, intended to shock the enemy into fear and flight. *There must be a thousand of us.* He felt Sylvan's iron shoes rip into turf. Fifty paces out, the hill's incline grew steeper. Sylvan fought to keep his edge, but neither his pure blood nor Orrin's spurs could maintain speed. Twenty five paces from the crest, the English chants overwhelmed everything else and a hailstorm of javelins felled men and horses. Orrin ducked behind his shield, and then used his legs, heels, and spurs to urge the horse closer. Ten paces away, he glanced over the wooden rim at his enemies.

This was not Bexhill. An unbreakable chain of oak shields spread across the ridge; the painted fronts of blue dragons, golden lions, chalky skulls, and bronze raptors writhed in surreal enmity. Over the din of dying cries and striking weapons, Orrin discerned a host of chants. "Ut! Ut! Ut! Holy Cross! Harold King!"

A javelin whirled over his helmet, forcing him below

his shield. When he raised his head again, the Devil's pincers clutched his chest. Huscarls stormed to the front; their axes hoisted high. Orrin turned Sylvan to the side; the horse almost tripped over a dead infantryman, but managed to stay upright. The huscarls flew in all directions, and a terrible wave of dying horse screeches deafened Orrin's ears. He flung his spear at the nearest approaching axe, wheeled around, and fled.

With momentum on his side, Sylvan flew down the God-forsaken hill. Other retreating men did not fare as well; the chevalier riding to Orrin's right spilled to the ground and nearly tripped Sylvan, but the horse veered at the last possible moment.

When he reached the valley floor, Orrin retched as the sights, sounds, and smells of the ridge infatuated his mind. *Man was not meant to endure such madness.*

Urse came flying down the hill after all the rest. He still wore his sick smile, even though blood smattered his face. "Sons of whores are hard to break. I'll give 'em that!"

Odo's voice returned with increased lather. "Never retreat! Never relent! Godwinson and his spawn do not deserve the flesh they inhabit! Rip the life from their ill-begotten bones! You are the army of Christ! You must not fail!"

Orrin hocked deep and spit to lessen the sour taste in his mouth. The ringing in his ears remained constant.

"Are you ready yet?" Urse asked, tipping his head toward the horns as they blared a double call. "Drink some strong ale and grab a new spear. We're going back up!"

Orrin charged five more times that morning. Sylvan died on the third attempt, and Orrin would have followed had he not fallen on a man's corpse. He recognized his savior as Richard Fitz Scrob, a petulant braggart not worth the land he owned; there would be no more bragging from him. Scrambling to his feet, Orrin spied Richard's horse wandering nearby. He rode this new destrier on the next two charges.

After the last attempt, Odo's voice rang out as the chevaliers regrouped. "Behold! The champion of Christ rides to his destiny!"

Still out of breath, Orrin looked to the slope. Duke William led a charge of the Norman's most powerful magnates. Like a swarm of locusts, they raced toward the English left. The engagement lasted just a few moments. The same riders plunged down the hill, reformed, and then charged the middle.

"They fall back too fast," Orrin said to Urse. "They're not searching for a fight; they're searching for a weakness." The English center repelled them once more. The Norman lords regrouped again in good order and mounted another assault; this one fell on the English right.

In this assault, Duke William's conroi held longer than the other sorties. Sword met axe amidst a gale of death. The line stood like a planted oak, but the strain could be seen on the rest of the defending army; their restraint flagged under the desire to aid their comrades.

"If they break, William'll call us up and we'll gain a foothold on the ridge," Urse said.

"Harold doesn't break," Orrin said in a whisper.

Then, as the Norman magnates battled on the right side, a band of Breton infantry rushed up to engage the left flank.

"What in the Devil are they doing? No one signaled for an infantry attack."

Fighting raged on the left slope. The infantrymen stood strong for several moments even as they used corpses as shields. But then, a stream of huscarls poured out from the English center.

"Beware!" Orrin cried, but it was too late. The huscarls cut through the unsuspecting Bretons. The remaining fighters broke and ran.

A great cry rose as the English streamed down the hill in pursuit.

Instinct took over. "Urse, rally the men around me. Now!"

The next instant, Orrin charged toward the retreating Bretons. He felt no pain, no fear. If the English routed the Norman left, all was lost anyway. He heard Urse and his men hard at his heels, but kept his eyes on the mustached, axe-and-shield wielding huscarls tearing down the hill a short distance behind the Breton force. He braced his spear under his arm and flew.

A flash caught his eye across the field. Duke William's conroi had fallen back in a disheveled mass. Terrified shouts sprang from shocked faces. "The duke's fallen! We're lost!"

Before he could react, Orrin slammed into his onrushing opponents. His horse reared as he thrust his spear. He felt the point bite into flesh just as a jarring crash shook his bones. White light blinded him and a searing pain shot from the base of his spine to the back of his head.

When the light faded, he found himself on the ground amidst a squall of hooves, feet, entrails, and dying men. Orrin covered his now helmet-less head with his hands and waited for the death blow, either from weapon or hoof.

A voice carried over the din. "Save Valmont!"

Keeping low, Orrin craned his neck. The battle shifted and a clearing formed around him. Bishop Odo's strained face loomed over him. "Rise! Return to the fray," The bishop said. "Neither God nor I have finished with you." He pointed to a fresh horse tethered behind his own.

Orrin spat gritty blood from his mouth. *My debt to this man grows beyond repayment.* "Is the day lost? I saw the duke's conroi break."

Odo gazed across the field. "No sinner's sword could defeat us."

He followed Odo's eyes. Two riders streaked from the mess of retreating chevaliers. One rider pointed to the other; even from this distance, Orrin could hear the shout, "William is here! He lives!" The other man removed his helmet and beckoned men to him. New riders detached from the Norman reserves to answer the helmetless duke. Without so much as a pause, he led his new conroi toward the beleaguered Bretons.

Emotion surged over the remaining ache in Orrin's body. Leaving Odo behind, he spurred his horse back into the melee and hacked down in unbridled wrath. Then, as if an ocean wave crossed onto the field, a force enveloped the fighting as Duke William's men smashed into the exposed, unsuspecting attackers.

In a blink, the chasers became trapped. They formed a defensive circle on a small plateau and fought on.

His battle frenzy ebbed and Orrin fell back. His mind raced to absorb the shocking turn of events; Harold's line had broken discipline. He strained to see if he could discern which English leader had failed.

"My God," he said with a jumping stomach. "Harold's brothers are as good as dead."

Chapter 27: Aidan

In the fenced pasture next to the English camp, Aidan retied Walter's saddlebag strap for the fifth time. Feeling the pulls and jostles, the gray donkey lifted his head, looked at his master with a coal-black eye, and voiced an annoyed grunt.

"I'm as eager to leave as you are." Aidan said. "Lady Edith's not finished reading yet. When she's done, we'll be off. I promise." In answer, Walter flapped his lips, snorted, and resumed grazing.

With every buckle and strap secured on his mount, Aidan turned to the stallion Lady Edith called Scramasax. He had tethered both mounts to the same post, expecting just a short time before the journey to Romney. Yet it had been three hours, and it seemed like a cruel joke to keep this black jewel of a horse next to the old, plump donkey. Next to such a perfect beast, both his and Walter's inferiority seemed to swell.

"Hello again, lord," Aidan edged closer with one hand on the tether. When he grasped the bridle, Scramasax raised his head from the grass and bristled. "I'll just bother you for one moment more. We can't have these bags open mid-gallop now can we?"

The stallion's two saddle bags were made of the finest, softest leather Aidan had ever touched. Dangling down from the horse's rib cage, the spacious carriers could hold several books in each. Aidan had packed everything from the traveling library he thought most important, but the bulk would need to accompany the army after the battle. He had saved space on the right side for the most precious cargo, which now sat in Lady Edith's lap atop the muster hill.

After folding the cover flaps and knotting the chords, Aidan glanced to the sky. The sun had passed its apex and filled the afternoon with light heat. If they didn't leave soon, they'd be travelling in the black of night. "I'll go see if she's ready," he said to the horses, "again."

The first two times he tried to spur Lady Edith into the saddle, his pleas met with complete silence. The third time, she lifted her head from the book and turned the page. This time, he swore to hold firm; his orders left no room for more delay. He needed to escort her to safety before the king's arrival later in the night.

Shuffling up the well-trodden hill, he resisted the urge to look south. The battle lay more than a mile away. From here, a cascade of hills and valleys blocked any view, but his imagination bit at him. Yesterday, the king ordered Aidan to follow him and his brothers to a vantage point overlooking the selected battlefield. As they discussed strategy, Aidan depicted the scene for his battle chronicle. Now, he yearned to be there like he was at Stamford

Bridge. The army had waited for the Normans all summer. Even after the grueling fight outside of York, most warriors reacted to the new invasion with determination, just as King Harold did. After two weeks of constant marching, camping, and preparation, the day had arrived. Unfortunately for Aidan and his chronicle, however, Lady Edith's safety took precedence.

Sighing, he gazed beyond the hill to the east. The green hills leveled off and gave way to golden farmland. Since the middle of last month, Aidan had traversed the length of England twice with countless side journeys thrown in. Bursts of pain needled his rump and calluses formed on parts of him he never thought could form them. The half-day journey to safety seemed insurmountable, yet he had to try. He couldn't fail the king, not on this day.

After reaching the hill top, he found Lady Edith unmoved. She sat with her back resting on the base of the lichen-covered muster tree. Her red gown sprawled across the tree roots as gnarled limbs loomed overhead. Holding the book in her lap with one hand, her eyes darted across the page and her other hand covered her mouth.

"My lady?"

Nothing.

He cleared his throat. "My lady, we've dallied here far too long."

Just as he stepped closer, she closed the book with the tenderness of a mother putting a child to sleep. When she looked up, her chestnut eyes were glassy. "God have mercy on us all."

Knowing the book's contents, Aidan stood silent and still. Even the hardiest soul would need time to comprehend the implications. After a long, hair-raising pause, her eyes fixed on him. They held more questions than one mouth could ever voice. Aidan, however, knew there was no time to answer any of them. "My lady, we *must* go."

Still searching him with her eyes, her head began to shake. "All this time, he fought for a cause…a noble, true cause."

"He did," Aidan closed the remaining distance between them. "We can talk more about it on the way. Please come."

"My dream. I finally understand my dream."

Not knowing what to make of that, he lowered his hand to help her rise. "Many dreams will come true once we win, m'lady."

"Victory. I can see it all now."

"We'll learn all about it from the king once he joins us. The horses are packed and ready."

"To the horses…" Ignoring his hand, she pushed herself up. Cradling the book in one arm, she dusted off her gown.

Aidan began walking. "With any luck we'll still arrive ahead of the army."

"We aren't going to Romney."

Wheeling around, he found his foster mother staring straight at him. The previous questions blooming in her eyes had vanished. He tried to speak, but she cut him off with a raised hand. "We will stay here and that's final."

"Now just one moment—"

Edith took a step towards him. "I have lived without my husband for ten months. I will not be separated from him again. Not now. Not after this." She shook the cradled book.

"But Lady Edith, that's why King Harold wants you to ride to safety. If something should happen, your life and the confession would be at risk."

"There are no copies?"

Aidan shook his head. "Bishop Wulfstan forbade it."

After glancing toward the distance, she breathed deep. "I can't leave. I *know* we'll win."

"How can you be so certain? I spent all summer with the army. I watched them crush the Norwegians. Even still, these Normans are a different breed of warrior. The king spent many nights speaking of them. If they break through, we're lost."

"They won't break through, Aidan. I know this is hard to believe, but I saw our victory in a dream. Harold...Oh Good God, Harold gets wounded. I remember now. He gets wounded, but the book brings you and me together and we help him...somehow. I don't know how, but we help him beat these monsters."

He had never seen Lady Edith act this way. She stood five paces away, rooted to the ground like the tree behind her. Her face held part elation, part derangement, and part dread. Looking at this new woman, Aidan realized he could not change her mind. He let out a breath, trying to figure out what to do. Then, he struck on a possible idea. "Well, if you're so determined, perhaps we can compromise. The king showed me a vantage point yesterday. It's just a short ride to the Romney trail from there anyway. If it looks like we're winning, we'll watch on. If it looks like anything else, we ride away immediately."

Her face and posture softened and her lips curled up. "Thank you, little firebrand. I promise to follow wherever you lead, but Harold's danger will pale in comparison to the Norman plight. We fight for more than personal glory, more than protecting our kingdom. We fight to rid the world of a horrific future. If God has any fairness, how can we lose?"

Riding behind and just off to the side of Lady Edith and Scramasax, Aidan let Walter meander down the path, all the while hoping for a fyrdsmen to appear with news of the victory already in hand.

"I'm just going to ride ahead," she said. "You can catch up to me."

"Lady Edith, please don't." He made his voice sound tender. "If you go ahead and take one wrong turn, one wrong step, you could get swept up in the conflict."

His tone worked; her grip on the reins lightened. "You say you came here yesterday?"

"We did. Knowing the Normans meant to fight on horseback, the king had targeted the hill as his battlefield. It's not the highest, but it's one of the steepest. I have a drawing I could show you. It's for the king's battle chronicle."

Her brow furrowed. "Between confession books and battle chronicles, I'm hesitant to ask if there's anything else you've been up to, Aidan."

"Well, there was another book. The king and I worked on a falcon bestiary all summer. It..." He paused, fighting back the memories of the knife ripping through the parchment. "It was lost during the march from York."

He must have hid his pain well; Edith did not sense it. "A falcon bestiary to go along with a falcon confession..." When she looked at Aidan again, her smile stretched wide. "Your work is exquisite, young one. Wulfstan trained you well."

Despite himself, heat rose in Aidan's cheeks. He looked away. "He did. Thank you, my lady."

"Aidan, look at me."

Grudgingly, he looked up.

"Harold told me about the goldsmith's daughter. Did you get her with child?"

"No!" He rose up in his saddle and Walter grunted once more. "You must believe me! We only...we only kissed. The bishop found us before anything more occurred."

"I see."

His heart raced. It had been so long since he spoke of the night of the red star with anyone. "I couldn't live my whole life without knowing, Lady Edith. I just couldn't. And because of my one curiosity, God and my mentor cast me out."

Her smile turned devious. "God has favored many men who have at one time or another ran off to kiss a girl when they shouldn't have. But I know what you're going through. Churchmen's fangs bite deep and inject long-lasting venom. Wulfstan, however, is a different sort. Yes, he is strict, but the man has a good heart. No doubt he regrets his anger. Do you regret your kiss?"

Aidan's mind and heart pulled from opposite ends of a rope. "I...I regret the pain it caused."

"That doesn't answer my question."

He wanted to say "no." He wanted to fly to Worcester, steal Ebba away, and live as far from swords as he could. Yet these desires burned as soon as they appeared in his mind. Wulfstan had set him on a path of belief, learning, writing, and exploration. The kiss had blocked this enlightenment, and he felt lost ever since. "I...I don't know."

She shrugged. "I hardly knew where to walk when I was fifteen. My question may have been unfair. And since you won't spur your donkey forward, let me ask you this: do you wish to return to Worcester?"

This time, he did not hesitate. "I pray for the bishop's forgiveness every day, Lady Edith. His anger was just, but it haunts me nonetheless."

"Well I won't let you be haunted," she said. Her smile now quivered. "I owe your mother that much, at least. After the victory, we'll seek Wulfstan out and address this...this situation."

His mind crept back into control as they reached the base of a wide, gradual hill covered in fescue of gold, green, and gray. His foster mother's words revived a hope buried long ago. *I wonder if I'll ever be able to repay her kindness.* Then, his mind seized on a way. He could try to heal her anger over the king's marriage to Queen Alditha.

Just as he started to speak, however, an unexpected breeze carried a sinister sound under the rustle of leaves. Aidan's skin began to tingle. He recognized the unbridled, uncaring, brutality of battle. His thoughts of love and redemption shattered. "The watch tree is at the ridge top."

Edith set her posture. "Don't be frightened, Aidan. This is our day. Our triumph."

When they reached the top, they found bristly, leafy bushes scattered about and the scent of cloves in the air. After tethering their mounts to saplings, Aidan withdrew the battle chronicle pages from Walter's saddlebag along with his writing kit. He hoped the work would help steady him during the fight. He also hoped he would record another victory.

They walked in a trance-like silence to the tall, thick oak tree tilting over the far end. Covered in shade, the vantage point lorded over the whole battlefield.

He could not discern King Harold, but his banners –

the Dragon of Wessex and the Fighting Man of Godwin – flew behind a thick wall of English warriors set across the London road. From their position behind and above the fight, it looked as if God had draped crimson rushes atop the ridge, but Aidan knew it was blood, not straw. Inanimate bodies of men and horses were strewn everywhere, but most heavily on a small plateau at the bottom of the hill.

As he watched, a wave of mounted warriors galloped headlong into the line. The echoes grew louder, and the hell the army endured assaulted Aidan in a way he could never have prepared for. Dropping his chronicle materials to the ground, his breath hardened and he covered his mouth. Then, chunks of salted beef mixed with warm ale spewed from his gut onto the base of the watch oak.

"This is no place for either of us, my lady," he said between spits. "Can we please move on to Romney? If the Normans crest the hill, we could be seen."

She walked to him, straightened him up, and used her sleeve cuff to clean Aidan's face. She then held his upturned head in her hands. Her palms felt cold on his balmy cheeks. "No, sweet one. The battle is awful, but Harold's banners still fly. He is a true champion, and these demons cannot prevail as long as God watches the world."

When she turned back to the vantage point, Aidan collected the pages onto his writing board, settled on the dry grass, and prepared his ink vials. His trembling hands clinked the vials, and unlike Stamford Bridge, he could not make them stop.

The Confession

July 1, 1065

   The earl: I remember the damp stone walls with their crusty mortar, for that's where my shaking hand gripped. I remember the smells of urine, rose water, and fungus, for I breathed through my nose to calm my heaving chest.

Guilt still shoots through my veins when I think about Odo's plot. True, I had no weapon, but the torch could have cudgeled his skull easy enough. My hands...Look at them Wulfstan. Have you ever seen any man with stronger hands? Why didn't I burst in and choke his life out?

Fear. God help me, but at the moment when future's fate hung in the balance, I heard a door latch open and I fled. As a result, I have endangered countless lives from England to the Levant.

I swear, here and now, I will never run from another chance to kill them. With God as my witness, I vow to kill William and Odo...or die in the attempt.

Chapter 28: Orrin

They were East Anglians by the look of them, warriors from his homeland. To his surprise, the wave of guilt he expected never came. Instead, Odo's chilling voice dominated his mind. "God is watching you through my eyes, Orrin. He will know your worth by your deeds this day."

Ever since Gyrth and Leofwine Godwinson perished in their ill-fated charge, the tide of battle had sided against the English. Now, the Normans battled time as well. If the English held the ridge at nightfall, Duke William would be forced to retreat in dark, foreign territory with Englishmen harrying every step. Harold knew this too, and his army had found a renewed vigor in the last hour.

"Are you ready, Urse? I fear this last charge may be the worst yet."

D'Abitot, whose chain mail now held a blood-stained sheen, snorted a laugh. "How can one shit smell worse than any other? Let's have it done."

Urse led half the conroi as Orrin held the others back. When the charge hit the shield wall, they held their ground without throwing too many killing blows. Had this happened just a few hours ago, a scourge of huscarl axes would have cut them down. But it had been a long, blood-thirsty day and Harold had gathered his remaining huscarls to the center, leaving inexperienced fyrdsmen in their place on the flanks. It didn't take long for those undisciplined men at the end of the English line to grow impatient. They left their posts to run down the slope so they could catch the first attack from the side.

Just as they did so, Orrin screamed, "Now!" They did not rush to Urse's aid. Instead, they bypassed the entire fight to crest the hill. The East Anglians tried to turn and fight, but they were caught between two sharp-toothed jaws. One fyrdsman lunged at Orrin's torso with a bent, rusty sword. He blocked with his shield and then sliced down in a diagonal arc. A fountain of blood met the air. Without pausing, he spurred the horse onward. Moments later, he met Urse and the rest of the conroi atop the ridge.

"Ha ha! Every shit should smell this sweet!"

Orrin ignored the blood-crazed warrior and wheeled his horse around. *Are you watching me now, bishop?*

Soon, dozens of fresh warriors rushed up the hill to bolster the Norman position atop the ridge. As this occurred, the English retreated in good order to form a half-circle of spears and shields around the snarling Dragon of Wessex and the gleaming Fighting Man banner of the Godwin clan.

Orrin marveled at his former friend's determination. *He cannot think to stay afield. Not now.*

The Norman chevaliers hovered several paces from

this last stand, waiting for the duke's command. The English shields stood strong as if the fight had just started.

"Attack at will!" The duke's order crashed through the air.

Unleashing a terrible cry, Orrin and the remaining chevaliers obeyed. His horse pulled up when they hit the wall, unable to force through the spear-bristling defenders. "Die damn you!" Orrin screamed as he hefted his sword onto a shield. The jarring impact shivered deep into his shoulder. An Englishman appeared through the shields and would have run Orrin through with his spear. But at the last moment, the force of battle surged to the side, and he twisted his shoulders so the spear point hit the air just under his nose.

The mounted warriors disengaged from the fray. They had lost dozens more and the defensive formation still held. All the while, the sun crept nearer to the horizon.

"Re-form the attack," Urse yelled. "We have precious little time."

Orrin held out a hand. "In a moment. Let the men rest. Why doesn't he retreat? Even a blind man could see he's almost surrounded."

Urse made to answer, but Harold beat him to it. Over the din of battle, the English king's bellow cracked like thunder: "WILLIAM!!! Come get your empire!"

"My God," Orrin said. "He won't leave without fighting William first."

"You told me he was brave. You forgot to mention his obsession with death." Urse pointed to the hill. Four mounted chevaliers trotted up the slope. Orrin recognized them as the best the invading army had to offer: Eustace of Boulogne, Robert of Beaumont, William de Warrenne, and Egenulf D'Laigle.

Urse swore under his breath. "This is madness. The day is won! Why endanger our best warriors now?"

Orrin just shook his head in disbelief.

Another pause took the field. Then, Harold called again. "Odo of Bayeux! Come get your heart's desire!"

He could see Harold now, standing tall in the center of his warrior circle. Orrin was a devout man, but if he ever believed in the Norse gods, he would have thought Thor had come to stand in Harold's stead.

Duke William did not rise to the bait. Instead, he issued a vehement order with his own voice. "Hold your positions! No one attack!"

Orrin barely heard the command; his attention was stolen by two figures standing next to a giant oak tree in the distance. One was short, a boy by the look of it; he seemed oddly familiar. The other silhouette in the encroaching dusk took his breath away. She had long hair and the form of an angel without wings. *Edith. It must be!*

With her capture, he could win the duke's trust, the respect of Bishop Odo, and maybe even his passage home to Hesilia. *I may even stop Harold from pursuing this heroic folly.*

Orrin broke away and raced toward the onlookers. The sun darkened as he did so. Orrin thought it had gone behind a low-lying cloud at first, but a quick glance caught the duke's plan in action. No Norman attacked because archers unleashed a hail storm of arrows.

Orrin hastened his charge. The robed boy pulled on Edith's arm, but she stood rooted to the ground with her gaze fixed on the battle. Half-way there, he heard a familiar shout. "No! NO!" But then, the voice cut short.

The urgency in the call could not be ignored. Orrin pulled on the bridle, his horse reared to halt, and he looked back to the fight. The defensive circle had caved in. Norman warriors attacked like diving vultures. *Harold's been hit!* His heart beat like forge bellows.

In an instant, the four Norman champions exploited a breach. A flurry of limbs, swords, and shields obstructed his view. He saw Egenulf pulled from his horse, and heard the tell-tale scream soon thereafter. Beaumont pulled back, a spear jutting from the haunch of his horse. Just when Orrin thought Harold may cut his way through, the remaining Norman champions hacked away with a shower of killing blows. Then, as the sun faded below the horizon, the last English banners fell to the ground.

Shocked by the cataclysm, Orrin looked back to the oak tree. Edith and her boy had vanished.

Chapter 29:
Edith

She ran through branches and brambles without knowing where she headed. A weight tugged at her extended right hand, leading the way. Low light poured through the tree tops, but it held no warmth, no feeling at all. Her mind hung in a mist; she was too baffled to cry, too shocked to yell, and too scared to think. She heard birds welcome the fast approaching dusk and a rambling, nervous voice, but she couldn't comprehend anything except her own rigid breath.

Scramasax appeared; the horse snorted a welcome and nudged Edith's hand with his muzzle. The voice grew more urgent and the force shifted to her back, pushing her toward the saddle. Her heart beat louder to match the voice's intensity, but two words managed to break through: "Harold" and "alive."

Her mind replayed the scenes: the Normans had gained the ridge; Harold held the field, cornered; Aidan pulled her arm, but she could not rip herself away; a rider bore down on them, but she stood and waited for God's justice to prevail; one word, "no," floated through the air amidst a storm of arrows; and finally, Harold's banners fell in a sickening flurry of death.

Pressure fell on her shoulders and her head shook back and forth. Snapping from the memories, she looked down to see Aidan's burning eyes.

"Lady Edith! Please! The king may yet live. We must escape to Romney before that rider comes back!"

He may yet live. Edith pursed her lips as sensation returned to her body. Aidan was right; there was no way to tell who lived and who perished. She signaled her readiness with a nod.

They had just reached the road when Edith heard a cry from behind. She turned and found a bloodied huscarl stumbling toward them.

"Rand!" She wheeled Scramasax around and flew to him. "Have you fled with the king?"

The huscarl regarded Edith with a cold, distant stare as other warriors appeared behind.

She dismounted. "Are you hurt? Tell me, is the king here or has he fled to the forest?"

Rand swallowed several times, unable to utter any words.

Dread filled her body. She grasped his gore-covered cheeks. *"Tell me!"*

"I...I'm sorry, m'lady. He...he fell."

Aidan appeared at Edith's side. The boy lowered her trembling hands from Rand's disoriented face. "God save us all," he said.

Save us? He's abandoned us. "This cannot be happening.

Tell me, one of you, any of you, did you see my husband fall?"

No one answered. A glimmer of hope remained in Edith's heart. "Could he just be injured? Speak now, for if he needs rescue and we do not act, we will all rot in Hell this day."

"I saw it," Rand's voice was a whisper, but it rang in Edith's ears like a scream. She fell to the ground.

The beleaguered huscarl stood over her, staring off into the distance. "He had the retreat organized. We had him covered and the demons couldn't break in no matter how hard they charged. But he kept sticking his head up to issue orders...challenges. Something caught his eye, 'cause he stopped and shouted 'No!' That's when the arrow nipped him under the eye. He fell. Some of us lost courage and scattered. It was all the dogs needed. Four of 'em rode in, trampling and slicing as they went. I tried to cover him, Lady Edith; truly I did. I killed one of 'em, I think. But a damned horse kicked me in the head and I went blank. When I came to, he lay next to me, face down...no movement...no...life."

A small cry escaped her lips. She covered her face with her hands and rocked back and forth. Nothing she could think of could provide an escape. She just sat on the ground and rocked and thought. The vilest beasts on earth had ripped the man she loved away from her. Her husband, the father of her children, was no more. Her children's lives now stood in danger and she was helpless to protect them. And her children were just the beginning. The children of innocent families around the world now faced attack, according to Harold's confession.

The confession! Looking up, Edith had no idea how long she had sat on the ground. The countryside now sang to the sound of night birds and insects. *Aidan was right all along. I should have gone to Romney. I was just so sure...* The need to escape felt like a fever. She could not fail Harold now, not after God had already done so.

Wiping her face, she rose from her grassy seat. She was shocked to find Rand, his warriors, and even Aidan all seated with her. "Friends, we must see to the king's wishes and flee to Romney." The words almost caught in her dry throat. "We can collect our thoughts there. Rand, can you and your men find horses?"

"Aye m'lady. We'll be right behind you."

Aidan went to mount Walter, but Edith stopped him. "Leave him behind, Aidan. I fear he's no match for Norman stallions. You can ride pillion behind me."

The yellow and silver of dusk had retreated into the blue of night as they began to rush off. After just a few trots, a new voice called out. "Lady Edith, Stop!"

She turned Scramasax. Lit by the last dregs of day, Osgod rode an exquisite roan stallion down the path from the English camp. "May I have a word in private?" he said, fast approaching.

"A word? My husband lies dead along with his army and you want a *word*? If you weren't a clergyman, Osgod, I'd run you over here and now."

"God has left us today; there is no doubt," he sounded breathless as he pulled alongside Scramasax. "We all are in great peril now. But your work here is not yet done, I'm afraid."

"What do you mean?"

"After Duke William took the field, I went to him under a banner of peace and begged him to release King Harold's body for burial. He denied me, but agreed the king's remains should be found as proof of the day's victory."

"Even now, you take sick pleasure in tormenting me. Be gone you lecherous snake! I'll have no more to do with you!" She tried to go around Osgod, but he reached out and grabbed Scramasax's bridle.

"I do not mean to give offense, Lady Edith. I just explain the situation, for they have ordered me to bring you to the field so you could find our slain king."

Edith tried to kill the clergyman with her stare. "Impossible. How did they even know I was here?"

"I know not, my lady. But Duke William said they would hunt you down if you did not come willingly."

"The rider must've recognized you, m'lady," Aidan said. "How else would they've known."

She winced and squeezed the bridge of her nose. The blunder of going to the watch tree knew no end.

Rand and his men had gathered around. "This is foul, m'lady," he said. "Do not do this...this bidding. It will mean your certain death."

"You're right, Rand. If I go, they'll kill me the moment I find Harold. But if I don't, they'll come after us..." She forced her mind to concentrate; no escape presented itself. Instead, her failure kept circling back. *I cannot protect the confession anymore.* Then, she recalled something Harold said just before the battle: "The hands I trust are yours and Wulfstan's." The bishop would know what to do. *But how can I get the book to him?* She regarded Osgod. "Will the Normans to change their minds about the burial?"

"They dismissed me without a second thought, m'lady, although I think they made a grievous mistake. If they want people to know of the king's death, holding a funeral makes the most sense."

Her raised hand silenced him. Wulfstan would exhaust every horse in Mercia and Wessex to attend Harold's funeral. If she could convince the Normans to change their minds, she would just need to get the book to the ceremony. *But who?* Surveying the faces before her, she found no one. When she felt the hands around her stomach reset, however, the answer dawned.

After one last resolute breath, she spoke to Osgod. "I will return to the tents and wait for more of the battle heat to cool. In the dead of night, we'll go."

"Lady Edith, NO!" Rand snatched Scramasax's bridle from Osgod's hand.

"There is more to this than you know, my warrior. King Harold must receive a proper funeral, attended by all the leading magnates and clergymen in the land. He should be put to earth by his most reverent supporter, Bishop Wulfstan. Promise me, Rand. Promise you will see this wish through or die trying."

"M'lady, please—"

"*Promise me!*"

His posture wilted. "I...I promise."

"Good. Now, leave us for the moment, all of you. I must speak to Aidan alone."

The scribe trembled behind her. "There must be some other way," he said when the others left.

"There is none, little one. I must protect the book, even if it means sacrificing my life."

"What will happen to the book if you...if you..."

"It will be up to you, Aidan. I'm giving you the book, Scramasax, and Rand's protection. You must get the confession to Wulfstan."

She felt his chest flex. "I...No. Lady Edith...please!"

She forced her voice calm. "Harold's funeral is the

fastest and most assured way of drawing Wulfstan to us. Harold trusted him almost as much as he trusted me. I know you're at odds with the bishop, but now is not the time for petty grievances." Aidan made an attempt to argue but she shook her head. "I do not mean to belittle the strife between you two. If the Normans had not summoned me, things would be different. But the cold, hard truth is they know I'm here. And as long as I live, I'll be watched. If they find this book, they will destroy it; I cannot bear that. The confession is all I have left of him. You and Rand will go wait in the forest. If I succeed, Osgod and I will follow not long after with Harold's body. If I don't make it, Aidan, swear to me now that you'll make sure Wulfstan gets the confession."

She felt the boy's hesitance, but she also knew he had more sense than to argue any more. "I...I swear, m'lady."

"Good. Now come give me a kiss. I fear it will be the last act of tenderness I receive this day."

*

She sat on the furs and skins of the tent floor with her arms wrapped around her skirt-covered knees, entranced by a burning beeswax candle. Set on a small wooden table, the faint flame's bold, sun-colored tip and thin blue base danced in front of her eyes. Its honey scent wrapped her so tight in a cocoon of warmth, safety, and memories, she never heard Osgod enter.

"My lady, it's time to perform your duty."

Ripping away from her vigil, she found Osgod hunched down in the small canvas tent holding a bundle of rolled-up cloth. The flame cast the clergyman in shadow, showing Death himself carrying a black funeral shroud. "Duty...or torment?"

With no words of reply, the clergyman offered the bundle. "Please wear this. Venturing into the camp in your present garb would be most unwise. We had best leave at once; they are expecting you."

"I will be out when I am ready," Edith said, knowing readiness was out of the question. She lifted her hands to receive cloth.

A gust of fresh air entered through the tent flaps as the clergyman left. She put the bundle down and cupped the flickering candle. *Too many lights have been dashed this day.* She thought of her children. Their safety was her last comfort, yet even that solace would be short-lived. Godwine, Magnus, and Edmund were bound to a life of vengeance from this day forward.

Forcing those awful thoughts away, she unfurled the cloth to discover a dusty monk's habit and sandals. The rough spun woolen fabric felt coarse and unforgiving. Her slim frame would never fit the disguise, but it would serve. With the cowl pulled over her head, no one would suspect a woman.

After removing her soft, warm gown, she lofted the plain, mud-brown robe over her shift. She then removed her headscarf, tied her hair with a chord of leather, slipped into the new sandals, and wrapped the thongs around her calves. Lastly, Edith found a pocket inside one of the sleeves where she could hide her deer-bone *seax*. Harold had given it to her as a wedding gift. With this small blade, she had cut thread for her children's clothing, cultivated herbs in her garden, and carved servings of meat for their dinner. After a last deep breath, she left the candle burning and exited the tent.

Outside, the chilly autumn night paid its respects. A gentle breeze pushed the heavy, almost mournful air.

Countless stars glimmered in the silent moon-lit sky. Atop the hill's crest, the large apple tree reached for her with black, twisted fingers. *What a difference between day and night.* Earlier that morning, Harold had rallied the pride of England for battle around the tree. The camp roared as his voice ushered in hope, vitality, and passion. Now, the tree sat as calm and quiet as a burial cairn.

Clopping horse trots combined with rickety sounds of a wooden cart to shatter the silence. Compared to the tent's gentle candle flame, Osgod's torch seared her vision. He gestured to the back of the cart; his plentiful girth left little room for her up front. "God will protect us as we labor to grant King Harold a proper Christian burial."

Edith moved to the back of the cart, infuriated by Osgod's words. She had no doubt he desired to bury Harold, but whether that desire stemmed from true devotion or avarice she could not tell.

After crossing a small plateau, they descended another large hill. The path continued on, but the view struck Edith's heart. Torch lights scurried across the black hillside like lines of fireflies as English women searched in the night for their dead family, friends, and lovers.

"I should have warned you," Osgod said. "The field is no less horrific than this afternoon."

Edith wiped tears away. "Are we to begin the search now?"

"No. They asked me to bring you to a public audience first."

"You mean a public humiliation." Osgod began to reply, but Edith cut him off. "No matter. Let's be done with it."

With a sharp shake of the reins, he urged the horse toward the Norman encampment.

As they drew near, the agonized cries from the battle-field faded underneath the roar of laughing men, singing scalds, and braying horses. One man waited for them by the camp entrance. He was diminutive in stature, with close-cropped dark hair and a stubble beard. His suit of mail reflected the campfire and his rich crimson cloak lent him a lord's authority. Edith knew him at once.

"Greetings, my lady," Orrin said. "You'll be safe with me."

"You dare show your face now, Orrin, after what you've done? How many times did Harold take you into his counsel? How many times did he prize your friendship? Your way of repayment is sickening beyond words."

His face showed no emotion. "A choice needs to be made when a wife's homeland goes to war against a mother's. For me, my wife's lands and welfare made the choice for me, albeit not easily. For what it is worth, I," he paused to swallow hard, "I grieve for your loss."

"Your grief, sir, will not return Harold to me. Your sword, however, could have saved his life. Now lead the way. I have to find my husband whom you helped kill."

The traitor opened his mouth, but then turned his back and started walking. Osgod fell in with Edith and they followed in silence.

The Norman nobility had gathered for their victory feast in a large canopy tent just below the battlefield. These foreign demons gorged themselves with French wine, English meat, and uninhibited rapture. The light and smoke from the feasting fires bathed them in a ghoulish orange haze and the smells of the foreign spices burned the back of her throat.

Orrin led them to the head table covered with glass wine jugs, silver goblets, and chewed bones. Behind it,

Harold's personal standard stood propped up by spear points. Excrement stained the magnificent white linen background. The Fighting Man – a warrior woven out of gold thread who wielded magnificent, jewel-encrusted battleaxe – hung slashed from head to navel. With all her soul, Edith wanted to take the banner down and fold it in her arms, but she could not. The man sitting in front of it scared her too much.

Duke William of Normandy sat at the table's center in a wooden chair larger than any other. His skin looked pale as milk. He kept his face clean-shaven and his hair cropped, so just a dark shadow covered the crown of his head. He still wore his battle armor and stared straight ahead with a mailed fist propping up his long, chiseled chin.

Following Orrin's gesture, Osgod approached the head table. "Duke William, may I present Lady Edith Swan-neschals." He then retreated off to the side.

She walked to the duke. His stare descended on her soul. "Do you speak this tongue?" he asked in Latin.

She nodded.

"Then turn and kneel before your conquerors, Lady Edith."

Gathering all her remaining dignity, she turned from the head table, put both her knees on the ground, and placed her hands behind her back. She did not, however, bow her head. Instead, she set her face in stone and leveled her stare at the murderers.

Edith heard William speak in calm, hoarse Norman. The entire crowd roared the moment he finished. Some bellowed unintelligible cries of triumph as they pointed at her. Some sank their teeth into haunches of roasted meat, eyeing her with hunger. Others hoisted goblets above their mouths and gulped down streams of wine.

Her chest fluttered. *With each moment, Aidan rides farther away. Let them mock me all night.*

The feast started up again and the man sitting to William's left approached. Judging from his rich crimson garb, he was some type of clergyman. He spoke Latin almost in a whisper.

"My name is Bishop Odo of Bayeux. The duke has sent me to instruct you."

Edith willed herself to show no reaction, even though the name sent jolts of hatred through her. Pretending to adjust her sleeves, she reached for the *seax* hilt.

Odo continued. "Your lover was last seen defending his army's dragon standard, which fell just past the crest of the battlefield hill. You have an unenviable task, but do not fail or play us false. Finding his body will save countless English lives. Godwinson represented England's sole chance to defeat us; with his death proven, your countrymen will think twice before they take arms again."

Edith met Odo's stare. "What will become of him?"

"You should not have asked, Lady Edith. But if you must know, we intend to parade his corpse to the sea cliffs and throw him to the ocean depths."

Edith ignored the barbarism and appealed to Odo's religion. "Harold must receive a Christian funeral. I beg you in the name of God. Let us take him from this place and lay him to rest with respect."

"Speak not of God, Lady Edith; you were Godwinson's whore, nothing more. I will not grant your request. His grave could create a shrine where rebellion may grow."

When her appeal failed, she tried negotiation. "He was

vastly wealthy. I have means as well. I offer his weight in gold…"

Odo shook his head. "Why render a service when the gold is there for the taking anyway? No. We will do what we wish with Godwinson's corpse."

When her bargain failed, she used her last option. Looking away from the bishop, she said, "But you have to find him first. I will not search unless you swear to treat his body with respect."

"You dare make demands?"

Edith shot the man a cold look. "If you do not agree, kill me and find another who can verify your victory."

Odo glanced up and stroked his upper lip. "If I swear," he said, "you must not rest until the body is found. This task *will* finish before dawn."

Run Aidan, please! "I will not rest."

"Fine. I swear under God's watchful eyes that your lover's body will receive a proper funeral. I will discuss the arrangements with your clergyman—" Edith began to rise, but Odo's hand grasped her shoulder and forced her back to the ground. "But I will make a demand of my own. Tell me where to find his book."

"What?" *How does he know?*

The bishop released Edith's shoulder. "My sources tell me the usurper worked with a certain crippled scribe above all others. I've often wondered what this scribe wrote that interested him so much."

Edith's mind flew. *Speak. Say something before he suspects.* Then, she struck on something and forced the tension out of her voice. "King Harold employed scribes to write letters to his councilmen, dispensations for his army, and correspondence to his family." Edith paused to let her nerves settle. "He also kept a book of falconry to describe the habits of God's most glorious creatures. Perhaps your *spies* caught him working on that."

"Perhaps," Odo said with doubt spilling from his face. "And what has become of the scribe?"

The first lie had been the hardest. Once done, the rest dropped like rain. "The last I heard, Harold kept his writing office hard at work in London. In truth, I don't know. The king did not involve me in matters of hunting or scholarship. I was his most prized whore, not his counselor."

Odo sighed. Edith felt like a sow being appraised at market.

"Make no mistake, I will keep a keen eye out for his scribe and his *falconry* book. And if I learn you have lied to me, I will hunt you down, in this life or the next. Now go find your dead husband. Already, rumors of his survival spread and prolong our invasion."

Rising from her knees, Edith gripped the seax hilt and looked at Odo. Her body tensed and she prepared to strike, but he had already moved too far away. Then, she felt another stare. Turning to the head table, she saw William assail her with his eyes. She relaxed her secret grip and turned to Osgod.

"Stay with the duke and negotiate Harold's burial at Waltham. I will go ahead." Without waiting for his reply, she pulled the cowl over her head and fled.

The monk's habit proved its worth during the brisk walk through the tent maze. The hordes of victory-drunk warriors never glanced at her.

Emerging at the base of the hill, the wallows of her dying countrymen renewed their attack on her fortitude. She remembered the hill as she had first seen it this night. *I am to become a firefly.*

She grabbed a torch from a nearby sconce and picked her way up the slope. Halfway up, she spied Norman guards trailing behind. Releasing a seething breath through her nose, she continued her climb.

After reaching the crest, the stench of death threatened to overwhelm the bonfire smoke. Naked, looted bodies lay stacked atop the blood-slicked ground. At the far end of the ridge, the remains of the English army's banner hung limp from a planted spear.

Edith headed toward the banner and started her search. Undaunted by the smell and sight of butchers' work, she brushed hair back from stiff faces, closed lifeless eyes, and said continuous prayers for these lost souls.

In a heap nearest the banner, she found a body fitting the right height and build. An arrow protruding from his right eye had turned his face into a debauchery. His right leg bore a wicked gash from hip to knee. Edith wiped his left thigh clean, searching for the final, damning piece of evidence. The birthmark on the inner part of the leg broke her. Falling on top of Harold and cradling his bloody corpse to her breast, her mouth opened in a silent scream. The sobs came next, deep and forceful. Those she could not keep silent.

Edith sat on the cool, damp earth and let time pass by without consideration. At long last, the familiar sounds of horse and cart returned to her ears. She had stopped weeping, but blood and gore covered her hands, arms, face, and robe.

Before Osgod got within earshot, she whispered, "I've done the best I could, my love. Aidan will get the book to Wulfstan. Rest now. Rest."

When Osgod reached Edith, he crossed himself. She heard several more footsteps. In an instant, Duke William appeared next to Osgod; his face showed no emotion. "You swear this is the body of your dead lover?"

She was almost too weary to respond. "I have come too far to cradle someone else's corpse in my lap, Norman. Where will he be laid to rest?"

"Waltham," Osgod said. "We have settled all arrangements. The escort begins at dawn."

"Will you Normans follow?"

"No," the duke said. "My men need rest. We will not march for a few more days."

Edith nodded in sullen agreement. Everything had gone as planned.

"My lady, it grieves me to say this, but your duty is fulfilled," Osgod said. "It is past time you prepared for the journey home."

I am prepared at last. Her mind jumped to a different time to summon Annora's bravery. "Home," she said, laying Harold's head on the ground and reaching into her sleeve, "is gone."

In one fluid motion, she pounced at Duke William and swung the blade. A hand pushed on her chest, roars of fear filled the morning, and her knife continued downward. *Die Beast!*

But then, just before she expected the point to dig into flesh, a hand ensnared her arm and snapped her wrist bones. The knife fell from her grasp. Edith had no time to scream before her assailant placed the blade at her throat. Turning to look at her murderer, she found Bishop Odo wearing a sick grin.

A quick rush of pain filled Edith's body; her back hit the soft earth and her eyes found the lightening sky. She reached for her throat, expecting a gush of blood, but instead found the dry, rough fabric of the monk's robe.

Then, a sharp heat burst from the back of her head. As total blackness took over, she heard the words, "A fate worse than death..."

Chapter 30:
Aidan

October 15, 1066

As the band of weary, desolated warriors sat in silence or dozed around their campfire, Aidan stared into the leaping light. The calamity, as far as he could tell, was total. Since Bishop Wulfstan cast him out of Worcester, his service to King Harold helped lift the darkness. He remembered arriving at the king's tent at Tunbridge, holding Wulfstan's letter of condemnation. For the months leading to the battles, the king treated Aidan more like a son than a scribe. How could God take such a man?

As an answer, the fire offered a loud POP followed by a lingering wheeeeez. Blanching, Aidan leaned away and tried to comfort himself with thoughts of a dark, dry room, a soft straw pallet, and an even softer kiss from Ebba. But then, the burning logs caved in and a plume of embers lofted into the pre-dawn sky.

He rose from his piled leaves and glanced toward the

horses, which were tethered to trees nearby. Scramasax's eager whicker overcame the sounds of the burning logs and made Aidan smile despite himself. *Even now, he wants to fly.*

For a moment, Aidan thought to check the saddlebags again. He doubted any of these men could read, but confession would prove a tempting treasure nevertheless. The best way to protect it would be to sleep with it, and the idea tempted him to no end. But he turned away from the horses and the fire. *If I take it out, even for an instant, someone could see. Best to leave it alone until I think of a better hiding place.*

As he shuffled away, Rand's head lifted, the warrior's first movement since he sat and stared into the flames hours earlier. He was Lady Edith's huscarl, yet she made him swear to protect Aidan. Now, as she ventured into the Devil's den, he could do nothing but sit and think and drive himself mad.

"To the stream," Aidan said in a whisper. "To wash my face." They had found the fresh-cut path to the stream soon after arriving at the clearing. Some hunters or pig herders must have maintained the site. Now, their bodies most likely littered that accursed hill.

"Be quick," Rand said before resuming his fiery vigil.

Away from the circle, thousands of insects sang their nocturnal calls in unison. Every moment contained a rustle of leaves or a flutter of wings. Aidan no longer believed in grumpkins or demons, but wild boar and wolves posed more pressing threats. God's wrath could manifest itself in any number of ways. The lone surety in his mind was that the wrath would come soon.

Aidan reached the trickling stream and felt cold, damp mud seep into his leather shoes. Well beyond caring, he leaned down and splashed the water over his face. Momentarily calmed, the task Lady Edith assigned him unfolded in his mind's eye. In the morning, he would join Osgod, travel to Waltham Holy Cross, and wait for Bishop Wulfstan. His breathing grew rapid and his fingers tensed as they pressed against his wet face. The thought of seeing the bishop again sent a shudder through him. Maybe there's a better way. Perhaps someone else should protect the book?

He lowered his hands and noticed silver light had fallen over the stream. Glancing up, he saw the bright half-moon through a hole in the tree canopy. Perhaps this was a sign to leave Rand and make his own way?

Splashes in the stream tore Aidan's eyes from the sky. He found a black outline of a deer taking a drink just paces from where he stood. The deer caught wind of him as well, and stiffened. He could sense the doe's fear and strength. Lady Edith exuded the same instincts when he last saw her. "I must protect Harold's book, even if it means sacrificing my life," she had said.

A sudden breeze picked up and filtered through the forest. He thought he heard a woman's desperate sobs carry on the wind. But then a wolf howled and several pack mates answered. The silhouette of the doe's ears pricked. Without the slightest hint, she bounded away. He opened his mouth to call her back, but no sound emerged.

Standing on the stream bank, fear for his foster mother heaved in his chest. *There's no way they'll let her go.* He shook his head as the tears fell.

The frigid water seeped through and his teeth began to chatter. He thought of the colossal task of escaping Rand: interminable nights, no protection from man or beast, no guarantee he could find another protector, and most of all, the guilt of breaking his oath. With a thousand arguments to the contrary, duty compelled Lady Edith to venture into the Norman camp. Compared to her task, his fear seemed trite. After a deep sigh, he climbed up the stream bank.

When he returned, the horses appeared undisturbed and all the men lay in their same positions. Just a few glowing coals remained of the once-roaring fire. If God's wrath lurked therein, Aidan could stamp out the danger easily enough. He fell into his leaves, turned his back to the smoldering glow, and let exhaustion take its course.

They rose from their slumber in the rising blue light of pre-dawn. The air felt moist and chilled. Morning dew had settled onto Aidan's robe and into his bones. Walking to the tree where Scramasax stood tethered, he fastened the bridle straps and secured the saddle bags once more. *At least the confession made it through one night.*

Footsteps approached from behind. "How you faring, lad?" Rand asked in a tired voice.

"I..." Aidan paused, thinking on how to respond as he shut the flap. "I feel lost," he said at last.

"Aye," Rand said, pinching the bridge of his flat, filth-covered nose. "A good way of putting it." The fyrdsmen had gathered around and Aidan could see the same defeated, guilty, uncertain look in them all. Their friends and dreams lay dead on that cursed battlefield. They had begun to wonder if they too should have died in the fight against the invaders or if the rest of their families would survive after their failure.

These miserable eyes regarded Aidan with veiled contempt, as most eyes did. He was a twisted, weak adolescent who couldn't hold a trowel any better than he could hold a sword. Had it not been for him, they could have fled to their homes. But now, by a lady's pleading and a huscarl's orders, they embarked on another dangerous venture. The least Aidan could do is hide his weakness. "But I'm doing fine under the circumstances. No need to rest on my account."

"Well then," Rand said, shaking off the melancholy. "We should return to the forest edge. Lady Edith and Osgod will no doubt leave the Norman camp at first light."

Aidan remembered the deer in the stream and the cries on the night wind, but Rand's countenance left no room for second-guessing.

The band set off with the huscarl leading the way. In front of them, a brown, sunken rut between two thick tangles of green led to the London road. In the past weeks, Aidan had ridden more than he ever thought possible. He feared infected sores would develop on his chafed haunches. His arms, shoulders, and back screamed with pain after a thousand jolts, bounces, and turns. Yet Scramasax proved a special gift. The stallion responded to commands as if they were holy orders and his stamina seemed endless. In fact, the stallion possessed too much fight. Just after they set out, the path widened and Scramasax bolted for the lead. Yanking the reins with all his might, Aidan forced him into a bristling halt. "Let's just leave Rand alone," he said into the horse's ear.

An hour after setting out, the path narrowed so only a column two riders wide could pass. Aidan pulled in beside Wynchell, an albino miller from Lincoln. After riding in silence for some time, the squat, round-featured man spoke in a whisper. "Is it true what they say, that you used to be a novice at Worcester Abbey?"

Aidan gave a slight nod. He could barely think about those days even in the best of times.

"Will God punish us for failing?"

Seeing the gloom in Wynchell's gray face, Aidan summoned his most uplifting words. "God knows the truth. He knows you fought bravely. He's rewarded you by allowing you to fight another day."

"But if God knows the truth, then why did King Harold die?"

"Well, sometimes the best of us are sacrificed so the rest may be saved. Perhaps, by fighting to the last, King Harold weakened the Normans so they won't withstand out next attack?"

"Yes," Wynchell said, stroking his stubby chin. "We'll skewer the bastards good in the next fight. All their loot'll be ours and King Harold'll be lauded as a hero, maybe even a saint. I can see God's plan now. Thanks, boy."

As the London road appeared before them, Wynchell began speaking of his home, family, and friends. Aidan listened, noting how his interpretation of God's Will brought new hope. All the while, he prayed he had not offered the miller, or himself, a cloud-built castle.

Chapter 31:
Orrin

October 15, 1066

With the sun climbing over the horizon, Duke William led his army from the battlefield. He rode alone, stiff and stately atop a black stallion. The English clergyman steered the cart behind him, displaying Harold's mangled corpse for all to see. The curia came next, led by William Fitz Osbern and Bishop Odo. Orrin followed the nobility with Urse at his side. The caravan cut through the red horizon like a black dagger, striking its way toward Hastings.

As the wind swept through the rolling hills and grassy plateaus, Orrin's apprehension stoked to a new height. *We're going the wrong way.*

Urse turned to him. "What makes you so glum, Englishman?"

"He's still bitter about the filly that got killed from under him," Reginald Fitz Alan said, slapping Orrin on the back. Fitz Alan was a young wisp of a chevalier under the command of Fitz Osbern. "That, or he's bitter the bishop had to save his hide before an axe nipped him."

"Peace, both of you." Orrin couldn't stand the banter. In truth, the battle had turned disastrous for him, even though his side won. Rumor spread like a plague throughout the camp that he lost his fortitude and ran just before Harold's final stand. This falsehood coupled with the truth of Bishop Odo's heroics to further enflame the suspicion surrounding him. Even the sighting of Lady Edith turned against him. He had expected her capture and ransom, not the horror William and Odo put her through. "I'm fine. Let me ride in peace."

"I think his pain goes deeper than that, Urse. Look at him. He's cross as a clergyman."

"True enough, Reginald. Tell us Orrin, what ails you?"

"I told you. I'm fine." Lady Edith's words rang in his head: *I have to find my husband whom you helped kill.* "I just don't wish to return to Hastings."

"Well, it makes sense to me," Reginald said. "We need rest and reinforcements. I, for one, am dying to shed this armor and wash the English grime away. Can't do that in the muck of the battlefield, can you? Come friend. Soften your sharp face. We ride as conquerors!" He spurred his horse forward and Urse followed him with a happy roar.

As the others galloped ahead, Orrin kept his horse at a trot. He wished for nothing more than to be left alone.

The sun had risen when the caravan arrived at a sheer cliff. Between land and horizon lay a frothing, white-capped sea, the same one they tamed eighteen days ago. The waves were audible now and the wind picked up in sudden, menacing gusts. In the southern distance, Orrin spied Hastings' wood shacks and wattle and daub huts.

The charred, leaning church tower sprang up like an accusatory finger.

Commanders called for their ranks to form up. As men jostled and weaved into place, Orrin saw a group of bedraggled prisoners being led to the cliff-side. He recognized them as the few stragglers caught in the hills after the battle. They wore chains around their wrists and bruises on their skin, but their faces seemed relatively untouched. A dread seized Orrin's stomach as he tried to figure out why they had been brought here, but he said nothing.

When Duke William reached the cliff's edge, he dismounted and faced his army. The edges of his new bearskin cloak fluttered in the wind.

"My friends and fellow conquerors, I'll be brief, for our quest is not finished. In truth, it's just begun.

"We came to England to right several wrongs done to me and to God most of all. The usurper stole my rightful crown. He lived in Godlessness, kept concubines, and broke holy oaths. He supported pluralist bishops, whose avarice and heresies have enraged our mother church. The man was not fit to be king of a pig sty, much less this bountiful country."

A sinking feeling emerged in Orrin's stomach. He forced his face to remain neutral as the duke continued.

"I set before you an arduous task: to cross the sea, to invade the wealthiest kingdom in Christendom, to break the fabled English shield wall, and to remove the usurper's stain from existence. Yesterday, in a battle destined for songs and stories for ages to come, you proved your mettle. You killed the treacherous letch and his brothers. You killed the strongest warriors in England. You won the greatest victory since Caesar defeated the Gauls at Alesia."

In unison, the crowd shouted, "Dex Aie! Dex Aie!"

Orrin frowned as the sinking feeling grew more tangible. *God's help indeed. We'll all need it if William does what I fear.* Out of the corner of his eyes, he saw two Normans make their way to the clergyman's cart.

"Yet brave warriors, while you achieved all these blessed victories, the Godwinson stain still exists. Just last night, the usurper's whore begged me to give him a Christian funeral." For a moment, the duke and Orrin met eyes. "Of course, I refused and sent her off to a wench's fate."

Cheers and sniggers rippled through the crowd. Orrin stood tall even though he felt an imaginary rope around his throat. *Dear God, she's dead...dead by my actions.*

"The woman thought her plea could persuade me. But here and now, I will prove nothing can shelter the sinful from God's punishment." He nodded and the two soldiers carried the bloody corpse to the cliff's edge.

"By my command, Harold Godwinson's eternal rest shall be here, so he can strive in death to guard the shore and sea he failed to guard in life." With a heave, the soldiers tossed the body head first. Orrin covered his gaping mouth. He knew William could be hard, even ruthless at times, but he never dreamed the duke would resort to such depravity. The imprisoned English onlookers, however, held nothing back. The grown men fell to their knees and wailed like children.

Bishop Odo began the cry, "Normandy! Normandy!" The entire procession picked up the fervent chant, casting the words up and down the coast. As he mouthed the words of his fanatic brethren, Orrin watched Duke William gaze down at the waves.

After Odo concluded with a prayer for the Norman dead, the army headed toward Hastings. Confounded by the shameless display, Orrin started that way as well when a servant approached him. "The bishop orders an audience, Lord Geirson."

He waited for the servant to move off before letting his wince show. *Now I learn the value of my debt.* Praying to God for fortitude, Orrin urged his horse onward and found the mounted bishop near the cliff edge. Garbed in a crimson, embroidered mantle, Odo was handing his high-pointed red mitre to an attending servant.

"Ah, Orrin. How are you this glorious morning?" He gestured for the servant to leave. "I noticed a most somber countenance on your face during the ceremony. Perhaps you're still recovering from the conflict..."

"Not so, lord bishop. I'm as fit as the next man. Last night's revelry is weighing on my head, nothing more."

"You may be as fit as the next man, but you're more English than most."

"Not today, my lord. There was no shortage of Englishmen at the ceremony."

"Ah yes. You noticed our prisoners then."

"I did, but I'm still confused as to their purpose."

"All will be explained in good time. Now, do you remember what I said to you on the battlefield?"

"That you weren't finished with me, lord bishop."

"Yes. That's good. Come with me. I will show you the task I have in mind. Your Englishness will no doubt help in its execution."

They rode to a near-by hilltop. As Orrin approached, his eyes bulged. The English clergyman sat in his cart and a plain coffin lay in the cargo hold.

"I know not whom William threw over the cliff," Odo said. "Godwinson, or what is left of him, is ready for his journey."

Orrin's mind pounded in confusion. "Why go through with that farce?"

"If there is one thing my brother believes, Orrin, it is this: fear is an effective weapon. By watching Godwinson's unshriven corpse fly out to sea, those English prisoners know the dire consequences of challenging us. As we speak, they're being set free. In a few days at most, all of Sussex will know what they witnessed.

"At the same time, his whore would not search for the corpse unless we swore to arrange a proper burial. To break that now may have repercussions in the near future. So, Godwinson will get his funeral, although it won't be an extravagant affair, to be sure."

"How can you be assured of that, lord? The clergyman will want everyone in England to know where the fallen king is buried."

"Because you will accompany the body."

Orrin recoiled. "What? Me? You must be mistaken."

"Questioning me is not good policy, Englishman. That is my only warning. You speak their tongue. You know their leaders. Besides, you won't travel alone. Urse and his conroi will go with you. Our scouts say the remnants of the English army are fled, so you should be safe."

Mind racing, Orrin could almost touch the opportunity before him. He could make an honorable end to his friendship with Harold by escorting him to his final resting place. At the same time, he could earn enough Norman trust to make a name for himself.

Odo led him to the despondent clergyman. "My lord bishop," the fat man said, "This is most egregious. When we negotiated last night, we agreed no escort would be necessary."

Odo leveled a tired, angry stare at his fellow man of

God. "I am being more lenient than my wont, Osgod, and acquiescing to more than I need to. We have changed our minds, and we swore you no oath. You will follow this man's orders or you'll suffer my wrath. Is that clear?"

The clergyman bowed his bulbous head.

"Be grateful we did not throw the usurper's actual corpse off the cliff...and yours along with it."

The bishop sent Osgod off to prepare for the journey. He then turned back to Orrin. "These are my instructions: First, ensure the body arrives at Waltham Holy Cross. That blithering oaf is a canon there, so he should know the way. Second, ensure no great gathering is called for the funeral. I want him put in the earth as fast as they can dig a hole. Lastly...enquire about Godwinson's scribe."

He did not risk asking why the scribe interested Odo so much, even though the look on the bishop's face made his skin crawl. "What should I do if I find him, lord bishop?"

After making sure no one was in earshot, Odo leaned in and spoke soft. "What I tell you now can never pass your lips again. Swear this to me and I will continue. Decline and this opportunity will slide through your fingers. I can assure you there won't be another."

Orrin didn't allow himself time to think. "I swear, my lord."

Odo nodded. "The usurper owned a book. My sources tell me the text has a crimson-dyed cover ornamented with a most splendid falcon medallion. This book is most precious to me. I must have it. With the usurper dead, the scribe should be willing to divulge its location. You said yourself that Godwinson stored many treasures at Waltham. It may be there."

"What does this text contain, Lord Odo?"

Odo's mouth curdled. "I asked the whore about it last night. She said the usurper worked on a book of falconry, but I know differently." He shook his head. "The book's location, not its contents, is your chief concern. Find where the book resides, and you will earn our undying trust."

Chapter 32: Aidan

As Rand reached the end of the forest canopy, he flung out his hand to signal a halt. "Aidan, come here." An odd edge filled his voice.

Moving Scramasax forward, Aidan asked, "Is something wrong?"

Rand pointed. Clouds had moved in and the mist-covered low lands spread out before them in dull greens, browns, yellows, and grays. From this vantage point above the rolling hills, Aidan could see the London road wind its way through the valley for several miles. Far down this distant view, he spied a caravan led by a large pull cart. "They're still too far away to tell."

"It's them."

Aidan squinted to get a better look and caught a glimpse of silver surrounding the cart. He settled back in his saddle, but continued to squint as the ramifications set in. "They've sent an escort..." Half thinking, he reached down and secured his saddle bag flap. The presence of Norman warriors changed everything. Lady Edith said nothing about this complication. How could he join Osgod if they held him hostage? "We'll have to return to the forest. Perhaps we could follow them at a distance, although I'm not sure if they're going to Waltham or not."

Rand made no reply. Instead, he regarded Aidan with blood-hungry eyes.

Sensing the warrior's passion, Scramasax began to stir. Aidan had to yank on the reins to stop him from charging then and there. "It's too dangerous. We're exhausted. If we lose, all of Lady Edith's sacrifice will be wasted and we'll be food for crows. Let's leave before they realize we're here. We'll find Wulfstan some other way."

Rand snatched Aidan's wrist in a rough grip. "Do not lecture me of sacrifice, boy. Those whoresons killed my king. They're holding Lady Edith prisoner. I won't skulk behind them like some scolded dog!" He threw Aidan's wrist away in disgust. "We'll either free her or die trying."

With the memory of the deer and the agonized cries filling his mind, Aidan spoke without thinking. "But what if she's not there? What if they've—"

The huscarl quieted him by drawing his sword and pointing it toward the caravan. "Then they'll find a pain Lucifer himself would quake from."

Chapter 33:
Edith

She woke to the sounds and smells of the sea. Before opening her eyes, she let the salty, spray-filled air carry her away. She saw herself aboard a lean, powerful vessel with a full white sail. In the distance, the gates of Heaven loomed and she felt a prick of excitement. Would Harold be waiting for her? Would the pain of the past day burn away like a morning mist? She breathed deep and opened her eyes to welcome her hard-earned afterlife.

A blurry face loomed above her. *Harold?* Reaching up, her fingers brushed the man's clean-shaven cheeks. She jolted back in anguish and shock.

"Your charms won't work on me, whore." Bishop Odo said. A sudden twinge hit her stomach, followed by searing pain. Edith yelled and curled up before another kick could land.

"Lord bishop," a new voice said. "The ship's ready to sail."

"No," Odo said. "It's not ready yet." He leaned down

to whisper in Edith's ear. "Take your last look at England, whore. You'll never see her again."

Shaking, Edith tried to get her bearings. She lay at the end of a dock. A small punt bounced in the waves below her and its moorings rubbed against the dock post. Not far out to sea, a large merchant vessel lay anchored. Fighting back a seizure of pain-induced nausea, she rolled to look toward the shore. Down the dock, sailors and soldiers loaded punts with crates, barrels, and chests. A town loomed in the distance, but Edith didn't recognize it.

"Now get up," the bishop said.

Agony wracked her body, but she knew inaction would draw more punishment. The moment her hands touched the spongy wood, a new sensation struck her right arm with lightning's intensity. She crumbled back down, her head and torso smacking the dock. She braced her right arm against her side as the memory of Odo's crushing grip streamed back. The pain and terror forced her to weep. "I can't. My arm. You broke my arm."

"Feeble woman."

Footsteps clunked and then four uncaring hands clenched her shoulders and hips, lifting her as if she was a sack of dirt. The pressure from the hand on her right shoulder sent searing bolts through Edith's entire body, causing her to cry out. Her legs shook and she would have fallen again had it not been for the hands. Her last semblance of strength came from the grimy monk's robe she still wore. Some of the blood caked into the fabric was Harold's.

She looked up and found Odo's impatient glare. "Why don't you just kill me," she asked between quiet sobs.

"Were it up to me, I would have thrown you to the

army as a victory prize. My brother, however, seeks to make a different sort of prize out of you."

Edith thought she was beyond fear, but Odo's face held a pleasure that made her heart catch fire. "What do you mean?"

"After being presented to the ducal court as proof of our conquest, you'll spend the rest of your days as a nun at the Abbaye aux Dames in Caen. The good sisters will mend your arm, calm your aching stomach, and teach you to repent for your lifetime of sin."

When they locked eyes this time, Edith could not hide her abhorrence. This response fueled Odo's gut-shaking cackle, but she turned her attention to the merchant ship floating in the harbor. She remembered William's haunting words just before she fell unconscious. *A fate worse than death.*

"From your face, Lady Edith, I can see my brother's sentence is...unappealing."

Edith could not stop her tears. "My children. Please. In the name of Christian mercy, let me return to my children."

"You should rejoice, Lady Edith. You daughters will soon be married to Normans. As for your sons, they'll soon be with their father."

Anger erupted from deep inside her bones. It coursed through her veins and overpowered the pain for a quick moment. She broke away from the sailors' grip long enough to spit in Odo's face. After a surprised, angry bellow, he lashed out and slapped her face with the back of his hand. The blow sent Edith reeling back into the arms of the sailors, who pushed her to the dock. The pain emitting from her arm threatened to throw her into unconsciousness again.

Odo's tepid breath fell on her ear once more. "You impetuous slut. I was going to offer you a respite so you could say farewell to your kin, but your actions have cost you that opportunity. Instead, I will make a different offer. Tell me where the usurper's scribe is holed up, and I'll put you on the punt. Refuse and the sea will welcome another corpse."

Pushed beyond her limit, Edith lost all fear. "You are nothing but a blustering monster, Odo. I will say nothing more about the scribe. Do your worst. I hope you enjoy robbing your brother of his proof."

The bishop growled and Edith braced herself for the end, but it never came.

"Take this Satan's spawn out of my sight!"

The hands lifted her again. This time, one of the sailors lifted her over his shoulder and descended the ladder to the punt. With each step, she thought of her sons rallying all of western England against these Norman curs. She thought of her daughters safe and warm by the hearth Harold built in Nazeing. And she thought of Aidan racing through the forest with Rand at his side. *If the Normans had caught them, the bishop wouldn't be asking me about him.* As the sailors paddled the punt toward the merchant ship, tears returned to Edith's eyes, but she refused to wail. Odo watched from the dock, and if he insisted on ripping her soul away, she would not give him the gratification of seeing the damage.

The big merchant ship set sail an hour after Edith boarded. Too weak to move from the stack of barrels and boxes where the sailors threw her, she watched as England's shores grew smaller.

By midday, they passed Dungeness and her land disappeared. Wider and deeper-hulled than a longship, the merchant vessel displayed a massive striped sail that caught the wind in full. Looking over the rail, Edith saw the ship had no escort. *Why should there be an escort? The Normans now own both sides of the channel.* The thought made her arm ache even more.

All around her, crewmen managed lines and cargo. Most of them ignored her, while some sniggered as they passed. Filled with wariness, her instincts proved correct after they reached open water. The captain, a white-haired and black-toothed warrior, stepped before her. He looked like an old, grizzled pig as he pointed to his chest. "Fulk D'Amber." He then pointed to Edith, smiled, and undid his belt.

"No!" She tried to scramble atop a stack of wood boxes, but Fulk grabbed the hem of the monk's habit and yanked. She crashed to the deck, shuddering in pain. A huge weight impacted her back as Fulk fell on top of her. His manhood rose as he licked the back of her neck, pulled the monk's habit up, and ripped off Edith's undergarment.

Her strength failed and she began to weep. "Please God!"

As she braced for the defilement, an urgent cry rose up from the ship's starboard side. The captain paused, and then asked a question in the Norman tongue. Edith turned her head and saw all the crew watching and pointing over the gunwale. Many of them quaked in fear. After a frustrated grunt, the captain rose and strode toward the crew. He bellowed instructions and the other men scurried to follow.

Edith struggled to her feet and looked over the rail.

God be praised! A fleet of longships closed in fast. The lead ship cut through the water like a raptor slices through the air. Yet it wasn't the ship's speed or blazing sail that made Edith's heart leap. It was the dragon carving on the prow. *The Dragon of Wessex* was descending on the merchant ship at the head of an English fleet.

It didn't take long before the first grappling hook crashed onto the merchant ship's rail. "Pull!" Edith heard some blessed Englishman shout. She couldn't revel for long, for Fulk stormed to her and snared her by the throat. A dozen more grappling hooks caught the merchant ship. The Norman crew drew their swords. Edith and Fulk stood at the ship's center, next to the mast. He held a knife to her neck and turned in a slow circle, showing all he was prepared to kill. After what had befallen Edith, her life was of little concern. Inside, she glowed in the knowledge that this Norman monster would not long outlive her.

After heartbeats of dead quiet, the English stormed. Steel rang against steel as men yelled, ran, and died. Edith watched where she could. A few of the men who sniggered at her earlier lay writhing on the deck in pools of blood.

The fight lasted just a little while, and then the English surrounded Fulk. He stayed silent, but kept the knife at Edith's throat as he turned in circles.

"If he kills me," she said in her calmest voice, "hang his entrails from *The Dragon's* mouth."

The English warriors erupted in a cheer. She felt Fulk's arm muscles constrict. Edith said a final prayer, but the sharp metal never reached her skin. Looking up, she saw a gray-gloved hand locking Fulk's arm from behind. Englishmen pulled Edith out of harm's way as others descended on the quivering Norman leader. She heard him plead, but the words suddenly gave way to shrieks as swords punctured his flesh from all angles. Edith watched with leaden eyes as the final cut severed head from body. Fulk's still-shocked face hit the deck with a *thunk*.

A young, confident voice filled the air. "That man had no idea how to treat a queen."

Edith's jaw dropped. She stumbled forward in disbelief. "Godwine!"

She fell into her son's arms, wary that she may wake up in the hands of the Normans at any moment. His warm embrace and wet tears never disappeared and Edith realized God had finally heard her.

The Confession

July 1, 1065

The earl: With the words of Odo and Egenulf haunting my every step, I snuck back to my cell. If I tried to run or got caught wandering the palace, my men would have paid with their lives. I could not have their deaths on my head, not after the terrible trap I stepped into. The roosters welcomed the day just moments after I slipped into my pallet and my guards stumbled back into consciousness.

The bishop: I think I understand the depth of your madness. This is a harrowing predicament.

The earl: I'm sorry old friend, but the true reason still slithers inside me. The web entangling me is fearsome. My enemies are formidable beyond measure. But nothing is as terrible as the path to victory.

The bishop: The solution is the burden that attacks you? What path could be so daunting?

The earl: One I'm scared to even utter, but it must be performed for England to survive...

Chapter 34: Orrin

An autumn wind had begun to howl across the low lands and angry clouds churned across the afternoon sky as the caravan neared the Andredsweald. As Orrin rode, he looked up the steep incline to the forest entrance. The road cut a hole in the thicket of trees, forming the yawning mouth of some green and brown demon. He swore under his breath as his uneasy feeling returned.

"You said you came to the battle via this road?" On any other day, he would never torture himself by engaging this plump clergyman in conversation. Today, he had little choice. Urse and his men compared battle triumphs all morning. Orrin neither cared about nor could compete with their stories. Riding in silence was also out of the question, for too many emotions swirled within him.

"I did, my lord," Osgod said. Every word dripped with self-importance. "I'm afraid my slow-pulling pack horse elongated my journey. I arrived just moments before the battle began. Of course, my encounter with the Jezebel Lady Edith delayed me as well."

Another emotion pounded in Orrin's chest at the mention of her name. She was too beautiful, too strong, for the fate that befell her. "You knew her?"

"Oh yes. Her manor sits not far away from Waltham. God is good to free me of her. My heart still throbs from the fright she gave me after she found the usurper's corpse."

Orrin doubted Osgod called Harold "the usurper" yesterday. But the sacristan piqued his interest. "You saw her die?"

Osgod ruffled his bushy eyebrows. "That daughter of sin invited the Devil into her flesh and, using his evil strength, attempted to cut good Duke William through with a concealed knife. My eyes could not believe the speed with which she struck. My old bones couldn't react fast enough, but Bishop Odo, blessed with the vigilance of a hawk, thwarted the she-devil. The last I saw, ten men had carried her off to send her back to her fiery pit."

Orrin looked deep into Osgod's round face and saw no hint of deception. It made more sense that a woman with Edith's strength would fight to the end. Still, the damning images of Osgod's story made Orrin's chest ache even more.

The caravan crested the incline and plunged into the dense forest. Orrin used the terrain change to break away from this sickening lickspittle. "Men," he called to the fifteen other chevaliers surrounding the cart, "keep your guard constant. The English retreated to these woods after the battle. Some may still lurk within."

As they readied for the arduous trek, Orrin glanced back to Osgod. The sacristan darted his eyes all over the forest. His posture had grown rigid and he gripped his reins so hard his hands turned red.

"Ease your worry clergyman. No harm will befall us. With no leader to unite them, the remnants of Harold's army have fled far away already. The remaining packs won't have the courage to threaten us."

Osgod did not ease. "And what, pray tell, might happen if one such pack finds its courage?"

Orrin had asked himself the same question before setting off. The prospect of fighting their way through the forest was grim. Their best hope for reaching Waltham lay in a different course of action.

"I can talk to them. This is no foraging expedition. We aren't raiding homes or raping women. We're carrying out a Christian service for the dead English king. If anyone doubts me, I have the proof in the back of the cart."

Osgod regarded him with a look of sheer incredulity. "Your tactics are most unique, Lord Geirson. I would have thought the Norman answer to any English challenge would be a barrage of swords, not a shower of Christian brotherhood."

As the caravan delved farther into the wood, a light, misting rain began to fall. Orrin wrapped his cleaned red cloak around his shoulders. "You're right. Most Normans would choose to kill their way into the duke's good graces," he gestured toward Urse. "But I am not Norman. If I can keep our swords sheathed, I will. There are other ways to win favor."

"What do you mean by other ways, my lord? If the duke aims for the throne in Westminster, he'll still have to fight to get it. Earl Edwin of Mercia and his brother, Earl Morcar of Northumbria lead all the power of the north country. True, the usurper had to save their hides from

Tostig and the Norwegians, but the earls are still powerful, and moreover, unconquered."

Orrin did not rise to Osgod's bait. His quest to find the scribe needed to be kept secret. If others knew, they may start their own search and, God forbid, find him first. "I've met Edwin and Morcar. Eels have stronger spines. Duke William loses little sleep over them, I promise you."

Osgod began to reply, but Orrin quieted him with a raised hand. A sharp, narrow bend had appeared down the muddy, leaf-covered track. "Walter, Roger," he called out. The two chevaliers came to attention. "Ride ahead and make sure the road's clear on the other side."

As they spurred their horses forward, Orrin motioned for Osgod to continue. The bloated fish of a man looked perturbed that he had been interrupted. "The earls may not be fierce, but their Mercians and Northumbrians most assuredly are, my lord. The blessed King Edward feared these unbridled clans so much he never journeyed much farther north than London."

As Osgod prattled on about the ferocious north men, Walter and Roger disappeared around the bend. Orrin signaled for the caravan to halt. He preferred not to move ahead until he knew what lay on the other side. "The duke will deal with the north men in good time. The throne sits in London, not York. Tell me, do you think the Witan will name the young Atheling as king now?"

With Harold dead, the young Edgar stood next in line for succession thanks to his kinship to old King Edward. Harold and Edith did have sons, Orrin remembered, but they did not have the Witan's support, in part because they were products of a handfast marriage. Edgar the Atheling, however, was a pliable wisp of a lad with royal, church-sanctified blood.

"No doubt, my lord," Osgod said as he released the reins and rubbed his hands. "Many in the Witan, including Edwin and Morcar, thought young Edgar should have succeeded King Edward earlier this year. The usurper, however, won the Witan's support by arguing that England needed a war commander as king, not an untested boy. The invasions proved him right in many ways, and wrong in many others."

Walter and Roger had not returned, nor did Orrin hear their horses. Urse noticed their delay as well. "Too long," the warrior said, drawing his sword.

"I'll take ten men ahead of the cart," Orrin said. "You guard the rear with the rest. Do not attack until my order. Is that clear?"

"Clear," he said, frowning.

Orrin turned to Osgod. The sacristan's face held an unnatural paleness. "Follow my pacing. If a fight does ensue, be sure to move the cart over so my rear guard can pass." The clergyman nodded and strangled his reins once more.

Surrounded by ten mounted warriors, Orrin signaled for the caravan to move forward at a walk. As they advanced, he raised his voice loud and clear. "Peace! We ride in peace! Hold your weapons for the mercy of King Harold's soul!" He continued his chant as they reached the bend. He hoped an answer lay on the other side. Maybe Walter and Roger continued down the road. Maybe the English would hear him. Maybe —

Halfway around the bend, a loud crack followed a quick rustle of leaves. Orrin snapped his head to the sound. He saw Osgod shaking the reins with all the power in his fat body, but the cart sat square in the road. He realized in a flash their attackers were either too stupid to understand him or did not care. "Urse, they've blocked the road with the cart," he said in Norman. "Dismount and come to me. Quickly!"

Orrin breathed hard as he gripped his wolf-bone hilt. The forest was quiet save for pattering of rain, the nervous bristle of horses, and the jingling of armor. He swiveled his head, yet he saw no one down the road and the thicket on both sides held nothing but brush.

Then, Orrin heard the terrible word: "Loose!"

"Shields!" he cried as javelins rained down from above. Orrin's horse screamed in pain, as did men and mounts all around. Bucking in agony, his horse threw him from the saddle. He crashed to the soft ground, landing on his back. Breath flew from his stomach and his helmet slid over his eyes. Amidst the screams and screeches, Orrin heard the word "Attack." In a wave of excruciation, he pushed his helmet up and rose. Six Normans lay dead and just two managed to stay horsed. The stink of fresh entrails and shit floated in the air as the road lay covered in horse and human corpses. Urse and the remaining men had formed a defensive circle at the head of the abandoned cart. Just as he assessed the damage, a chevalier screamed and toppled from his horse with a spear sticking from his back.

"To me!" Orrin cried as he pushed himself up. Every joint screamed in pain. "Rally to me!" Urse whipped his head around and signaled for his men to advance. They surrounded him and crouched with their weapons at the ready. His head cleared and battle rage took full hold. He scanned the tree tops, the source of the javelin attack. "Show yourselves! Quit your hiding and fight like men!"

Four opponents answered his challenge. They appeared far down the road, armed with swords, shields, and sick smiles. From their leather tunics and dirt-covered faces, Orrin guessed they were well-trained fyrdsmen, most likely a band of hunters and trappers. The last mounted chevalier saw them as well and charged in a fury.

"No!" Orrin yelled, but the man didn't hear him as he raced down the road with his spear couched under his arm. The Englishmen held their ground with unreal confidence. As the chevalier crossed a line of piled leaves across the road, his horse's front hooves fell into the covered ditch with a stomach-twisting SNAP! The Norman flew from his saddle and crashed down at the English fighters' feet. They fell on him like wolves.

"Steady," Orrin said to the remaining conroi and to himself. "Stay calm."

Four more Englishmen joined the four in the road. Is that all of them? He glared at his attackers. The Normans were outnumbered by one. Before his mind could produce another thought, the English charged.

"Form a line! Make short work of them!" These fyrdsmen had fought well to this point, but the charge would be their undoing. Even without their mounts, seven Norman chevaliers could overwhelm twice their number.

The Normans spread across the road with Orrin and Urse at the center. "FOR NORMANDY!" Urse bellowed and led the men forward at a run. The two lines crashed together. Orrin's first attacker poked at his torso in a weak thrust. He knocked the rusty blade aside with his shield and lunged forward with his own sword. Steel sliced through leather, flesh, and bone. The man gargled a prayer through bloody lips and flopped to the ground. Orrin twisted his sword from his opponent's stomach just in time to block another attack. All around him steel rang against steel in an eruption of whirling limbs. Urse cleaved through an opponent's sword with a two handed thrust, and then lopped his head off with a clean swipe. Just one Norman had fallen, compared to four fyrdsmen. He and his conroi advanced on their remaining enemies. Just as he began to feel safe, he heard footfalls behind him.

Terror seized his soul even as he wheeled around. He had broken his defensive circle before making sure all the enemies had shown themselves. Now eight more warriors charged at their unprotected backs, led by an axe-wielding huscarl.

"Urse!" he called. "Behind you!"

Orrin, Urse, and another warrior turned to face the new threat, leaving three Normans to fight the first attackers. His mind flashed to Hesilia, and he prayed that God would protect her after his death.

The fight dissipated into a flurry of death blows. As he fought off two attackers, Orrin heard swords bite into mail, followed by anguished Norman cries. He tried to look and see who fell, but spear thrusts flew at his torso, legs, and head. Back-pedaling away from the onslaught, he tripped over a dead limb. He stumbled and cried out as a spear point rammed into his shoulder. Panic overtook his warrior training. He imagined his flesh slicing from his bones and lost control of his bowels. Life became superior to honor. He flung his sword to the ground and clasped his hands before his chest. "I yield!"

The pitiful words stayed his attackers' blows. Recognizing Orrin's lost nerve, they raced off to finish the last Norman standing: Urse.

The surrounded Norman resembled a baited bear. Releasing a guttural roar, he knocked away strike after strike. "Rise Geirson! Rise and fight!"

Orrin's strength failed. All he could do is watch. Urse continued to bat away blades and retreat until the huscarl descended upon him. "GET UP!" Urse yelled as he lunged at the English leader. The huscarl deflected the blow with his shield, knocking the sword from Urse's exhausted hand. He then hoisted his axe high in the air for the killing blow.

"Stop in the name of God!" The voice froze the combatants. Still on the ground, Orrin followed the voice to its issuer. Osgod stood in front of the cart, caked in mud. He held a cross in his outstretched hand and his eyes dared anyone to challenge him.

The huscarl lowered his axe, but never took his eyes off Urse, who lay face down on the forest floor. "They killed Lady Edith," he said through heavy breaths, "or she'd be with them."

"I know, my son, but this is folly."

"What folly, father?" One of the fyrdsmen asked. "If they had us surrounded, we'd see no mercy."

Orrin tried to speak, but his disorientation combined with humiliation to silence him.

"You are no doubt right, my son, but this is a folly of a different sort." He walked to the huscarl, who watched Urse like a dog regards a haunch of roasted meat. "These men have value. That one," he said, pointing at Orrin, "is privy to Duke William's council. And this tamed pig is his second in command. Kill them and you gain nothing. Keep them hostage, and you stand to gain ransom...and information."

The huscarl's mouth twitched. He never tore his gaze from Urse, but his breathing burdened his whole body. The field returned to silence as every eye watched what he would do.

"RAHHHH!" In a flash, his axe swung. Osgod cried out and Orrin closed his eyes. Yet instead of the death sound he expected, he heard a loud CLACK! Opening his eyes, he caught a glimpse of three men dragging a groaning Urse toward the cart.

The huscarl stalked toward him. "Don't worry, m'lord," he said, hate filling every word. "We didn't forget 'bout you."

Before he could react in any way, a hand ripped his helmet off. Then, the butt of the huscarl's axe slammed into his head, turning the misty forest black.

A sharp jostle shattered Orrin's sleep. Blinking his eyes open, he saw trees limbs pass by in rapid succession. He heard the rhythmic creaking of a rolling cart combine with steady rainfall. Shooting pain pulsed down his shoulder and thick cords of rope wrapped around him. When the memories flooded back, he cried out. His captors must have thrown him in the cart after he blacked out. He also knew who lay next to him in the casket.

Thirst attacked his throat, mouth, and stomach. "Water," he said in a cracked, defeated voice.

A face loomed over him. "Here," a blond, brown-eyed adolescent said. "Take some from my water skin."

Orrin's pulse thumped in his wrists and chest, even as the cold water poured down his throat. I've seen him before.

"Careful now. Don't take too much or you'll choke."

The scribe! Dear God, why is the scribe traveling with these butchers? The realization, not the water intake, made Orrin choke in violent coughs. Each convulsion caused eruptions of pain in his shoulder.

The sound of horse's hooves ushered in another voice.

"Don't waste good water on this snake, Aidan. He's not worth the shit in his breeches."

"He woke when the cart hit a bump," the boy said. "I didn't know what to do."

"Woke up, did he? Well, there's a quick answer to that."

A sharp thud impacted his temple. The surge raced from shock, to searing pain, to a return to darkness. Orrin had time for just one thought: Aidan. His name is Aidan.

Chapter 35: Aidan

October 16, 1066

The campfire roared once more as the warrior band drifted off to sleep. Aidan tried to close his eyes, but nerves wouldn't let him. Both the smell of burning logs and the visions of the ambush surrounded him. Having watched Rand's attack from behind a thick maple tree, he had witnessed merciless killing right before his eyes. Maybe it was the proximity to the clash or the deranged glee shining in Rand's eyes, but somehow this fight had shaken him almost as much as the Norman victory.

Osgod's presence added to Aidan's unease, for certs. The clergyman's eyes seemed to dart everywhere at once. A few times, Aidan caught him glancing toward Scramasax as they set up camp. Even as Waltham's canon lay snoring next to his cart, Aidan could not chase away the distrust.

Unable to take any more, he rose, cleaned off his cloak,

and headed toward the horses. From now until they reached Waltham at least, Aidan would sleep next to the saddlebags. If anyone asked why, he would tell them the truth; he was sick of sleeping near fires.

All the fighters' mounts had let their heads droop or had found a flat patch to lie on, but Scramasax stood tall with pointed ears. As Aidan dragged his foot across the leafy floor, the stallion offered a docile whinny in greeting. "You see," he said, reaching up to rub Scramasax's muzzle. "We're fast friends already."

In response, the horse brayed and side-stepped away from his tether tree, pulling the rope almost taut. "What's got you on—" He saw the flames glinting in Scramasax's black eye and felt the horse's neck muscles strain. "Oh. Believe me, I don't like it either. We'll find a more comfortable resting place in a moment."

He walked to the saddle and unbound the bag straps. King Harold's book still lay nestled inside the soft leather. He ran his hand over the jagged parchment edges and felt an upwelling of strength. With the unknowing help of this warrior band, he and Scramasax at least stood a chance to get the book to safety.

After securing the saddlebag, Aidan led the horse down the path. The farther they walked from the fire, the more the horse and Aidan relaxed. The half moon lit the forest, and as Aidan's eyes adjusted the trees and leaves began to glow in an ethereal blue.

"Boy. Aidan. Where do you think you're going?"

His head snapped around to the source of the desperate whispers. Down a break-off from the main path, Orrin Geirson stood against a thick oak tree, enwrapped in rope from hip to neck line.

"It's none of your concern." Aidan walked Scramasax farther down the path.

"Aidan, I beg you. Fetch me a drink. In the name of Christian charity. Please. My throat's scorched."

Pursing his lips, he pushed a seething breath through his nose. The phrase "Christian charity" echoed in his head. After a long pause, he yanked a half-filled water skin from the bundle behind the pommel. "Stay here," he whispered to Scramasax. "I'll be but a moment."

"Thank you Aidan," the traitor said. "Dear God thank you."

When he got near, a whole new wave of irritation swept through. The prisoner's arms were locked underneath the chords of rope, disabling him from lifting the water skin. "Open your mouth," Aidan said, not bothering to hide his disgust.

The traitor did as ordered. Aidan lifted the skin and poured a stream down.

"That's better," Orrin said after choking away the last drips. "Thank you. I'll repay your kindness. When William takes the throne, find me. I'll protect you."

Aidan made no response. The thought was too terrible to contemplate and safe harbor with a traitor was not safe at all. He turned and started to walk away.

"I remember you, Aidan. Do you remember the day at Fritton?"

Stopping in mid-stride, Aidan said, "It was the day you broke your faith with the king. I'll never forget that."

The bound prisoner lowered his head. "So it was. I've revisited that day a thousand times...and made the same choice each time. They had my wife, Aidan. Even Harold would've understood that."

The boy swallowed hard as unbidden images filled his

mind: the red night; Ebba's intertwined fingers and nervous giggles; the smell of spring wildflowers and the sounds of the rushing stream; and the tenderness of her lips combined with the slight smell of clove. *What would I do to protect her?* Glancing through the trees to the camp, he decided to stay for just a few more moments. "Are...Are you willing to die so she can live?"

"If it comes to that, I'll go gladly. My life is a small price compared to my family. I don't expect you to understand, boy. You're bound for a cloister, no doubt, not a marriage bed."

Aidan lowered his head. Orrin just saw him as a monastic scribe, and a broken one at that. Resentment, shame, and to Aidan's surprise, a modicum of pride welled inside. "Monastic life's been closed to me. I can marry if I wish."

"What? You look more pure than an angel. What happened?"

Aidan studied the leafy ground. "I...I made a mistake." With his face shielded from the prisoner, he winced.

Orrin stifled a chuckle. "It seems I was wrong about your purity, boy. I've felt that sheepishness more times than I can count. What's her name?"

Unable to restrain himself, he said, "Ebba." The utterance jolted his body more than jumping into a cold lake ever could. The tips of his fingers and toes prickled.

"A pretty name. Since your chosen life is denied to you, will you pursue her instead?"

Aidan pondered this forbidden future for a heartbeat: a house, a hearth, children running and laughing and Ebba; Ebba stood at the center of it all. But that future was closed to him just as much as monastic life. His lone path lay with the book.

"You look like you've seen a spirit, boy."

"I...I'm not sure what I'll do," he said, shaking his head and frowning. "Why do you care anyway? Can't you realize your life is over? Rand won't let you breathe a moment longer than necessary. Your traitor's reasons will be lost on him."

"True enough, but his blade has been stayed once. I daresay it will be again. It may mean nothing to him, but Osgod fears a Norman reprisal with all his soul. One way or another, the clergyman will secure my release."

"And what then? Will you return to your family?"

"After I'm freed, I will finish my mission."

A sudden chill filled Aidan's bones. "What mission?"

"I'm looking for a book Harold once owned. It has a gold falcon affixed to the cover. Do you know of it?"

Air rushing from his lungs, Aidan said, "No...no. I've never seen the like."

The traitor's eyes narrowed. "Are you sure? Think boy. There's no use protecting it now with Harold dead. Just tell me where it is. London? Winchester? Waltham?"

Aidan raised his voice. "I said I don't know. I wrote messages and charters for the king, nothing more. Why are you so interested in this book anyway?"

Orrin still wore his reticent gaze. "It's real, Aidan. We both know it. And I'll find it one way or another. I have to. My wife and child's welfare depend on it."

"Well I can't help you. Now, I should retur—"

A snapping twig turned Aidan's head. Rand appeared behind him. The bedraggled warrior's beard framed his deep scowl. "You can't help him do what? Was the traitor begging for escape?" The warrior paused at Aidan's shoulder and unsheathed a dagger. "He should know better." In three fast steps, Rand held the blade at Orrin's throat.

"You swore you wouldn't try to run. Looks like you have one more lie to atone for."

To his credit, Orrin didn't panic. "I don't need to escape, Rand. I'm under Osgod's protection. The boy just gave me a drink of water. Tell him, Aidan."

He knew the truth. He also knew what Rand would do if he stayed quiet. Aidan had no idea why Orrin wanted the book, but Rand could solve the problem with a quick stroke.

The first hints of desperation crept into Orrin's voice. "Aidan? Speak up boy."

"Quiet now, Orrin," Rand said, pressing the dagger flat onto the prisoner's skin. "Don't go wakin the other men. This is between us."

"Aidan! For the love of God, tell him I wasn't trying to escape."

His tongue froze and his hands began to shake. Bishop Wulfstan's voice bellowed for him to tell the truth. Lady Edith begged him to let Rand's blade fly. Visions of Orrin's wife and son flickered between memories of King Harold, Ebba, and Worcester.

Rand's lips curled into a wide, thick-lipped smile. "Looks like your bribes scared the boy stiff."

"I didn't *bribe* him! Aidan, why are you just standing there? Call off this mad dog!"

An invisible force made Aidan step forward. "I couldn't sleep because of the fire. When I came this way, he...he asked for a drink of water. And then..."

"And then what boy?" Rand's eyes glowed with hunger. "He offered protection, didn't he? He said the Normans wouldn't hurt you if you helped set him free."

The boy's heart cringed at the opportunity. Orrin had offered him safe harbor. All he had to do was say "yes."

Orrin grew frantic and struggled in his bonds. "Aidan, think of my family. Think of Ebba! What would they think? For the love of all you hold dear boy, tell this man the truth!"

Rand tilted his head as he loomed over Orrin. "One more moment of silence boy, and it's his death warrant."

Ebba's voice fought through the myriad of visions stalling Aidan's mind. "There's goodness inside you, Aidan. Don't ever let it go."

Rand raised the dagger high in the air.

The scribe managed a feeble whisper. "He asked for a drink, nothing more."

The warrior turned his unblinking stare onto Aidan. "*What?*"

"He...he wasn't trying to escape. He broke no agreement."

Rand shook with anger. "I should kill him anyway."

Aidan stepped forward again, praying for Rand to act on his hatred. Just then, however, a cry came from the camp. "What the Devil is going on out there?"

Rand pulled the dagger from Orrin's throat. "Here comes your savior," he said before hocking a glob of spit onto the ground.

Osgod waddled down the path. "The prisoner is under God's protection. *He* is not *yours* to kill."

As the fat clergyman blustered on, Aidan glanced back to Orrin. The friendliness had fled the traitor's face as he stared back.

October 18, 1066
Orrin's head swung back and forth. "You're making a terrible mistake, Osgod."

"I'll not be upbraided by a Norman cur," the sacristan adjusted his voluminous seat atop the cart's bench. "Nor will I curb the dignity of our fallen king just because your duke has asked me to."

As the rain abated and the chilled air of winter took its place, Aidan listened to the argument as he rode Scramasax next to the cart. He wished he could have ignored them, but that would have left him alone with his thoughts and with the growing mortification smell emitting from the casket. Patting his horse's neck, he asked for patience, both from Scramasax and himself. They had crossed out of the Andredsweald yesterday afternoon and now rode through the flat river lands of the Thames estuary. The journey would be over by nightfall.

"Soon enough, he *will* be king," Orrin countered. "And then what'll you do? William of Normandy won't care one fig about your church if it contains a shrine to Harold Godwinson. Do you want its destruction weighing on your conscience the rest of your life?"

"Blasphemy! Hold your tongue you devilish nag, or I'll let these men cut it out!"

Aidan wished with all his heart Osgod would make good on his threat. Never before had he wished for someone's death, but Orrin's quest for the book had to be stopped. Unfortunately, Osgod protected Orrin like the prisoner was made of gold, and they both watched Aidan constantly.

The other Norman chevalier, Urse, lay in brooding silence on the other side of the casket. He had not said a word since waking yesterday morning. After attempting to speak in his Norman tongue, a blow from Wynchell's staff silenced him soon enough. Orrin had felt the same justice many times as well, but didn't stop talking. His current argument with Osgod seemed to entertain the miller, so the staff lay dormant for the time being.

The sacristan loosed an irritated sigh and jostled his reins. "King Harold's benefaction helped turn Waltham Holy Cross into an ever-lasting tribute to the Almighty. After a ceremony worthy of England's greatest hero," he paused to glance at his English escort, "he'll be laid to rest in his rightful place, a beautiful shrine in our sanctuary. As for your duke, I'm sure our English nobles will rally around King Harold's shrine and chase the bastard from our shores before he ever gets near Waltham."

As Orrin fumed and Osgod bristled, Aidan rode in contemplative silence. He didn't share Osgod's faith in the English nobles, but the sacristan's view on King Harold's burial made sense. A stately ceremony would offer a proper tribute. It also would attract important people from far and wide, including Bishop Wulfstan. *If Lady Edith were here, she'd agree with Osgod too.*

At noon, the walled city of London appeared in the distance. Wurt, a stick of a boy who chose army life over his career as a cutpurse on London streets, whooped with joy. "Ha ha! Never thought I'd say it, but that's a sight to warm the heart!"

"Will we stop in London before heading to Waltham?" Aidan asked. The church lay another ten miles north. Aidan's whole body ached, Scramasax needed rest, and a little delay might offer an opportunity to pursue his solution for hiding the book. All he needed was a needle, some thread, and enough privacy to sew a hidden pocket into his cloak.

"No." Osgod and Rand said in unison.

The clergyman spoke first. "I dare not take the king's body too close. The city elders will no doubt wish to hold the funeral at Westminster. I have not undergone this hardship to have my prize snatched from me now."

Disgust filled Rand's face. The look alone cowed the fat clergyman, who retreated into his shoulders and rubbed the crucifix pendant dangling around his neck.

The huscarl looked back to the city. "You men fought well...did your king proud. But we promised Lady Edith we'd see Aidan and the casket safe to Waltham. She died so this could happen. We won't stop 'til it's done."

Aidan stared at the city as well, masking his dread with a slow nod. Rand was right. No amount of personal cowardice could defeat the courage of Lady Edith's sacrifice. To delay now would do her a disservice.

In the end, no one left the caravan. They passed the eastern side of London and forded the Thames at Barking. Dusk had crept into the gray sky when Waltham appeared before them. All the men rejoiced at the sight, except Aidan.

Waltham displayed its wealth with pride. Sturdy wooden houses with fresh-thatched roofs lined straight, wide streets. As the caravan proceeded toward the church, townsfolk emerged with wary looks on their faces. Osgod told them to return to their suppers, but none listened and Aidan couldn't blame them. The cart escort was a spectacle to behold; blood and mud-caked men rode strange horses alongside a cart carrying two foreign hostages and a casket. By the time the church tower rose before them, a following of dozens had formed. Aidan watched as they whispered, pointed, and grumbled at Orrin and Urse. There was little doubt these townsfolk had heard of King Harold's defeat. If they didn't get the Normans out of sight fast, a riot could break out.

"Come along," Osgod said, disembarking from the cart

with a graceless thud. "I need six men to carry the casket inside. The rest of you take our captives to the storage shed behind the church. I'll deal with them in good time."

Rand, Wynchell, Wurt, and three others lifted the casket from the cart in silence. If they were affected by the smell, they had the grace to hide it. Darkness had risen, and the townsfolk lit candles and torches as they watched the makeshift procession. Sniffles and small cries lofted into the night air as people began to realize who had come to his final home. Aidan followed the casket bearers, whispering a prayer for King Harold's eternal soul.

"This way." Osgod's voice sounded urgent and out of breath as he climbed the stone stairs to the double oak door entrance. He gripped the bronze handles and pulled them wide open. A cascade of white light shined out.

"Curious," Osgod said as he ushered the casket bearers inside. "One of the other canons must have run ahead and prepared the church. Good, good. Place the casket down quickly."

Aidan entered the church. He had never seen such beauty. Thousands of bees wax candles illuminated the empty nave. The raised sanctuary dais spanned almost the width of the building. Covered by fine white cloth with embroidered gold borders, the table presented golden chalices; jewel-encrusted reliquary boxes; an open, illuminated bible; and a rich mahogany staff topped with a gleaming silver cross. The Holy Rood – the life-size crucifix that supposedly bowed its head to the king – loomed like a giant silver star in the back of the sanctuary. Smells of incense and fresh flowers emanated from the clean floor rushes. Tapestries of red and gold lined the stone walls. For a moment, this beauty allowed Aidan to escape the journey's pain and his fear of the future.

The astonishing scene even breached the proud fyrds-men. After lying King Harold down, Wurt wiped tears from his eyes. Wynchell blinked and shook his head in disbelief. Rand, however, remained stoic.

Aidan stepped to him. "Thank you...For everything."

"The pain won't cease, lad," he said, transfixed by the candles glowing before him. "I thought laying him to rest would help, but it hasn't."

Aidan began to reply, but Osgod cut him off. Stepping to the doors, he gestured for everyone to leave. "Well and done. Your service is performed. Now, if you don't mind, preparations need to be made. Everyone out now. I'll instruct the cooks to slaughter an extra sheep for supper. You too boy. Away with you."

Too exhausted to resist, Aidan took a last look at the scene and began to exit when a voice boomed from the choir. "The boy stays. If anyone should leave, it's you, Osgod Knoppe."

Aidan froze in the doorway. Even with his back to the sanctuary, he recognized the speaker.

"Bishop Wulfstan?" Osgod's voice held no semblance of Christian fellowship. "What are you doing here?"

"I was in route to London when I heard of Harold's defeat. It is no secret he wished to be buried at Waltham."

"Do you make a habit of hiding in choirs?"

Aidan remained stuck in the doorway. He'd never heard anyone speak to the bishop with such disrespect.

"I make a habit of prayer, you greedy miscreant. Your lecherous voice disturbed my vigil. And now I see that you've made a most interesting acquaintance. Aidan, turn around and greet your bishop properly. I did not raise you to be a statue."

Aidan could hardly breathe, but obedience won out.

He turned and found Wulfstan standing behind the sanctuary table. His shoulder-length gray hair and wiry beard now showed streaks of white. His blue eyes could still level a mountain and his erect posture radiated authority. Holding his staff and wearing an immaculate scapular of natural wool, he portrayed the picture of God's shepherd on earth glaring at two troublesome sheep. "Lord father," Aidan said as he fell to a bended knee, shaking all the while.

Osgod shook out of anger, not fear. "Your bishop's staff may hold sway elsewhere, Wulfstan, but not here. You'd do well to remember —"

"I remember well, you vile locust!" Wulfstan vaulted the altar and strode toward a recoiling Osgod, pointing a tense, straight finger. "I remember how you clung to Harold's cloak hem, begging for gifts as a child begs for honey." Wulfstan stopped with his finger almost touching Osgod's flared nose. Aidan lowered his head and closed his eyes. "You're lucky your fellow canons have more honor in their hearts and sense in their heads. They've agreed to cede Harold's burial arrangements to me, which means your presence here is no longer necessary. Now be gone!"

Aidan heard Osgod's gasps, followed by footfalls of leather sandals. "I will return once I've convinced my brothers of their madness," he said from a greater distance than where he stood before. "You had best be gone by then, you condescending crone. You and your crippled mouse."

Still on bended knee, Aidan clasped his hands together and pressed them against his chest. He heard Wulfstan take a few steps. *Please spare me God!* But then, the most unexpected sound Aidan could have imagined reached his ears. The shock stayed his fear for a moment, allowing him to glance toward the source. Wulfstan stood at the foot of Harold's casket, weeping.

"What have I done?" The bishop said, shaking his head and closing his pained eyes. "Dear God, this is all my fault." He crouched down and placed his hands on top of the casket. His staff clattered on the floor. "Forgive me, dear friend. Please forgive me."

Aidan watched, blinking away astonishment. A wave of sympathy doused his fear. Without thinking, Aidan rose and crossed the nave. He placed a caring hand on the crouched bishop's back and let his own tears flow.

They remained there for some time. At long last, the bishop rose and engulfed Aidan in a fierce embrace. "I thought you dead, boy. Gone from this world without hearing my plea for forgiveness." Aidan's heart fluttered at the words. He returned the embrace and buried his wet face in the bishop's robe. The familiar smells of must and lavender beckoned memories of home.

Holding Aidan by the shoulders, Wulfstan said, "Let's rest those ghosts for now. How on God's earth did you manage to travel here with Harold's body? From what I gathered, the decimation was absolute."

The question sent a flare of realization through his mind. "I have something for you that will help explain my story. I'll be but a moment." Gesturing for Wulfstan to stand still, Aidan turned and dragged his foot out of the church. His emotions still ran hot after the reconciliation. It felt like an anvil had been lifted from his shoulders.

He retrieved the book from his saddlebag and hurried back to the church. Out of the corner of his eye, he spied a shadow of a man scurrying away, but Wulfstan's appearance at the entry doors returned his attention to the church.

"This is for you."

The bishop received the book with a confused glance. Then, his jaw fell open and his eyes went wide. He looked from Aidan to the book and back to Aidan. "Dear God in heaven. How did this come to pass?"

"The king gave the book to Lady Edith at the battle-field. We tried to flee, but the Normans caught her before she could escape. So, she tasked me with bringing it back to you. It's all there. Every word."

The book absorbed Wulfstan. He held the crimson covers to the light and weighed the wax seal in his hands. "Remarkable," he said. "And Lady Edith?"

Aidan told him the whole story: the battle, Edith's heroics, and the skirmish in the Andredsweald. He spoke of Orrin, Osgod, Urse, and Rand. Wulfstan listened to the whole harrowing tale.

"So you see, father, you're the only one left whom the king and Lady Edith trusted."

"Their trust honors me, Aidan, more than you know, but there's a flaw in your thinking."

"What do you mean?"

Wulfstan showed a small smile. "They trusted you too."

Aidan stood speechless for a moment. He had never thought of it that way. His voice slowly came back. "I guess they did. But I can't protect this gift like you can, father."

"You're right. You can protect it better." He pressed the book back into Aidan's hands. Confusion swept over him, but the bishop quieted him with a pat on the shoul-der. "I live by God's Will, my son, and he has given me no indication that I should become the protector of a potent legacy. You, on the other hand, live by your mind's guidance and it has proven to be a capable defense against many a hardship."

Aidan remained baffled. "So, you're leaving me alone with...this?" Panic and anger began to stir inside.

"I never said that, you impetuous boy. It may not be God's Will for me to protect the confession, but He made it plain long ago that I should protect you. I seem to have forgotten that. So, if you're amenable to rejoining your brothers at St. Mary's, then you'll have a home protected by God and by me."

"A home..." Aidan's heart skipped a beat. King Harold had treated him well during his months with the army, yet he never felt at home. One reason lurking in his mind made him hesitate. *Ebba...*He summoned the vision of her auburn hair, emerald eyes, and soft white skin. It almost broke him, but he knew she was beyond his reach. Thunor would never agree to a marriage, not after the night of the red star. *If it was meant to be, Wulfstan would not have caught us.* As he stood in the abbey with the confession book in his hands, the choice seemed clear. "I'd like that more than anything. Will the brothers take me back?"

"They will do my bidding. Are you prepared?"

Aidan nodded his agreement. *Goodbye, Ebba.*

Wulfstan led Aidan to the altar. "God works in amazing ways, my son. Even now, as he walks through the valley of the shadow of death, Harold reconciles old friends and bears witness to your rebirth."

Aidan knelt before the bishop and rededicated himself to the solemn vows of obedience, chastity, and poverty. All the while, he hugged Harold's book to his breast. Then, Wulfstan took his *seax* from its belt sheath and cut tufts of hair from Aidan's head, creating a rough tonsure.

After the short ceremony, Wulfstan bid Aidan to rise.

"On a day I dreaded with all my heart, my son, you've made me —"

"*MON DIEU! MON DIIIIEEEEUUUU!*" The base cry echoed in the open church.

Aidan recognized it straight away. He rose up and rushed outside. Another sickening scream unleashed into the night, and he followed it to the sheds behind the church. What he found shocked his soul.

A huge bonfire roared in a small clearing in front of the wooden sheds. Next to the blaze, Orrin and Urse lay naked on their sides with their hands and feet bound together behind them by rope. Rand loomed over Urse, holding a glowing iron poker. The Norman's skin smoked and the air held the thick smell of scorched flesh.

Wulfstan flew past him. "These men yielded under God's eyes! You cannot do this!"

Giving the fire a wide birth, Aidan crept closer. "Rand, please stop. The price for this is Hell."

"They killed our king, Aidan! They *killed* Lady Edith." The huscarl's eyes gleamed.

"I loved Harold more than anyone," Wulfstan said, "but it matters not. They have God's protection."

Rand began to shake as rage collided with sense. The bishop approached and removed the poker from his hand. Wulfstan then cast it into the fire, sending up a shower of embers that made Aidan shy away.

Overcoming his fear, he looked back to the prisoners. Urse had collapsed, maybe even died, but Orrin lay on the cold ground and stared straight back with a look that held more than relief, more than thankfulness. Then, he looked down and noticed the falcon book still in hand.

Chapter 36:
Orrin

From the time he arrived, Bishop Wulfstan took charge. He hid Orrin and Urse in a small, clean barn outside of Waltham, and paid for a local midwife to tend their wounds. A few times, Wulfstan would tend to them himself. During his first visit, Orrin told him of Duke William's wish for a quick, private burial ceremony for Harold. The bishop listened as he removed a pus-stained bandage from Urse's arm and replaced it with a clean strip. Wulfstan rose without giving any indication of what he would do. "Rest now, Orrin. Your body and your conscience need rest."

Beaten to a bloody, bruised pulp, Orrin had no choice but to follow the bishop's orders. Still, he counted himself lucky because Rand's scalding iron never touched his flesh. Urse, however, had been roasted like a haunch of mutton on a spit. In the immediate hours after Rand's devastation, Orrin prayed for the chevalier's death. No one could return from such an experience, even if God kept his heart beating.

The next day, Wulfstan snuck into the barn after night had fallen. Harold was buried in a quiet ceremony during the morning, he reported. No other magnates attended, and the tomb lay under an unassuming stone behind the church sanctuary.

Orrin cried tears of thanksgiving. Had Harold's burial turned into an English rallying point, his mission would have failed. Over the next days, Orrin healed and Urse's heart kept beating. In fact, the chevalier showed signs of recovery. His bandages cleared, his dreams became less feverish, and he even managed to eat a little.

During these days when he felt like a wounded, caged animal, Orrin set his mind to work. The vision of Aidan standing next to the bonfire holding a decorated text always bolted to the forefront. That Harold's scribe would be caught holding a book was not out of the ordinary. But the shocked look in his eyes and the speed with which he hid the text behind his back screamed to Orrin that Aidan, indeed, hid something of great import. He studied every aspect of the vision, looking for a clue that could help unlock its meaning. A small detail emerged and then slowly grew into a revelation. As the little, crippled scribe moved to hide the book, the cover decoration flashed in the firelight. The view may have lasted for a quarter of a heartbeat, but Orrin saw the etching of a golden falcon. He was positive he saw it. Combined with the look of sheer dread on Aidan's face, could there be any doubt this book was the mysterious falconry text Edith Swan-neschals mentioned?

When Wulfstan visited next, Orrin asked to see Aidan, but the bishop refused. "Having rejoined my monastic brotherhood, he is hard at work at prayer. If anything, he has spent too much time around soldiers already."

"I could demand to see him, Wulfstan. I have orders from the duke that involve him."

Wulfstan's countenance turned to ice. "I have orders from God that involve him too, Orrin. And until your duke is king, I owe him no allegiance." He stormed from the barn without looking back.

Over the next days, just the midwife came. On the tenth night, Wulfstan returned.

"Our time has come to an end," he said with more chill than the wintery air. "Horses and provisions are prepared and waiting."

Orrin rose from his straw pile. He couldn't leave yet. Not without finding Aidan. "You call yourself a Christian, yet you'd cast Urse out in his condition? Look at him. He can barely sit up!"

"This is not of my doing, Orrin Geirson. Word has arrived from Sussex. Your duke has marched. Townsfolk are descending into a fear-induced frenzy. It won't be long before Waltham takes its anger out on you. You must flee, now."

Orrin stared at Wulfstan for long moments. He could not tell if the bishop attempted a bluff, but the risks of staying outweighed the rewards. No matter how important a book may be, it could not stop a farmer from skewering him with a pitchfork.

He turned to his sweating, anguished companion lying on a mass of straw. "Urse, could you manage to ride if we hoisted you into a saddle?"

He answered with a slight nod and groan. "I'll summon

some of the lay folk who still have their head," Wulfstan said. "They can help lift him."

In the end, Wulfstan's actions proved their worth. Armor, sword, cloak, and horse waited for him in a small clearing. He mounted and watched four farmers push Urse into his saddle and secure him with chords of rope tied to the pommels. "Man's 'eavier than ten stone sacks," one of them groaned after they finished.

In the distance, Orrin heard yelling and the crack of wood. "The townsfolk are looking for you," Wulfstan said. You had best be on your way."

Orrin flushed with guilt for doubting this man of God. "I owe my life twice over to you Wulfstan. How can I repay you?"

The stare the bishop cast pierced Orrin's soul. "The boy. Swear that both you and Urse will leave him out of any future dealings. Whatever your duke wants of him, he does not have it."

Orrin swallowed hard and stood tall in his saddle. *Anything but that.* He nodded and accepted the oath.

Chapter 37:
Aidan

October 30, 1066

Brother Aidan rode next to Rand on the short trip from Waltham to Nazeing. The huscarl took his time, keeping his old gelding at an easy trot. Aidan didn't try to force the conversation, for he knew Rand would speak in good time. Nor did he ride ahead to escape the drizzle, even though Scramasax begged to be unleashed. Aidan contented himself with riding alongside the warrior and enjoying their last moments together.

While all the other men left for their homes after finishing King Harold's escort, Rand stayed in Waltham as a hollow echo of his former self. After days of wearing a hair shirt, washing beggars' feet, consuming unleavened bread, and drinking stream water, the huscarl had finished the penance Wulfstan assigned him for torturing a fellow Christian. Aidan helped nurture the man back from the abyss, talking with him through cold nights, leading him in prayer, and wiping tears from his eyes. Now, for the first time Aidan could remember, the huscarl smiled.

"It'll be good to go home," he said, bundling a woolen cloak over his tunic to ward off the weather. "You sure you don't want to stay with me, boy...I mean Brother Aidan?"

He didn't fault Rand for the tongue slip. His new status still felt strange, even when he heard Wulfstan's joy at pronouncing it. And the name wasn't the only change. With Wulfstan's protection, Aidan had found the time to sew a leather-lined pocket inside his robe. Constantly nestled against his ribs, the book felt like an unwieldy growth.

"I envy you," he said. "Wulfstan says we're not returning to Worcester until after Duke William's intentions become clear." The news of the Norman march sent a shiver through London. With winter fast approaching, the invaders now lurked southwest of the city, and no one knew where they would strike next.

"Damned Normans are keeping everyone locked down," Rand said. "When our army gathers again, we'll break their damn lock with our axes."

It was Aidan's turn to smile, for Rand had healed at last. During his penance, the huscarl confessed he found no joy left in the world, save his hidden love for Gytha, Lady Edith's daughter. Wulfstan counseled him to repent his sins. A successful penitent, the bishop said, stood a chance for great rewards.

"God will bless you for your efforts," Aidan said as they rode. "I know He will."

Rand tilted his head and spurred his horse into a canter. "God can bless me by findin a lass to warm my bed. If He needs a suggestion, tell Him she's just 'round the bend." As he spoke, Nazeing Manor appeared in the distance.

After riding into the compound, they dismounted by the barn. Aidan noticed a powerful silence for such a welcoming, warm place. *Perhaps it's just the rain.*

"Gytha!" Rand called out. Neither the rain nor the silence had dampened his spirits. "Gytha, where are you?"

The door to the great hall cracked open. Both Aidan and Rand turned, but the beautiful maid Aidan remembered did not appear. Instead, a stoop-backed, aged servant descended the wooden steps. Aidan broke into a wide grin nonetheless.

"Renweard!" Rand embraced him. "It's good to see a familiar face."

"Aye, good ta see you too, lad," the old servant said. "Gave you up for dead, 'long with the rest of our men folk."

"Our men fought to the last, old friend. "For a long time, I thought I should've died with them. But God kept me alive for a reason." He glanced at Aidan.

Renweard's mouth fell open. "Is that you, Master Aidan?"

"Hello, Renweard. I'm a brother of St. Mary's Abbey in Worcester now. So please, no more 'master' for me."

The old servant gave a twisted smile and light nod. "Well it's good to see ya too, whether you're master or brother or otherwise."

Aidan watched Renweard's countenance. *Why does he look so scared?*

Rand almost bounced with excitement. "Is Gytha inside?"

Renweard shook his head. "She's gone, lad."

"Gone? Gone where?"

"To 'er brothers in Exeter. With their mother dead,

Gytha and Gunhild needed kin to protect 'em, not weak-kneed serfs."

Rand's posture fell and his eyes dimmed. "Gone to Exeter?" His voice just broke a whisper. Not knowing what to say or do, Aidan hurried to his friend's side.

"Sorry, m'boy," the servant said. "Whole manor knew you shined on 'er. Lady Edith even asked me once if'n I thought you two a good match. I told 'er you'd be the best husban' this side of 'eaven."

Rand stood rooted in place. "Gone to Exeter."

Aidan's chest fluttered but he forced himself to speak. "I'm sorry, Rand. You're welcome to return to Waltham with me. Wulfstan would be happy to take you into his service."

"You might want ta stay a few nights with yer folks, lad," Renweard said. "Your ma hasn't stopped cryin since she 'eard 'bout the fight. Filthy Normans. I'm gettin out of the rain. Feel free to join me if'n you like."

Rand snapped out of his trance long enough to thank Renweard and agree to visit his parents. He then turned to Aidan. "Perhaps I should've worn the hair shirt another day." To Aidan's surprise, Rand flashed a smile.

"What will you to do?" He tried to keep the eagerness from his voice. Aidan wanted Rand to make up his own mind, but he also wanted the huscarl to stay with him.

"If Gytha's gone to Exeter, then that's where I'll go. I did my penance for her. If God's good, she's still waiting for me, just a bit farther away than I expected."

Aidan felt a surge of pride. Rand could have fallen back into despair. Instead, he kept his head and his faith. "Will you leave soon?"

"Relax those lines on your face, friend. The bishop's a fiercer protector than I could ever claim to be. Besides, I'll be here for another night. After I visit my parents, I should go back to Waltham, say my thanks to Wulfstan and..."

"And what?"

"I...I feel I should pray to King Harold for a blessing. If I'm to cross the country for his daughter, I'd feel better if I knew he favored the trek."

"Well, even if you had arch-angel Gabriel's blessing, you'd never make it to Exeter on that old grunt," Aidan gestured to Rand's gelding. "You should take Scramasax. Lady Edith would've gifted him to you at your wedding, most like. Besides, he's sick of me always holding him back."

Rand looked honored. "Thank you, boy...brother. Christ on the cross! I won't ever get used to that."

Laughter erupted from deep in Aidan's gut. "I'll tell you a secret; neither will I."

Aidan was helping Rand stand after their vigil in front of Waltham's altar when the ghost walked in the door.

"It can't be," Aidan said.

Rand looked up. "Glory to all saints present, past, and future."

The ghost stood in the doorway. A sling held her arm close to her chest. She looked pale and large bags hung from her eyes. Her floor-length dress of natural wool muffled her steps and her white veil covered her expression. Behind her, a strong, blond, young man stood smiling.

Lady Edith's sob of joy broke the silence. "Come here my friends, my heroes. I still need your strength."

With a quickness he hadn't shown since the Andredsweald, Rand flew to his lady. Aidan dragged his foot across the nave as fast as he could. When the three reunited, tears flowed without impediment.

"They told us you went to God," Rand said.

"They tried to send me, but Godwine stopped them."

Her son stepped forward. "Rand, your service to our family can never be repaid. The best I can offer is another chance to fight. Will you join us?"

The warriors clasped forearms. "Service to your family is my life, Godwine. You need not ask."

"Rand isn't the only warrior in your midst, Godwine," Edith said, tilting her head toward Aidan. The new monk felt his cheeks blush.

"How could I forget him, mother? His mind is mightier than the sharpest sword. I cannot thank you enough, foster-brother."

Aidan bowed his head, humbled. Godwine had never spoken to him with such respect. "It was my honor, lord."

"We'll have time to talk later," she said, "But right now, my son and I need to pay our respects to the king. Would you two join us? I don't think Heaven will contain Harold's smile once he sees us all together again."

Rand and Aidan followed them to the unmarked stone slab behind the altar. The four stood in a silent prayer.

After several moments, Godwine slammed a fist into an open palm. "The bastards will *pay!*" Lady Edith rebuked him with the smallest glance. His head sunk down and he folded his arms across his chest.

They stood for some time, each person lost in their thoughts. Aidan remembered King Harold's advice: "Love is not a mistake." He also remembered Lady Edith's willingness to help him reconcile with Ebba. A part of him fretted over telling her about his return to monasticism, but he focused on divulging a long kept secret instead. "Lady Edith?"

Her wet eyes glanced up.

"Before...before we parted, there was something I should have told you."

"Oh?"

"He loved you very much...King Harold did. Much more than Queen Alditha. He...he didn't love her at all, actually. He said so many times. You deserved to know that after all you've been through."

Her smile widened as she reached out to clasp his hand. "Thank you, dear boy. From the depth of my soul."

Blushing, he put his head back down. A crushing weight flew off his shoulders with the admission, although the part about Alditha's pregnancy still lingered. *I promised to carry that secret to my grave. Besides, it would just cause pain on this happy day.*

No one heard Wulfstan approach. If Lady Edith's appearance shocked him, he masked it well by offering her a warm nod and falling into the quiet observance. Just then, sun burst through the church windows.

"You see, my friends," Edith said. "Harold's smile is breaking through the sky."

The story of Lady Edith's rescue amazed everyone, even Wulfstan. Disobeying orders, Godwine had left his brothers in Exeter and rushed to London to join his father's army. He'd arrived too late to join the land force, but the fleet had yet to disembark. So, he joined the crew of his father's ship and sailed out the morning before the battle. As they rounded Folkestone, a wind picked up and smashed several ships against the cliffs. The remaining fleet was forced to shelter in coastal inlets for the night. The delay proved disastrous, for they reached Hastings the day after the battle. The spotting of Edith's merchant ship provided the lone consolation.

"It was a complete accident," Godwine said. "We recognized the ship as a Norman vessel, so we attacked. I almost fell overboard when I saw my mother on deck."

Aidan told the tale of the Andredsweald next. When he spoke of his monastic vows, she received the words with no smile, head nod, or kindness. In fact, she let the development go without saying anything. After he finished, however, her jaw flexed. "They'll all pay: William, Odo, and the rest."

Wulfstan grunted. "One night, while Orrin Geirson recovered from Rand's attack, he screamed Odo's name in a tortured sleep. I thought nothing of it at the time, but now..."

Edith held up a hand. "Godwine, Rand: Will you excuse us? I need to speak with the bishop and our new monastic brother alone."

As the two men stayed in the church, Edith pulled her cowl overhead before leading Wulfstan and Aidan into the square outside. The encroaching night had brought a heavy chill. "Those walls have too many interested ears and eyes for me," Lady Edith said. Since learning Aidan had become a monk, an ice had entered her voice to match the chill outside.

"I agree," Wulfstan said. "I don't know where Osgod Knoppe lurks, and that makes me uneasy. Perhaps we should retire to Nazeing?"

"Not yet," she said. "I cannot bear to go home just now. If we stay outside and speak softly, no one can hear us."

She walked shoulder to shoulder with the bishop as Aidan trailed behind. "Now tell me: is the book is safe?"

"It's as safe as we could make it, my lady," Aidan said. "After we reached Waltham, I sewed this special pocket inside my robe," Aidan patted the bulge on his side. "It's lined so the wetness can't seep through and since I'm a new monk, people assume it's a bible."

"You, little firebrand? Why doesn't the bishop keep it?"

"I refused ownership, my lady," Wulfstan said, marking every step with a plant of his staff. "God has called me to protect Brother Aidan, not the confessional. And besides, since you've returned, I think we should honor Harold's last wish." He halted and they formed a small triangle at the far end of the square.

"Here? Now?" Glancing at the bishop, Aidan reached inside his cloak.

"No," Edith said. "As far as I'm concerned, Harold wished for all three of us to take care of his legacy. As long as one of us tends to it, I'm at peace. Unfortunately, I think our secret is beyond us. Odo asked me twice about it. I told him the first time Harold worked on a book of falconry. It was all I could think of. The second time, I was too broken to answer him."

Aidan's heart fluttered at the remembrance of the bestiary. Wulfstan, however, looked confused. "Book of falconry?"

"Yes, father. I forgot that part. The king had me create a falcon bestiary over the summer. It...it was ruined during the march from York."

Edith began to speak, but Wulfstan interjected. "We can discuss the lost bestiary another time. The confession is the pressing matter. Orrin Geirson saw Aidan holding the book. During his recovery, he begged to speak with the boy. Despite the oath he swore, he'll come back the first chance he gets."

Aidan pulled his arms in and the book pressed against his body. His first act as a new monk had been his most careless. Now, the Normans would stop at nothing to find him.

"They'll come," she said, her complexion filled with red heat, "but I'll be damned if they catch him."

Wulfstan's face deadened. "I agree, save for the blasphemy. I think it's time for our new monk to return to Worcester."

Aidan's heart jumped. *Ebba!* Then, the excitement flipped to fear. "But lord father, I thought we couldn't leave for Worcester on account of the Norman advance."

"Then listen with more care. I said *you* would return. I said nothing about myself. Before, I could not just send you home without my protection. Now..."

"Godwine and I can take him," Edith said, picking up on Wulfstan's thinking. "We'll spend a few days in Worcester before traveling to Exeter."

"But I don't understand," Aidan said. "If you don't come with me, lord father, that means..."

"I'll stay in London. When the Normans enter, Odo will focus on me, not on Worcester, at least for a while."

"But he'll try at some point." Lady Edith regarded Aidan out of the corner of her eyes. "I have an idea, but it can only work if we're sure no one else has read the confession."

"Orrin saw it, my lady, but there's no way he could have read it," Aidan said.

"Good. Then my plan might work. How long would it

take for you to recreate the falcon bestiary with the same cover as Harold's confession?"

"At Worcester? It would take me a few months, at most."

Her breath misted in the air. "A few months...What do you think Wulfstan? Is there enough time to create the text Odo believes is a farce? If you can present such a book, it would quell any search for Harold's secrets."

"The plan has merits, my lady," Wulfstan said, "although I'm unsure about the time remaining. My faith in the English forces is miniscule."

"You think London will fall easily?"

"My friend Archbishop Eldred is the only leader of substance left. The northern earls bluster and beat their chests, but they'll fly like crows the moment William's army appears. Even so, there may be enough time. Given our circumstances, I think you've struck on the best way to placate Odo's voraciousness."

"Then why do you look so wary?"

Wulfstan stepped between Aidan and her. "What do you plan to do with the confession, my lady? The text is dangerous. Harold should never have given it to you—"

"But he did, lord bishop, and I intend to guard it. But don't fret. I won't commission hundreds of copies or send messengers to read a version in every town square. I know it's not for every ear."

Her words appeased Wulfstan, but Aidan remained on edge. Something in her tone told him she had other plans. *The Lord will punish us all if she frees such a devastating secret.*

The Confession

July 1, 1065

The bishop: The time has come. Tell me how you've decided to combat Odo's unconscionable campaign.

The earl: Not yet, Wulfstan. It's still too new, too raw. The mere attempt to whisper it sends stabs of agony coursing through me.

The bishop: Let your fear go, my son. You are in God's loving arms. We will talk it through together. Now, if the realization tormented you so, how did the Normans react?

The earl: They never knew. The morning after the feast, my guards escorted me to a small port just outside of Bayeux where my ship and men waited. I had purchased my release with my soul.

Before I boarded, my guards handed me a message from William. It included a list of demands to be carried out: marriages to take place, castles to garrison, and hostages to exchange in preparation for his arrival. William had wasted no time in listing tasks for his new servant.

The bishop: Ludicrous. Even a child could see he has neither the right nor the authority.

The earl: A child perhaps, but not me. As my ship floated into the great strait, I began to break as the future assailed my mind. The duke and the bishop had stitched me up in a pretty embroidery. After my pledge, I was sworn to help them.

The bishop: There are less laudable callings, Harold. Battles between Christians and Mohammedans grow more vicious, more desperate with every passing day. Our pilgrims travel more like armed convoys than penance-seekers, while their city garrisons strike every passing caravan. Many swords in Christendom will view an attack against the Mohammedan as long overdue.

The earl: As we crossed the channel, I brooded over the same thought. The incursions against our pilgrims must cease, but our pilgrims must stop pillaging innocent towns as well. I realized the only solution is peace. Instead of making a whole territory suffer for the actions of a few, both Christians and Muslims should lay down their swords. The people of the Islamic faith do not deserve a scourge of Norman swords. Their scholars understand arithmetic, the stars, the human body, and even the written word in ways our scholars cannot.

Standing on the deck of my ship in the calm, clear night, I realized my English people should try to learn from the Mohammedan, not enslave them. Yet if the Normans take control, a campaign to rid Islam from the world would soon follow. Any refusal to join this conflict will meet with anathema from Rome and persecution from the Normans. These thoughts combined with my fury to form the terrifying solution.

The bishop: What is it, Harold? Go ahead. Let it go...

The earl: A new course for England. One close to God, but free of papal tyranny...

Chapter 38: Orrin

November 2, 1066

Finding the duke took less time than Orrin expected. Norman movements dominated the tongue tips of everyone south of London, and a blind man could follow the army's path of carnage. Yet it wasn't total, even according to the skittish Sussex villagers Orrin sought out. True, William had ravaged the fortified town of Romney. In Canterbury, however, the magistrates submitted without a fight and William rewarded them with a complete pardon. As Orrin and Urse followed the army's path to the southwest, the pattern held true; those places that tried to defy William now lay demolished and those that surrendered remained whole.

The threat of attack loomed around every bend. He pushed the horses as fast as Urse's beleaguered body would allow. To keep his friend's spirits up, he spoke about the sweet smell of wine, the salty taste of female skin, and the joyous clinking sounds of a full purse. At one point during the second day of riding, Urse faded to the brink of unconsciousness. Seeking to relight the man's spirit, Orrin spoke to him of the book in Aidan's hands and the rewards this knowledge would earn at journey's end. "You'll drown in rank and profit and I'll return a hero to my family." Somehow, Urse regained some energy and continued riding.

They followed the Pilgrim's Way – a dilapidated Roman road that crossed the width of southern England. They passed rolling golden fields and trickling streams, up shallow green hills, and through small verges of leaf-shedding woods. The November winds blustered strong and cold. Several times, Orrin and Urse had to place their trust in their horses' speed to escape roving bands of Englishmen. Other times, Orrin thought Urse had died in his saddle. Every time he checked, though, he felt warm, short breaths under his nose.

Four pain-staking days after setting out from Waltham, they met the army's rear guard outside the ancient city of Winchester, the capital of Wessex, the country's richest earldom. In previous decades, King Alfred the Great and Canute, Emperor of England, Norway, and Denmark called Winchester "home" much more than London.

Upon seeing the army, Orrin raised a clamor. "Physicians! I need physicians! My friend is near death!" Servants rushed to help the two bedraggled chevaliers. They untied Urse from the saddle and hauled him off to the camp's infirmary. After saying a prayer for his friend's soul, Orrin sought out the captain of the rear guard.

"We're holding outside the town, m'lord," the warrior

said, "out of respect for the widowed Queen Eadgifu who sits in residence."

"She's still here?" Orrin asked, trying to stifle his amazement. Two women had dominated Harold's life. Edith Swanneschals, his handfast wife, filled him with joy. His sister, Eadgifu, filled him with constant irritation. Still, she was the scion of a proud, fierce family. "Have we begun siege preparations? With the dowager queen here, Winchester won't be an easy log to split."

"No, m'lord," replied the captain. "We've just arrived, and the duke called a halt. He didn't want to insult Queen Eadgifu by arriving in battle array. In fact, a delegation has arrived from the city to discuss our intentions."

They walked the short distance to William's command tent. Orrin thanked the captain for showing the way. He thought for a moment of finding somewhere to wash, but decided against it. *I look more convincing this way.* He set his shoulders back, corrected the broach that clasped the tattered red cloak to his chest, and entered the tent.

A silent crowd several rows thick had gathered inside. Grateful for the cover, Orrin peered through the assembled heads to see what grabbed everyone's attention.

William sat in a chair, looking relaxed with one leg crossed over the other. He dressed in chain mail but wore no helmet. The dowager Queen Eadgifu knelt before him in much the same way Edith Swanneschals had in the tent below the battlefield, but without dignity or defiance. This woman seemed intent on displaying her misery.

"My queen, please sit down," the duke said as William Fitz Osbern brought over a stool. With a nod of gratitude, Eadgifu rose from her knees to sit. She was taller than Orrin by a full grown man's outstretched hand. She had pale, sad features and deep bags under her lifeless brown eyes. Her hair was raven black and her shoulders and hips were wispy and narrow. In fact, her only distinguished feature was her nose which stuck out like an oversized spearpoint. She wore a fresh, woad-stained over tunic and an unwound wimple of the same rich blue color.

"You'll want an explanation, I'd imagine," she said in impeccable Norman. "No, this is no trap. I do not have huscarls leashed inside the city waiting to ambush you. This is real. I wish no more bloodshed so I will raise our gates."

"Honored queen, we never doubted your honesty," Fitz Osbern said. "Your brother may have usurped the throne, but you also spent many years married to King Edward of honored memory. But, if we may inquire, why did you submit to us and not one of the remaining English factions? Our sources say the northern earls have placed Edgar the Atheling on England's vacant throne. Why align yourself with us instead of Edgar?"

She leveled her eyes and furrowed her brows at the seneschal. "You've never met the earls, have you? Edwin's a boar without tusks. All bristle, no bite. His brother'd rather look at himself in polished bronze all day. My brothers held more bravery in their snot than those two preening pheasants."

Fitz Osbern nodded politely and continued. "And the Atheling?"

Eadgifu smiled. Orrin thought it a defeated, ugly look. "The boy's a pretty enough lad, I suppose. But a leader of men? A hero of a kingdom? God did not bestow in him those traits. So, even with my father and my brothers raging in heaven, I have no choice but to throw my lot in with you."

Fitz Osbern tried to continue, but the duke gestured

for him to stand aside. "This submission demonstrates your intelligence. Perhaps you're inclined to show some more?"

The crestfallen queen craned her neck, winced, and then nodded her ascent.

Duke William leaned in. "We will need information: troop counts, supply levels, morale status, and anything of a military nature you can think of. Edwin and Morcar have just had a few weeks to recover from the Norwegian invasion, so their strength must be sapped. We will also need to know who truly rules London. Our spies say a thane named Ansgar has assumed command of the defense. Do you know this man? Is he made of iron, linen, or coin? And what of your nephews, the usurper's ilk? Are they gathering troops to revenge their family?"

The duke continued on, but a pull on Orrin's cloak drew his attention away. He turned to see Bishop Odo standing next to him.

"Come with me," the bishop whispered. Orrin nodded and followed him out of the tent, grateful to be rid of Queen Eadgifu's pathetic display.

Outside the stuffy tent, Orrin breathed in the cold, gray afternoon air. Bishop Odo led him down a path to a small plain overlooking Winchester's city walls.

"I'm surprised at your resilience, Orrin. A foraging party found the remains of your conroi in the Andredsweald. We assumed you had either turned traitor or been killed. The latter appears false. I pray the former is as well?"

Inside, Orrin roiled. He knew the loss of his men would spark even more questions about his loyalty. "An English warrior band ambushed us, m'lord. Only Urse and I survived."

The bishop sighed and cast his eyes to the city. "And the usurper's corpse?"

"They listened to me and held a quiet ceremony for him."

The bishop nodded. Some aspect of the ancient city distracted him. "And did you progress in your search for the scribe?"

"I found him, m'lord."

The bishop turned to Orrin, his eyes alight. "And?"

"He's a boy named Aidan. Not much to him, really. A cripple. Scared of fire."

"*Where* is he?"

"In Waltham, under Bishop Wulfstan of Worcester's care."

Odo sneered at the mention. "I've heard of this bishop. They say he lives solely for God's Will and that no man can understand the Almighty better than he."

"I met him as well, m'lord. A rigid man, it's true, but honest." Odo grew more displeased with every mention of the Worcester bishop, so Orrin pressed forward. "The scribe had the text with him; he held a decorated book with a falcon on the cover."

"*What?* You saw it? Did you read it?"

"I saw it, m'lord, but couldn't read it."

Do you think it's the usurper's falconry book?"

Orrin breathed deep. "I think it is."

The bishop began walking again, rubbing his chin with one hand and holding his staff with the other. "You've done well, Orrin. We'll occupy London by month's end. And at my bidding, William has issued a decree naming any act to harbor writs, charters, texts, and ledgers pertaining to the usurper as treason. All such documents are to be surrendered by the coronation. If our all-too-pious bishop is as honest as you say, I should possess my book before Advent concludes."

Orrin's heart beat strong as his confidence returned. He seized the chance dangling before him. "I'm yours to command, m'lord. After we confiscate the book, will it be possible for me to see my family? My wife had just given birth when I left and I'm eager to return to her."

"My dear son, if events unfold as you say, I'll send you home with a hero's bounty."

Chapter 39:
Aidan

November 8, 1066

"What is going on here," Lady Edith asked as the small group rode into Oxford. A swirling, rumbling tumult of humanity filled the clearing outside the city's famous church, St. Frideswide.

Aidan had stopped here on his previous travels with Wulfstan and enjoyed his stays. Several parish churches offered soft sleeping straw and plentiful bowls of lamb stew. And with the Thames on its western side and Watling Street to the east, Oxford boasted one of the most vibrant markets in the kingdom. Besides all of the merchants arriving by river or horse, the city's thick earthen ramparts encircled almost a thousand dwellings, the bishop once told him. *And judging from the look of it, the head of every household is gathered in front of us.*

Stopping here had made sense when Lady Edith suggested it to him, Rand, and Godwine. The journey to

Worcester would take two more days at least, and Aidan learned long ago that overextending on the first travel day led straight to a sore rump. Now, a feeling in his bones begged him to sacrifice Oxford's comfort. "Maybe we should find a tavern or a church farther down Watling Street?"

Rand took the lead. Despite the city law preventing men to draw weapons inside the ramparts, the huscarl looked ready to kill any aggressor. Scramasax added to this menace. Lady Edith had denied Rand's attempts to return the stallion before the journey. "After all you've done, my warrior, Scramasax is a small debt to pay," she had said. Aidan agreed; even though he felt a deep kinship with the horse after the forest trek, he also recognized Rand fit atop Scramasax like a well-made glove fits a hand.

"Something's amiss," Godwine said. He wore a thick woolen cloth around his neck and mouth. Combined with his cloak hood, the garment served to fight the chill and conceal his face. "Mother: you stay back with Aidan. Rand and I will see what the uproar is about."

Lady Edith nodded and pulled her cowl low overhead. "Very well then, but be careful. We need no undue attention."

They had agreed to this before setting out as well. Godwine had wanted to raise swords as they crossed the realm, but Edith refused, saying: "They think I'm dead and that Aidan is in Waltham. We should let them think that for as long as possible."

Now, she led Aidan to the side of the street while the two men approached the crowd. No sooner had they reached the back row when the uproar fell quiet. A faint voice penetrated the air. When the speaker finished, the rumbling started again, but without any of the previous anger.

Before Godwine and Rand could ride back, the crowd parted and a stream of horses cantered from the square. Aidan's eyes bulged and his throat stopped in mid-swallow. A Norman conroi bore down on them, swords and spears at the ready.

His arms flailed atop his plow horse. A thousand thoughts rushed through his mind. Part of him wanted to run and protect the book in his hidden pocket. Another part screamed at him to protect Lady Edith. He had a notion to scream for help. Another thought pressed him to yield before blood was shed. Ebba's smiling face flashed by. All these thoughts, however, did nothing to spur his useless limbs into action.

The Normans drew within five paces and the smallest cry escaped his lips. He tensed and shut his eyes, bracing for capture.

Their horses shook the ground for several moments. Lady Edith didn't scream. The crowd didn't surround them with shouts. He couldn't hear Rand or Godwine or anyone else. Then, the hoof falls receded.

The quieting caused him to open his eyes. Lady Edith still sat atop her mount. Her mouth gaped open and one hand shook as it covered her chest. "It's okay, little firebrand. They're gone," she said with a heavy breath and growing smile. She shifted in her saddle, and to Aidan's shock, he found his arm braced against her. Somehow, he had moved between her and the Normans during their charge. "Moreover, they weren't here for us."

Aidan had somewhat recovered when Rand and Godwine returned. "It was a Norman messenger," Edith's first-born said through a snarling mouth. "He nailed a proclamation to the door of St. Frideswide, and then addressed the crowd. William's army has taken Winchester without a fight and now sits on the Oxfordshire side of Wallingford."

Aidan flinched in his saddle. The Normans were less than a day's ride from Oxford.

"There's more. The archbishop of Canterbury has submitted and ordered every God-fearing Englishman to do the same."

"Stigand dares to order God-fearing men," Edith said with an incredulous laugh. "If Christ the Lord came to earth and asked for an indulgence, the beloved archbishop would charge him double the price. Still, I like this news not at all. Did the Norman say anything else?"

"He did." Godwine pinched the bridge of his nose. "The northern earls have deserted London. The city is guarded by church prelates, merchants, and beggars in the street."

Aidan's head whipped to Lady Edith. "We can't leave Bishop Wulfstan there alone, my lady. We *have* to go get him."

"The bishop can take care of himself," Rand said. "You and Lady Edith are in too much danger to waste another moment. We're ahead of the storm, but just barely. If we leave now, we can still reach the West Country. Tomorrow, it may no be so."

Edith regarded Aidan with caring eyes. "Rand has the right of it. Wulfstan wanted to stay and did not fear the Normans at all. Now, if there's nothing else, I think Aidan's original suggestion was well made. Let's quit Oxford straight away. Take a good, restive breath, friends. We won't stop until we reach Worcester Abbey."

She began to turn her horse but stopped when Godwine's head tilted. "There's something else. The proclamation didn't pertain to Stigand or the Norman march. It pertained to father."

Edith's head snapped around. "What of him?"

"The Normans have deemed his reign as an interdict between rightful kings. As a result, any man possessing evidence of his kingship will be declared a traitor the moment William takes the throne. The proclamation orders every man to relinquish charters, writs, or other written evidence before William's coronation. If such evidence is found later, the owner will die."

Aidan couldn't help himself; his hand reached under the fold of his cloak to grip the corner of the confession book. "When...when is the coronation?"

"If they take London soon, it could be in a matter of weeks."

He stole a glance at Lady Edith. Her eyes darted to every face in the group and her lips twitched. "They seek to eradicate *my husband* from existence!" Her eyes rested on Aidan for a long moment. "Well, they'll find it takes more than harsh-sounding proclamations to kill the memory of a great man. Come, let's be off to Worcester. The more distance we can put between us and them, the better I'll feel."

After setting off down Watling Street, Aidan let Godwine's words roll in his head. They made him forget fear, exhaustion, and hurt. They painted a clear picture of the future, one Lady Edith must have realized as well. The Normans had demanded the confession. If they did not receive it by the coronation, Wulfstan would die.

Three days later, the burgh of Worcester appeared on

the horizon. It looked no more than a brown crown on a rise above the winding green Severn River. The outer walls resembled a ring of old teeth that had chewed on too much stone. But inside the ramparts, the citizens were raising churches, houses, and road ways. The two churches in the cathedral close – the ramshackle stacked-gray stone of St. Peters and the more symmetrical stone of St. Mary's – loomed high above everything else.

"Home," Aidan whispered as knots formed in his throat.

The band paid the city toll and raced down Sidbury Lane. Since dusk had fallen, few people meandered outside. They charged forward until the lane forked with one branch running north and the other continuing straight to the cathedral close.

The approach occurred so fast, Aidan could not keep his emotions in line. He had tears in his eyes when the horses stopped. His previous banishment had set him free; it was a mixed blessing if there ever was one. Now, the walls loomed before him once more and crossing the threshold would be permanent. *I have to for Bishop Wulfstan's sake...and for King Harold's sake as well.*

After saying goodbye to Rand and Godwine, he walked with Lady Edith to the precinct gate. "I had better head in, my lady. Will you be staying in Worcester long?"

"A few days, little one. Godwine wants to meet with some of the local thanes and I need rest." She patted her slung arm. "Are you sure you're up for this?"

After Oxford, she and Aidan had spoken deep into the night. The Normans advanced faster than they ever thought possible. The falcon bestiary creation would have to match their speed if they were to save Wulfstan and the book. "With the brotherhood's help, the bestiary could be ready in four weeks."

"That's not what I meant. Are you ready to join your brothers?"

A gale of unease swept through him; he gripped the book inside his tunic for surety. "I need to do this; the brotherhood is Bishop Wulfstan's best chance."

She embraced him. "No one can ever doubt your heart, Aidan. If they do, they'll answer to me. Now, if you're certain, go to your fellow monks. Tell them you speak with Wulfstan's voice and act to save his life."

"Right. I'll let you know how we progress. Where will you lodge?"

"I remember Harold telling me of Worcester's market tavern long ago. I'll rent the loft if it's free. Unless you hear otherwise, you can find me there."

Entering the precinct grounds, he focused on his task to avoid the pressure in his heart. He'd need two brothers to help prepare the parchment. Another would cure the leather for the cover. Only Aidan could perform the writing. As for the falcon ornament, he'd need Thunor, the goldsmith. His heart jumped at the thought. *I've said my vows. That life is closed to me now.*

He had taken only a few steps when a surprised call went up. "Aidan? Is that you?" Before he could answer, dozens of monks streamed out from the surrounding barns, stalls, and sheds. They greeted him and pestered him with questions. Then, one voice rose to calm them. "Is this a passing visit, or have you come to finish your novitiate?"

Prior Alfstan parted the crowd and approached. Wulfstan's younger brother was a rounder, jollier version of the bishop. His eyes were larger, lighter, and less piercing. He also smiled as much as his brother scowled.

"I'm here for as long as you'll have me, Father Alfstan," Aidan withdrew a folded message from his tunic pocket. "I've come from Bishop Wulfstan. We reconciled at Waltham Holy Cross and he initiated me into the brotherhood. So, with your permission, I'd like to join you for the rest of my days." The request sounded odd in his ears, even as he said it.

The surrounding brothers felt no awkwardness. They erupted in joy as Aidan handed Alfstan the note.

The prior raised a hand for quiet. "What are you two up to, Aidan?" He pointed to the note.

"I'll explain it all, father. I promise. Perhaps we should hold a meeting in the chapter house after Vespers? That way, all the brothers can hear."

Bells tolled the call for prayer. Alfstan slapped Aidan on the back and smiled. "You haven't lost your knack for timing, my boy. Come you scurrying mice. First, we'll pray. Then, our new brother will regale us with a tale. I'm sure we won't be disappointed."

The cathedral's chapter house was a round, wattle-and-daub walled, thatched roof building set right next to the church of St. Mary's. The brotherhood met here to discuss matters of enterprise and faith. Due to its round shape, they sat on benches surrounding a gilded pulpit.

After Prior Alfstan initiated the meeting and said the introductory prayer, he invited Aidan to speak from this center stage. The young monk dragged his foot to the pulpit, thanked the prior, and addressed his brothers.

"The bishop asked me to speak with his voice today.

As you all know, Duke William of Normandy is marching through the land unabated. The bishop's concluded it'll be a matter of time before he assumes the kingship. And when William gains the throne, all of us will be subjected to the harshest scrutiny. So, Father Wulfstan wants us to create a coronation gift the new king will cherish. If we don't succeed, our father's life may hang in the balance." The half-truth stung, but he could not reveal the real reason.

"What type of gift?" one monk asked.

"We have little enough money," a panicked voice said. "How can we pay a ransom for our bishop's life?"

"The Norman has more gold than he can count," Aidan said. "The bishop has asked us to make a much more appropriate gift: a book."

Alfstan's booming voice rang out. "We'll supply any book the Norman desires. We just want Wulfstan returned safely!"

"I understand your worry, good brothers. To truly succeed, Wulfstan orders us to create a new book for the coronation, one Christendom has never seen before. Like King Harold before him, William has a passion for hunting birds. He believes them to be God's favorite being, next to man. So, the bishop has asked us to create a bestiary; one that describes the habits and nature of the splendid raptor."

Shouts erupted. Some monks found the idea blasphemous; others found it divine. One voice, however, spewed with doubt.

"Brother Aidan, how can we trust you?" He recognized Coleman's voice. The same monk who caught him with Ebba still did not trust him. *He senses my weakness, my hesitation.* Bracing for the upcoming challenge, Aidan turned to confront his petulant, wispy-haired brother face-to-face. Coleman's brown eyes beamed in defiance. "Trust me, Brother Coleman? I've arrived with Wulfstan's sealed note. He has accepted me into the brotherhood, so trust him."

His adversary approached the pulpit. "Listen to me, brothers. I am not questioning Aidan's return. The bishop's note is valid by the look of it. However, the note says nothing about helping Brother Aidan with this task." He held the note aloft. Alfstan had let Coleman read it. Making matters worse, Coleman was right; Wulfstan did not mention the task because he wrote the note before learning of the Norman advance.

Aidan tried to break in, but Coleman kept his attack. "Am I the only one who finds it strange how this erstwhile novice has just miraculously returned from his...crisis of faith? Now, he claims to speak with the bishop's voice. True, he speaks well and describes a wondrous gift fit for a king. But why would the bishop ask us to break our sacred rituals, strain our cattle supply, and subject ourselves to this gift's construction? To me, it sounds more like the rash plan of a thief rather than the well-thought out plan of a wise elder. The safer, and smarter, decision is to ask the bishop directly. I volunteer to ride to London and confirm the bishop's desire for this undertaking—"

"No!" Aidan shouted. "There's little enough time as is. Listen to me, brothers. This is what our lord bishop wants."

"I wish I could trust you, Brother Aidan, but the risk is too great," Coleman said. "Without the bishop's consent, I'm afraid I cannot go along with your plan."

The room descended into a storm of voices. Alfstan tried to regain order, but could not salvage the argument.

When the monks settled down, Alfstan's spite showed on his face. "Aidan has offered one path; Coleman has provided another. Go and pray on this solution, brothers. The answer will be provided by God."

When the brotherhood reconvened, God's answer incensed Aidan. By a vote of thirty-three to seventeen, the brothers decided to wait for the bishop's explicit order before helping to create the bestiary. He could not blame his brothers; monks were trained to follow a strict schedule. He could not even blame Coleman. *What have I done to earn their trust?*

The failure fell to him. His ill-conceived plan had faltered before it ever got going. With a heart heavier than a boulder, he left the cathedral close to ask for Lady Edith's forgiveness.

Fuming all the way to the market tavern, Aidan shoved the door open with a shoulder. Inside the smoky, hot hall, a raging hearth fire drew his immediate attention. Men on trestle tables laughed and mumbled as the tavern-owner bellowed for him to shut the door.

Aidan did as ordered, and almost knocked into a tall girl when he turned back to the hall. His focused mind shattered when he looked up.

"Aidan! I heard you'd come back!" Ebba stepped close and opened her arms for an embrace.

She looked more beautiful than ever. In the past months, she'd grown taller, thinner, and stronger. Her brown hair had thickened and her chin, nose, and cheeks had sharpened. He wanted to take her in his arms, fly away to some remote village, and live the rest of his days next to her. But in these months, he'd pledged his service to God, Bishop Wulfstan, and to King Harold's eternal soul. He could pledge nothing to Ebba, save regret. Using every bit of fortitude in his body, he held out a hand. "Hello, Sister Eadburga. It's good to see you."

A brief flash of shock passed across her face. "It...it's good to see you too." Her smile dulled.

"I wish I had more time to talk," he said, "but I've just now come from a brotherhood conclave and need to find someone."

"Brotherhood? Didn't Wulfstan banish you?"

"He did, but he also found it in his heart to take me back." Aidan looked deep into her eyes and tried to speak in soft tones. "I've taken my vows since we last spoke. Once, uncertainty clouded my mind. But I've realized I spent my entire life preparing for this. Any other life, no matter how tempting, is wrong for me. Does that make sense?"

Her eyes darted to the nearby trestle tables before she stepped closer and whispered. "But those things you said in the grove..."

"I let my passion get the better of me; we both did. The red star was not God's sign to avoid my chosen life. It was His sign of warning."

Ebba began to shudder. Her eyes turned glassy and she shook her head. "A warning to avoid me, you mean."

"No!" Every word felt like a wedge splitting his soul. "A warning to both of us to resist our deluded thoughts."

A single tear streaked down her cheek. She no longer met his gaze, but stared down to the rush straw. "Well, I don't wish to delude you anymore."

"That's not what I meant. Please..."

She knocked his shoulder as she fled the hall, sobs floating in the air. Aidan took a step to run after her, but then thought better of it. *She needs time to understand my words. And so do I for that matter.* He turned back and saw

Lady Edith standing across the way. She stared in the direction Ebba had run, her face full of concern.

They found two spots at a trestle table and he told her of the meeting. "They don't trust me, my lady. They want to hear the order from Wulfstan. It'll take two or three weeks before we start. At that rate, we won't finish before the coronation."

Lady Edith let out an exasperated sigh. "What if we rip the pages out and bind new ones?"

"We'd risk damaging the cover. If any Norman has two eyes, they'd be able to tell."

Laughter in the hall crashed around them, but they sat with sunken shoulders. "I need you to think, little one, for I have no answers," Edith said. "Think back to all of your lessons. Is there anything we can do to create the bestiary in short order?"

Aidan sighed and begged his exhausted mind to work once more. After several silent moments, he jumped. "I think I know a way. The bishop won't be happy, but we don't have any choice."

"What do you have in mind?"

"In one of the bishop's first lessons, he showed us a treatise on the Eucharist, written by a monk of Glaston-bury. The author was a fool, he said, and not because he disagreed with the arguments. Rather than enduring the effort and cost of creating a new book, the brother had scraped away some previous text and used the blank pages to write his thoughts."

"I don't follow," Edith said, her head shaking in confu-sion.

Aidan began speaking with more fervor. After this day of heartache, it felt joyous to seize on something. "The bishop said the monk acted foolishly because he sacrificed someone else's hard work just to finish his writing faster. Don't you see, Lady Edith? We can use the same book! All I have to do is copy the text onto a parchment scroll. Then, I'll scrape off the ink from the original book and write the bestiary. No one will know and it'll save time. It'll work, Lady Edith. At least we have a chance..."

Edith leaned back. "And what of your brothers? How will you perform this task without them noticing?"

After thinking for a moment, he began to see the plan unfolding. "Well, I can copy the confession and clean the pages in my cell. As for the bestiary, that work can only be done in the cloister...maybe Prior Alfstan can help there. He wanted to help me, but the other brothers decided against it. If I show him the cleaned book, he wouldn't stop me from doing the work."

A small, pained smile creased her lips."If you say so, Aidan."

"What's wrong, my lady? You're not pleased."

She grimaced before looking at him with her familiar care. "Are you sure you want to live like this? The brothers may have welcomed you, but they didn't trust you in the end."

"I can't blame them. My request was too much to put on them. In time, they'll learn to trust me. Besides, I don't know how else to live."

"Living is not about knowing, little firebrand; it's about learning. For instance, I learned today that the brotherhood doesn't trust you, whereas that poor girl would have fallen into your arms if you let her. You broke her heart. I daresay you broke your own too."

A sudden heat rose under his skin. "Wulfstan's taken care of me. He's prepared me for this at the sacrifice of many efforts. I got confused once; I can't let it happen again."

"I know you love the bishop. And you're a grown man now. I won't question your decisions any longer. It's just..." she pause to sigh, "sacrifice can turn to despair if you lie to your heart. But enough of my doting. It sounds like we have a new plan. Go back to your bookmaking, Aidan, and remember: I believe in you with all my soul."

"I will, Lady Edith. And thank you." He rose from the table. A new energy filled his mind even though his heart felt cleaved in two.

Chapter 40:
Edith

November 13, 1066

In the dead of a cold, clear night, Aidan emerged from the precinct with the scroll. Distancing herself from Godwine, Edith held out her hand to receive the confession copy. When the rolled parchment hit her palm, Edith felt a surge of strength. She also felt a lighter weight than she expected.

"Harold's seal isn't fixed to the pages, Aidan. Is that wise?"

"I dare not remove it from the book, my lady. If Orrin caught a good look at it, the Normans may expect the seal as well. Besides, Wulfstan will vouch for the words after we've saved him."

"You've given this much thought. And you are right as always. Now, how is the bestiary progressing?"

The young man kicked the gravel. "The past day was lost as I made the copy. But I looked at the original parchment. It's thick and dry, so a sharp knife should be able to scratch off most of the ink. I also spoke to Alfstan, and he'll let me skip all duties save prayer to create the gift."

"Have you shown him the book already?"

"I didn't have to. He's still furious about the vote and wants the book done almost as much as I do."

As Aidan spoke, she noticed he seemed bereft of the zeal he had when the idea first dawned. "Something's troubling you. Tell me now, for I won't see you until after the journey to London."

"It's the journey, Lady Edith. I'm scared. Why do I need to deliver the book?"

Her heart begged to embrace her foster son, but now was the time for strength, not coddling. "I know it's daunting, but it's also the best way to clear your name. If you don't deliver the bestiary, Orrin, Odo, and maybe even William himself will search you out. This way, the matter is settled once and for all."

"It's just the prospect of another cold trek across the kingdom..."

"We'll don't worry about that, little firebrand. I've given Rand a heavy purse. You won't have to sleep by a campfire the entire way."

Aidan nodded but did not lighten. "Is there something else?"

"I know I must, but destroying the original..." he grimaced. "I have Wulfstan's voice in my head screaming at me every time I think of it."

Edith smiled. "I pray to God you hear that voice yelling at you Aidan, for that means you've saved him."

Aidan nodded and rolled his eyes. "I see your point, my lady."

"Now," She slapped the parchment roll into her gloved

hand, "speaking of journeys, Godwine and I must be off. Advent starts in a few days, and I want to be in Exeter well before then."

After one last farewell, Edith and Godwine rode out. Her heart ached with every step the horse took down the road, but she had done all she could for her foster son. Rand would protect him from any harm, and as a secondary precaution, she also assigned another protector to her beloved monk.

As they passed through Worcester's gates, she remembered the look on Ebba's face in the tavern hall. It had pained her more than she felt possible. In truth, she did not see the girl's face. She saw her own. And in Aidan, she saw a guilt-stricken Harold prizing duty over love.

No one deserved that anguish, so she sought out the young goldsmith's daughter hours before their departure.

As Rand distracted her father at the market stall, Edith perused the goldsmith's wares. "Your father's work is amazing, child," she said to Ebba, who stood near the back with her head down. "You should be more proud."

"I'm very proud, my lady. Does anything catch your eye?"

"In truth, I'm having a terrible time picking one. So, I think I'll have to buy it all."

Blinking, the girl stepped forward. "I...are you sure?"

Edith hefted a full purse onto the stall counter. In the flight from Nazeing, she had taken all the coin the horses could carry. The jewelry was not only a good investment – the rings and bracelets would help Godwine bestow gifts to his new men – but it would also buy her some time with Ebba.

When her father learned of the sale, the happiness

blinded him. He let Ebba help carry the jewelry back to the tavern without a second thought.

"Do you know who I am, child," Edith asked as they walked with Rand trailing behind.

"No, my lady. But you seem wise."

Edith could not help but laugh. "I've made more than my share of mistakes, but thank you for the kindness. My name is Lady Edith Swanneschals and I'm—"

Ebba stopped in mid-stride. "Your Aidan's foster mother. You were married to King Harold before he…Oh my lady, I'm so sorry!"

The girl dropped to a knee, but Edith gestured for her to rise. "My husband died defending his land, Ebba. That helps combat the sorrow. But come, we're well beyond formality even though we've just met. My foster son loves you more than life, after all."

Ebba's posture dropped from underneath her brown dress. "I…I don't think so. Not anymore."

Spying a bench just outside the tavern, Edith gestured for Ebba to join her there. "Do you love him?" Even though a white shawl covered her mouth, Ebba's bulging eyes showed how much the question stunned her. "Forgive me, child," Edith gave her arm a reassuring rub. "After my recent trials, I'm afraid I've lost all sense of tact. Still, the question hangs between us, and I wish it answered. A passing fancy is to be expected from a girl your age. If it's so, just tell me and I'll be on my way."

With her hand still on Ebba's arm, Edit could feel the girl's body jolt. "Passing fancy?" Her head shake was short and definite. "He…we…I can't explain it, Lady Edith. It's something in the way he speaks with me. How he looks at me. I've never known anything like it. Before he left, we were going to get married. Now, he's come back as a brother of the Abbey and wants nothing to do with me."

The quivering arm, the incredulous eyes, and unwavering words were more proof than Edith expected to receive. Sitting on the bench in the cold, late autumn day, she realized Aidan had more friends than he knew. "I know your pain, Ebba. Believe me I do. Aidan may be acting strangely, but you must not let it destroy your love for him."

"He doesn't want anything to do with me, Lady Edith..."

"He said the words, but he doesn't feel that way. Right now, he's caught in a vicious web. He's scared and lost and his lone savior is Wulfstan."

"I want to save him too, my lady. I don't know what he's caught up in, but—"

"It's best to bide your time, dear. Aidan's work in the monastery is vital to more lives than just his. If you truly want to help, watch from afar and tell Rand if you see anything suspicious."

"Suspicious?"

"Anything out of the ordinary. A new face in the city. An open gate when it should be closed. Anything. Dark forces grow closer with every passing moment. The Normans..." Edith looked at the bewildered girl and suddenly smiled. "I'm sorry. You deserve to be spared the horrific details. Just know the Normans are after Aidan. He needs all the protection he can get."

"I...I will do my best, my lady."

"Good. If Aidan succeeds, we'll all earn a respite. Perhaps then he'll realize his mistake."

"I can't ask him to leave the brotherhood, Lady Edith.

Not for me. My father won't let him within fifty paces of me."

"Your father is a good man. If he's worried about losing the abbey's patronage, I could always use a skilled smith. Rest assured, dear girl: I would be more than pleased to see Aidan leave God's calling for more," she looked deep in to Ebba's eyes, "earthly pursuits."

Ebba's eyes slanted, meaning she smiled broadly from under the shawl. "Thank you," she said. "With all my heart, thank you. But I should be going. Father'll be wondering where I've been."

"Well then I'll bid you farewell. My son and I will be leaving after dusk."

"Aren't you going to stay here and protect Aidan too?"

"I wish I could, Ebba, but my son and I must get to Exeter. We have our own task to perform."

Now, as she rode next to Godwine with the confession scroll tucked in her saddle bag, Edith turned her mind to that task.

The Normans arrived under a papal banner, claiming they fought to right a tremendous wrong done to them by Harold. The confession, however, proved them to be liars. If the remaining English magnates knew the Normans' true intentions, there would be no end to their anger. The knowledge could unite them into an unstoppable force.

Yet the last part of the confession troubled Edith as much as Wulfstan. She could not make the confession known without revealing this terrible secret. Or could she?

Her gaze fell on Godwine. He looked just like a young Harold. England needed a champion, someone with the ability and passion to unite the separate factions into a full scale rebellion. *Godwine could do it.* Armed with the knowledge of the Normans' true intentions, he could convince Edwin, Morcar, the Atheling, and everyone else to resist the invaders. *I'm sorry Wulfstan. Harold vowed to keep the confession secret, but I did not.*

They rode south toward Gloucester. With any luck, they'd reach the city before the midnight office. After a night's rest, they would hire a vessel to sail them down the mouth of the Severn to Godwine's lands in Somerset. From there, they'd be just a day's ride from Exeter.

She could see it all. The west country, the center of the Godwinson family's power, lay unconquered. With her sons at the head of a new, desperate army, the Norman occupation would be short-lived.

Yet as they raced through the quiet, pastoral town of Great Malvern, a rush of doubt clouded her plans. *Do I want to assign my sons this lifetime of bitter fighting?*

She glanced again at Godwine. He no longer hid his face and rode with a look of sheer determination. He would take his vengeance, whether she assigned it or not. The best she could do is bestow upon him every possible weapon.

They reached the forested path that led to Gloucester and charged on without pause. The speed made Edith feel like a feather caught in a gale. Her lone control lay in the saddle bag and it too would vanish when she showed the pages to her sons. The moment of its unveiling, she realized, would need careful planning. Reveal it too early, and they may act before they're ready. Reveal it too late, and the chance may be lost. *Reveal it at the right moment, and the Devil himself would not withstand our power.*

The Confession

July 1, 1065

The bishop: You have lost your wits, my son. Breaking from the papacy is a path to Hell, not salvation.

The earl: When I caught my first glimpse of England's shores, I thought so too. The suffering involved in the pursuit would be catastrophic, and I cursed my foul mind for daring to conceive it. The fear overwhelmed my anger at William, my euphoria at returning home, even my desire to live.

The bishop: But God sent me here to save you. "Save the truth," he said.

The earl: He knows my mind. If He wanted my thoughts forgotten, He would not have sent you.

The bishop: I shudder to ask, but what is in your mind?

The earl: The mother church is broken and I intend to fix it. This blood-hungry papal court must be replaced with men who respect peace. If I can defeat William and Odo, I will gain enough power to overthrow Hildebrand, Pope Alexander, and their minions. Only then will the world be safe from interminable war.

The bishop: The madness still grips you. Repent now, Harold. I beg you to chase these evil thoughts from your head. The Pope is God's emissary. Defying him will mean excommunication. No sacraments. No solemn burial. Darkness on earth...

The earl: My soul is a small price to pay. If I don't resist, countless innocents will suffer at the hands of these mad men.

The bishop: But it's not just your soul. England will be placed under interdict. Children won't be baptized and sins won't be confessed. Masses will cease and churches will shutter their doors.

The earl: No. I will prevent it. Once Hildebrand and Alexander are ripped from St. Peters, the men who take their places will understand my actions and absolve my people of any wrongdoing.

The bishop: You denigrate the church of your ancestors. You threaten the very foundation of our lives. Defying the papacy is madness.

The earl: It's my chosen quest. Hildebrand views the Normans as the papacy's sword arm. Now, that sword is pointed straight at my heart. I can either bow down or fight. You've known me a long time. Has my knee ever bent easily?

The bishop: This is not about the church. You would threaten the afterlife of every Englishman to prove your righteousness in this petty squabble.

The earl: No. I am trying to protect every Englishman from William's cold clutches and Odo's disastrous campaign. I ran from one chance. I won't run again. England must be protected from this horrid future, no matter the cost.

The bishop: I can stand no more of this. You have lost your senses. I absolved you from the oath you made in Bayeux. I agree that the Norman invasion must be stopped at all costs. As for the rest of this...this confession, we will speak when your head is clear.

The earl: I'm feeling stronger already, father. Thank you for hearing me out. But I must ask: have you lost faith in me?

The bishop: You have uttered horrific words, my son. But despite it all, my loyalty to you is second only to God, and it always will be. Now, Aidan, for the love of saints in heaven put down your quill...

Chapter 41: Odo

December 10, 1066

As William and his curia rode up to the snow-blanketed fortress of Berkhamstead, Edgar the Atheling stood shivering in front of the entrance gates. Behind the wispy boy, dozens of English nobles, church prelates, and London burghers waited with cold breath and nervous coughs. Odo's glance passed them all until it fell on a gray-haired man in a plain Benedictine robe who stood apart from his delegation. The man planted his staff in a vertical line from the snow-pack and watched the approaching Normans with restrained neutrality. The look held so much condescension and moral righteousness that Odo recognized him straight away. *I will wipe the arrogance from Wulfstan's face if it's the last thing I do.*

He turned back to the Atheling. No man made a sound and the snow muffled the horse trots, so the two parties faced one another in a tense silence under a flurry-filled sky. Then, as William dismounted, his stallion unleashed a ferocious whinny. The boy pretender jumped so hard his thick fur pelt fell from his slender shoulders. Snickers emitted from the curia ranks with Odo's among the loudest.

As the rest of the curia stayed mounted, William turned to his pathetic rival after calming his stallion with a muzzle pat. "Well met, cousin," he said in Latin. "I understand you have something for me."

Odo kept his demeanor light even though he seethed inside. The kinship between William and Edgar was as thin as an insect wing, yet William chose to acknowledge it nonetheless. Odo had argued for no such kindness, but William thought differently. "Until the crown is on my head," the duke had said, "we must give them no reason to distrust us."

Flanked by two men Odo assumed were the northern earls, Edgar advanced until he met William halfway between delegations. He opened his mouth to speak, but no words came out. Redness filled his cheeks as he glanced over his shoulder. Odo followed the gaze to a person he missed in his first glance. A willowy, black-clad woman stood among the English nobles and she now flung her fingers at the boy. Odo shook his head in bemusement. *With all the remaining power in England around him, he turns to his mother.*

The fingers, however, served their purpose. Edgar turned back to William. "I...I have brought my undying love for you, cousin, and an offer. If you find it in your heart to accept England's crown, I promise to follow you as loyally as I followed King Edward." The boy then knelt in the snow and lowered his head.

William turned his gaze to the men standing next to the prostrated boy. "What say you, lords? The Atheling has offered me the crown and his allegiance free of condition. Do you do the same?"

The squatter, more pig-like man to Edgar's right spoke first. "Duke William, while neither I, Edwin, earl of Mercia, or my brother Morcar, earl of Northumbria, have had the honor of meeting you before, we have heard tales of your fairness and honesty. We want it known that we had no hand in the usurper's rebellion against your rightful claim. In fact, we tried to prevent him from his destructive path, but his Devil's ways proved too powerful. Now, we speak for every noble in the realm and offer the crown into your benevolent hands." The brothers knelt next to the boy they had proclaimed king just weeks ago. Edwin had forgotten to include that little treason in his speech. William's act of forgiveness for Edgar's brief kingship was another thought that made Odo's blood boil.

"Well said, loyal Edwin," William spoke in a voice loud enough for all to hear. "The offer from the nobility touches my heart, but I could never accept without the clergy's blessing."

Odo craned his neck to regard the back of the English delegation. Wulfstan followed an aged, purple-robed prelate to the spot where Edgar and the earls still knelt. "My lord duke, I am Ealdred, archbishop of York. Speaking on behalf of the English dioceses yet to succumb, I can say with all honesty we seek an end to this bloody invasion. So, if we agree to offer you the crown, will you promise to do everything in your power to cease the violence ensnaring our beleaguered realm?"

Odo's chin retracted into his neck. This archbishop dared to make a condition. *It must be Wulfstan's doing.*

William's countenance darkened. "This violence would never have happened, had anyone in the realm stopped the usurper. But since no one showed the courage, the task was left to me. And as you can see, I finish my tasks." He sighed and thought for a moment. "Thanks to the usurper, England declared war on me. He has been dealt with, but his followers have not. Therefore, everyone who pledges their allegiance to me and my council will be pardoned. Those who choose not to pledge will be viewed as my enemy. It is an easy enough choice to make." Turning back to the archbishop, he softened his voice. "I have done all I can do, Ealdred. Do I have the clergy's support or not?"

Odo's breath suspended. This was the moment he had waited for.

The archbishop licked his lips and then bowed his head. "If it pleases you, lord duke, I offer to preside over your coronation ceremony as a gesture of our loyalty to your reign." Bending to his old knees, Ealdred took William's outstretched hand and kissed the back of his palm. When Wulfstan followed suit, Odo forgot his previous frustrations and almost howled in joy.

The power of the moment swept William away as well. "Excellent," he said, clapping his gloved hands. "Now, let's adjourn to the fort. We can warm our limbs by a hearth and discuss my coronation in London."

He kept talking as he walked past the kneeling nobles and led the way into the fortress. The Norman curia began dismounting and following their king-in-waiting, but Odo stayed mounted. He wanted one last triumphant glance at the beaten Wulfstan. Yet when the crowd cleared, Worcester's bishop had risen from his prostration and now glared straight into Odo's soul, smug and arrogant as ever.

After William dictated his coronation plans, the Englishmen begged their leave to return to London. Odo stood aside as they exited and nudged his head in Wulfstan's direction. He then excused himself and rushed to his pavilion tent outside Berkhamstead.

A little while later, he rose from his cushioned chair when the guards escorted the English bishop inside. "Come in, Brother Wulfstan."

Standing just a pace inside the entryway, Wulfstan searched the well-furnished tent with open dismay. "I was not aware, Lord Odo, you had taken monastic vows. Only those men of God could ever call me 'brother.' And I assure you, no brother of mine would send armed guards to drag me to his lodging."

"Forgive me if my guards offended you, Wulfstan, and allow me to disagree. We *are* brothers in arms. We both fight to preserve God's reign on earth do we not?" Odo gestured to a small table covered with trays of fresh roasted quail, pig, and beef.

Ignoring the invitation, Wulfstan leaned his staff on a tent post and clasped his hands behind his back. "I fight nothing, save the Devil. You, on the other hand, seem willing to fight every creature under the sun that does not conform to your will."

"Oh, you have me there." Odo sat and thrust his hand into the tray of steaming pig loin. "I'm afraid my nature savors a good fight more than most. In fact, I daresay I crave them from time to time. A good battle is cleansing for the soul. Take our victory over the usurper, for instance. Can there be any doubt our world is cleaner now?"

"It appears God decided against the English. It also appears we are still plagued with filth."

Odo pushed the trays away and fixed his light gaze on Wulfstan. "No question. Enemies abound and threaten our good cause. This kingdom is sick and I intend to heal it."

"I was unaware you cared so much for England's spiritual well-being..."

"Oh I do." Odo filled his face with earnest. He wanted to enjoy riling Wulfstan before striking the final blow. "For my first order of business, I seek to punish the many clergymen here who have taken a wife. Service to Our Lord should be all-consuming, don't you agree?"

The old monk grimaced. "I fear many have taken wives, but they are no brothers of mine, either. I do not think, however, this problem is England's alone. I've heard many clergymen in Normandy also have wives. How come you haven't healed them?"

Shifting in his seat, Odo admonished himself for leaving Wulfstan an opening. "I cannot control what happens in other bishoprics. In Bayeux, I promise you, churchmen are married to God alone. Yet England has more problems than just lustful clergymen. Prelates collect bishoprics like they collect lice, while the mother church condemns plurality. Your own archbishop of Canterbury, for instance, also holds Winchester's bishopric." Odo clicked his tongue in disapproval.

"Stigand is a deft politician, it's true, but a daft clergyman. Depose him at your will. The country will be the better for it. Yet our country has an archbishop of York as well. And with him, even your harshest investigations will find no wrongdoing. Ealdred is beyond reproach in the eyes of God and man. Depose him, Odo, and you'll have full scale revolt."

Odo waved a hand across his face. He knew Ealdred could not be attacked. He also knew no attack was necessary because one, maybe two summers awaited the ancient prelate at most. "I'm glad your mentor is so loved, Wulfstan. But what about you? How would the populace react if you lost Worcester's seat?"

"I have no idea how the people would react. God, on the other hand, would no doubt avenge my aggressors for the wrong."

"Wrong?" He favored the old monk with his most disarming smile. "Since arriving in England, my dear brother, I've learned much about your diocese and monastery. Is it not true that your monks produce texts in the local dialect instead of preserving the church's Latin?"

"That is no crime."

"Not yet. Once William takes the crown, this hideous English tongue will be chased away like an unwanted dog. Your monastery's practices will be treasonous soon enough."

Wulfstan glanced at the tent flaps. "Bishop Odo, there are many poor, scared people in London looking to me for solace. I have neither the time, nor the patience to listen to your accusations. So either say your peace or let me go. Now."

"I was warned of your viper's tongue and I see it's still dagger sharp." Odo rose and patted his full belly. "But someone in your tenuous situation would be well-advised to dull the edge of their attacks."

"My tenuous situation, Odo? I hold no seat beside Worcester. I am unmarried. My monks translate some writings to English, but that is not a crime until the king says it is. So, as far as I can see, my situation is safe."

"Safe?" Odo walked to a nearby desk and held up the proclamation. "You are aware of the decree to surrender all writings involving the usurper?"

"I've relinquished all the charters and writs I possess."

"Do not accentuate your treason with lies, Wulfstan." He slapped the parchment back on the desk. "You did not relinquish everything and you know it. There is a book with a falcon on the cover. It was Godwinson's before his death and was last seen with you."

"Ah yes. The bestiary."

"The what?"

"The falcon bestiary. One of my monks helped Harold construct it. A most beautiful text that pays tribute to rap-tors. I have not relinquished it because it doesn't pertain to Harold. It was his gift to the world, not a testament of his reign."

"My sources tell me the book contains a different story, and I would like to see it."

"What, pray tell, did your *sources* say the book con-tained?"

They locked eyes and pure hatred lurked just behind Wulfstan's calm expression. *He knows. This man could ruin me with a word.* "A fantastic tale about Godwinson's travels two summers ago. I've always wondered what caused him to defy the oath he swore in Bayeux and I hoped this text would explain it to me."

"Harold forswore the oath, Odo, because he was forced to make it. You don't need a mythical book tell you that. As for the text in question, I'd love nothing more than to show it to you. Then, mayhap, you'd leave me alone."

"Then why don't you? From what I'm told, it sits just a few miles away at Waltham."

"I will send for it, my lord, although it may take a few days. The book was damaged some during the campaigns in the fall. My monk works to restore its glory."

"Restoring it, you say? This has gone on too long. I have had enough of your lies. Guards! Take Bishop Wulfstan to Wallingford. Keep him comfortable, but make sure he stays in place."

"You *cannot* do this!" The good bishop's fingers stretched out like hawk talons.

"I am doing this, you conceited weakling. Until the coronation, you will be my honored guest. After the coronation, you will be my prisoner. The only way you'll escape is by producing the book to me."

The guards re-entered the tent and grabbed the bishop by the shoulders. As they pulled him away, he wrenched his neck around. "How can *I* produce the book if you keep me prisoner?"

Odo smiled wide. Fear had taken over the arrogance in Wulfstan's face. "Pray, good bishop. I understand you can do that better than anyone."

Chapter 42:
Orrin

December 11, 1066

A twinge of nostalgia bit at Orrin as he halted his conroi outside Waltham Holy Cross. Just two months ago, he stood outside Bexhill with different warriors at his back, trying to effect a bloodless invasion. Today, he brushed his fingertips over his wolf-bone hilt with a different sensation coursing through him.

He filled his voice with all the spite in his soul. "Forward at a gallop. Anything you find is yours. Any man you kill is a traitor. Any woman you see is ripe for the picking!"

Like a pack of ghosts, the fifty soldiers rumbled toward the town. *Urse would be proud.* Thinking of his fallen friend who still lay teetering on Death's threshold made him kick his spurs harder. With the sun peeking through wind-driven clouds, Waltham looked every bit the serene English village. Snow drifts covered roofs, entryways, and the church tower. As he approached, Orrin imagined how it would look in just a few moments: a ring of smoke, cinders, and ash. *They brought this on themselves.*

While the English nobles swore their allegiance to William just yesterday, Waltham sent no representative. As a town beholden to Harold Godwinson, it should have bowed down to avoid this fate. When Odo told him about Waltham's defiance, he jumped at the chance to prove his loyalty once again. "To win your passage home, destroy the scribe's falcon book," Odo had said. "Burn down the entire place if you have to."

When the horses reached the first row of houses, Orrin opened his ears and braced for the telltale scream of town folk. The blood-curdling cry would give him a long-sought revenge on this town that nearly took his life. It would also tell him where the women hid. This time, he would not hold his men back from their winnings. Yet the first row passed without a sound. So did the second and the third. Shaking, Orrin held up his hand and signaled for a halt. The Norman horses reared as the riders yanked on the reins.

Head swiveling, Orrin noticed how most of the houses had fresh timber nailed across the doorways. No livestock could be seen and none of the thatch roofs showed hearth smoke. Before he could react, an unexpected sound floated on the wind. Deep, urgent voices lifted a prayer song to the Heaven. "They're all in the church!"

The conroi dismounted in the clearing by the entry steps. The last time Orrin arrived here, thick chords of rope rendered him immobile. This time, his free limbs would not be idle. "You stay out here," he told his soldiers, "and begin ravaging at my signal. I want to tell the town folk their reaper has arrived."

Drawing his sword, Orrin raced up the steps and

kicked the door in. He yearned for the panicked swirl of chaos. He imagined a church full of quaking, broken people begging him for mercy. They would find none. *The days of brokering peace are over. I will sail home on a ship made from Waltham's timbers and paid for by the falcon book's destruction.*

Stepping through the tattered threshold, he found a dark, empty room, save for twelve old men holding candles by the altar. He knew them at once as the church canons, both from their rich vestments of charcoal and crimson and because he recognized the sot standing near the edge of the altar dais.

"Where are all the people?"

"Gone...fled." Osgod looked scared enough to soil himself, but his fear did nothing to console Orrin. He fought down the mounting disappointment, knowing his job in Waltham could still be accomplished.

"I've come for Aidan. If you give him over, we may spare your church."

The sacristan's face blushed and his head lolled toward his shoulder. "Wulfstan's boy? You've brought a host of soldiers for..." He jolted into action. "Stay here my brothers. I fear this is just a dangerous misunderstanding. Lord Geirson, please speak with me in private. I beg you." Walking to the side wall, he gestured to the door.

Orrin followed, knowing Osgod could not hope to outrun him. Once outside, the fat man led him around the back to the sheds where Rand performed his torture.

The sight of the sheds renewed his vitriol. "Captain!" A Norman chevalier came running from the front of the church. "Torch the town. If you find anyone alive, make sure they watch their house burn before killing them."

"No! Please Lord Geirson. Just a moment of your time. I promise it's worth your while."

Staying his order with a hand gesture, Orrin regarded Osgod with hatred plain on his face. "Where did the town folk go?"

"Most fled north. Some ran to London." He hung his head. "The church has not collected a penny in days."

Anger spewed from his gut, but Orrin controlled himself. "Is Aidan still here?"

"No. He and a band of rebels left for Worcester after Wulfstan chased you off."

The mention of the bishop's name made him blink. He and Urse escaped Waltham because of Wulfstan's kindness. "I know the bishop submitted at Berkhamstead yesterday. Did he return here or go to London? I'd like to thank him for his help once more."

Osgod's head bobbed on this thick neck. "Thank him for helping you escape, is that it?"

"Yes."

"My dear Orrin, who do you think incited the mob?"

"What do you mean?"

"Wulfstan concocted the whole scene. He wanted you to fear for your life so you'd agree to leave."

"He incited the mob himself..."

"Why would I lie?" Osgod spread out his hands. "The blessed bishop stirred up the entire town with tales of Norman atrocities. He then let you hear them howl for your blood."

"But why didn't he just let the mob kill us?"

"You claimed God's protection. Wulfstan is scheming and misleading, but he does not violate God's Will...at least I never thought he did."

The realization hit him like a lightning strike. *Even Wulfstan plots against me.*

As he stood in shocked silence, Osgod looked at him.

"It was all he could do to separate you from Aidan. Of course, I'd protect the young boy too. He carried such a valuable treasure."

"What are you talking about?"

"The book, of course."

Orrin prayed his face remained unexpressive. "I did not know he carried a book."

The thin smile spreading across Osgod's flabby cheeks told Orrin his attempt at secrecy had failed. "We both know he did, Lord Geirson. But before I continue, we must come to some understanding. If I tell you my small secret, will you call off your raid? Waltham's people may yet return and I'd rather them toss their pennies into our collection plate as opposed to a reconstruction."

Stalking to the clergyman, Orrin pointed his sword tip at Osgod's stubby nose. "You are in no position to broker for anything."

To Orrin's surprise, Osgod did not even flinch. "I must disagree. What I have to say will interest you...greatly."

Osgod's calm demeanor made him pause. "Tell me then. But you had better offer *tremendous* value."

The clergyman intertwined his fingers over his chest. "I do, I assure you. At first, your unexpected appearance in our church baffled me. Your quest for Aidan, however, explained it all. It seems you and I are of the same mind in this regard. We both seek his falcon book."

"How do you know I'm after the book?"

"Well, I don't think you wish to pat the boy on the back. And since the text contained such treasonous words, I figured your Norman overlords would want to obtain it at all costs." His eyebrows raised high.

"You *read* it?"

"How could I have resisted. You didn't notice how

Aidan fidgeted with his saddlebag every few trots in the Andredsweald? While he and Wulfstan talked in the church, I dared to untie the straps and glance in. I just got through a page or two before Aidan came out. It was dark and my eyes have regressed over the years, but the text was clear enough. Aidan and Wulfstan recorded some confession Harold Godwinson made about his journey to the continent..."

Every muscle in Orrin's body pulsed at once. Now, this stupid clergyman had thrust himself into the middle of the tempest. "Osgod, I shouldn't have doubted you. Your information is worth a mountain of gold and Bishop Odo of Bayeux would pay it. I will stand my men down if you agree to go to him and tell him what you told me."

"I'd be most honored. Are you not coming with me, Lord Geirson?"

Orrin glanced over his shoulder. The Norman soldiers awaited his order to raze the town, but the anger he felt at Waltham fled under a wave of excitement. If he wanted to catch Aidan, he didn't have a moment to spare. He also didn't want to bring any soldiers with him. They would draw unwanted attention to his secret mission and he knew he could travel faster by himself. "I'm going to Worcester while my men escort you to Berkhamstead. And please tell the bishop that as well."

Chapter 43:
Aidan

December 15, 1066

Aidan sat in his backless stool and smoothed the blank pages before him. The mere gesture energized his weary soul. For as long as he could remember, writing had been his solace. And on this most frightful of nights, the gift again proved its worth.

Rand had visited just before Vespers. Without mincing words, the huscarl told Aidan the Normans had taken London without a fight and planned to crown William on Christmas day. He also said Wulfstan had disappeared after an audience with Bishop Odo. The news added even more tension to his throbbing head, yet he steeled himself to the idea of another sleepless night. *One more line. One more word. One more page.*

His knuckles cracked and his back screamed in agony, but the physical pain didn't hold a candle to the job itself. The worst was the cleaning of the parchment. He had turned to that task after making the copy for Lady Edith. With every scratch, his most beautiful creation crumbled. Sometimes, tears would fall as he scraped. A few times, he became so angry his knife nearly ripped the parchment. He wept openly when the last word vanished.

As he started the bestiary, however, the work became less taxing. Remembering King Harold's falconry lessons took Aidan to a different, happier time. The writing had become enjoyable, until Rand's news. Now, he still had dozens of pages to fill and time grew desperate.

As unrelenting snow descended on the cloister green, Aidan picked up his quill and delved into another lesson. He envisioned a scene on the sea bluffs and his right hand unveiled the visual counterpart in steady, unwavering lines and curves. His soul moved in perfect symmetry with his mind, thinking, writing, praying, and learning. The outside world dissipated. The night no longer seemed cold. His foot no longer felt deformed. The world made perfect sense; a vision existed which needed a new form, a new outlet for understanding. With each line, circle, and slant, Aidan created a new path of enlightenment.

The Normans respected just French and Latin. Writings in English were deemed trash at best and treason at worst. Most bishops and prelates bent to Duke William's will and halted their English writing production. Wulfstan did not. In his last message before he disappeared, Worcester's bishop mandated an increase of English texts as way to preserve a now-threatened way of life. Aidan loved the bishop for a thousand reasons, but this one above the rest. Where thousands of English swords failed, a small unnoticed rebellion with quills defied the Norman might.

Aidan had finished his twentieth page of the evening

when a tap on his shoulder broke his concentration. Looking up through bleary eyes, he found the bald, bucktoothed Brother Tovi. The Rule of Saint Benedict prohibited talking in the cloister, so Tovi clasped his hands together, signaling the time for Compline. The bestiary had engulfed Aidan and he hadn't heard the church bells chime. He nodded his thanks to Tovi, rose, and followed his brother out of the cloister.

Compline focused on preparing the soul for its final rest and its passage into eternal life. It began with an examination of conscience. Here, his thoughts fell on Ebba once more. He had been harsh to her in the tavern and hadn't seen her since. He wished he had time to seek her out, but the bestiary took up every moment. *One day, I will help her see what a mistake we made...*

After Compline concluded, Aidan retreated through the still dense snow to his cell. There, he changed into a dry habit and collapsed into his straw pile...yet no rest came.

He dreamed he guarded a treasure chest atop an open, grassy plain. An army of fierce, faceless warriors protected it too. The perfect blue sky held no sun. White-capped mountains encircled the plain and formed an arena, in which Aidan and his chest held the center. With a log-splitting *CRACK*, earth began falling into a roaring black chasm, starting from the mountain line and closing inward. The warriors charged, hacking and chopping with their swords, yet the blackness swallowed them all. Before Aidan could even scream, the yawning chasm licked at his heels. Alone, he frantically searched for something, anything to help stave it off. Then, he drew out a white feather quill from his habit sleeve. The black abyss halted. He flung open the chest and lifted manuscript pages to the sky. The rumbling intensified, but the abyss grew no wider. Then, the mountains collapsed in a burst of dust and earth and snow. When the landslide settled, Aidan remained where he stood, holding his quill and his pages. The hole had vanished, as had the mountains. In the distance, a city of white stone appeared atop a desert of red-gold sand. Within the walls, a golden-domed church glistened atop a steep hill. Its church bells sounded so loud, Aidan looked to Heaven to see if arch-angels answered its call.

The church bells kept ringing as the dream ended. He snapped awake. *Vigilis.*

As he shuffled toward the church, the dream clung to his mind. He relished the feeling of holding his quill and his pages. This feeling refreshed his heart and renewed his constitution. Just before entering St. Mary's, he noticed an auspicious sign; the snow had stopped.

Aidan shut off his mind and lost himself in the rhythms of prayer. When the midnight office concluded, he took a single taper, dragged his foot through the snow to the cloister, and continued the bestiary writing.

On the Friday of the third week of Advent, Aidan sought out Rand in the monastic precinct's guest quarters.

"It's done," he told the warrior. Under his arm, he carried the bestiary in a soft cloth sack.

The warrior regarded him with a solemn nod. "Let's go to the stables. There's no time to lose."

They had just cleared the city walls when a lone horseman approached. Sensing danger, Rand pulled Scramasax in front of Aidan. "Off to the side. Now boy!"

At fifty paces, the rider charged. As Aidan yelled in

warning, Rand drew his sword. The attacker closed and a single steel *clang* echoed in the night. After a hefty grunt, the huscarl toppled to the snow-covered ground. Aidan scurried off his horse and started to run to his friend, but the sound of pounding hooves stopped him.

Darkness draped over the assailant's face, but his voice was unmistakable. "This is your end, Aidan." Silver glinted in the night and Aidan's horse unleashed a hideous scream. Blood showered over his habit as the gelding collapsed. He just managed to dive out of the way before the horse's weight crushed him.

Shaking off a wave of snow and pain, Aidan looked up. Orrin had learned from his previous mistakes. He ran straight to the saddle bag, pulled the bestiary out, and let the falcon glimmer in the moonlight. "I knew you'd try to run. It was just a matter of time."

Sprawled on the snow, Aidan's whole body shuddered. He lifted his head in time to see the traitor open the book.

"No!" Rand flew in, his sword slashing through the night air. Orrin looked up just in time, dropped the book, and blocked Rand's strike with his blade. Then, Aidan realized Rand's sword had bent.

"Stop!" He stretched out his hand. "Just take the book to Wulfstan. You'll see."

"Wulfstan?" Orrin spat in the snow. "I answer to a different bishop, boy." The traitor cast a disparaging eye toward Rand. "You look a far cry from the day when you scalded my friend's flesh with a poker."

"Aidan," Rand said, keeping his gaze fixed on Orrin. "Run back to the city. The traitor and I have some matters to settle."

"The boy will stay where he is and watch you fail, rebel." Orrin prowled around the stationary huscarl.

Then, Aidan's heart jumped. The Norman's first slash met solid steel and then he unleashed several more. Some Rand parried. Others he blocked. Hard and fast cuts flew, from high and low, from right and left, and each one Rand evaded.

"Stop now! Rand, let him take the book!" Aidan scrambled to his feet, but the warriors ignored his pleas.

The huscarl counterattacked, filling the air with curved silver flashes, driving the bigger man away from the road. Orrin caught one blow high, and then jammed his blade down to halt a vicious undercut. Hard on the Norman's heels, his blade sang in the night. The swords clashed and sprang apart and clashed again. The traitor moved to his right, but Rand blocked him with a quick sidestep and drove him farther off the road.

Aidan raced forward, begging for them to stop this madness.

Orrin's back hit a tree and snow fell in large clumps. "RAHHHH!" He bulled his way forward once again, swinging his blade in a horizontal arch that made Rand jump back.

"You fucking scum," Rand said. "You will rot in hell for all you've done." His sword whirled and slashed. In one wild flurry, the huscarl took back all the ground Orrin had fought so hard to claim. Focusing so much on the sword play, Orrin lost control of his feet and staggered for a brief moment.

"Filthy whoreson," Orrin screamed as he regained his balance and charged headlong toward his foe. He breathed deep and swung hard, trying to smash the younger man down. But the crooked blade parried every attack, and countered with vicious snips to Orrin's head, armpits, torso, and legs.

Aidan gave up trying to stop the fight and prayed for Rand's blade to win. One of the huscarl's strikes grazed Orrin's neck, causing him to stagger to a knee. At once Rand closed, his down cut screaming through the air. Orrin flung his sword arm up in the split second before the onslaught. Aidan's heart leapt. *Mighty God in Heaven, Rand is going to win.*

The huscarl spun and Orrin lost sight of him. Then, the butt of Rand's sword slammed into his opponent's spine. The traitor wailed in pain and fell to the ground. His back crashed into the snow just as his final cut sliced through the air.

Aidan's protector held his blade in perfect position and his stance could have absorbed a much stronger cut. His sword, however, snapped like a twig.

Aidan lost control of his senses. He howled and rushed forward. Orrin's heavier sword cut through steel, cloth, leather, and skin. It sank deep into shoulder bone and flesh. Rand's knees folded. His head turned to Aidan. "I'm sorry," he said. He tried to say more, but couldn't. He fell forward. Orrin jerked back, and Rand's body collapsed on top of darkening snow.

"No, no, no, no..." Aidan rolled the huscarl into his blood-soaked lap and felt his chest. Rand's heart still fluttered.

"Why! Dear God! You didn't need to kill him! The book's yours! *Take it!*"

Orrin stood over Aidan, chest heaving. He gripped his sword and stared forward with a hell-possessed look. "I'm not who you think I am, Aidan. I'm a Norman now, and I have orders."

Aidan's eyes went wide as he realized what Orrin meant. He raised his arms in a futile attempt at protection as he saw the sword rise in the air for the killing strike. He said a quick prayer and readied himself for death.

"Stop!" A girl's voice floated in the night.

Orrin turned to face his new opponent and found Ebba standing a mere ten paces away.

"Little girl, I will kill you too if I must." Orrin lifted his sword once more.

Aidan let his base instincts take over. He grabbed the hilt of Rand's broken sword. It still had half the jagged blade. Orrin turned from his distraction, but he was too late. Aidan sprang and sank the broken blade into the Norman's chest. The two toppled over. Pressed against Orrin's chest, Aidan felt the sensation of a beating heart arrest.

When he pressed himself up, Orrin Geirson's body lay unmoving beneath him. Aidan crawled away, shaking, retching, and denying what he just had done.

Ebba rushed to him. "Are you hurt? Where did he cut you?"

"No. I'm unhurt. I killed him. My God, I *killed* a man!"

"You had to," she said, cradling him in her arms. "He almost killed you first."

"But...but Rand!" In an instant, worry for his friend washed away the significance of his sin. He sprang up and raced to the huscarl's side. "Can you hear me, friend? Can you ride?"

Rand coughed up a glob of blood. "With...With me slowing you up, you wouldn't make it to London before Easter, much less Christmas Mass."

"I can't leave you here. It's unthinkable." Aidan felt panic close in.

"Then don't think and just go. Listen boy, my...my

fighting days are done." The light from Ebba's candle illuminated Rand's caring, hopeless eyes.

"You can't give up," Aidan said. Tears poured down his cheeks. "Not after all we've been through."

"I'm not giving up, Aidan. I'm just passing the torch to a much better rebel."

Unable to trust his ears, Aidan looked to Ebba for confirmation. She cried just as much as he did, even though she'd never met Rand before. She walked over and embraced the stricken warrior. "I...I should go get you help," she said.

"You saved Aidan's hide, lass. That's help enough. But there is," Rand coughed, "one thing, you could do. After...afterwards, let...let the monks know where I lie. I'd...I'd like to rest in Worcester's graveyard. Maybe Gytha can come visit me there. I'd ask Aidan, but he's off to London just now."

Ebba nodded her agreement, sniffled, and stepped away. Her candle still lit his face, which now wore a contented grin.

Aidan tried to maintain some amount of strength. He clasped the warrior's hand between his own. The emotion welled up from his stomach and exploded up his throat and into his eyes. There was nothing he could do to stop it. "You saved me when I was in trouble, and I couldn't pay you back in kind."

"No, friend," he said, with his eyes now closed. "You...you've paid me many times over..."

Aidan made the sign of the cross with one hand and held Rand's arm with the other. "God's peace be upon you, friend."

The warrior answered with complete stillness.

Ebba led him away by the hand, but Aidan watched

Rand the entire time. The lump in his throat felt like a boulder. His foot kicked something soft and supple in the snow. The feeling pulled Aidan away from the abyss. He bent and dusted the book off. *I must get this to London...for Rand's sake.* He then walked with Ebba to Scramasax. "How..."

She managed a light smile as she wiped her eyes. "Lady Edith told me to watch over you. I followed you to the city gates and then saw that man begin to follow."

"Lady Edith?" He shook his head. "I...I can't thank you enough."

She reached out and rubbed his shoulder. "I don't want your thanks, Aidan. I never have."

His mind reeled as guilt collided with something stronger. "I know I've treated you poorly since my return, but I—"

"Hush now. Hush. Lady Edith told me what I needed to know. I'll not stand in your way. Just promise me one thing."

"Anything Ebba," he said, clinging to the book in his hands.

"Come back soon."

Chapter 44: Edith

December 24, 1066

"Raise the banner," Edith said.

The red Dragon of Wessex climbed high above Exeter's stone walls and billowed in the winter wind. Behind the walled town, the morning sky clung to the first edges of dawn. The raw air felt dry and unmerciful, like Edith's heart. The Godwinson clan had marked their final stand. From this day forward, there would be no escape, no turning back.

Edith glanced at her sons as they watched their flying symbol of defiance. Godwine wore a look of sheer determination, Magnus watched with awe, and Edmund smiled with expectations of glory. *My sons. My warriors.* Behind them, Edith knew, stood the power of Somerset and Cornwall. Thousands of men had answered Godwine's call to avenge his father. By the time the Normans could answer this challenge, they expected thousands more.

Godwine stepped forward, turned, and regarded his army. Nodding in pride and power, Edith's eldest son raised his arms high and unleashed his lungs. The fighting men answered him again. The howls rumbled through the morning like thunder, reminding Edith of her last morning with Harold and his army. This muster did not hold the strength and passion of Harold's, but Edith told herself not to panic. Godwine was still young, still learning.

"Go to your families and celebrate our Lord's birth in good cheer," he told the assembled thanes, huscarls, and fyrdsmen. "For you are God's vengeance. He knows our land has been stolen from us. And He also knows the righteous can never fail as long as their hearts remain true. When we gather next, we will bathe our axes with Norman blood and take back our kingdom. God be with you all!"

Another cheer echoed through the morning. This time, Edith joined the cacophony.

After the banner-raising, Edith and her sons returned to their manor hall inside the city. Harold's family had kept a hall in Exeter for decades and Edith felt near at home within its sturdy timber walls. Gytha and Gunhild had been busy while the rest of the family attended the ceremony. They had covered the feasting board with pine branches, scented the hearth with incense, and set out a succulent feast. The most important thanes and city officials would arrive at any moment to join them in the Christmas celebrations and Edith's daughters had done her proud.

"Before the guests arrive, let's exchange our gifts."

Edith went first. She gave Gytha and Gunhild red-dyed dresses and told them to go try them on.

Alone with her boys, she prepared their gift: their

father's legacy. She walked to a nearby chest and unlocked it with the key around her neck. Withdrawing the scroll, she took a deep breath. For weeks now, she had stood back and watched as her boys became men. They could champion Harold's cause. She knew they could.

"For you three, I have a special present. It's your father's gift to you." The boys' eyes went wide as she presented the scroll Aidan created. "This is a scroll documenting a confession—"

A servant flung open the door to the manor house. "Lady Edith, a visitor has arrived early."

"Get him a mug of ale and ask him to wait a few moments, Renweard. I'm not done giving my sons their Christmas gift."

The servant swallowed hard and hesitated. Behind him, Edith heard a clamor of horse hooves and shouts. "Make way for the queen," one man said.

Furrowing her brow, Edith took the scroll and walked toward the door. She had not expected Harold's sister. "What is Queen Eadgifu doing here? I thought the Normans kept her at Wilton Abbey."

"It's not Queen Eadgifu, my lady," Renweard said meekly.

Looking out to the courtyard, Edith saw a company of huscarls surrounding a golden litter. One of the huscarls opened the door for a young, pale, red-haired girl. She had green eyes and wore a tunic the color of harvest wheat. When she stepped out of the litter, Edith's chest convulsed.

"It's Queen Alditha," Renweard said.

Edith could do nothing but stare. It wasn't Alditha's beauty that transfixed her, nor was it her golden circlet crown. It was her walk. As the girl approached the great hall, she smiled as bright as the summer sun and rested both hands atop her round, pregnant belly.

The Confession

July 1, 1065

Aidan watched Earl Harold rise from his supplication in front of the altar. His foster father looked spent and sore in one respect, replenished and renewed in another. The confession had worked to calm his nerves and pull him back from the frenzy of grief. At the same time, they had delved into England's darkest future, and the effort had left them all exhausted.

The earl spoke softly. "Did I talk too fast for you, Aidan?"

"No, m'lord. I think I caught everything, though I was down to my last page."

"You hear that, Wulfstan? Your novice says we talk too much."

Wulfstan had begun to douse the torches in the quenching bowl. "My novice," he said from across the church, "needs rest if he's to be of any use today."

Harold smiled and nodded. "I think the boy's of good use no matter the day. If you ever get tired of praying,

Aidan, you can come to me. I've always got need of good men. With the trials lined up on the horizon, I'll need as many as I can get."

Wulfstan had assigned the earl no prayers to recite or good works to perform as penance for his sins. The earl's forgiveness would be earned through the protection of the kingdom. What greater assignment could there be?

Still, the bishop looked like a part of his soul had died as he walked back toward the sanctuary. Neither he nor the earl looked ready to pick up the argument.

Only one torch kept the church alight. "Don't fill his mind with delusions, Harold. Aidan's not some thane's son in training to wield an axe. He's got a different calling entirely."

Aidan held the door as Wulfstan and the earl walked from the church. Outside, the sky began to show its first hints of lightening.

"Not all battles require axes, Wulfstan," Earl Harold said as he descended the stone steps. "Callings aside, Aidan's a fighter. He'd go to the end of the earth to save those he loved. Wouldn't you, boy?"

Lowering his head as he followed his two fathers, Aidan hid a brimming grin. Swords, axes, and shields were a mystery to him, and would be for the rest of his life. But the Almighty needed more than swords to fight the Devil, and Aidan wanted nothing more than to enter this battle. *There's more than one way to protect loved ones.* "I would do my best, Lord Harold."

Chapter 45: Odo

December 25, 1066

Horns blared from the choir of Westminster Abbey, signaling the start of Mass. Standing where the stone narthex opened to the cavernous nave, Odo waited for the fanfare and the bells to stop. Then, he wrapped the butt of his staff on the floor. "Glory be to God, Normandy, and England." The murmuring died and every neck craned in his direction. He drank in the awed attention for a heartbeat. "The coronation will now begin. The congregation will remain standing until all the celebrants have progressed to the sanctuary."

With the crowd inside quiet, the sole disturbance came from outside, where London's merchants shouted and cursed at the top of their lungs. In the weeks since the nobility's submission, the city residents had grown restless. Led by the contemptible Ansgar, these upstarts demanded more assurances for their safety and begged for favors from the new royal court. William tried assuring them the same rights they enjoyed during King Edward's reign, yet the disquiet continued. Now, as his lips fell into a deeper frown with every shout, Odo clung to the hope of the day. *In just a little while, their dissatisfaction becomes treason.*

With a stiff nod, he signaled for the *Te Deum.* The melodic chant sung by the abbey monks settled the attendees and opened the progression. As befit his high honor, Odo walked first. He wore vestments sewn for the occasion. His crimson chasuble was embroidered with flowers of golden thread. The center of every flower displayed an oval jewel. The miter he selected added five hand-lengths to his height and displayed a cross of encrusted rubies on its gold fabric. The stole draped over his shoulders held an embroidered depiction of the victory over the usurper; golden warriors fighting on a field of crimson. Timing his walk to the music, Odo could not break decorum to look at the crowd. So, instead of seeing their impressed faces, he gained satisfaction through their sharp intakes of breath as he passed.

Every step brought him closer to safety. After the ceremony, Odo would use William's new kingship and Orrin's surprise gift to condemn Bishop Wulfstan. Combined with the destruction of the falcon book and the wretched scribe, Wulfstan's demise would wipe the horrid night in Bayeux from existence and ensure Odo's grand calling remained secret. In fact, his lone agitation stemmed from Orrin's delayed return from Worcester, but snows had made several roads impassable. *He chased after a crippled boy. How could he have failed?*

After progressing to the altar, he could look over the assembled nobles. Edgar the Atheling clung to his mother's skirts. Stigand, the leech-like archbishop of Canterbury, leaned on his staff with eyes half-closed. His white robes and soaring bishop's hat set him apart almost as much as his flock of choir boys. The brothers Edwin and Morcar stood as far back as possible with their arms crossed over their golden-mantled chests. It was the strongest defiance they could muster, yet they managed to botch this as well. Either from too much nerves or drink, Edwin heaved over to regurgitate his breakfast on the church floor. Instead of holding his posture or helping Edwin, Morcar scrambled away from his spitting brother to save his leather shoes. Most attendees paid the Earls of Mercia and Northumbria enough dignity to ignore their antics, but Odo heard the chuckles sneak out.

Of all the conquered Englishmen, only Bishop Wulf-stan looked composed. He stood against the south wall, wearing a simple cloak of natural wool. Two of Odo's guards bracketed him. *Soon you will be in your precious Heaven, you self-important simpleton.*

No English aristocrat walked in the regal procession. After Odo, Roger of Beaumont led a host of Norman baronage down the nave. They wore silken tunics of sage, azure, silver, gold, and crimson, but their dress paled in comparison to the excited gleam in their eyes. After the barons filled the front of the nave, the foreign dignitaries entered, led by Count Brian of Brittany and Eustace, the count of Boulogne. These men, wearing caps adorned with feathers of a dozen colors, had accompanied the Normans on their conquest and no doubt expected a mountain of riches in return. *My reward will dwarf all of theirs.*

The King's chaplain, William of Poitiers, sauntered in next. Just last week, he had shown Odo the first few pages of his *Historum Normanum*. The words pleased Odo greatly. With no English account to contradict him,

Poitiers would relegate the usurper to the shadows of history.

After the chaplain, William Fitz Osbern walked down. Wearing a clove-colored tunic embroidered with silver thread, he acted with an appropriate amount of solemnity, but Odo saw the superiority in his eyes. Odo hid his bristle. *I walked down first, servant. I have the honor.*

As a last face slap to the conquered, Archbishop Ealdred walked next to Geoffrey, bishop of Coutances. Geoffrey's official role was as a translator, but even a child could tell his position equaled Ealdred's.

The second-to-last entrant filled Odo with more joy than he could imagine. Dressed in flowing robes of crimson silk, this man embraced a bible to his chest. His plain black skull cap combined with pale cheeks and a grizzled graying beard to present humility, but his eyes made up for it. The two, green-gray jewels set against their backdrop of bright white radiated pure power. As he advanced, he sang the *Te Deum* with such passion that he could be heard over all others. Odo had invited him without expecting his acceptance. Yet his master surprised him. Hildebrand, the papal chancellor who promised to effect Odo's grand calling, had fought the winter seas to witness Normandy's achievement firsthand. *This is just the beginning, master. Afterwards, you will witness my triumph over Wulfstan as well.*

After Hildebrand took his place next to Odo, the conqueror entered Westminster. The tunic sleeves of brocaded gold and purple fell to a nice length down his arms, and the blood-red cloak hung down his back, creaseless. He walked slow, and even paused to share some words with Edwin and Morcar. William talked; the dolts nodded their heads. When he passed the Norman lords and vassals standing closest to the high altar, they made such a clamor the mob outside must have thought Christ himself had risen. Instead of quieting his countrymen, William stood and accepted the acclaim by smiling and standing amidst his warriors. The reaction did nothing but incite his men further.

When he reached the altar, the conqueror knelt and the ceremony commenced. During the claim assertion, more general phrases, such as "hereditary right" or "right of blood" replaced William's specific kingship ties. This removed any insult to the Atheling, who held a much more direct tie to old King Edward. Also, the salutation at the beginning of the litany read "to the most serene William, the great and peace-giving King crowned by God, life, and victory." No other monarch, save the Holy Roman Emperor and the King of France, received such holy honors.

To Odo's surprise, the archbishop's voice did not falter, nor did he stumble on a single word. Had it not been for the infernal Bishop Geoffrey repeating every word in Norman, Odo may have lost himself in the moment.

Just before the anointment, Ealdred turned to the audience and asked, "Do you, loyal English and Norman subjects alike, accept William as your new king?" Geoffrey translated the question, and the ensuing response erupted inside the church. English and Norman proclaimers stepped forward. Standing on either side of the altar, the two men shouted at the top of their lungs in obvious competition.

Then, the church doors flung open and a stream of guards poured in. They swiveled their heads to find the source of the disturbance. Odo screamed, "No you fools! It's just part of the service!" but it was too late. The ceremony dissolved into a tumult of panicked motion.

"It's a trap," Morcar yelled as he rushed to escape. "They'll kill us all!"

The screaming reached feverish levels. Then, cries turned anguished outside. "Fire! The church is aflame!"

"The mob'll kill us all," bellowed William Fitz Osbern. "Stop this madness!"His pleas fell on deaf ears, however, and the attendees spilled into the streets.

Shielding Hildebrand from harm, Odo rushed forward. As William sat on his throne holding a jewel-encrusted scepter in one hand and his head with the other, Odo growled to the remaining Norman retainers, "End this fighting and squelch the flames. Do it now or you'll be granted lands in Hell, not England. You," he pointed to Ealdred, "Perform the anointment."

The archbishop wiped sweat from his brow and signaled to the boy holding the holy oil vessel. The boy scampered to the altar, doing his best to avoid the anarchy. Ealdred crossed himself, doused William's crowned head with oil, and then shouted, "With this holy anointment, God, and all members of his office here on earth, now recognize William, Duke of Normandy, as King of England."

Odo stood breathing hard before the altar. *It is done. Wulfstan cannot escape.* Glancing back to the nave, he found the docile bishop unmoved by the south wall, watching with open disdain. In response, Odo gifted him the broadest, most sincere smile he his lips would allow.

Rising from the throne, the new king stormed toward the main doors, shoving attendants out of the way. When he reached the arched entryway, he turned back to the altar. The crown sat firm on his head and Odo could see the flames burst behind him. "Lord Odo, gather the remainder of the Witan and lead them to the West Palace. This chaos ends now." He then stalked into the brawl.

Chapter 46: Aidan

With his composure breaking outside London's closed gates, Aidan tried to appeal to the sentry's faith. "I'm a brother of Worcester Cathedral. If you let me into the city, your soul will ascend to heaven."

The Norman chortled. He was a short, squat young man with black stubble covering his cheeks. "City closed," he said in lilting Latin. "Go run away now." Smiling wide enough to show finger-width gaps in his teeth, he mimicked Aidan's limp. His three fellow guards sniggered.

Aidan curled his fingers in disbelief. He had learned of the unrest earlier in the afternoon, but didn't expect London to be closed off completely. *I've come too far to be turned away now.*

"I have coin," he said, hefting the purse of silver pennies tied to his rope belt. "Let me in and I'll pay you."

The smile fell from the sentry's face. But before he could speak, a voice called from the gate's other side. The four sentries scurried over and helped push open the doors. A litter of polished wood carried by four burly men emerged. The litter carriers wore fur pelts to ward off the cold, and each carried an axe slung on his back. The litter rider was veiled behind thick cowhide curtains.

Aidan stepped aside as the litter raced past. He figured it was some rich merchant escaping to the country until peace was restored. Moments later, the squat sentry returned with an honest look. "Coin?"

"Yes. Here." Aidan untied the purse and dropped it into the Norman's gloved hand.

The smile returned as the man tucked the pouch into his belt. "Yes. Here." He gestured to the road leading away from the city. This time, the sniggers grew to open laughter.

Aidan's eyes went wide. "Let me in!" He tried to walk past the sentry, but the snickering man grabbed him by the cowl and pushed him down the road to where Scramasax was tethered.

Rage filled his every extremity. He imagined what Rand would do to this imbecile, and the pain of the thought fired his cold blood. Yet just before he turned around, he noticed the litter had halted some twenty paces away.

"Come here, brother," the voice in the litter said. The speaker sounded tired to the bone. "What are you doing here?"

After his frantic race to London, Aidan was well beyond manners. Standing half way between the litter and the gate, he said, "What does it look like? I'm trying to get inside!"

"These Normans only listen for authority or profit,

and you offer nothing now. Tell me: what task is so urgent that you'd risk entering such a volatile place?"

The more the man spoke, the kinder and more familiar he sounded. "My bishop's inside. He's in trouble and I can save him, but I can't wait *another blessed moment!*" Flushed with anger, he picked up a pebble and hurled it at the Norman sentries. It clicked on the harmlessly on the gravel. Their ensuing laughter infuriated him all the more.

A noise from inside the litter turned Aidan's head. The man who exited made his jaw drop. Ealdred, Archbishop of York, stepped out and stood as tall as his stooped back would allow. His coronation garb and golden mitre gave him a saint's authority. "You're Wulfstan's boy, aren't you?"

Falling to his knees, Aidan managed to say, "Ye...yes, your grace. Brother Aidan Bardanson."

"I remembered your face and gait from last year's Christmas service, but wasn't entirely sure."

"But holy father, we...we didn't speak at last year's service."

"No, but I remember anyway. And Wulfstan's spoken so much about you I feel as if you're a brother of York Cathedral. I have good tidings for you, Aidan. I saw your bishop earlier today at the coronation. He seemed well enough."

"You *saw* him, your grace?" Aidan's heart skipped a beat. *Did he somehow elude Odo's clutches?*

"Yes. He stood in the gallery, as he's wont to do...although..." Ealdred's head tilted as his eyes squinted in thought.

Tension flooded back to Aidan's chest. "Yes, holy father?"

"Now I'm not so sure. He had been absent for weeks. I

assumed he was holding a vigil or helping a parish church outside the city walls. I meant to ask him where he'd been, but he was nowhere to be found after the riot."

"That's not like him, your grace. He's in real danger. If I don't get to Westminster this instant, it could mean his life."

Ealdred glanced at the gate. "Get in the litter. These fools know better than to defy the man who just anointed their king."

Aidan scrambled onto a cushioned seat and the arch-bishop climbed in opposite him. His servants lifted the carriage like it was made of feathers. When they reached the gate, the Norman captain tried to argue, but Ealdred castigated him until he pleaded on his knees for God's forgiveness and paid back Aidan's coin.

Once inside the city, the uprising's effects were immediate. As the litter bearers jogged down the street, a smell of charred flesh and wood clung to the brisk night air. Aidan and Ealdred bounced inside the litter, but they made good time wending their way toward the Strand.

Once, Aidan heard a desperate female voice begging for help. Daring a look toward the archbishop, Aidan found him shaking. "I helped as many as I could after the riot," Ealdred said. "But there were so many...If I stop now, crowds would form and we may not start again."

"What happened today, your grace?"

He frowned at the closed curtain. "The work of beasts and cravens, boy. Since King Harold fell, a man named Ansgar has led the city. Today, he meant to spark an uprising at the steps of Westminster. Yet he lost his nerve and failed to appear. Norman guards held the leaderless mob at bay for a while. But during the coronation proclamation, the guards grew confused and stormed inside the church.

The mob broke free. Church outbuildings were burned and swords clashed in the square. The fire spread...pushed by the devil's hand. It climbed the city walls and laid waste to half of Cheapside."

"Dear God," Aidan crossed himself.

Ealdred looked as shaken as Aidan felt. "Today scared me more than any other," the old man said. "I could think of nothing save my own escape...and then I saw you outside the gates. God has shown me the error of my cowardice. Now, we have little time before we reach Westminster. Tell me of this trouble surrounding Wulfstan."

As the litter bounced, Aidan measured his words. He trusted the archbishop, but couldn't tell him everything. He started by stating the danger. "I think the bishop of Bayeux will accuse him of treason."

Ealdred waved the words away with his bony fingers. "Preposterous. We've done everything they've asked."

"Yes, your grace, but Bishop Odo is convinced Wulfstan harbors proof of King Harold's reign."

"Wulfstan may have loved Harold dearly, but he wouldn't risk his life over a worthless charter."

Taking a deep breath, Aidan reached into his robe and produced the new bestiary. "You're right, holy father. The Normans search for this. They think it some book of secrets, but it's not so."

Blanching, Ealdred received the book. Even in the dark litter, he looked through all the pages. "I'm at a loss for words, Aidan."

"As you can see, your grace, the Normans are clearly mistaken, but I had to retrieve the proof from Worcester. While I was away, I fear what Odo's done."

"But I saw him today..."

"Maybe they wanted him to witness the coronation.

Maybe—" Before he could say anything else, the litter stopped and lowered. Ealdred handed the book back to Aidan and said, "We're here. Let's get to the bottom of this."

After sliding the book back into his hidden pocket, Aidan took a final peaceful breath and followed Ealdred out.

A throng of torch-holding guards lined the steps to the palace entrance doors. When Ealdred tried to walk past them, a chevalier in mud-covered chainmail answered him in rich-sounding Latin. "No one's allowed in the palace, archbishop. Not even you."

"Lord Fitz Osbern," Ealdred said, motioning for Aidan to stand behind him. "You've returned from punishing today's outlaws."

"I performed my orders, your grace, and do not wish to discuss them with you. Now be gone."

The archbishop stood his ground at the foot of the steps. "You strike me as a man of intelligence. Don't be unbending. God is watching and my audience with the king cannot wait."

The guards gathered closer and Aidan tensed. These men were not simple sentries who would cow easily.

Head shaking, the Norman named Fitz Osbern said, "The king's meeting with the Witan leaders right now. In fact, he expressly forbade your attendance. Whatever you have to say, it'll have to wait."

Glancing to the sides, Aidan saw three lines of Normans surrounding the entire palace. Either they gained entrance through these doors, or they'd gain no entry at all.

The archbishop kept his voice calm. "Tell me, lord

seneschal: is Bishop Odo also attending this mysterious meeting?"

At the mention of Bayeux's bishop, Fitz Osbern's eyes flickered. "He is."

"It's good to know the king is attended by his most loyal servant." Ealdred paused as Fitz Osbern shifted his shoulders back. "And did Father Odo bring anyone along?"

"As it happens, he arrived with Bishop Wulfstan."

"Ah. I thought as much. Allow me to explain. The boy behind me is Wulfstan's monk. They got separated during the recent tumult. If you were to let him pass, at least, your orders would be intact and I'd be most grateful."

Fitz Osbern paid Aidan a cursory glance. "Sorry, your grace. No one can enter."

Aidan felt sweat in his armpits and forehead. He grabbed the back of the archbishop's robe, but bony fingers knocked his hand away.

"Lord Fitz Osbern," Ealdred said, turning his voice honey-sweet, "he's just a young, crippled monk who poses no threat to anyone. Besides, he carries a manuscript Bishop Odo would be quite surprised to see."

"What do you mean, old man?" The Norman descended a step.

"Well, I make no promises, but Brother Aidan's arrival at Wulfstan's side may force our king's honored half-brother to answer a few questions of his own." He dared to unfurl a knowing grin.

As Fitz Osbern stared at them, Aidan remembered what the archbishop said outside the city gates: "These Normans only listen for authority or profit..." *This is profit at Odo's expense...and Fitz Osbern relishes the notion.*

After a lingering silence, the Norman stood aside.

"The boy can enter, but four guards will surround him at all times. If he makes one questionable move, they'll slit his throat."

Aidan's breath caught in his chest when he heard the threat, but Ealdred grabbed him by the shoulders and leveled their eyes together. "The door opens, Aidan Bardanson. Go quickly and remember that righteousness is on your side."

Nodding his understanding and thanks, Aidan watched as the giant oak doors creaked open. Four long, limber Normans formed a guard at the stair top. In the torch light, they looked like shadows preparing to escort a soul to Purgatory. After one last bow to Ealdred, he wrapped his arms around his sides, secured the book in its hidden pouch, and climbed the stairs.

Chapter 47: Odo

English nobles filled the hall of the West Palace. After they found their places around the large feasting board, Odo entered with Wulfstan in tow. They had just reached the table when King William appeared in a gust of swirling cloaks and clinking chain mail. Everyone in the hall bowed deep.

"Well met, my lords," William said. "You may rise."

"Well met indeed, Duke Wil...my king," Ansgar said. This burly middle-aged thane had fought in the usurper's army and still carried his left shoulder in a sling. After the battle, he had taken control of London's defenses, but his bluster amounted to nothing when the Normans bore down on the city. Now, he stood next to the broken, distant Atheling. "What's the meaning of this summons? Surely, you cannot blame us for the riots earlier today."

"No, Ansgar," William said. "I attribute this morning's disturbance to the divergent cultures melding into our new kingdom. A bit of unrest is to be expected. My men have dealt with the most serious of the transgressors and everything has been set right. I bring no blame with me to this moot, just rewards."

Edwin and Morcar leaned in. "We've been nothing if not loyal, my king," said Edwin.

"And it's been appreciated," William said, his face showing no emotion. "In fact, the whole Witan has proved its worth. Be assured you have my thanks, all of you."

"King William, it's known far and wide that your Norman court is filled with thieves and serpents," Morcar said. "We English stand by our words as strong as we stand in a shield wall."

"My good Morcar, such strong words are not surprising from such a well-built youth. But you have never experienced a day in my Norman court. Perhaps after the upcoming Easter celebration, you'll view it anew."

The confusion spread on the earls' faces. "Forgive me," Edwin said. His voice strained. "Is it wise to bring your Norman court here and leave your duchy unguarded?"

"You misunderstand me, loyal Edwin. You and your brother may learn to enjoy my court after you spend Easter in Rouen."

Murmurs filled the hall as Odo chuckled.

"King William!" Morcar's head shook. "You *cannot* do this! Not at such a fragile time. Who will help lead the recovery?"

The king looked at the earl with a curled lip. "I will see to the recovery; do not doubt that. And do not fret. You'll be in good company. The rest of the Witan shall attend you."

The Englishmen sat in the hall, staring dumbfounded into nothingness. Even when the guards entered and lined the room, they were too shocked to notice.

King William stepped into the void, "What say you

lords? I believe this is the first time I've caught you speechless."

Edwin, red-faced and bleary-eyed, lurched forward. "God damn you, William. You won't take me or my brother anywhere we don't want to go. You promised fair treatment."

"Quite right, son of Aelfgar. You and your brother are free to stay. Let me assure you, however, that you'll not be mistreated in my duchy. Who knows, you may even end up betrothed to one of my daughters. But if you choose to stay, I'm sure another, more eligible suitor could be found. Any refusal could be seen as treason, of course. And I would hate to remove such able men from their birthright."

Edwin rubbed his temples as if a rat nibbled at his brain. Morcar grasped him by the arm, whispering in his ear. After nodding twice, Edwin shouldered his brother away. "We'll speak more of this *proposal* later," the elder brother said. "But still, William, you cannot take the entire Witan to Normandy. Not now."

"Ah, forgive me. I did indeed misspeak," William said. "Not all of you will be going. Keeping to the terms of a prior agreement, Ansgar will stay behind. As for the church, Archbishop Ealdred and his most ardent supporter, Bishop Wulfstan, will remain as well."

The thane rose up. "Be comforted, my lords. The King and I have settled all arrangements. I'll remain as the leader of London's defenses for the rest of my days."

William nodded. "Indeed you will." Then, turning to his guards, he said, "Take the honored leader out to the yard and kill him."

For a moment, Ansgar didn't hear. He still puffed his chest out and held his chin high. But when the realization hit him, his face twisted in horror. "Never!" At once, a knife appeared in the hand opposite his slung arm. He had taken two steps toward William when the guards descended on him. One used his spear butt to plunge into the thane's ample gut. The blow sent Ansgar plummeting to the ground.

William approached the broken man. "You must think of me as quite a pretty fool, Ansgar. If you plan an uprising, it's best not to boast of it in your cups or to your whores."

The guards seized Ansgar and began to drag him away. "Friends," he wailed, "Rise up! Stop this! Save me! Countrymen! DO SOMETHING!!" His pleas fell on deaf ears. The other nobles turned their heads in fear. Wulfstan stepped forward, but Odo held him back.

The slamming door echoed in the stone hall. Then, the Atheling rushed toward William. Guards converged, but could not react in time as Edgar yelled, lunged, and fell right at the king's feet. A smirk filled William's face as he held his guards back with a hand.

"I beg you," the boy prince said in a squeal. "Please stop, in the name of our royal blood ties. It wasn't supposed to be this way. Ansgar's my protector. He's the last one…"

"These trying times have left my little kinsman spent. In fact, you all have exhausted yourselves in excitement over my reign. Guards, see our esteemed Englishmen to their quarters, but don't let them leave the city. They'll need to be close at hand for the upcoming voyage."

As the northern earls and the Atheling trudged away, William said, "Bishop Odo, please hold back a moment. You and Bishop Wulfstan."

Odo bowed. *The time has come.*

With a smattering of guards lining the walls in the otherwise empty hall, the king regarded Odo down the bridge of his royal nose. "I learned this afternoon that you've been quite busy, brother. What's the meaning of Wulfstan's incarceration?"

"It pains me to say this, my king, but I've discovered a situation...involving treason."

Wulfstan stood with an unbending posture. William, however, looked fit to bend him. "I had hoped he would help solidify my reign amongst the people of the west. Should I alter my thinking?"

"Lord king," Wulfstan said, clearing his throat, "I've committed no crime, yet this...man of God...has held me hostage on the basis of these unfounded accusations."

Odo started to pace. "The hostage part is true enough. Once his crime came to light, I held him until after your coronation to prevent escape. He's been treated fairly, so far. As you can see, he speaks without inhibition."

"I don't care a fig about the incarceration anymore," William said with his jaw flexing. "What treason did he commit?"

"It's best if you hear from the source." Odo turned to a nearby guard. "Call in the witness."

A morsel of fear-laced uncertainty crept into Wulfstan's countenance. The look turned into outright misery when Osgod Knoppe waddled into the room.

"Greetings, King William," the canon bowed as much as his fat would let him. "This is the greatest of days for our realm, God strike me if I lie."

"I will strike you, Osgod, if you lie," William said. "Now, what did you witness?"

The Waltham canon did not hesitate. "One of Wulfstan's monks possesses a book containing the confession of Harold Godwinson, my king."

"A *confession?*" William prided himself on never showing surprise. Upon hearing Osgod's words, however, even Odo's mighty brother looked shocked. "What did he confess?"

"As God as my witness, lord king, I just read the first few pages. He confessed to great crimes, but then digressed to speak of his love of family. Aidan...the monk interrupted me before I could read more."

William flew to Wulfstan and grabbed him by the scruff of his habit. "I'm sure you are aware that possession of such a text is treason, Wulfstan, so I will ask you once: Do you reject Osgod's claim?"

"With all my heart, King William. Neither I nor any of my monks possess this book. One of the brothers did bring a text from the battlefield, but it contains a bestiary, nothing more."

"William," Odo said, stepping up to Wulfstan and his half-brother, "I know you respect Worcester's bishop, but I believe he's playing us false. He was the usurper's confessor and Osgod *read* the confession. Tostig Godwinson mentioned it to me as well. Against these witnesses, all you have is a weak denial."

"Your witnesses are an avarice-filled canon and a crazed traitor." Wulfstan said, staring straight into the king's eyes. "How could you believe them?"

"I saw it, my lords," Osgod said in a low, damning voice. "This man is a liar."

William looked ready to cut both Englishmen's heads off. Shoving Wulfstan away, he said, "I have had enough. Odo has the right of it. A witness is proof. Your denials, Wulfstan, amount to nothing. I therefore order you to—"

A guard ran up to the table. "My lord king, there is a monk outside requesting an immediate audience. He says he has the falcon book."

Odo's chest cracked. "*What?*"

"Let him in," William said, turning his gaze to Odo.

Feeling the weight of his brother's stare, Odo rushed to the guard. "We were not supposed to be disturbed. You have—"

"He's done his duty, Odo. Step away and wait...*now.*" Head lowering, Odo stepped back.

The guard signaled and the hall door opened. Wulfstan's bedraggled, crippled monk limped in carrying a book. Odo rushed to his brother as panic made the room spin. "Take the Englishmen away. This has gone beyond them. Let us read it in peace."

"No. You have accused Wulfstan of treason and brought Osgod as a witness. We will settle this, now. Bring the book to me, good brother."

After the monk exchanged a warm look with Wulfstan, he set the book on the table. An invisible vice squeezed Odo's heart, but he could do nothing. The falcon glimmered in the firelight. *He will kill me.*

William opened the book and exhaled. Osgod and Odo rushed to it. After just a few words, Odo shivered in relief. Each page contained pictures and descriptions of raptors, just as Wulfstan and Lady Edith said.

Osgod, however, began to whimper. "This is not the book I saw, King William. I swear it. Some evil magic is at work here."

Odo's mind flew. This trial was by no means over. Looking at the boy who had almost destroyed him, he searched for some new way to attack. Orrin said the boy's name was Aidan. What else did he say? His mind rushed back to the day Winchester submitted. He had marked a small detail in Geirson's story. It seemed so minor he now fought to recall it. Then, as the hall fell into a hair-raising silence, a log in the hearth burst apart.

The sound jolted Odo's memory. "The clergyman may have a point, my king. He has described this book in detail to me, so much so I did not doubt him for a moment until the bestiary appeared. The bishop and his monk may indeed have altered the text. But what to do? We must settle this. Therefore, I suggest a trial by ordeal."

"What is there to decide?" Wulfstan railed with more vehemence than Odo thought the old man could summon. "I produced the book in question. By what right do you declare this trial?"

William regarded his brother with cool calculation. "You have both sworn to me your version of the story is correct. We'll let God decide."

The boy blanched and Wulfstan fumed. "Out of the question. We are leaving this Godless place." Odo could not withhold a smirk as Wulfstan stormed toward the door after collecting the book and his monk. *Wrong move, old man.*

"Enough," William said in the merest whisper. The word stopped Wulfstan far short of the door. "I am well within my rights of arresting you on Osgod's word alone. Now come back here and listen."

With hate leaping from his eyes, Wulfstan led his monk back to the hall. For his part, the boy looked ready to disintegrate.

Odo advanced. "Since he brought the book, the monk should perform the ordeal."

The English bishop stepped forward and started to speak. Before he uttered a word, however, the monk shuffled in front. "I'll do it," the boy said, squeaking like a mouse.

The king tilted his head. "What did you say, brother?"

"Lord king, I will champion Wulfstan in whatever trial you choose."

Turning to the monk, Wulfstan stooped down. His voice carried pure, unaffected tenderness. "This challenge, my son, will not be for the faint of heart."

The monk breathed heavy. "I'm ready, father."

"Thank you, my son. Thank you..." Wulfstan rose and turned to the king. "I accept Brother Aidan Bardanson as my champion, although your view of justice sickens me. Now, what ordeal have you selected to decide this...matter?"

King William squeezed the bridge of his nose in frustration. "Odo, what venue will judge the matter fairly?"

I have him. He gestured to the blazing hearth. "I propose a trial by fire."

Chapter 48: Aidan

Aidan knew he should pay attention to the powerful men in the room. He also knew his limbs shivered, betraying his dread to everyone. Most of all, he knew the people he loved more than anything now depended on him and no other. Yet despite all this knowledge, he stood rooted to the palace floor and stared straight at the giant hearth burning in a fireplace at the back end of the hall. Every crackle of scorched wood sounded like the Devil's laugh. Every flicker of flame seemed a demon's dance. The smell of charred pine, oak, and ash transformed into the stench of Hell. And behind it all, Aidan could hear the low, trembling voice of Death calling to him, begging him to embrace the flames as Jesus once embraced Judas.

He tried swallowing, but his throat had run dry. Breaths in this hot, damp hall supplied precious little air to his aching lungs. Beads of sweat cascaded down his forehead and armpits. Nothing he tried could break the spell cast over him by the tower of burning hate.

Wulfstan broke the spell for him. *"Preposterous!"* His shout echoed high into the rafter-beam ceiling and tore Aidan's eyes back to the great hall. "Such trials just prove one truth; fire burns flesh. Your ravaging of Sussex proved that well enough already!"

Odo paced once more. His gait reminded Aidan of an affectionate cat begging for scraps of meat. He began to speak, but Osgod stepped forward. "It proves more and you know it, Wulfstan. In fact, a trial by fire would be most appropriate."

"Oh? How so?" William said. In this moment, Aidan quaked. *My nights in the Andredsweald were watched closer than I thought.*

Osgod licked his lips and a little smile formed. "Worcester's bishop may rant all he wants, but he knows that English nobles held a similar trial for Queen Emma of blessed memory. This queen, I'm sure you recall lord king, is a distant ancestor of yours."

Wulfstan crossed his arms over his chest, but William's attention stayed with the now-composed canon. "My great aunt...I have never heard this story before."

"Allow me to share it," Osgod said. "After your ancestor married King Ethelred, the English nobles grew to hate the power she gained. So, they accused her of having an affair. Subjected to a trial by ordeal, she walked barefoot over nine glowing hot ploughshares. God protected the innocent woman from injury. After she had finished her march, she stood proud in front of her accusers and asked them when the real trial would begin. Where fire-torched iron proved your ancestor's innocence, King William, let fire prove this issue as well."

The king now turned to Aidan and Wulfstan. Regarding them with open disdain, he said, "How do we proceed?"

"There is nothing complex about it," Odo said with a flourish. "Let the boy retrieve your ring from the hearth and place it on the table. If he performs the task and is deemed uninjured, Wulfstan will be vindicated. If not, he'll be proven a traitor."

The words echoed in Aidan's ears: *Retrieve your ring from the hearth.* Unable to speak, he glanced back at the fireplace. The flames leapt and bounded about, as if they rejoiced at the idea.

A sudden movement drew his eyes away. Wulfstan reached for a clay cup and hurled it against the wall. "This is a travesty! The only way to test if the boy is injured is to wrap his scalded limb in sanctified linen and judge the injury three days hence. If you wish to pursue this trial, nothing will be solved, at least not tonight."

King William seethed in frustration. "That is your *last outburst*, you riotous old man. My guards are not the patient type." He turned back to Odo. "Is there any other way to judge this matter?"

"Wulfstan raises a valid point, my king. But an alternate solution presents itself. A judge can be assigned to oversee the trial and determine if the supplicant succeeds."

Aidan looked at Wulfstan with pleading eyes. Choked with anger, the bishop snarled and stepped forward, but the king silenced him with a daring stare.

"Whom do you suggest as a judge, Odo?"

"I believe I have the perfect man in mind. Since this monk is beholden to an ordained bishop, he must be judged by a clergyman. But who? Luckily, we have a clergyman in the palace guest house unsullied by bias. Call Hildebrand to judge this trial. God will no doubt guide him to the fair sentence."

"Yes! Chancellor Hildebrand would make a fine judge," Osgod tapped his fingertips together.

Aidan seized the name from his memory. *It's the chancellor. Odo sent him a message the night of the oath.*

Wulfstan's incredulous voice echoed off the walls. "I'd rather ask a wolf to guard a sheep flock."

With a click of his fingers, four guards knocked Aidan out of the way and wrenched the bishop's arms behind his back. "I warned you, Wulfstan. My patience is at an *end*. If you dare to interfere again, you'll die. If you slander the papal chancellor again, you'll die. If you stay quiet, you *may* live. Now, you," he pointed to the guard closest to the door, "go summon Hildebrand to us. I like this solution well enough."

The guard hurried off and the hall fell into quiet. William took a seat at the head of the trestle table closest to the fire as Osgod took a poker and stirred the logs. The *pops* and *cracks* made Aidan's head swirl, but Wulfstan's danger almost eclipsed his own. The Normans pulled his arms so hard his chest thrust forward.

"Lord king," Aidan said, trying to muffle his panic.

William craned his neck.

"I need to pray before this trial begins. I ask you, in Christian mercy, to allow my bishop to lead me in this most imperative supplication."

Pursing his lips, the king flicked his wrist and the guards threw Wulfstan to the ground. "You may pray," he said, "but if you raise your voice above a whisper, there will be no need for a trial at all."

"Yes, lord king." Aidan bent down and helped Wulfstan to his feet. "Are you hurt, father?"

"My body's fine, boy. My soul is wrecked with anguish. Come with me. We'll pray by the wall farthest from the flames."

They walked the length of the trestle table and knelt in the corner. It smelled of urine saturated hay, but Aidan thought it was Heaven compared to the other side of the room.

"We'll pray in a moment," Wulfstan whispered. "First, I need to know what you're doing. There's an idea bubbling in that mind of yours."

Glancing down the hall, Aidan bowed to keep up the pretense of prayer. "It's not an idea, father. It's the truth. The Normans are wrong...in a way. If God is good, he'll side with us, or at least there's a chance he will. How on earth did they learn of my fear?"

Wulfstan patted the crown of his head. "Orrin Geirson, no doubt."

The mention made Aidan's eyes flinch.

"You had an encounter with him, I gather," Wulfstan said.

"Yes, lord father. He would have killed me but Rand and Eb...some townsfolk saved me. Rand died in the fight, but Orrin got distracted in the aftermath. I...I killed him, lord father. Will God forgive me?"

The bishop cupped his chin, lifting Aidan's eyes to meet his. "My son, God rewards his greatest champions, either on earth or in heaven. By sending Orrin to Hell's gates, you performed a saintly service. He rejoices in your courage, so you—"

The creaking door made Aidan and Wulfstan look to the entry steps. A man in virgin white robes streamed into the hall. His eyes looked demonic. After a quick glance in their direction, he approached King William. "I came as fast as I could. The guard said something about a trial."

"Indeed," Odo said, bowing on one knee. "We have an impasse. Father Osgod here says he read a book containing Harold Godwinson's confession. This book was last seen in the hands of Aidan Bardanson, a monk beholden to Bishop Wulfstan of Worcester. Asked to produce this treasonous book, Wulfstan and his monk instead produced a bestiary." He pointed to where the book lay open on the table. "Osgod, however, swears the confession exists and that this substitute is meant to trick us. So, with conflicting proofs, we think a trial will settle the matter...a trial by fire."

"A confession given by the usurper..." Hildebrand turned to face Aidan and Wulfstan. "You did well to summon me, lords."

The king spread his hands open. "What will we do about the judgment?"

"Ah yes," Hildebrand said, throwing his arms behind his back. "I assume you want this settled in short order. Very well. I am aware of a method, but first I must interview the supplicants. Please approach, Father Wulfstan and Brother Aidan."

Rising from his knees, Aidan followed Wulfstan back toward the hearth wall. With every step, Aidan's muscles grew tighter.

"How did your monk get caught up in this messiness, Wulfstan?"

"Lord chancellor, Brother Aidan helped construct the bestiary. He has done nothing wrong, I swear."

"I will be the judge of that, father. Now, if this monk

helped create the bestiary, he must have some scribing talent..."

"Yes, lord chancellor."

"Would you say his talent is immense?"

"Yes, lord. God has blessed Aidan with an ability to write and draw with surpassing beauty."

"Excellent." He turned back to the Normans. "My method should be acceptable, gracious king. With your permission, I will send for parchment, quill, and ink. When they are delivered, the trial will begin. After the supplicant has fought the blaze, he must prove his welfare by writing and signing a declaration of innocence. If he is able to write afterward, he will demonstrate God's favor. If he stumbles at any point, well then, we'll know him for a liar."

As Aidan tried to grasp the chancellor's words, Wulfstan stared in disbelief. "No man, not Charlemagne, not Saint Cuthbert, not even Saint Peter, could overcome such a challenge."

Odo strolled to his half-brother's side. "If your monk is as pure as you think he is, Wulfstan, you should have nothing to fear."

"He has every right to fear," Osgod said, lurking by the burning logs. "He is about to burn."

"Silence...all of you," King William said from his seat. "Guards: fetch me a quill, some ink, and a blank scroll."

As Hildebrand assumed a seat facing the hearth, Odo held out his hand and William placed a silver ring into his palm. Aidan looked up to his bishop and beheld two helpless eyes. "I...I don't know what to say, boy. I've failed you as much as God has failed us."

It was the first time he ever heard the bishop lose faith. The words sparked rage in Aidan's blood. "We're not going to fail, father. We've come too far." Stepping past the puzzled Wulfstan, Aidan addressed King William. "I am ready to begin."

After one last embrace, Wulfstan walked to the side of the room opposite Odo, Osgod, and the king and started mumbling a prayer. Just then, the door latch opened and a guard brought the writing supplies to the trestle table and laid them in between the king and the chancellor.

"We begin," Hildebrand said.

Standing alone some fifteen paces from the hearth, Aidan closed his eyes as Bishop Odo began the ordeal ritual. "O God, just judge, firm and patient, who art the author of peace, and judgest truly, determine what is right, O Lord, and make known Thy righteous judgment and sanctify this fire." He threw the ring into the blaze as the logs crackled and sizzled in welcome.

Odo then walked to Aidan, lifted the boy's right arm, and said, "Behold, the arm that will act as a vessel for this ordeal. Does any man here doubt the purity of Aidan Bardanson's arm?"

"Not his arm's purity," Osgod answered back. "His book, however, drips with dishonesty."

"It's time," the king said, rising from his seat.

Aidan crossed himself, opened his eyes, and wiped the sweat dripping from his face.

Osgod chose then to strike. "Aidan, there's no need to endure this. Your master's played you false. I know the text exists. Don't continue with this! You're risking your livelihood, your future, on a fool's errand!"

"Silence that man or I will declare the trial invalid," Wulfstan yelled. "Do you want me to tell the world how Osgod of Waltham intervened with God's judgment?"

"Desist Osgod." Hildebrand's cold voice brokered no argument.

Growling under his breath, the clergyman fell back. Aidan shuffled closer. His head had fallen during the exchange, and his limbs shook. "I...I..." The boy's hands rose to his face, his fingers clawed out like hooks.

"Yes boy, say your peace," The chancellor said.

"I..." A tremendous sigh lowered his shoulders and wobbled his knees.

"If he falls, he fails," Osgod said, storming toward the boy in rapture. "Fall, boy. The weight's too much to bear."

Wulfstan's words were soft. "Aidan, follow your heart. Your future actions are defined by you and God."

William's wrath erupted. "Silence priest! Osgod, return to my side or I'll have your skin flayed from your body! Boy, either retrieve the ring or forfeit the trial!"

A vision of Ebba sitting in a red star-lit grove wrapped his mind in a cocoon. "I must follow my heart to Worcester."

Aidan dragged his foot to the hearth and reached in up to his armpit. Without even a cry he searched the smoldering floor. The smell of burned flesh filled his nose, but he closed his eyes, maintained the picture of Ebba in his mind, and kept searching. With the last dregs of sensation in his palm, he felt something small, circular, and too hard to be charred wood. Forcing his fingers to close, he emerged with a handful of coals, a burning ember, and the silver ring.

Everyone stood in shocked amazement as, without hesitation, Aidan approached the king with his charred right arm and placed the ring on the table. He then used his left hand to guide his gnarled right hand to the quill. Using the same technique, he scrawled his declaration.

Under the grace of God, I, Aidan Bardanson, hereby swear that I brought this book from Harold Godwinson to Wulfstan of Worcester.

When the last stroke finished, his feet gave way and he spilled to the floor. Like a barbarian horde battering a gate, the pain broke in at long last. It surged from his unmoving fingertips to the crown of his head. It enveloped his mind, body and soul. He couldn't think nor could he understand his senses...except for hearing.

"The boy is innocent," an awed King William said.

"My king, this can't be—" A loud slap cut Osgod's objection short.

"Take this lying pig from my sight. He'll answer for his false claims at my leisure. As for you, Odo, you'd best Leave Bishop Wulfstan alone from now on. If you accost him once more, you'll answer for it directly."

As Osgod wailed and Bishop Odo begged for forgiveness, the slightest smile crossed Aidan's lips just before darkness took hold.

The sensations floated through Aidan's mind in a litany of tempests: Osgod's scream, Wulfstan's abhorred face, and the charred skin on his arm. He floated in and out of consciousness. During his few lucid moments, he'd retch any of the elixirs the physicians crammed down his throat. Many times, he felt certain he would die.

Then, one morning, he woke in a plush straw mattress to the sound of church bells.

"Do you hear that, my son?" Aidan could hear the concern in Wulfstan's voice.

"The Epiphany," Aidan whispered. "One of my

favorite feasts." He raised his head and looked around. He lay in an infirmary. His bishop sat in a chair by his side.

Wulfstan showed a slight smile. "Are you hungry?"

For the first time since the trial, his mind turned to something besides pain. "I could eat a horse, father."

"How 'bout some simple broth to start? We'll work on the horse for supper. I'll go fetch a physician. I think you may be on the path to recovery."

Wulfstan rose. Before he walked away, however, he turned back.

"How'd you do it, boy. I've been baffled all this time."

"The bestiary *was* King Harold's confession, father. I...I didn't have time to make a new book, so I...I copied the confession for Lady Edith. Then I scr...scratched out the words to make the bestiary. The confession was there the whole time...just hidden underneath..."

A look of consternation seized Wulfstan's face before he waved it away. "Well, despite my misgivings, God must have sided with you. Your writing with your left hand has much improved in recent months. Our novice master would be pleased with your progress."

Smiling, Aidan nodded. "What happened after, lord father?"

"William sent Osgod to the gallows. We will no longer be plagued by him. As for Bishop Odo, William is taking him and several English nobles back to Normandy. They'll be gone until Easter, if not longer. In the meantime, the king's seneschal, Fitz Osbern, will administer the kingdom. This seneschal won the reward Odo sought all along: the title of *Subregulus*. His plans for the Holy Land will have to wait...thanks to you."

Aidan's heart fluttered in his chest as he pictured King Harold smiling at him. "What...what will happen to us?"

"Home, my boy. We are free to return home. Storm clouds lay in the distance, but we have God's sun shining on our shoulders for the moment. So take your well deserved rest. We'll travel when you deem yourself ready."

Two weeks after the Epiphany, Aidan and Wulfstan returned to Worcester. They travelled slowly, for Aidan's arm ached and itched every time he moved. Yet the pains of travel paled in comparison to the idea of staying in Norman-occupied London, so he gritted his teeth, focused on Wulfstan's prayer assignments, and resisted the urge to tear his healing flesh away with his fingernails.

As they made their final approach to the city, a small wooden cross sprouting from the snow caught Aidan's attention. It was set amongst the same patch of trees where Rand and Orrin had dueled and it had a strip of blue fabric dangling from the top. "Lord bishop, someone's marked the place where Rand fell."

After glancing at the cloudless, crisp sky, Wulfstan said, "We have some time before Prime. Let's go pay our respects."

They dismounted on the roadside and trudged through the snow to the marker. Aidan and his bishop sketched the cross over their chests and lowered their heads in contemplative silence. Standing in the forest once more sent shivers up Aidan's spine and made him forget about his slung arm for the moment. He could still hear the echoes of metal scraping, hateful shouts, and pain-filled screams. Most of all, he remembered the feeling of the dagger sinking into Orrin Geirson's heart. His mind recoiled in fear, shame, and a morsel of power. Raising his eyes from the cross, he looked to see if anyone marked where Orrin's body was found. When he found nothing, he nodded his approval.

At long last, Wulfstan said, "This is just a marker, is it not? Didn't you say Rand wished to be buried in the Cathedral close?"

"He did, lord father." Aida wiped a tear away with his unburned hand. "Someone must've set this cross here as a tribute to his final glory."

"I should thank the brother who did so. Standing here, at the place of his sacrifice..." Wulfstan shook his head. "I owe Rand a debt almost as large as the one I owe you."

A slight breeze caught the blue ribbon dangling from the cross. Aidan watched it wave in the wind and hid a smile. "No brother needs your thanks, father."

"Mayhap," the bishop said. "I can best offer my thanks by returning to the monastery. Come, Aidan. Your bandages need changing and the diocese needs my guidance."

Unable to hold back, Aidan stepped to the marker and took the ribbon in hand. The dyed wool felt light and gauzy and smelled faintly of spring wild flowers.

"Hurry along, Aidan," Wulfstan called from the horses. "The faces of the brotherhood will lift your spirits."

Aidan began to follow, but not without taking the ribbon from the cross and placing it in the pocket that used to house King Harold's confession. He then trudged back through the snow to Scramasax, all the while picturing the one true face that would lift his spirits higher than any other. *I'm coming Ebba...as quick as I can.*

Epilogue: Odo

January 14, 1067

The ship set out for Normandy at dawn. As the chalk cliffs of Dover faded behind him, Odo stood at the prow, letting the icy breeze fill his robes and limbs. Leaning on his staff, he closed his eyes and tried to think of anything but William Fitz Osbern waving to him from the dock.

The large merchant knar bore through the waves, its sail full and billowing. This was the first ship of William's triumph and its cargo was anything but rich. In the vast hold below, the moans and whimpers of wounded men drowned out the gulls and the waves. They also ruined any chance for Odo to find peace. "Ship master!"

The burly, rheumy-eyed man who had been lounging by the mast sprang to his feet. "Yes, Lord Odo. How may I serve you?"

"Is there any way to quiet those whining crones?"

Glancing toward the stern's hold hatch, the ship master's face scrunched. "Quiet them, m'lord?"

"Yes. Shut them up or you'll moan loudest of them all."

The confusion vanished instantly. "Yes, m'lord. Right away." As he scurried off, his boots pounded the deck boards.

Odo looked back to the pink horizon. In all his dreams of this journey, he sailed aboard Godwinson's *Dragon of Wessex* or William's *Mora*. Upon his arrival, the holds would burst with gold coin. Matilda would be waiting at the quay, eyes bulging and color filling her cheeks. Now, because of William's anger, he traveled aboard the wounded's ship. Upon his arrival, the holds would burst open with dying, gangrenous men and Matilda would be nowhere in sight.

The ship master's growls floated up from the hold. The words were muffled, but his tone wasn't. The wounded men hushed for a moment, but then began to moan once more.

Odo gripped his staff even tighter. *I tempted ruin all because of that damned monk.* In addition to William's punishment, Hildebrand had fumed and Godwinson's confession had slipped through his grasp.

When I return, they will pay. Because he blamed Osgod for the calamity, he at least salvaged that much. Hildebrand whipped Odo bloody and William sliced his reward from *Subregulus* to the earldom of Kent, but he escaped the gallows.

And the bestiary's appearance did have one silver lining. It convinced William that Harold Godwinson's confession was a lie. Still, it lurked out there somewhere and it needed to be destroyed at all costs. So, Odo dared one glance over his shoulder to the island that brought him such hope and such pain. *Death himself could not keep me away.*

England had not yet been truly conquered, so opportunity remained. Just before the fleet set sail, scouts reported a gathering of English warriors in Somerset. Fitz Osbern promised to look in to it, but he had neither the mettle nor the men to quell the uprising. If Odo could somehow undermine Fitz Osbern, William may yet assign him the title. *I just need to find men with unquestioned loyalty to me...*

Just then, a deep, monstrous voice emerged behind him. "My lord bishop," the shadow's guttural voice said. "May I have a word?"

Odo turned. A giant stood on crutches before him. Splotchy linen covered his face except for his left eye."Who are you?"

"Urse D'Abitot. We spoke in the church at Hastings just after our landing."

Interesting. "Yes. You also traveled with Orrin Geirson, if I recall. Speak, brave warrior. How can I help such a renowned champion?"

Even though Urse hobbled, Odo could sense the man's power. "I've come to see if you've heard from Lord Geirson. He's not visited in several weeks."

"No, I'm afraid. He left on a mission to Worcester, but I've heard no word since."

"Worcester." Urse almost growled as he regarded Odo with his uncovered gray eye.

"You know of the city?"

"I know the bishop, and the men he keeps company. They were responsible for my torture."

"Yes. I remember Orrin's tale. He had given you up for dead."

"Once he returns, I hope to get well enough. He promised me a large purse."

Odo nodded and kept his face sullen. "I think, D'Abitot, Orrin is dead. He should have returned from his mission long ago."

Urse looked into Odo's eyes. "Did the mission involve the cripple's book?"

Odo smiled. "Yes. And if you return to health, D'Abitot, I will offer you anything you want to continue what Orrin started."

"The only thing I want, Bishop Odo, is vengeance."

Odo made the sign of the cross as a gale blew at his back. "Then God has brought us together as brothers in arms, my son..."

THE END
**The story continues in book two of the Raptors of
Fate trilogy:**
The Dove Rebellion